MORYAA RE!

Mark Manuel

MORYAA RE!

Mark Manuel

JAICO PUBLISHING HOUSE

Ahmedabad Bangalore Bhopal Bhubaneswar Chennai
Delhi Hyderabad Kolkata Lucknow Mumbai

Published by Jaico Publishing House
A-2 Jash Chambers, 7-A Sir Phirozshah Mehta Road
Fort, Mumbai - 400 001
jaicopub@jaicobooks.com
www.jaicobooks.com

MORYAA RE!
ISBN 978-81-8495-796-9

First Jaico Impression: 2017
Second Jaico Impression: 2017

Page design and layout: Inosoft Systems, Delhi

Printed by
Rashmi Graphics
#3, Amrutwel CHS Ltd., C.S. #50/74
Ganesh Galli, Lalbaug, Mumbai - 400 012
E-mail: rashmigraphics84@gmail.com

The city in this story is Mumbai, 2011. Descriptions of it are absolute. The police procedure is adapted from information shared by IPS and Crime Branch officers. The characters are all fictitious; but they are inspired by people from the city.

– MARK MANUEL

Foreword

In an interview he did with me in May 2017 for my film *Sarkar 3*, Mark Manuel curiously asked if I had read *The Godfather*, because it was widely believed my character Subhash Nagre in the film is loosely based on the Mafia kingpin Don Corleone from that crime thriller. I hadn't read Mario Puzo's book; but I had seen Francis Ford Coppola's screen adaptation of it for Hollywood several times over in which Marlon Brando plays the Godfather.

The thing is, I am not a big reader of books. Time constraints prevent me from thoroughly enjoying them. But I find myself attracted to bookshops at international airports when I travel. And if there is an interesting title on the bestseller stand, I pick it up. To be on the Top 10 list anywhere in the world, I know the book would have had to pass the literary critics' test. I have collected fiction, autobiographies, works on social and moral norms in society, stories on recent inventions, they all look impressive on my bookshelf at home.

I go back to them whenever I read about an issue in the newspapers, or see something on TV, that I know is reflected in a book I bought. And if I could grasp in just a para the probable answer to what I am searching for, that would be my takeaway from the title. I would not feel like I had lost out. Yes, when I have the time I will go through my books, they will help me improve my language and style of writing when I want to put it to use. People spend very little time reading these days. The world of communication is becoming concise. But I know many who take pleasure in reading a book of 800 pages even today.

So what am I doing with *Moryaa Re!* then?

The subject is unique and makes exciting reading. A bipolar with psychopathic traits chillingly stalking Mumbai during Ganeshotsav, brutally and cold-bloodedly killing eminent citizens and disappearing without a trace after mocking the police, a city on edge, the Crime Branch struggling to detect today's gruesome murder in order to prevent tomorrow's from happening, the capricious monsoon providing the perfect dark and rain-spattered backdrop for the homicides, the sights, sounds and smells of Mumbai evocatively described through its glorious festivals and colourful people, a team of tough and gritty cops doggedly following the sinister serial killer's bloody footprints through dilapidated chawls and modern high-rises, at Mahalaxmi Racecourse and Shivaji Park, on bus and train, and right into the pulsating heart of the Ganpati festivities at Chowpatty. Do they get their man? It requires a great acceptance of psychopathy in a criminal justice system for any police force to successfully detect crimes committed by serial predators like killers, rapists, pedophiles and terrorists.

I find *Moryaa Re!* captivating for a number of reasons.

In my courtroom drama *Pink* of 2016, I played a bipolar lawyer. I was intrigued by the part and would have liked to expand on the grey shade of this character. My director wisely advised me to keep it subdued. He feared the bipolar activity would sidetrack the main issue – which was a social viewpoint on women empowerment after three girls get trapped in a false criminal case. I was given much reading material on the subject and saw plenty of videos of individuals suffering from the disorder. So I was familiar with bipolars and already on the side of the sadistic antagonist in *Moryaa Re!*

But I also sympathised with the protagonist, because I have huge admiration for the Mumbai Police, I believe it is a very efficient force and on par with any in the world. I have tried to play the cop on screen convincingly in a few of my earlier films. There was not much effort put into detailing those days. Whatever reference was required for the role was done through visual observation. The audience was not aware of the finer points. Later, policemen came up to me and said they liked the film – but they were embarrassed by my long hair, unbuttoned shirt, and wrong badge.

The cops in *Moryaa Re!* are not the indefatigable crime busters of cinema and TV serials who lead bohemian lifestyles, get into shootouts and fistfights and rescue gorgeous women who later fall in love with them. They are not heroes, they have wives to go home to, children to send to college, bills to pay, aged parents to look after, they are harassed by never-ending court appearances and failing convictions, hounded by the media, not trusted by the public.

I understand *Moryaa Re!* could be India's first police procedural. And I am positively influenced by the knowledge that many distinguished former Police Commissioners of Mumbai, some veteran Crime Branch officers, celebrated Encounter Specialists, experienced beat constables, and hardnosed cops on the Anti-Terrorism Squad and Anti-Narcotics Cell have helped the author in researching this book.

There's also the Ganpati angle that, well, strikes a chord in me.

The bad guy in the tale is a Ganpati devotee. There's no reason why a serial killer should not be one. All psychopaths march to some religious beat. I believe in Lord Ganesh myself. But I don't know if I could be called a Ganpati *bhakt*. Ganpati is looked upon as the ultimate God of Blessings. All over my house and office, I have Ganpati paintings and idols, they make me feel protected. I am not an exhibitionist in my beliefs and religion, I practice my faith behind closed doors with my family, and I will not take it out on the streets. But I will not deliberately avoid walking on Tuesday to the Siddhivinayak Temple at Prabhadevi where Ganeshji is the presiding deity because that is my right. Just as I go to the Haji

Ali Dargah in Mumbai, the holy shrines at Badrinath, Kedarnath, Vaishnodevi, Tirupati and Varanasi, the cathedral in Kolkata where I shot for *Te3N*.

I sang the powerful and divine *Ganpati Aarti* for Siddhivinayak Temple last Ganeshotsav and felt privileged and blessed when it was later used in a dramatic scene in *Sarkar 3* this year. So I guess my connect with Lord Ganesh is strong. And I love Ganeshotsav. Having grown up in Allahabad, I had never seen anything like this, the big festival there was Dussehra. Only when I came to Bombay in the 1960s did I realise how big Ganpati is here. Millions welcome Him into their homes and give Him a place of honour. Which other God has such a friendly and informal relationship with His devotee?

And as in real life, all the Ganeshotsav action happens in *Moryaa Re!* during the rains. That's another unique thing about Mumbai, its incredible monsoon, the entire south-west coast suddenly turning green, thunderclouds settling on the road to Pune. Today it's all about leakages. But I love the season. I have sang and danced with my heroines in the rain for films. I like going out and getting wet. You can hear the clatter of raindrops on the roof in the story, the wind as it howls around the house like the serial killer looking for a crack to get in; you can feel the earth-shaking claps of lightning and thunder and smell the heady aroma of a parched earth gratefully receiving the first showers. The romance of the monsoon is as poetically brought out in *Moryaa Re!* as the murders are terrifyingly described or the festival of Ganeshotsav is riotously portrayed and the police investigation tenaciously detailed.

The essence of English is its simplicity. That has always been Mark Manuel's style. I have known him, as journalist and friend, for 25 years and closely follow his work. I enjoy talking to him. In our interactions he throws up questions that provoke me to look beyond myself as an artiste out to promote my film. There's a level of comfort I feel when I sit with him. There's honesty and great trust in our relationship. It gives me confidence because I know if I were to officially say anything not worthy of being published, he would gently guide or warn me. I guess that is what the top brass of the Mumbai Police also felt when they worked with him on *Moryaa Re!*

Amitabh Bachchan

"I am the punishment of God. If you had not committed great sins, God would not have sent a punishment like me upon you."

– Genghis Khan

THURSDAY

1

WHISPERING DEATH...

... that's what he was.

An everyday man out to commit murder. Stooping slightly with every step, then dragging one foot behind. Dressed fully in black. This city, nobody gave a shit. One hand fingered the Rampuri lying among loose currency and small change in his hip pocket. Its 8-inch blade was single-edged and exceptionally sharp. It ended in a wicked needle-point stabbing tip. The blade folded into a brass handle. It opened with a soft, menacing click. Bollywood exploited the terror of this sound in its gangster flicks.

It was a killer's weapon.

But he was not *yet* a killer.

This would be his first murder.

And also *the* first, he chuckled to himself.

In another pocket was a Philips transistor. For cricket commentary. He was mad about cricket, the old five-day format of the game, with players turning out in whites and playing on green grass under the sun. Not this T20 *tamasha* with its limited overs, sponsorship and showbiz under lights.

Today, Australia was playing the first of three Tests against Sri Lanka for the Warne-Muralidaran Trophy at Galle International Stadium. But it was raining in Galle. Stumps had to be called. A pity.

However, at the Queens Park in Bulawayo, Zimbabwe was batting against Pakistan in a one-off Test.

He was reaching for the transistor, when…

"Allah hu Akbar, Allah hu Akbar!"

… the muezzin's call at sundown. Rising melodiously out of Minara Masjid, hastening the faithful to prayer, it interrupted the momentary quiet that was part of the city's noise 24/7.

He was on Mohammed Ali Road in South Mumbai.

And he had been thinking that sometimes the city slowed down so that you could almost hear its heartbeat, when everything was still, and you could put a finger on its silently throbbing pulse. Like this rainy Thursday evening at the start of September. Till the muezzin came on the air. Issuing the same summons that Muslims around the world obeyed. From Mohammed Ali Road in Mumbai to Marrakech in Morocco. He could hear it further down the road too, like a distant echo, coming from Bhendi Bazaar. Where there were many more Muslims and many more mosques.

Disturbed by the sound, the pigeons roosting in the minarets and cupolas of the masjid took flight with an angry clattering of wings. He watched them circling the sky, like planes waiting to land at a busy airport at night, as the muezzin's voice gently faded into the dusk.

That's when he saw it – the waxing crescent moon.

A curving silver stroke on twilight's lavender-orange monsoon sky. He stared fascinated, afraid it might disappear if he blinked. Knowing he shouldn't be doing this. Not today. It was bad luck. But the moon had just floated into his vision. Like a black cat crossing the road. He couldn't tear his eyes away. It was breathtaking, suspended above the darkening rooftops. Like a painting hung up in some art gallery.

A painting… Haider!

It was time. He shuffled and limped away, switching on the transistor. The commentator's rasping voice came on the air at once.

Pakistan was playing two uncapped bowlers, Aizaz Cheema and Junaid Khan. Its premier pacemen Umar Gul, Tanvir Ahmed and Wahab Riaz had been rested for the Zimbabwe tour.

He had no opinion on them. They were not in the class of Imran Khan, Wasim Akram and Shoaib Akhtar. Those former Pakistani greats. He admired fast bowlers. Especially the West Indies speedsters of the 1970s. Joel Garner, Andy Roberts, Colin Croft and Malcolm Marshall. He missed them. Above all Michael Holding, the Rolls Royce of fast bowlers, whom umpires named Whispering Death in awe because of his deceptively quiet and deadly approach to the crease.

Soundlessly creeping up on them like a ghost. They didn't know he was coming. Like an unknown, unforeseen assassin. He wanted to spread fear over the city. Leave a trail of blood, death and terror. He had waited long for this, this… *no*, it wasn't poetic justice, murder wasn't justice, it was an unlawful killing. But to him it was plain and simple revenge. His hand closed around the Rampuri.

HAIDER ALLARAKHA Khan laid down his paintbrush.

From his fourth floor studio apartment beside the J J Flyover the iconoclastic, 75-year-old painter could see Minara Masjid from where the muezzin had just reminded the faithful that it was time.

He hadn't been there in years, to the mosque.

Not even on *Jummeraat* – like today.

Thursday nights were significant in Islam. No *duas* were refused. All sins of the week were forgiven by worshipping Allah tonight.

Haider couldn't be bothered.

He wasn't an atheist – who rejected the presence of Allah and doubted the central tenets of Islam. He was agnostic, with no beliefs. And also eccentric. *Newsweek* counted him among the '50 Most Powerful Indians'. It said the maverick painter straddled the Indian art scene with works that were the spontaneous eccentricity of an original genius. *GQ* wrote that Haider, in his starched *kurta-pajamas*, hand-stitched moccasins and rimless bifocals, and with his ice-white hair and salt-and-pepper moustache, was the toast of Mumbai's society.

An underprivileged childhood, in which an interest for art was sparked off by the living canvas beneath his home, inspired Haider to look beyond the squalor and misery of people's lives and recognize the sense of fulfillment they got from simple joys and celebrations.

His metamorphosis was rapid.

From boy to struggling artist, from man to eminent painter, from creative genius in India to internationally celebrated art legend; picking up the Arte Laguna Prize and invitations to show at the Musee d'Orsay in Paris and Tate Modern in London; also, to Sotheby's and Christie's where his auctioned works excited the art critic of London *Times* and the business editor of NYC's *Wall Street Journal*.

His paintings were dramatic and colorful.

Like the clamor and chaos of Mohammed Ali Road.

His canvases screamed for attention. He painted them with bold and authoritative strokes, in bright oranges, vivid reds, shrieking yellows, neon greens, shocking pinks and electric blues. Never muted browns, dull grays and sober blacks. His themes ranged from the spiritual to the mundane. He pushed all boundaries with color and shape to create controversy and stir people's emotions. Like in his exhibition 'Ganpati Tantra' opening on Sunday.

The title suggested sexual imagery.

People thought Tantra was the Yoga of sex, black magic and witchcraft. Haider's exhibition exploited this fallacy. His series of 14 oils on canvas erotically interpreted an ancient Buddhist art form of the Himalayas that was as rich in tradition as it was esoteric. Its specialty was ithyphallic deities: the provocative and shocking sexual depiction of the Buddhist and Hindu Gods Vajrabhairava,

Yama Dharmaraja, Black Jambhala, Mahadeva and Ganpati with an erect penis.

Haider's muse was Ganpati, a deity of peculiar persuasion, whom he painted indulging in wild sexual acts. The Himalayan Buddhist masters believed this state literally and symbolically depicted an intense passion to accomplish specific tasks. Like gaining power and wealth, overcoming the ego and other obstacles on the path to enlightenment. They painted their ithyphallic deities performing powerful and wrathful activities like in an orgy.

Haider believed that Ganpati was a Tantric God.

And that Ganpati Tantra itself, though taboo in India, was erotic and unapologetic. The Tantric sex in Haider's paintings was not figurative. Or tame. It was X-rated.

Art critics described his ithyphallic collection as surreal. Which meant fantastic. Or bizarre. They feared Haider would face a violent backlash.

Sure enough, a right wing Hindu group objected vehemently.

But Haider was insensitive to religious sentiments. He asked the Hindutva brigade if it had the power of attorney to act on Ganpati's behalf, creating further controversy. God did not exist for him. Therefore, insulting a non-existent entity wasn't a crime.

"There has to be an understanding of Tantric physiology and theory before an appreciation of art," he informed these thought thugs.

They didn't know what he meant.

HE WAS enjoying the walk.

Under the arches of old dilapidated buildings with matchbox houses and dormitory hostels. On unpaved footpaths where dingy holes in the walls sold disturbingly vivid clothes in shiny velvets, silks and satins. Past a barber's saloon audaciously named 'Bollywood' with an unflattering painting of Shah Rukh Khan on its signboard in which the actor would have difficulty recognizing himself. Inside Minara Masjid, men were taking their places on floor mats, their bodies facing Mecca, adjusting white skull caps. Soon they would be praying, a sea of bodies rising and bowing piously like a team of Olympic synchronized swimmers.

Outside, street food vendors were laying out tables with checkered pink and white plastic sheets. On *sigdis,* soft, flavorsome kebabs were smoking while sweaty young men fanned the flames. Chicken shawarma dripping fat lazily rotated on vertical spits. *Tavas* sizzled with exotic curried meats. In small eateries which had stone platforms with large *handis* embedded in them, tongue soup, lamb trotters and brain fry slow-cooked on coal. And in a cauldron of bubbling *ghee*, an ancient with a dirty orange beard fried *jalebis* under halogen lamps. Perfumers displayed colored decanters of Islamic *attars*, hakims promised cures with *Unani* medicines, shopkeepers rattled crockery, mysterious characters with fake branded watches popped in and out of darkened doorways, beckoning.

He cringed as bikers zoomed by ignoring the traffic cop's whistle. The signals blinked amber. They had been switched off. Nobody heeded the lights here. Motorists honked, cabbies abused and an ambulance trapped between a post-van and bus wailed in protest. In some distant gulley boys shouted for a last innings of cricket. A traffic jam coiled itself sluggishly around the pillars of the JJ Flyover. They were illegally occupied by hawkers; dug up to lay phone lines, gas pipes and electric cables; and, closed down to construct flyovers, skywalks, the Monorail and Metro.

In the midst of this grand disorder was the constant surge of people impatiently on the move. Muslims going about their duties, gourmands attracted by the cheap food, curious tourists with cameras, Jewish backpackers with *Lonely Planet*s searching for the 18th century Gate of Mercy synagogue in the vicinity where a lamp still burned, and weary commuters taking this congested route home.

THE BEAT constable was on Mohammed Ali Road.

Over his khaki uniform he wore a yellow raincoat with 'POLICE' written in blue on the back. He had a .38 Tiger Titan revolver holstered to his belt and a walkie-talkie hanging around his neck. He stopped beside Minara Masjid that was now garishly illuminated by blinking fairy lights. Strung up outside was a Muslim politician's banner wishing constituents "Eid Mubarak" for the festival just gone by.

Far out to the west, the sun had sunk in the Arabian Sea. But here on Mohammed Ali Road, and in Bhendi Bazar, a purplish-pink glow struggled for continuance in an overcast sky of frowning monsoon clouds.

At the muezzin's call, this sprawling ghetto had begun to stir. Soon it would rise, yawn and scratch itself. This was the heart of Muslim Mumbai. This is where it all was. After Babri Masjid in 1992, after communal riots and serial blasts ripped apart the social fabric of Bombay in 1993, the minority began facing exclusion when it came to buying, selling or renting houses. Those who were economically weak and without influence sought security in Muslim ghettoes like these.

But the ghosts of 1992-93 were buried, *inshallah*.

This was Mumbai in 2011; an uneasy truce prevailed.

A gutter gurgled with rain water by the constable's feet reflecting the masjid's flickering green and red lights. A signal's reflection blinked in it with a jaundiced eye. Shattering this kaleidoscope into liquid splinters was the rubbish floating down the gutter. The constable sniffed. There was the aroma of *jalebis* in the air. Overpowering it was the fetid stink of human sewage from narrow alleys between buildings where broken septic pipes eternally awaited repair.

The constable was lost in thought.

When the bomb exploded, his heart stopped. Blinded by its incandescent flash, deafened by the earsplitting blast, he thought it was a terrorist attack. Then somebody detonated a braid of firecrackers that sizzled and popped in colorful pyrotechnics, sending orange, yellow and white sparks flying and raising thick, smoky clouds of gunpowder. The staccato *bang-bang-bang* sounded like AK-47 gunfire. But the constable realized thankfully that it wasn't.

Aerial shells soared skyward in a fountain of sparks before time-delay fuses re-ignited them to explode in stunning emissions of light and a rainbow of colors. A series of small bombs burst violently, the dull thud of each explosion rocking the tightly-packed buildings, the acrid odor of gases rising high in a tremendous release of sound, light and heat.

The constable was wondering what–

When suddenly there was a loud shout, "*Ganpati Bappa...*"

HAIDER PAUSED in his painting.

Like all finicky artists who are never done until their paintings are ready to go up on view, he was messing around with a large canvas and giving it finishing touches for the exhibition.

The firecrackers outside were disturbingly loud. Shrieking rockets whizzed past his window with flaming tails, the smell of gunpowder came in like an uninvited guest and hung around uncomfortably. He was reaching for the paint brush when he heard a tentative knock on the door.

A CHORUS of voices joyously yelled, "*Moryaa!*"

And musicians began to play. A long and quavering note from the *tutari*, that royal Maharashtrian bugle, penetrated the night. Drums rolled, war-like and thunderous – like the skies unleashing another downpour. Cymbals clashed. And the tinny sound of an electronic keyboard attached through an amplifier to speakers scratched the air. The virtuoso tickling the keys was giving an appalling rendition of *Mera Hi Jalwa*, the Bollywood song on Ganpati from the box-office hit *Wanted,* that its music directors would not have cared to hear at all.

Uniformed *lezim* dancers leaped about energetically, each carrying small cymbals, one beating the *dholki* – the main percussion instrument of this folk dance of colorful costumes and calisthenics. Children twisted their bodies in frenzied imitation of films stars dancing. A huge Ganpati majestically made its way at the heart of this celebration. The Null Bazaarcha Raja, banners on the truck bearing the idol said, being taken late in the day for installation by merchants of the market and vendors of the road.

The constable clapped a hand to his forehead.

Of course! It was Ganesh Chaturthi.

HAIDER WASN'T sure if he had heard the knock.

He was turning back to the painting, when… *there* it was again! This time he was certain he had heard it. A soft, hesitant tap, as if this late evening caller was unsure whose door he was knocking.

He sat still, waiting; head tilted expectantly. Straining now to listen over the racket the Ganpati procession below was making. He heard a soft snuffling sound at the door and the gentle knock again.

Irritably he wondered who was knocking.

He was expecting nobody.

He went to the door slowly, stretching his 6'1" frame that was stiff from hours of sitting on the floor and painting, and was about to open it when suddenly he halted with his hand on the bolt.

Somebody outside was listening to cricket commentary!

The ball-by-ball narration made compelling radio. It took cricket to the masses, carrying the highs and lows of the game, conveying the roar of the stadium among runs and the silence in between wickets.

He opened the door and looked out inquiringly.

"Moryaa Re!" a voice in the dark said softly.

Haider didn't see the Rampuri coming at him.

He gasped, not realizing what was happening.

At first, he only felt a sharp pain below the ribs.

Didn't know he had been stabbed and was already bleeding. And he was looking down curiously to see what was causing the sudden warm and wet sensation, when he received the second slashing blow. This time viciously across the throat, it sent him staggering back, leaving a gaping wound that almost severed his jugular.

In astonishment he opened his mouth to protest… to ask the man who was slowly advancing, shuffle-limp, shuffle-limp, and forcing him back into the apartment, *who, what, why…* ?

And was shocked when he violently coughed up blood.

He saw with terror the blood spurting out of the horrifying gash on his throat, drenching his clothes, spattering the floor. Suddenly frightened and feeling faint, life's juices draining out of his body, Haider turned to get away, his feet stumbling across a stone floor he knew every crack and imperfection of in the dark. His hands clawing the empty air for support.

When he felt the knife entering again.

High on the back this time.

Again and again in silent and savage fury.

He turned to face the man, a terrible look on his face, and saw the knife raised. Hopelessly he lifted his hands to ward off the attack and took it on his palms instead. The wicked Rampuri slashing blindly at his open fingers, cutting them to shreds, cruelly mutilating the hands of the great painter and leaving some fingers dangling, the palms slashed to ribbons.

And yet it kept coming…

… razor sharp and ripping into his flesh, the blade going *shhhhhunk* with each stabbing thrust, grating when it struck bone.

He was sobbing now, fighting for breath.

"Moryaa Re!" the man said softly, the knife plunging deeper with each shuffle and limping step he took closer to Haider.

"Moryaa Re!" the knife swinging in wide glittering arcs, throwing up dark splashes of blood each time.

"Moryaa Re!" the knife relentlessly stalking the painter, closing in on him, the Ganpati procession below drowning Haider's gasping breaths.

The Rampuri followed the grievously wounded painter as he careened drunkenly across the room in a trail of blood, knocking down a huge painting, leaving two bloody palm prints on the face of the Ganpati before collapsing torn and bleeding onto the canvas.

It moved in for the kill.

His blood was pouring onto the canvas from several wounds, mixing with the colors in the painting in one gruesome binge. Feebly Haider raised his head, felt his chin being pushed back, and struggled to focus through a blinding red mist of pain and blood.

He felt unbearable, unspeakable agony again.

A red hot streak of fire blazed across his tattered throat.

He gagged, felt fresh warm blood pouring down his chest that ruined the painting further, and thought in a daze that the gallery would not accept this canvas and only 13 paintings would go up. But 13 was an ominous number. Foreboding evil and threatening ill fortune.

With his dying breath, Haider gasped, *"Allah..."*

And realized that he was seeing only blackness all around, which was frightening for a painter whose world was full of color, and then all was darkness.

BABURAO NAWALKAR was a much harried man.

People thought the Commissioner of Police's job was a stroll in the park.

They were welcome to join him, the fucking jackasses.

Them and their mothers!

It was all the damned media's fault.

One pesky tabloid photographer – a *paparazzo* – had taken a picture of Nawalkar on his morning walk at Colaba Woods, four carbine-toting constables trailing him, and that scandal sheet of a tabloid had run it with a clever caption.

"Guns N' Roses," it said.

He happened to be passing a rose patch when that *gandu* shutterbug had got his frigging picture. The tabloid accused the CP of "taking time off to smell the roses while criminals ran the city". Shootouts, robberies, extortions and contract killings were on the rise, it alleged, and the Mumbai Police looked like it was losing in the battle against crime.

What shit!

Half of Mumbai's crime was the people's fault.

Senior citizens got murdered in their beds not by criminals, but their own relatives; grandsons were slitting the throats of their grandmothers for jewelry to sell and buy drugs; nephews strangling their aunts to usurp property; middle-aged men bludgeoning elderly parents and claiming insurance; fathers committing incest with their daughters. Women were being raped or killed (or both) by domestic servants, watchmen and tradesmen they trusted and allowed into their homes.

And then the media blamed the police!

Nawalkar was an old school cop.

In his day, he had the reputation of being short of temper and handy with his fists. He had a squat, broad-shouldered and muscular body, a tight face with a magnificent moustache, and flinty, darting eyes.

The CP's post was a political appointment.

Nawalkar had to ingratiate, lobby and claw his way up. He feared the job would bring his gray hairs with sorrow to the grave. Right now the CP had the Home Minister in his hair. The *mantri* was a *halkat!* He didn't know his ass from his elbow. Yet he bullied the police, threatening them with arbitrary transfers to undesirable postings.

The Mumbai Police was on its toes. Ramadan was over, but Ganeshotsav had begun. There was tension at Azad Maidan because of that energetic crusader Anna Hazare's hunger strike against corruption. Auto-rickshaws were off the road over a fare hike. The civic administration was picketing. Political rallies were turning violent. Rains were flooding the city. Senior citizens were being murdered. Terrorists and the underworld were planning attacks. And the Monsoon Session of the Maharashtra Legislative Assembly was beginning on Monday.

This evening, Nawalkar had to attend an Eid party at Haj House organized by a shady Muslim developer. The Home Minister would be there. In white *kurta-pajama*, wearing a fez cap and shawl, appeasing the minority voter. Nawalkar hated socio-politico-religious gatherings. He would leave when the Home Minister's convoy had set out from Mantralaya.

His cell phone beeped.

He looked at it. An unknown number.

"Nawalkar."

"Moryaa Re!"

"Huh," said Nawalkar, not hearing clearly, there was such a commotion in the background, so many different noises all at once, "Wh – who is this? Mario… who?"

There was a dry chuckle.

"I have a question for you."

Ever since his number had appeared in a public campaign created to boost the image of the Mumbai Police, all kinds of crackpots had started calling Nawalkar. A short while ago somebody called for train tickets to Yavatmal! He looked at the big clock silently throwing minutes into its chamber. It was 7.50 pm.

"What can I do for you?"

"Would you be able to catch me if I murdered someone and–"

"*Mur...*" sputtered Nawalkar. "You said murder... who?"

Again that chilling chuckle.

"You'll find out when you check this number."

"Who are you?" demanded Nawalkar irritably.

"Oh, you'll find out soon enough."

"You think the police–"

"I'm making it easier for you, but also challenging."

"Is this a joke?" Nawalkar thundered.

"Murder is never a joke. *Moryaa Re!*"

And the line went dead.

Fucking jackass, Nawalkar thought.

He buzzed his Reader.

Police Inspector Sudhir Shinde was the CP's assistant and liaison officer. Why the cop holding this sensitive post was called a Reader nobody knew. It was a designation favored by the British. Shinde took Nawalkar's calls, handled his correspondence, read complaints that came and forwarded them to the concerned police stations, followed up the action taken by officers on the CP's orders. This evening he was also tracking the Home Minister on the wireless.

He snatched up the intercom, "Sir."

"Shinde... has the *mantri* left?" asked Nawalkar. "Not yet! Okay, take down this number, 9821062106... I want to know whose it is immediately."

THE GANPATI procession had passed into the night.

The sweepers would have a time tomorrow, the beat constable was thinking. The litter of celebration was everywhere. Burnt wrappers and smoldering shells of rockets and atom bombs. Also firecracker residue, dull grey on the wet road in contrast to the bright red *gulaal* powder the Ganpati revelers had thrown.

The constable spat contemptuously in the gutter.

The reflection of the signal still blinked impotently in it. But the water had turned a curious crimson red. The constable thought it was the *gulaal*. Then he saw a plastic shopping bag of a popular store was blocking the rainwater from flowing freely down the gutter. Whatever rubbish was inside, was causing the water to turn red. He kicked the bag over.

Something heavy rolled out.

He bent to see and immediately gagged. Felt vomit rushing up his throat. Heard somebody screaming and realized it was himself. He reared up in horror and revulsion, feeling dizzy and suddenly weak, felt his stomach heaving and grabbed the signal for support. He pulled out his whistle, then fell on his knees retching horribly into the same gutter.

FIFTEEN MINUTES later Nawalkar was stepping into his car.

It was purring softly in the Victorian Gothic portico of the Police Commissionerate, a shiny white Indica, its orange dome light revolving, a uniformed constable with a gun on his hip holding open the door.

His cell rang.

"Nawalkar."

"Sir, Shinde."

"*Bola* Shinde."

"Sir, that number belongs to the painter Haider Allarakha Khan."

"Haider! You're sure? That didn't sound like him."

Shinde didn't know what the CP meant.

"Yes sir, the phone is switched off now, but we checked with Vodafone. From their cell tower locations we confirmed the last call was just made to you from near Haider's home."

"Hmm, okay. Where does Haider live?"

"Mohammed Ali Road, sir."

"So close? Ask the Pydhonie Police Station to check on Haider…

say I was inquiring, nothing specific. Also find out if Haider reported his cell phone stolen."

THE CONSTABLE got shakily to his feet.

He fearfully looked down and felt a fresh wave of nausea.

The severed human head that had rolled out of the plastic bag was still there, lying on its side, the tongue swollen and engorged and protruding horribly out of lips that were thick and blood stained. The eyes were bloodshot and open with terror. The nose dripped blood. Shards of torn muscle, fat and skin were loosely connected to the face that was severely cyanosed in death and congested. The cartilaginous structure of the windpipe stuck out from beneath the chin, the carotid artery and jugular vein hanging like tubular vessels, and behind, a little of the spinal column – mushy, soft and white.

The constable felt his body shaking uncontrollably.

He reached for his walkie-talkie and failed to switch it on. In panic, he raised the whistle to his lips and blew hard. Once, twice, a third long blast, before he threw up again.

At that moment there was a thunderous clap and lightning raked the indigo night, slashing it mercilessly, causing the heavily pregnant monsoon clouds to bleed torrents of rain.

The murder of Haider Allarakha Khan had been discovered.

But he was only the first victim.

2

MUMBAI WASN'T among the World's 50 Most Violent Cities.

The crime here didn't merit that disagreeable distinction. Two or three murders a day were par for the course. This city, more people got run over by trains daily. Or met their ends in road accidents. Sudden death was not unusual; but a decapitated head was unexpected.

The cops from JJ Marg Police Station hadn't seen anything like it. They waited uneasily for the forensic experts. A curious crowd, like buzzing flies, began gathering. So they cordoned off the area with crime scene tape. It said 'Police Line Do Not Cross'. They then informed the Control Room.

The Control Room was the police's nerve centre.

It took the homicide to the city's 93 police stations and the Crime Branch's Station House. All police vehicles with wireless sets, all cops with walkie-talkies, learned about it too. Some crimes involved a getaway vehicle. The Control Room would ensure *nakabandis* were organized and every policeman in Mumbai was on the lookout for it. The Missing Persons Bureau was also kept in the loop because sometimes an unidentified corpse turned out to be somebody from its files.

The heads-up on Haider had come from the CP.

The Pydhonie police, checking on the celebrated painter living in their jurisdiction, discovered the gory apartment with its headless resident. Just about the time the JJ Marg police were taking charge of the decapitated head a hundred metres away. The Control Room put two and two together. That's how the police came upon Haider's murder. Now they wanted to know whose case it was, JJ Marg or Pydhonie?

In Mumbai, densely populated areas had multiple police stations. Their territories almost overlapped. Turf wars were fiercely fought to defend jurisdictions. No cop in the world welcomed a murder investigation if it could be pushed next door.

But Haider's murder was not your everyday crime.

It wouldn't get buried on the inside pages. Crime reporters were already on the scene gathering information and reporting live to their newsrooms and TV channels. They were arguing with the impassive cops below Haider's building, waving press cards and government accreditations, and trying to bully their way upstairs.

This was big story night.

The murder's newsworthiness would be defined by the space and time devoted to its coverage. In newspapers tomorrow morning it would be measured in column inches. The rule was "If it bleeds – it leads". On TV tonight it would depend on how many minutes it got on prime time.

Baburao Nawalkar didn't want an investigation in the press.

The media influenced people's opinion. Investigations of major crimes were dramatized on TV channels and sensationally splashed across newspapers. The CP knew the media would lay siege to the police station handling Haider's case. Crime reporters would waylay the cops for information. TV cameramen would block the entrance. News channel vans would cause traffic jams on the road.

So Nawalkar gave the investigation to the Crime Branch.

When a police station was struggling with a sensational and complex case that had the city on edge and was attracting media attention, the CP transferred it to the Detection of Crime Branch – Criminal Investigation Department. The DCB-CID's cops specialized in crime. They ran parallel investigations into all major cases to support the local police. Like a midfielder shadowing the star centre-forward in a football match.

That's how Angelo Ferraz entered the picture.

The police divided Mumbai into 12 Zones and a Port Zone. The city's 93 police stations were among them. A Zone could have as few as three police stations and as many as ten. This was the uniformed force, it came under Joint Commissioner of Police (Law & Order) Arvind Mugbe. The Crime Branch had 12 DCB-CID Units in the 12 Zones whose plainclothes cops reported to Joint Commissioner of Police (Crime) Arun Rathod.

Mugbe and Rathod were Indian Police Service (IPS) officers.

Ferraz was the Senior Inspector of Police (Sr. PI) of DCB-CID's Unit I. Seven police stations came under Unit I. He was also looking after Unit II whose Sr. PI had suffered a heart attack. Unit II had six police stations under it. Both crime scenes linked to Haider's murder fell in police jurisdictions under Unit I and Unit II respectively. JJ Marg where his head was found. And Pydhonie where his body was discovered.

The Station House gave Ferraz the news.

The Crime Branch didn't use walkie-talkies. Its jeeps weren't equipped with wireless sets. The Station House was a 24/7 telephone desk whose operator took down and passed on messages. Communication was only on the phone. Maybe because the DCB-CID's work was too sensitive to be aired for every cop to hear. Or because it wasn't a fire-fighting police unit and didn't immediately and urgently respond to crime.

Ferraz was riding home in the rain.

He liked the anonymity and convenience of his motorcycle. Mumbai's traffic was unpredictable. Half the time it was gridlocked. The traffic cops switched off the signals and valiantly attempted to do the job manually. But they only caused confusion. To add to the motorists' grief, every road was pot-holed or dug up. Or they were a tricky maze of One-ways and No-entrys. But a plainclothes cop on a bike got by.

Ferraz halted at a Traffic Police *chowki* in Haji Ali to take the call. The iconic *dargah* of Sayyed Peer Haji Ali Shah Bukhari in the Arabian Sea was a blur of white domes and minarets dancing in the rain. Ferraz could not see the curving pathway to the shrine. It was submerged beneath the tide. He could hear the waves crashing against its marble walls. The traffic cops in the *chowki* recognized him. One nodded at a flask of hot tea. Ferraz shook his head regretfully. His raincoat dripped water onto the floor. In silence he listened to the Station House operator.

Haider Allarakha Khan murdered! Fuck!

His heart sank. He knew this was going to be a bad one.

Stepping out, he gunned his bike and hailed the traffic constable in a white raincoat at the Haji Ali crossroads. Ferraz gestured that he wanted to make an illegal U-turn and got ready. The constable nodded. He blew his whistle sharply and raised his hand. Magically the cars slowed down. Hitting the siren, Ferraz opened the throttle and cut into a gap in the traffic. As he roared off back to work, the constable threw him a salute.

DEATH HAS a presence.

You visit a murder scene and it registers at once.

The atmosphere is sad and heavy. And extremely tragic.

Cops are sensitive to this presence.

The abrupt, ruthless end to the victim's life didn't matter. That's how murder was, violent and frightening. Never pretty. To cops, murder is another crime. And they are only interested in the crime. They disassociate the victim from the crime.

But the sadness of Death gets to them.

It's as if the ghost of the person murdered has lingered behind to inform the police that once there were voices and laughter in this place, music and dancing, and he or she had been the life and soul of this party. Not anymore. Death had come by. They had been caught unprepared.

Now there's only an oppressive stillness at the murder scene.

And the all-pervading stench of Death. It's an overwhelming odor that can't be described, only experienced, and once you know what Death smells like you're never going to forget it.

Ferraz and his DCB-CID team weren't strangers to violent death.

Yet they hesitated outside Haider's door. It was midnight. But from homes in the building the tantalizing aromas of Mughlai food wafted up the stairs along with the voices of women in the kitchen.

This was their second visit here.

They had come with the Pydhonie police earlier. No sounds and smells then. The residents were in shock. The building had withdrawn into an eerie silence. It had covered its eyes in horror and turned its back in fright when the body was taken bumping down the stairs. And it had waited fearfully for the thud of doors being slammed shut on the road. Announcing the departure of the black police hearse with its creepy shrouded corpse.

Now they were back because the investigation was theirs.

"I want you to take charge," Joint CP (Crime) Arun Rathod told Ferraz at a meeting in the Crime Branch. "It's a serious case, press all your resources and get onto it right away. Let's wrap it up quickly."

Big and solid with gym muscles rippling beneath his short-sleeved shirt, a bespectacled hawk-eyed look in a strong, determined face and the calculating mind of a Chartered Accountant, which he was before he joined the IPS, Rathod impressively held the floor.

Also present was Additional CP (Crime) Nandkumar Sonawane, Deputy Commissioner of Police (Detection, HQ) Subhash Chakravarty and Assistant Commissioner of Police (Detection, South) Vikas Paonaskar. Supervisors and advisors. They analyzed the crime and nudged the investigation if the Detection team got stuck.

They also worked with the Public Prosecutor in making chargesheets stick in court.

Rathod told them about the anonymous call Nawalkar had got.

"From the victim's phone," Rathod said, "probably the killer, informing us about the murder and wanting to know if we could catch him!"

"What!" Ferraz said, astonished. "Who does that?"

At 5 feet 8, Ferraz wasn't tall; but he stood out with his presence. He was tough and no-nonsense. Good-looking in a rugged, unconventional way. With sharp features, soft brown hair and hard, piercing eyes that had seen a lot and not cared much for what they had seen.

"Underworld dons in hiding," PI Shadab Khan suggested. He was a burly and handsome Pathan. He had thick, short hair and an impressive handlebar moustache, both dyed brick red, and huge hands that ended in massive fists.

The Administration once objected to Khan's red hair.

"It's dye," the fiery Pathan argued, "if the Department can have cops who dye their hair black, why shouldn't I dye mine red?"

Now Khan was saying, "These gangsters call the media when they take a *supari* for a VIP killing. Also to claim responsibility for a bomb blast or for making an extortion threat."

"Yeah, but this chap was in Pydhonie. Not Bangkok or Kuala Lumpur. He advised the CP to check the number he was calling from," Rathod retorted testily. "That's how we discovered Haider's murder."

"What happened to his phone?" Ferraz asked.

"Switched off and missing," Rathod replied, "I've placed its IMEI number under observation."

Every cell phone has an unique International Mobile Equipment Identity number. If the phone got stolen or lost, the police and network service provider could track it through its IMEI number even if it was being used with another SIM card.

"Last week the MRA Marg police arrested a youth from Manish Market who is an expert at changing IMEI numbers. They seized Flashing software used to reinstall the Operating System (OS) of phones, his computer and hard disk," said ACP Paonaskar. He was a small, balding, bespectacled man with friendly eyes in a smiling face that belied his years of experience in dealing with crime.

"I know," the Joint CP (Crime) said. "But I really don't think the killer will switch on or use the painter's phone again with another SIM card."

"Why did he call the CP?" Ferraz asked. "To pass on a message or to tease us? Are we sure the caller's the killer?"

"Yeah, it's not like he wanted to confess," PI Navroze Daruwala agreed. "He tossed the painter's head on the road after the crime! Nobody saw him? No CCTV in the area?"

Navroze always sounded cross. He was a big, blustery Parsi with a red and angry face, he had thinning hair and the beak-like Parsi nose on which perched Gandhi spectacles that didn't suit him at all. He looked like a cranky baker or a finicky bank manager. But was more like a jovial liquor merchant watching stocks fly off the shelves on New Year's eve. Not strangely, the Daruwalas took their surname from the family business, which traditionally was the sale of wines and spirits.

"The caller had to be the killer," Rathod said again. "He knew the CP's number. He wasn't somebody who stumbled upon the murder. Such a person would have dialed 100 from his own phone. This man wanted to create a sensation. That's why he disposed of the victim's head in public."

"So what are you saying, sir?" PI Datta Salvi asked, scowling.

Salvi looked evil. He was sinewy, tall, had a thin-lipped mouth, spiky hair, and the coldest, blackest pair of eyes on any cop. Salvi was an Encounter Specialist. He had gunned down 32 gangsters in earlier postings at Oshiwara and DN Nagar Police Stations. Over the years the Mumbai Police had broken the underworld's spine, but the city was not totally free of organized crime, there were still gangsters at large. Maybe that's why Salvi was still malevolent.

"I'm saying whoever this caller is, he wanted to tell us *he* had killed Haider. And calling the CP was the surest way to do that," Rathod patiently said.

"He sounds like a crackpot," Navroze said.

"Why the painter?" Ferraz asked.

"The motive is unknown," Rathod said, "it could be a cash or property dispute, a fallout over a woman, revenge for something from the past, rivalry in the art world, fanatical payback for hurting religious sentiments, political agenda to create communal trouble. I don't see the underworld's hand. And I'm ruling out burglary. There was no break-in. The painter seems to have known the killer and let him in. Money lying around, a wad of thousand rupee notes, also an Audemars Piguet watch, was untouched."

"All he took was the painter's phone?" asked Ferraz in disbelief.

"Yes, maybe he's not as cracked as we imagine. Don't discuss the investigation with the media. Let's not warn or scare off the killer," Rathod instructed them.

Addl. CP (Crime) Sonawane had a suggestion.

Somebody had told Sonawane that he looked like Denzel Washington. Sonawane didn't know who Washington was. But he found out. And after seeing several of Washington's movies, he had to agree that the resemblance was not exaggerated. Since then Sonawane had begun aping the Hollywood actor. Fortunately, like Washington, he too had a genuinely dazzling smile.

Now Sonawane asked Ferraz, with a brilliant flash of white, "The Pydhonie police, have they covered all the escape routes?"

This was standard operation procedure.

After any sensational crime, the police sent teams to the outstation bus depots across the city and suburbs, to all railway termini, and the domestic airport, if they had a suspect in mind who might by fleeing the city.

But they had no suspect to chase this evening.

"Help them," Sonawane ordered DCP Chakravarty, a young, lanky IPS officer with a Hitler moustache and glittering eyes, "I want a list of all the buses, trains and planes that departed from Mumbai in the last two hours. Get their passengers' lists. Identify all single males who left the city. See if there are any names familiar to the police. Find out where they've gone."

"Thank you, sir," said Ferraz gratefully.

Sonawane smiled again, like Washington accepting the Oscar for his role as a cop in *Training Day*, then added apologetically, "But if it was the killer who called the CP, then he won't have plans to escape. He's bound to stick around and watch the fun."

They returned to the crime scene because it held the truth.

According to Dr. Edmond Locard, a pioneer of forensic science known as the Sherlock Holmes of France, "The perpetrator of a crime will bring something to the crime scene and leave with something from it, and both can be used as forensic evidence."

It was almost always true.

Forensic experts, using the physical and biological evidence available at a murder, rape or arson scene, and video recordings and photographs they had taken, were often able to reconstruct the crime. Sometimes they even guessed who did it. Every crime didn't have a witness. Or a suspect. But the evidence was there. The perpetrators walked free often because the police failed to adequately investigate the crime scene. Either they didn't know how to. Or the crime scene was contaminated by the weather, victim's family, the suspect, curious public, and the police themselves.

The Forensic Science Laboratory (FSL) at Kalina had sent a team to Pydhonie. It already had a huge backlog of rape cases and sexual assaults to investigate. This involved DNA testing of semen, saliva, vaginal and rectal cells, hair strands, fingernail scrapings, and other biological-serological tests. But Haider's murder got top priority.

They collected hundreds of fingerprints from his apartment. From which they would try and identify the killer by his genetic blueprint. It hadn't happened before. Habitual criminals didn't leave fingerprints. But the forensic experts never stopped hoping. They also took samples of blood, because sometimes in furious knife murders the killer lost grip of his weapon in the struggle and ended up cutting himself.

The Mumbai Police's Fingerprint Bureau was unlike the swanky office in the teleserial *CID*. The cops here maintained fingerprint records of over 95 lakh criminals manually. There were plans to digitize the fingerprint records of all criminals in Maharashtra on a central server at the state CID HQ in Pune. Police stations could then feed it prints lifted from crime scenes. Hoping the central server with its voluminous data would recognize them and identify the suspect if he had a criminal record.

The cops arrived at Haider's building in a white, unmarked Qualis. It had all the gadgetry of a police jeep but not the look. Yet all of Mohammed Ali Road knew who was here. It is the easiest thing in the world to identify a CID officer. The swagger and arrogance in their walk, the insolence in their stare, give the policemen away. Only the baddies in Bollywood films fail to recognize plainclothes cops.

Bollywood caricatured the Mumbai policeman ridiculously. It showed him with shoulder-length hair and unbuttoned uniform. He had a moustache and wore Ray Bans. He was forever getting into shootouts and fistfights and rescuing gorgeous women who later fell in love with him. Hackneyed as this screen image was, it was Bollywood's success formula. Show a superstar as a cop and the movie was a guaranteed 100 crore rupees box-office hit.

Two Pydhonie police jeeps were angled at the kerb outside Haider's building. About a hundred curious people watched from across the road. Ferraz looked up at the dirty grey building. Out of every window dish antennae gazed skywards to catch satellite signals. On clotheslines outside balconies, the day's washing still limply hung out to dry. He stared at the shops at the bottom. A hosiery store, dairy, shoe shop, crockery merchant, a furniture place, and a bookseller offering religious literature. He wished there was a bank. A bank would have had CCTV. Not these mom and pop stores. They would be afraid of somebody stealing their cameras. With Navroze and Salvi, Ferraz went up the rickety staircase in the dark.

Khan disappeared into the milling crowds.

Upstairs, they caught their breaths.

The apartment was in shambles. There was thick, fresh blood everywhere, giving off a sick coppery smell, they were squeamish about stepping in it. It made their skin crawl – the blood, sticky and horrible, on the floor and even on the walls, where the painter's palm prints remained from his death struggle. There was also paint, colorful and equally sticky, that had spilled out of overturned cans to mix with the blood. The painter's shit added to the stomach-churning scene, his sphincter muscles had relaxed after death and his bowels had let go. The apartment stank.

They thought of him, they referred to him, as the painter. Haider had got the Padma Vibhushan. He had wined and dined with presidents and kings. But to them he was the painter. This was a cop trick. Made it easy to deal with the crime if they depersonalized the victim.

They looked around. An Irani restaurant table lay on its side, its Italian marble top cracked. The accompanying Bentwood chairs, supposedly imported from Poland but painstakingly copied by crafty carpenters at the Oshiwara furniture bazaar, were strewn all over. Like in a western movie's barroom brawl scene.

They also found a coffee-maker broken on the floor. But a set of ceramic mugs, brightly colored by the painter himself, stood safely on a black stone ledge in one corner of the apartment next to a small maroon refrigerator. There was an electric hotplate on the ledge. They figured this was the painter's kitchen. Though they found a stack of takeaway menus and knew he was getting his meals delivered. A knife block of six high-quality Kaiserhoff knives with wooden handles meant for cutting, chopping and slicing also stood on the ledge. It had no empty slot. The killer hadn't picked up an opportunistic weapon and gone to work on the painter; he had brought his own knife. An ancient radiogram that had escaped the frenzied attack was standing precariously on a tiny table. But the painter's antique rosewood bar lay overturned, revealing bottles of single malt and some Scotch. Not one broken. The cops were surprised. They hadn't imagined Haider's eclectic tastes ran to whisky.

The 'Ganpati Tantra' canvases stood against a wall, mute spectators to the terrifying murder of their painter. Many were ruined by splattered blood. Like walls in public places defaced by the red spittle of *paan*. The cops stared at the paintings in silence. They weren't aesthetes, but…

… the writing on the wall suddenly caught their attention.

They weren't sure at first. Whether what they were seeing was the killer's work. Or the painter's. It looked so fresh. On one bare white wall in red paint the color of blood was printed:

'The flowers on the canvas have dried
Still life is never so still after all.'

Ferraz reached out and touched the writing hesitantly.

"Wet!" he exclaimed, drawing his hand back in revulsion, like he had touched fire. His finger was red.

"Is that paint or blood?" Navroze asked.

"Don't know," Ferraz said, wiping his hand on his trousers. "Why would the killer write that? Is he telling us something? First the call to the CP, then this. It's fucking creepy."

He took a photo of the writing on his cell. What the hell happened here, he wondered, sickened by the silently shrieking horror all around.

He spotted the faint outline of a bloody footprint near the front door.

Opening it, he stepped into the small dark landing. A barred window without panes looked down on the road. It offered little light from outside. A naked bulb dangled from the ceiling. He found the switch in the passage and put it on, flooding the landing with a harsh yellow light. The painter's was the only flat on the floor. The lavatory and bathing room was outside. He gingerly pushed the doors open and peeped in. Not expecting somebody to be hiding there, but…

… from below suddenly came the loud wail of a baby waking up from its sleep. Ferraz listened. TV sets were playing behind closed doors. Men's voices came up to him in some argument. A doorbell rang causing static on somebody's radio. When sound traveled so easily in this building, he was surprised nobody had heard the painter being done to death.

Maybe they had and weren't telling…

… because nobody wanted trouble with the police.

Or with the killer(s) if some local gang was involved.

It could also be that the painter didn't cry out… with his windpipe cut, how could he? And sometimes the body went into shock and post-traumatic stress when stabbed and the victim just helplessly watched himself bleed to death. Or he died of a cardiac arrest. At his age, such a frenzied assault resulting in blood loss and organ failure would easily have triggered a heart attack in the painter. The pathologist conducting the autopsy would be able to tell.

Navroze joined him and looked at the bloody footprint outside.

"Did Pydhonie call the Dog Squad?" Ferraz asked.

"They did. The dogs led their handlers down where they lost the scent. You saw how it was. Hundreds of people must have been around. And that rain, it would have wiped out the killer's tracks."

They looked at the apartment's door.

It was an old fashioned French double door. It opened inwards and was locked from out by a sliding bolt and padlock. There was no separate security grille. From inside, the door was shut by a simple hasp and barrel bolt. There was no Godrej nightlatch. There wasn't even a peephole.

"No sign of forced entry," said Ferraz, "the door was open when the Pydhonie cops arrived."

"The painter would have to open it when somebody knocked to see who was calling, and the killer must have known that," observed Navroze.

"How would he know that unless he's been here? And was familiar with the painter's habits? We need a list of all Haider's friends, associates, the names and numbers of everybody who was a frequent visitor to this place."

"Maybe the killer was one of the neighbors," Navroze said.

"Why do you say that?" Ferraz asked in surprise.

Navroze shrugged, "The killer's clothes will be blood-stained, how could he have just walked out of the building unnoticed?"

"He could have washed himself in the bathing room. But you're saying someone from this building could have committed the murder…"

"And just returned home and sat tight."

"… well, it's an idea, let's get a door-to-door done."

There was the sound of a heavy tread on the stairs.

Khan came up, panting.

They entered the bloody apartment again.

Khan stood silently, his head bowed and eyes closed.

"*Innaa lillaahi wa innaa ilayhi raaji'uun,*" he said softly.

Ferraz and Navroze looked at him.

"To Allah we belong and to Him shall we return," Khan explained, running his palm over his head. "When is the *janaza* – the funeral? According to the Shariat, the body should be buried as soon as possible."

"Who's going to do it? The painter has no family," Navroze said.

"Local Islamic organizations will make arrangements," Khan said. "They won't like the idea of the autopsy, though. It's unacceptable in Islam, the desecration of the body."

They looked at him again.

"Found out anything?" Ferraz asked.

The big Pathan shook his head regretfully.

"Nobody knows a thing," he said. "They're asking me. You know how it is. People figure they know a cop, they'll get the inside story."

"Nobody noticed a stranger entering the building?" Ferraz asked, "The local busybodies, the shopkeepers, women are usually alert and sharp."

"Who was looking! Nobody expected Haider *saab* to get killed."

Navroze said, "The killer had to be stalking the painter... to know he would find him alone this evening. It's taken some planning, this murder."

"Yeah," agreed Khan, "a place like this, the families are close-knit and an outsider would immediately stand out... even if he was a Muslim."

Salvi joined them. He had a telephone book in his hand.

"Look at what I found," he said.

"His telephone book," said Ferraz. "Put someone on it, call every single person listed and see if they spoke to the painter today. Ask them if they suspect anybody who disliked him enough to have done this."

Salvi asked, "Have the Pydhonie police informed his family?"

"I heard he has nobody," said Navroze.

"So who collects the body?"

Navroze nodded at Khan, "Ask him."

"Find out if there's any history of threatening calls, hate e-mails, any bad blood with the neighbors, professional jealousy with other artists, enmity with gallerists, art critics, buyers," said Ferraz. "Get Antone de Azavedo to do the door-to-door inquiry tonight. There aren't too many flats. Warn him the killer might be one of the neighbors. Get the names of people staying in each house. Look for a man living alone. Find out where they all were at the time of the murder. Did the painter have a maid? A *dhobi*? Who did the dishes and clothes?"

"Pydhonie picked up some history sheeters," Salvi said.

"Fuckall help that'll be. This isn't a professional job. Shadab, find out everything there is to know about the painter that nobody knows. Who inherits all this?" Ferraz said with a sweep of his hand, "Did he die intestate or is there a will? The paintings must be worth a fortune. Find out who his attorney is. Or his business manager. Also see which restaurants he was getting his meals from and talk to the delivery boys… *you never know!* Check those small lodges in the bylanes for any criminals from out of town. Take Dinakar Salian and Puneet Singh, what are they working on?"

"Those terrorist sleeper cells."

"Okay. Datta, some right-wing Hindu outfit objected to his exhibition. Find out from Special Branch which organization. I won't be surprised if some saffron blooded fundamentalist killed him. Use Sangeeta Kadam and Dhananjay Gadkari. Check everybody who ever had any opposition to his works. Tell Vishnu Shetty to follow up with forensics. I want to know if they looked at the lavatory and bathroom. Did the killer wash off the blood there? Ask Sanjay Chhabria to get a preliminary autopsy report and the painter's cell records for the last three months. Find out whether he was assaulted by one knife or more… the number of injuries seem to indicate there was more than one assailant… the autopsy will tell us from the stab wounds. See if the painter was social media savvy and had a laptop. Get his e-mail address from people in the art world. Was he on Facebook and Twitter? Who were his Facebook friends? Who was following him on Twitter? How do we get some history of his online activities? From the Cyber Crime Cell or the FSL?"

"I'll ask Tushar Pandit and Arun Sawant to find out," Navroze said.

It struck him that the DCB-CID's Unit I had the only Goan, Sindhi, Gujarati and Sikh cops in the Mumbai Police. Where did the Crime Branch find them? There were still quite a few Parsis like him in the Department. The Foreigners Branch even had an Irani cop. All kinds made the force. Ferraz himself was Mumbai's last Anglo-Indian policeman. At one time there were so many. There was also a Jew in Immigration. And a Nepali in the Social Services Branch. This was the most secular police force in the world, Navroze thought.

3

THE FIRST 24 hours in a murder investigation are important…

… because the killer has an edge over the cops.

He's the Phantom of this particular Opera, he secretly follows their investigation, dodging the police, playing Hot & Cold when they get uncomfortably close or drift too far. He knows what's happening. He reads the papers, he watches TV news; crime investigation is a reality show these days.

The cops don't know about this hot and cold game.

They think the killer is playing Blind Man's Buff – and they are 'It', the one blindfolded, twirled around and expected to find him. They don't like this game. So they invent one of their own. It's called the Timetable.

What helps the police in the 24 hours *after* a murder is a timetable of the victim's last day – the 24 hours *before* the murder. It's actually like a school kid's classroom timetable:

Monday: 8 – 9 am PHYSICS; 9 – 10 am MATH; 10 – 11 am ENGLISH; 11 – 12 noon HISTORY; 12 – 1 pm RECESS; 1 – 2 pm GEOGRAPHY. And so on for the rest of the day.

It tells them what the victim did in his or her last 24 hours, whom they met, phoned, texted and emailed; made love to, wined and dined or fought with. The timetable often gives the police clues that reveal *why* the murder was committed. And by *whom*.

There was nobody to help with Haider's last hours.

All they could do was go after a record of his phone calls.

Which was a pity, because in the early stages of an investigation, information is the police's only tool with which to dig further.

Ferraz was an old fashioned cop in a modern world of crime. The young Detection officers of today, they were post-graduates who had studied law, psychology and political science, they dressed like advertising executives and sat behind desks peering at their laptops through designer reading glasses. They were geeks who relied on technical intelligence. They were social media savvy. They carried two and three smart phones. And they networked on BBM; they socialized on Facebook; they Tweeted and they were on Skype. That's how they went about busting crime. Online, or on the phone. The old dogs went out sniffing the trail while it was still warm.

FERRAZ FORMED teams to follow all promising leads.

Navroze and he hit Bhendi Bazar looking for 'Cutting'.

This city, you could get 'Cutting' any time of the day or night.

It was available on the road. A small glass of strongly-brewed tea spiced with cardamom and ginger. Never served out of a cup. A big glass was too much to have. So roadside *chaiwallahs* cut the quantity by half and served it in small glasses. They also cut the price. Hence the name – 'Cutting'.

But Ferraz and Navroze were not on a tea break.

They were calling on Abdul 'Cutting' Patni. A police informer addicted to cutting tea with one ear to the ground. Dongri, Bhendi Bazar and Mohammed Ali Road were his areas, the heart of Mumbai's old underworld. But this was also their Zone. They didn't warn him they were coming.

Khabris networked with the cops over the phone. They kept their identities a secret. But sometimes they would go to the Crime Branch or Anti-Terrorism Squad office if they had sensational information. Ferraz and Navroze knew they were breaching a trust by approaching Cutting on his home turf. They went on foot, walking between the raindrops, because parking in Bhendi Bazar was impossible even for a police vehicle indomitable in Mumbai traffic.

Late at night, Cutting had dinner at Noor Mohammadi Hotel, a modest UP Mughlai eatery to which the actor Sanjay Dutt had once donated a family chicken recipe. In his honor they named the dish *Chicken Sanju Baba*. The best-seller here, however, was the *Nalli Nihari,* beef shanks cooked overnight in marrow with 29 spices. It attracted Muslim patrons as locally popular as Bollywood superstar Salman Khan and as internationally renowned as *tabla* maestro Ustad Zakir Hussain.

"Arre subhanallah, Ferraz bhai!"

Mohammed Khaled Hakim, the swarthy proprietor of Noor Mohammadi Hotel, big, beefy and bearded, and dressed in a loud Pathan suit, rushed up and embraced Ferraz in a bear hug of genuine pleasure. He then stepped back and held the policeman at arm's length.

"Aap toh Eid ka chand hain," he accused Ferraz, grinning broadly. "Why didn't you warn me you're coming tonight?"

"I didn't know myself," Ferraz admitted lamely.

He introduced Navroze.

"Actually Khaled *bhai*, we are here on work."

"About Haider *saab*," Khaled said, his dark, unshaven face clouding.

News traveled fast, Ferraz was thinking.

"But you cannot leave Bhendi Bazar without eating *Nalli Nihari!*"

Khaled *bhai* was being the friendly neighborhood restaurateur.

He told Navroze proudly, *"Allah ka karam hai* that it remains our monopoly. *Har cheez ka copy hota hai, Nalli Nihari ka nahi."*

That's when Cutting made a dramatic entry.

His scouts had told him the police were here.

Cutting was eternally beholden to Ferraz. Long ago, Ferraz had saved the *khabri* from arrest in an illegal firearms case that he was being framed in.

Cutting never forgot Ferraz's help.

Khabris were human intelligence. They passed on vital information about the underworld that helped the police detect cases and keep crime in check. The information could be about anything from fake currency and extortion to murder and terrorism.

Most *khabris* were small criminals themselves.

They were familiar with the underworld dons, the slum lords and drug traffickers; they knew the extortionists and gun-runners, the real estate mafia, brothel madams and *hawala* operators; also, the bookies, smugglers and professional hitmen.

Some were reformed junkies or alcoholics. Others, juvenile delinquents grown up into lives of crime. Many were ex-convicts. Some just got their kick by hanging out with cops.

The *khabri's* life was one of risk and danger.

He always walked the thin edge. With the police on one side and the underworld on the other. And because he belonged to neither side, the *khabri* was called a "Zero" – which meant he was a nowhere man. But the *khabri* knew something about everything in the underworld. He found this out by listening and not asking too many questions. And then he sold the information. No *khabri* was in the game to do community service.

The cops paid the *khabri* his price.

They had a Secret Service Fund for this. But the money was measly. Also, the Department wanted to know how it had been spent. No cop would ever reveal his source. So they created slush funds of their own. *Khabris* asked for cold, hard cash. And always a large sum. Most officers dealing in crime, narcotics and terror had sources for this sort of funding. It was usually some shady businessman they were blackmailing.

The 'Cutting' alias gave Abdul Patni a swaggering reputation. It hinted of vicious switchblade assaults in dark alleys, of victims left mutilated and bleeding, and created a deadly image that suited him fine. The real deal was that the *khabri* got his pseudonym from his addiction to *cutting chai* that he drank at Chiliya restaurants.

Strangely 'Cutting' in the underworld, which spoke its own hushed language, also meant 'tip-off'. The *khabri* wasn't concerned about this coincidence. Nobody suspected he was a police informer because he was a full-time 'Square Foot Bhai' in Bhendi Bazar.

The underworld was full of dark and mysterious players.

A Square Foot Bhai was the local goon who never operated outside his neighborhood. His writ ran large in a tiny area; he was a big fish in that small pond. He had neither love nor loyalty for any gang. His racket was petty extortion but he also ran gambling dens, controlled *matka* operations, and used muscle power to broker real estate deals.

The police knew Cutting was a Square Foot Bhai.

And he knew that they knew.

"Adaab, Inspector saab."

Cutting was full of old world Muslim courtesy.

He sidled up to them now, smiling in an oily manner, his head bent respectfully and right hand rising to the brow in greeting.

Ferraz and Navroze regarded him distastefully.

Cutting took the prize for dressing outrageously.

He had on a neon green silk shirt open at the chest to reveal a white netted singlet beneath. He wore peacock blue jeans and had tied a red handkerchief around his neck. The *de rigueur* white Muslim skullcap gave his rakish appearance an added edge, sitting at an angle on his red dyed hair. He was an undersized punk of 52 with a thin, vicious face, dark hooded eyes, a broken nose and gold caps on two front teeth. The rest of his teeth were the color of tea. His lips were stained red from chewing *paan*. An unlit 555 dangled from his mouth. He had rings on several fingers and a thick gold chain around his neck. On his thin wrist was a fake Rolex. When he grinned, the gold teeth gleamed.

He was either color blind or had dressed in the dark.

"You're here about Haider, right?" Cutting said smugly.

Everybody seemed to know, Ferraz was thinking.

"Why didn't you call us?" Navroze demanded.

Cutting smiled ingratiatingly.

"*Maaf karna, saab*, I have nothing at the moment."

They stared at him.

Cutting said hastily, "My sources are already at work. But nobody is saying anything about the murder, maybe nobody knows anything."

"What do you think?" Ferraz asked.

"This appears to be a solo job," Cutting said. "One man, in and out. With no fielding. More than one person would have attracted attention."

"An out of town contract killer?" suggested Navroze.

"There was no *supari* for Haider *saab.*"

"Know if he had any enemies?"

"No... everybody liked him."

Yet somebody hacked him to death, Ferraz was thinking.

"He was stabbed," Navroze told the *khabri*, "who uses a Rampuri? Could this be the work of somebody like Gupti?"

Gupti was a muscleman of a Byculla gang. Nobody knew his real name. In the underworld and in police records, he was known as Gupti because of his deadly precision with the *gupti,* a thin, long dagger. He was wanted for murder by several police stations and had long gone into hiding.

"*Arre nahi, saab*... Gupti won't accept a job like this. He takes pride in his work. Maybe the killer used a knife because it is silent. Imagine the noise a gun would make. But that beheading... no artist is involved here."

The pun was unintended.

In the underworld an 'artist' was a hired assassin; not a painter.

"Look Abdul," Ferraz said, unwilling to address the *khabri* by his alias, "I can't believe there's no history to this crime. It's not a random murder. Somebody went there with the intention of killing Haider."

Cutting looked around exaggeratedly.

"Let's sit inside," he said, nodding towards Noor Mohammadi Hotel.

Reluctantly, Ferraz and Navroze followed him.

Khaled *bhai* had kept a table for them on the mezzanine floor.

He placed their dinner order himself.

"*Nalli Nihari* is a must," he said firmly, "three plates to start with, full *boti*. With *karari roti.* I also insist that you try the *Chicken Achari,* it's new on the menu, and *Mutton Chaap,* the *Yakhni Pulao.*"

He looked at them for approval.

Getting none, Khaled *bhai* told his waiter, "*Javed miyan, do-chaar Firni aur cutting chai bhi lana.*"

Cutting selected a seat with his back to the wall.

He sat facing the policemen feeling very much at home.

At the other tables, the regulars were dining noisily.

Waiters were shouting out orders to the kitchen.

"*Teen plate Kheema! Do Shammi Kebab! Ek Dal Gosht!*"

Typical of Bhendi Bazar, this was an inexpensive eating house, the menu was written on the wall in Hindi and Urdu and the clientele was so-so.

Ferraz shut his ears to the slurping and burping all around.

A stray cat appeared under their table meowing for a handout.

The tea arrived first, steaming and in dirty glasses.

Cutting sniffed his as if it were a fine Cognac.

"You know Haider *saab* was a Mohajir?" he asked.

"What's that got to do with his murder?" Navroze growled.

"There might be a connection, *saab.*"

The way he told it…

Mohajirs were Muslims from the minority provinces of UP, Bihar and Hyderabad who had fled to Pakistan after Partition. They spoke Urdu but hadn't been accepted by Muslims of the majority provinces of Baluchistan, Sindh, Punjab and Pakhtun in Pakistan who spoke Balochi, Sindhi, Punjabi and Pashto respectively. Considered migrants, the Mohajirs hadn't been allowed to forge an identity with Muslims of the promised homeland. And they were denied employment despite being educated and skilled workers because a feudal system prevailed in Pakistan. Discriminated and victimized, denied basic fundamental rights, they faced a settlement crisis, religious and ethnic tension. The Mohajir label hurt their presence and participation in a country they hoped to make their own. Far from being accepted as Pakistanis in Pakistan, they were considered traitors and agents of India. When the killings began, by the Pakistani army and their own Muslims brothers, the Mohajirs accepted Gandhi's call to return and claim the properties and wealth they had left behind.

"Among them was Haider's family," Cutting said. "They were originally from Darbhanga in Bihar but settled down in Bombay when they returned."

"Then what?" said Navroze, wondering where this was going.

The food arrived, several plates, overloaded and spilling oily and spicy gravies on the table. Beaming, Khaled *bhai* supervised the service.

Cutting talked, answered his phones and ate at the same time.

His *paan*-stained fingers delicately wrapped pieces of crisp *roti* around the gravied meats and popped them into his mouth, while he sipped tea in between bites, keeping up the flow of conversation. He had stuck his showpiece 555 cigarette behind one ear. His three cell phones, all high-end models, kept buzzing intermittently.

It was fascinating to watch him.

The policemen nibbled at their food.

Cutting looked around meaningfully, then lowered his voice.

"Some time back the Indian Mujahideen (IM) visited Haider *saab*."

The IM was home-grown Islamist terror.

A shadowy militant group of indigenous Islamist jihadis who

were the cat's paw for Pakistan's Lashkar-e-Taiba. Its specialty was serial bomb attacks on shopping malls, places of worship and tourist interest, hospitals, markets, theatres, public transport systems, restaurants and even courts. The idea was to give Indians a taste of jihad. So far Mumbai, Pune, Delhi, Ahmedabad, Bangalore, Jaipur, Lucknow and Varanasi had been its targets. Since 2008, the IM had accounted for over 250 deaths.

Its activists were not hardcore terrorists.

They were educated and techno-savvy young Muslims trained in sabotage and subversion. All experts at using online tools in planning terror activities. The Crime Branch in Mumbai, the Anti-Terrorism Squad in Maharashtra and the National Investigation Agency in Delhi, killed many of the IM's operatives in encounters. But like the mythological Greek monster Hydra, it regrouped and resurfaced.

"Why did they call on the painter?" Ferraz asked.

"Coming to that," the *khabri* said picking up a clay pot of *Firni*.

He subjected it to the same sniffing test as the *cutting chai*.

"The IM is seeking financial and logistical support from sympathetic local Muslims, they want safe houses for sleeper agents, aren't you aware?"

Ferraz and Navroze said nothing.

"You remember the German Bakery blast in Pune last year?" Cutting asked. "Along with it, I'm sure you know, the IM planned to blow up the famous Shrimant Dagdusheth Halwai Ganpati Temple there. But that bomb attack was foiled by an alert flower vendor. The IM bomber escaped to Mumbai with the explosive. He dumped it in the sea at Worli. He was from Darbhanga in Bihar, Haider *saab's* birthplace. The IM sent this man to Haider *saab* hoping the hometown card would do the trick."

"Then what?" Navroze asked.

"But the IM didn't know Haider *saab* was a Mohajir and hated Pakistan."

"What did he tell them?" Ferraz asked curiously.

"He called the IM cowards... mentally sick retards, and drove them away."

The two cops looked at the *khabri* in silence.

Ferraz was thinking of the phone call the CP had received. That wasn't like the IM. The terrorist group never hesitated to claim responsibility for its bomb attacks in emails to TV channels and newspapers. If it was behind Haider's murder, why wouldn't the IM say so?

Cutting regarded the cops.

As he took the 555 from behind his ear and lit it with a cheap plastic lighter, he said carefully, "I cannot think of anybody else who would want Haider *saab* dead."

MEANWHILE, A kilometer to the east...

... Shadab Khan was cruising along slummy P D'Mello Road with Dinakar Salian, Puneet Singh and four Detection cops from Unit II.

It was pouring like tonight was the end of the world.

The Qualis' wipers jerkily fought back raindrops on the windshield. Khan sat next to the driver and scowled at the seedy outdoors. The traffic was crawling. It was 2 am. This was the port road. Monstrous trailers with shipping containers were slowly emerging from the docks. They had to crawl past a line of Volvo buses occupying half the road. The buses did the Mumbai-Goa run and had been brought here to be washed. P D'Mello Road also had a number of all-night petrol pumps with serpentine queues of trucks waiting to refill.

"We're going to be here for the rest of the night," grumbled Dinakar.

In front of the Qualis a gigantic crane dipped and pitched alarmingly as it hit potholes. Behind, a Navy tractor pulled a large boat on a trolley. Hedged in, the policemen felt trapped.

The road was named after P D'Mello, a stormy trade union leader of the 1950s who led a bitter struggle against the contract labor system for port and dock workers. It ran along the city's eastern waterfront and was used mainly to service the Mumbai Port Trust's three wet docks: Prince's Dock, Victoria Dock and Indira Dock. At its southern end was the Naval Dockyard where repairs and maintenance of the Indian Navy's fleet were carried out. At the northern end was Mazagon Dock, shipbuilder to the nation. On this 6 km road was also the General Post Office, St. George's Hospital, the CST Train Terminus, the ghostly Wadi Bunder Railway Yard with hundreds of broken bogies and miles of godowns, the Railway Police Commissioner's office, several shady eateries and permit rooms, marine service companies, freight agents, crane operators, and a weighbridge.

The pavements of P D'Mello Road were the eyesore.

Totally occupied by Bangladeshi immigrants whose shanties were hideous structures of wood, tin and plastic, with dish antennas on the roof and ladders from the road going up. Nobody evicted them when they should have. Now it was too late. The Bangladeshis had ration cards, electricity, voter ID cards, water connections, even cable TV network.

They were a dangerous and desperate people.

Also filthy – the road was an open slum. Drains overflowed. There was garbage everywhere. And the smell of sewage and signs of squalor. The Bangladeshis broke streetlights and dug up the road, forcing traffic to slow down in the dark, then siphoned oil and fuel from tankers, looted sacks of food grains from the tops of trucks. They also waylaid lone motorists and robbed them. And stripped parked vehicles of their cargo.

P D'Mello would have turned in his grave.

"Ghettoes are the same everywhere," grumbled Khan.

"*Enter the Dragon*," said Dinakar.

"What do you mean?"

"What you just said."

"What–"

"Jim Kelly tells John Saxon in the movie that–"

"Who the hell are they?"

"They are actors, sir."

"Discussing these slums?"

"Not these, sir! They are on a Chinese junk sailing among Hong Kong's famous floating slums."

"Famous slums!"

"Well, they are tourist attractions."

"Tourist attractions!"

"Yes, like Dharavi, sir."

"Who said Dharavi is a tourist attraction?"

"Anyway… it's a dialogue from the movie."

"What movie?"

"Come on, sir, surely you've heard of Bruce Lee?"

"I thought he was into kung-fu. What's he got to do with *these* slums!"

"Never mind," said Dinakar, sorry he had brought this up.

Since midnight they had been checking all the small hotels on P D'Mello Road. These were strictly boarding houses. Not rated for their service, food or luxury. None had a 24-hour room service menu. But the front desk could produce a call girl for a guest in five minutes flat. Cops from the Port Zone sometimes used these hotels when they were entertaining.

Khan wasn't looking for entertainment. He was searching for a killer.

He didn't think they'd find him holed up here. But in police work you never knew. They had finished checking lodges and guesthouses in Dongri and Bhendi Bazar which were more the underworld's class. Now Khan was stopping at every hotel on P D'Mello Road and questioning the night manager after checking his register. He was hoping to read a familiar or suspicious name.

But only foreigners used these hotels. European backpackers, Arabs come for medical check-ups, Russian technicians working offshore. Even some Chinese yachtsmen on the Indian leg of an international regatta.

Khan was sleepy and irritable. This had to be the shittiest road in Mumbai, he was thinking. But his cool grey eyes were suddenly alive, flicking this way and that curiously.

The Qualis continued its slow progress.

The rain had trickled down to a drizzle.

Khan had been a cop for a long time. And he knew, whatever its virtues, the BEST did not run buses through the night. The Brihanmumbai Electric Supply & Transport Undertaking believed its fleet of 4,000-odd red buses was Mumbai's lifeline. Maybe they were. But not at 2 in the morning.

The first bus rolled out at 5 am; the last one at 12.30 in the night.

"What bus are those black guys waiting for?" Khan suddenly asked.

Dinakar and Puneet thought they had heard wrong.

But Khan twisted in his seat. They turned and looked back. In the dark and between traffic they could make out two men, blacks as Khan rightly said, at the bus-stop. And with them was…

"There's also a woman," said Puneet excitedly.

"I saw."

Khan told the driver, "Switch off the lights and make a U-turn when you find a gap in the divider. Then come back but keep behind a big truck."

He dug out his mobile and called Ferraz.

"Angelo, who's that Nigerian wanted by the Anti-Narcotics Cell? We got an advisory from them last week, remember?

"Obado Emmanuel?" the other cops heard Ferraz saying.

"That's the guy," Khan said, "I just spotted somebody like him."

There was a sharp intake of breath.

Then Ferraz said, "Are you sure? Where?"

"We're on P D'Mello Road, he's with another Nigerian and a woman."

"What are you going to do?"

"If it's him – we make the arrest now or lose him."

"That guy's wanted..."

"I know, but we got no time."

"Okay, I'm calling the Anti-Narcotics Cell."

"That'll be too late."

"How far is Yellow Gate Police Station?"

"We've no time. It's a port police station."

"Shit... I'll inform Control Room."

Narco Nigerians...

... that's who the blacks at the bus-stop were.

The new drug lords of Mumbai. They started off with lottery rackets and online job scams. But drugs were the main reason they were here now. They trafficked cocaine.

The Nigerian drug cartel delivered the white powder from Colombia, Peru and Mexico via Dubai to the doorstep of Indian consumers halfway across the globe. Their couriers came on student, tourist and business visas, carrying 200-300 grams of cocaine each time, valued at 18-20 lakh rupees. Once they got past the Air Intelligence Unit of the Mumbai Customs, the Nigerian drug peddlers took delivery of the contraband. They sold it from abandoned buildings, empty mill compounds, railway yards and ramshackle warehouses in Wadi Bunder and Reay Road.

The Anti-Narcotics Cell's raids on these hangouts weren't successful.

The Nigerian drug peddlers were big men, ugly and physically strong. They were also fast runners. Four Mumbai cops couldn't hold one Nigerian down. The last attempt to arrest them led to a violent free-for-all outside Cotton Green Railway Station. It took members of the public, some traffic cops and finally a passing patrol van from Sewri Police Station to join the fight and pin down three Nigerians.

All the policemen suffered injuries.

The Nigerians didn't fear the Mumbai cops. They remained silent during interrogation. Arthur Road Jail had at least 50 Nigerians arrested under the Narcotic Drugs & Psychotropic Substances (NDPS) Act of 1985, awaiting trial in some 200 cases. They sniffed, snorted, smoked and even peddled behind bars. They picked up cocaine and heroin from other Nigerians when they were taken to court or hospital. The drugs were smuggled into the jail up their rectums in condoms. Undertrials paid cash. Or traded coupons meant for bread, biscuits and cigarettes available in the jail canteen.

Obado Emmanuel was also a killer.

He was wanted for murdering a Russian drug dealer on Arambol Beach in Goa. And for gunning down a Narcotics Control Bureau officer in Delhi. His picture had been circulated to all police stations in India. And here he was on P D'Mello Road this rainy night. Or so Shadab Khan thought.

The Pathan cop checked his gun.

But when they reached the bus-stop… no Obado Emmanuel!

"*Maa ki chooth!*" Khan swore bitterly.

He stared at the empty bus-stop, disappointed. Where had the Nigerians gone? P D'Mello Road was not the best place to go chasing after a killer Nigerian drug dealer in the dark.

He called Ferraz again.

"Angelo, they have disap–"

"Sir, the woman is there," said Puneet, spotting her in the shadows.

The cops leaped out of the Qualis, Khan in the lead.

Dodging the traffic, they ran across the road in the rain.

And then, a scene out of some horror movie.

The woman came screeching at them like a bat out of hell. She was all flesh, short and muscular, and she was wild-eyed and disheveled. She flew at them with teeth bared and nails flashing, like she was possessed.

Her black dress was open to reveal her grimy undergarments

in the blazing truck headlights. Which were also black, like the night.

Black skin, black dress, black lingerie.

Black as the Ace of Spades.

The cops froze. They weren't prepared for this.

She was disturbingly strident and creating a ruckus. The traffic stopped, truckers abused, motorists began yelling and honking.

In the confusion, the woman slipped amongst them…

… her teeth clamped down on Khan's hand, her nails clawed at Dinakar, narrowly missing his eyes and raking down his face, and at the same time she delivered a roundhouse to Puneet.

A multitasking wildcat, that's what they had on their hands.

With a yelp of pain, Khan clouted her hard on the side of the head, freeing his hand and sending her staggering.

He gazed at the bite marks on his forearm in horror.

Dinakar, who had only felt a sudden fire blazing across his cheek and not seen the woman's nails slashing him in the dark, now cringed as blood trickled down his face, thick, wet and sticky in the rain.

Puneet was shaking his head, dazed from the punch.

There was a flash of lightning and thunder rumbled in the sky.

The Nigerian woman bounced back into the fight.

That's when Obado Emmanuel with a gun in his hand, looking mean and mad, rose from behind the bus-stop. He was joined by the tall and muscular Nigerian in track pants and a red hoodie.

Khan, Dinakar and Puneet stared…

… like they were looking at Batman and Robin.

The two Nigerian split and charged at the cops.

Obado Emmanuel, even without a gun, was dangerous.

Not tall like the other man, he was short, thick and beefy.

He couldn't shoot with the woman in the fray, so he came roaring at them like a bull, 120 kg of muscle. The cops weren't prepared for this, too. Only Khan had his gun out. But there was no time to take aim. Or shoot. No place, too. Chances were he would end up shooting one of the other policemen.

Obado Emmanuel didn't give them time to think.

He launched himself at Khan, shouting "*Move Uche!*" to the woman and "*Drop him, Nwanakwo,*" to the other Nigerian, pointing at Puneet.

Khan swung his gun but Obado Emmanuel ducked.

Rising, the drug dealer kneed the cop in the balls, dropping him moaning. But Khan had been hit in the groin before. Rolling over in pain, he kicked Obado Emmanuel's legs out from under him, bringing the big Nigerian down, the gun still tightly clenched in his fist.

At the same time Khan bellowed in rage, "*Arre bhadvayano!*"

The four Detection constables from Unit II joined the tag team fight. They had been standing by uncertainly. Like pubescent teenagers bashfully waiting to be asked for a dance at the college jam session. In the Mumbai Police it was usually the sectional cops in khaki who saw all the action. The Detection staff came later. After the crime had been committed. They were used to beating the shit out of uncooperative accused during interrogation. Not this kind of rough-and-tumble.

Two ganged up with Puneet against the Nigerian named Nwanakwo. The other two grabbed Obado Emmanuel and hauled him to his feet. The woman Uche closed with Dinakar.

In pouring rain, the fight notched up to the next level.

Enthralled truckers, meanwhile, circled them closely. Like they were watching Brad Pitt and Edward Norton in *Fight Club*.

Nwanakwo came at the cops like a 100 meters sprint runner getting off to a flying start. He struck Puneet, doubling him over, then shoved one constable aside, knocking him off balance. He was making a dash for it, when the second constable grabbed him and they fell. Nwanakwo landed on his back. He was struggling to get up when Puneet took a flying leap and landed on his chest, all 6 feet 2 inches and 100 kg of him. The constables pinioned the Nigerian's arms down while the big Sardarji cop began pounding him with his fists till Nwanakwo was senseless.

Obado Emmanuel hadn't let go of the gun.

He swatted off the constables holding his arms like they were flies, smashing the gun into one man's face and knocking him down, then kicking him under the chin to keep him down.

He was turning to dispose of the other constable, when…

… *"Stop! Drop the fucking gun! Now, you black motherfucker!"*

Obado Emmanuel hesitated. He was staring into the barrel of the .38 Ruger Special held rock steady in Khan's outstretched hands.

Their eyes locked.

Naked hatred in the Nigerian's and the light of defiance.

And in Khan's something that Obado Emmanuel recognized.

He saw the deadly intent of a cop used to killing in cold-blood.

"I said drop it! Now, you black bastard!"

Khan's voice matched the murderous look on his granite-like face.

The Nigerian slowly lowered his gun.

Khan kicked him in the groin – neat, clean and swift.

Obado Emmanuel sank on his knees, dropping the gun.

Khan whacked him behind the head with the butt of his Ruger, hard.

Dinakar and Uche were still wrestling.

She fought him with animal strength, biting and clawing, elbowing Dinakar in the face, kneeing him about the body, and wriggling out of his grip by ramming her taut, muscular butt into his crotch and head-butting him each time he tried to grab her.

The truckers watched spellbound.

Dinakar socked her suddenly.

A sweeping punch aimed at her jaw that missed. It bounced off her shoulder and sank between the soft mounds of her breasts, drawing a gasp of pain. Her face distorted in fury, half naked, Uche attempted to flee. But she slipped in the rain and went down on her haunches.

Dinakar had represented Mumbai University in the javelin throw. He had powerful shoulders and a strong arm. Now he caught Uche around the waist with one hand, twisted his body and violently hurled her with all his strength into the bonnet of an Ashok Leyland parked by the side.

She crashed into the truck and collapsed with a soft cry.

The cops stood in the rain looking at one another.

Everyone was breathing very hard.

FRIDAY

4

FRIDAY MORNING...

... and her time was up.

He was hiding behind an old milk booth. He knew she would come. She always did, rain or shine. And *always* at this hour, at 6 am.

He was on Altamont Road.

It was the dog that brought her out; a fat and waddling pug that half the time she had to help, lifting it onto curbs that its short legs could not climb, and picking it up when strays came growling and snapping.

He was glad it was a pug.

What he was *going* to do would have a bigger dog like, say, an Alsatian or a Doberman flying at his throat! The dogs people walked around here had to be seen. One fellow brought a Great Dane. As majestic as a lion. And somebody walked a Rottweiler, madly straining at the leash. Another chap dragged a mournful Saint Bernard. And one girl walked with two lean Dalmatians at her heels, their noses to the ground.

It had rained earlier on Altamont Road.

Now the trees wept inconsolably for leaves they had shed. Municipal sweepers in green uniforms and orange jackets, gloves on their hands, masks on their faces, were clearing the wet road.

He touched the Rampuri... last evening had been *exhilarating*, the sensation of the knife stabbing, slashing and ripping Haider apart had been irresistible. The soft *shhhhhunk* each time. The spurting blood. It had been impossible to stop, he hadn't known when it was over. Who would have thought murder was so easy! This morning might be tricky, though. He was in the open. But she wasn't expecting him. He was Whispering Death. He licked his lips in anticipation and chuckled to himself.

He could see a police beat *chowki* next to the ING Bank. It was shut. A yellow light glowed dully outside. The beat constable's motorcycle rested on its stand. He was probably having tea with the policemen guarding the homes and offices of the consular corps on Altamont Road.

Many *firangs* lived here.

Altamont Road was among the costliest residential areas in the world even before Mukesh Ambani built his 27-storied Antilla here. It was old world, with heritage buildings and trees. The Municipal Commissioner lived here in a bungalow that outclassed the Chief Minister's residence on Malabar Hill. The Chairman of the Mumbai Port Trust also put up here, and the General Manager of the Western Railway, both in grand stone bungalows.

The consulates of South Africa, Indonesia and Japan were on Altamont Road, the Belgian consul general had recently moved to Worli. And Washington House, the residence of the American consul general, had been sold to Lodha Developers for 342 crore rupees over bids by realty companies like Tata Housing and Mahindra Lifespaces. But the British Deputy High Commissioner still lived on Altamont Road in a duplex.

And that's where she came from.

It was 6.05 am. He looked down the road. She *was* coming!

Wearing a grey track suit, its hood up, the pug disdainfully sniffing the crisp morning air. She wasn't walking with her usual zip but listlessly dragging her feet, as if suffering from a hangover. Probably had one too many Pink Daiquiris at her Ganpati party the night before, the *bitch!*

FERRAZ GOT up at 6 am with a start.

The rain had woken him up. He lay in bed listening to the familiar clatter on the roof. The rain sounded angry. Even the wind appeared to be in a temper and was howling with bared teeth. It rattled the windows and huffed and puffed at the door. Searching for a crack to get in. Ferraz hated waking up to cold, dark, rain-spattered mornings. He disliked going to work in squelchy, slushy and clammy weather. But the rain was pelting down. Non-stop. Like somebody upstairs was overturning bucket after bucket.

Ferraz was feeling blah! as Jackie would have said.

He had got home at 3 am in a torrential downpour. The rain chased him all the way, battering him on the motorcycle like a hail of bullets, drenching him to the skin. His hair was plastered down and dripping. His clothes were soaking. And his soggy shoes clung to his cold, shriveled feet. Utterly bummed out, Ferraz stood under a jet of scalding water in the shower till the chill left his bones. He then poured a peg of Vat 69 (the Pope's favorite Scotch, he always said to annoy Jackie) and had it with hot water. Whisky connoisseurs would have disapproved. But this was his nightcap. It gave him sound sleep.

Before turning in, he had looked at the time. It was 3.30.

Without hesitation he picked up his phone and dialed a number.

His call was peevishly answered on the fifth ring.

"Who the fuck is this?"

Dr. Yunus A Miyasahib, the celebrated psychiatrist, didn't sound pleased to be woken up at this uncivilized hour. In fact, he sounded extremely cranky.

"Doc, this is Angelo Ferraz."

"At this hour! Are you mad?"

"Do only loonies call you at this hour?"

Dr. Yunus considered this and found it funny.

"A cop calling a shrink at 3.30 am, this had better be good," he chortled.

"You heard about Haider's murder?" Ferraz asked.

"God – yes, on the TV!"

"You knew him?"

"He was my friend," Dr. Yunus said soberly.

"Okay, help me understand this," Ferraz said quickly, "the killer called the CP using Haider's phone..."

"To say what?"

"... informing him about the murder. And he left a strange message for us at the crime scene painted on the wall, in red, like blood."

"What kind of message?"

"A cryptic poem, just two lines, doesn't make sense. Something about still life and flowers drying on the canvas. I took a picture."

"How do you know it's a message from the killer for the police?"

"Come on, Doc, why would Haider paint this?"

Dr. Yunus sighed and was silent for a moment.

"What is it you want to know, Angelo?"

"Why did he call the CP and leave a message for us?"

"How would I know?" Dr. Yunus said irritably. "Maybe it's more fun for him this way, to thumb his nose at the police, show contempt."

"Fun? How can murder be fun?"

"He's got a double challenge. First, to commit murder. Then, to get away with it."

"A double challenge?"

"Yes, he's raised the odds and made things difficult for himself."

"How do you mean?"

"By tipping the police about the murder, Angelo."

"You really think so? We would have learned about it anyway."

"There's another possibility," Dr. Yunus said, yawning loudly, "maybe he wants to get caught!"

"You're joking!"

"No Angelo, I'm serious," the psychiatrist said solemnly, "maybe he dislikes killing and wants to get caught before he kills again."

"If he dislikes killing why the fuck did he murder Haider, then?"

"Maybe because he had to… but he doesn't want to kill again."

"Kill again? Why not turn himself in? Are you saying we got a crazy?"

"Angelo, what I'm saying is that the phone call, the message in red paint, there's nothing crazy about both," Dr. Yunus explained patiently, "they sound like a warning."

"A warning!"

"Yes, Haider had a horrible death, but there appears to be no motive for his murder, and the suspect brought the police's attention to the killing himself. He's made your investigation of a barbaric crime challenging as well as chilling by giving it an element of intrigue beyond the usual whodunits. He's a shadow in the dark right now, but he's seeking recognition and respect, which the police will not give. So he's daring you to catch him with these clues before he kills again."

"You really think he may kill again?"

"He *will*, that's what I'm saying," Dr. Yunus ominously said and hung up.

FERRAZ LIVED in police quarters on Carter Road in Bandra.

Between the office of the Additional Commissioner of Police (West) and Aashirwad – the bungalow of yesteryear Bollywood superstar Rajesh Khanna. From his third floor flat he had a grandstand view of the Arabian Sea. He could see its grey waters extending to Lakshadweep in the south and Karachi in the north-west. Like somebody had opened the Atlas across the road. When summer ended and the monsoon began, Ferraz witnessed the arrival of the rains from his window. They came one night in June across the sea, riding the waves, bringing with them thunder and lightning, and a wind that howled down the coast bobbing the fishermen's dinghies anchored close to the shore.

The seasons always changed at night, he noticed, as if the cosmos was embarrassed by this meteorological conversion and preferred to get it over in the dark.

The poet Dom Moraes famously said that the monsoon walked into Mumbai on silent feet, like English butlers and Russian diplomats.

Ferraz disagreed.

He had woken up to loud claps of thunder and lightning that crackled and illuminated the magenta sky like a photographer's flashgun. The rain followed, whispering in the trees. He had admired the *son et lumière*, breathing in the heady scent of the parched earth gratefully receiving the first showers. The air felt cool and moist against his skin. Like a splash of Old Spice. There was a poetic romance to the monsoon's arrival. After that it became a bore.

He went to the window now, like an athlete to the start of the race, big arms swinging, pajamas riding low over his flat stomach. At 42, he was in great shape. But his joints cracked, he felt cold and stiff and his lower back hurt.

That's what came from three hours' sleep.

Opening the window, Ferraz leaned out and tasted salt on the sea breeze. Across the road where *dhobis* spread their laundry to dry, he could hear the waves rising angrily among the rocks. There was no struggling light of dawn in the overcast sky. And morning hung between darkness and daybreak, a curtain of rain in between. He went to make himself some coffee.

At 6.30 am Ferraz was back at the window…

… with a steaming mug and the stub of a fat Cuban cigar between his teeth. He wasn't a habitual smoker. Of cigars or cigarettes. A

Cuban tourist, who the Crime Branch helped in a foreign exchange scam, had presented Ferraz with a box of Partagas Serie D No. 4 cigars. He described the cigar as a "robusto" and talked effusively about ring gauge, length, strength and flavor.

Ferraz hadn't understood a thing.

Going online he read about cigars. And got hooked. Now he was smoking the Partagas. He loved its strong, full-bodied flavor and the rich aroma of wood and spice that hung all over the house. Ferraz dragged each cigar out for days. There was two inches of the last one left. At night, it relaxed him and uncluttered his mind. In the morning, it jumpstarted his day. He struck a match and two things happened. With a soft 'plop' the morning newspaper fell through the letter-slot on the door. And his cell rang.

HE HAD come to Altamont Road last night…

… after watching the show on Mohammed Ali Road.

The constable spilling his guts out after finding the butchered head, then a flurry of police activity, more cops arriving and laying siege to Haider's building, the top brass in uniform and epaulets, and local politicians, then a battery of press reporters, photographers and TV vans, the gutter where he had derisively chucked the painter's head after taking it as a trophy being cordoned off, policemen holding back the heaving crowd.

He had been in the thick of it, but he had been wary.

He knew the police would be looking for him, *for the killer,* figuring he might be morbidly hanging around. They had no description of him. But they had experienced eyes. He also knew that plainclothes cops would be mingling with the curious onlookers on a fishing expedition for leads. Hoping to overhear any theories that were floating around.

But they didn't know he knew all this.

And he knew *nakabandis* would come up soon.

The police would be stopping every suspicious person, they would be looking for anybody carrying a knife, or with blood on his person, but they would never catch him; to catch him they had to find him and to find him they had to know who to look for.

But he wasn't hiding. He was like anybody else.

Not like Dr. Jekyll. Not like Mr. Hyde.

He was himself. Whispering Death.

FERRAZ PICKED up his phone.

It was Sub-Inspector Sangeeta Kadam. She had been working on the murder investigation through the night with Salvi. Why was she calling so early?

"Yeah, Sangeeta?"

"Sir, good morning!"

She sounded breathless…

… like he had called and got her out of the shower.

The Crime Branch cops, those lecherous, *chaalu* bastards, they were always imagining Sangeeta in the shower, Ferraz thought guiltily.

"Tell me?"

"Sir, we have a possible lead."

"Let's hear it," he said, sitting on the window ledge.

"Haider was involved with two women."

"*At his age!*"

Sangeeta giggled.

"There is a spurned lover here, sir."

Ferraz was amazed.

"Who is the gir– the lady?" he asked carefully.

"Her name is Abida Ashraf Rasheed, she is a Moplah of Kozhikode."

"*A what of what!*"

Sangeeta giggled again.

Outside, a crazy wind was bending the palms on Carter Road.

"She is a Malayalam-speaking Muslim of the Malabar region of

Kerala. They are called Moplahs. This community is of Arab descent. Abida is 45, she is well-to-do, her family is into pepper trading, they have a boat-building yard on Beypore River in Kozhikode."

"What's Kozhikode?"

"Calicut, it's the new name."

"How do you mean of Arab descent?"

"Arabs began using the sea route to Kerala to trade in silk, spices and other commodities after Vasco da Gama landed at Kappad near Calicut in 1498…"

"Uh-huh."

"… many settled there and took Malayali brides. Their descendents are Moplahs. The community in Kozhikode is Kerala Muslim but it retains its Arabian identity. The people continue to dress like Arabs and have a cuisine distinctly influenced by the Middle East."

"Hmnn, interesting. Okay, what about this… Abida? Is she married?"

"She's single and was, er, Haider's lover or muse since 2005."

"And?"

"They had a bitter fallout two weeks ago."

"Bitter? Why did they split?"

"Haider got involved with another woman."

"What a love life he's had! Never a dull moment. Who's the new woman?"

"Umaima Mulla, she's an NRI wealth management expert."

"*A what!*"

This time Sangeeta stifled a giggle.

"A kind of financial guru who plans an investment strategy for HNIs' money. She manages their portfolio trading activities and advises them on tax saving schemes or something like that."

"HNIs?"

"High net-worth individuals, sir."

Ferraz was astonished. He was a financial duffer. With no portfolios that needed managing. Or investments requiring strategy. All he had was a savings account in HDFC Bank and a debit card.

"Wow, these people need managers for their money?"

"Haider must have been worth hundreds of crores, sir."

Ferraz was silent.

Trying to count the zeroes in a crore, Sangeeta thought.

But Ferraz was imagining a woman in black with a veil masking her face creeping up on the painter with a knife in her hand. He felt a shiver going down his spine.

Quickly he took a gulp of coffee.

Jilted lovers who turned killers were almost always men.

But you couldn't discount the odd woman. You didn't require a criminal record to commit murder when you were spurned in love. The blind rage was a compelling reason. But he was finding it hard to associate the savagery of the painter's murder with the scorn of a woman.

He looked out. The rain had stopped. And early morning joggers were running down Carter Road, skipping over clay-colored puddles that looked like weak, milky Irani *chai.*

"Where did you get this goss?" he asked Sangeeta.

"From an eminent newspaper art critic, sir."

"Why did you say the parting between Haider and, and… Abida, that's her name, right, was bitter? Did she discover he was, er, bonking the investment banker as well and took it badly?"

"I think so, sir. She allegedly stole his art collection worth crores."

"Who, Abida? *When?* And this new Mulla woman, *Umaima – yes*, the financial guru, was she the one who discovered this rip-off?"

"Apparently, sir. The theft was realized only on Monday."

"Just three days before the murder! Where's Abida now?"

"Not here since her break-up with Haider. I suspect she's in Kozhikode."

"In hiding, hmm," Ferraz said. "You seriously think she killed

Haider? Love triangle murders usually happen among the illiterate lower middle class living in chawls and slums. But high society's had its share, too. I agree, the jilted Moplah woman had the motive. It also seems likely she took the paintings. Maybe to teach Haider a lesson. And her absence now is suspicious. But what about the man who called the CP?"

"He'd be an accomplice, sir. Calling to distract our investigation."

"Abida's accomplice?"

"*No sir, Umaima's!*"

HE HAD come to her party last night, uninvited.

To see chauffeured automobiles unloading what the Page 3 referred to as the literati and glitterati of Mumbai. Famous feet delicately stepping onto a red carpet at the foyer of the building. Media flashbulbs blazing. Each guest a recognized face, throw in a film star and a cricketer.

All come to celebrate Ganesh Chaturthi, if you please.

Yes, in the house of this distinguished English couple, self-confessed Indophiles and Ganesh *bhakts*, like it was the most done thing. This was the third year she was hosting this wildly popular Ganpati party.

"It's *de rigueur*," she told a lifestyle reporter, coyly revealing the names from her 'A' list of socialite friends invited for cocktails and canapés in honor of Lord Ganesh – her guest at home!

He had hung around, listening to the clinking of glasses and the titter of laughter coming from her first floor flat, watching from the shadows how gaily she chatted with friends in the balcony that had been decorated with lights and lamps.

A glass in her hand. Cigarette between painted lips.

A dowdy woman with a pale, freckled face untouched by the Indian sun, behaving in a most sickening, condescending manner.

Raising a toast to Lord Ganesh!

Meanwhile, retro played inside dimly lit rooms where people drunkenly danced with their shadows and waiters in white coats and gloves passed around the smoked salmon and Vietnamese grilled chicken.

No devotional music. No Ganpati aarti. Not even a *Ganpati Bappa Morya.*

He would show her tomorrow.

And tomorrow had come this morning on Altamont Road.

Everywhere, the evidence of a brand new day.

A Gokul milk van rumbling down the road. Cars being washed. And people out for their morning walks. A group of old men with creaky knees and paunchy bodies, in shorts and tees; couples strolling; young girls with bouncy breasts and flashing legs, iPods on their hips, earphones clamped on their ears; young men pumped with testosterone taking the slopes easily; school children waiting for their bus; the Laughter Club cackling over some silly joke, unmindful of signs that said 'Quiet, Birds Singing'.

He shuffled and limped across the road in front of her now, pretending to drop a letter into the squat red postbox standing stolidly opposite the grey Income Tax Colony. She didn't even look up as he passed. He followed her till they came to a fork before the Municipal Commissioner's bungalow: one lane twisting and sloping down to Peddar Road; the other continuing straight ahead, past grand mansions with sweeping driveways, each with a garden, a Christmas tree in one leaning over the tops of the other trees, as if peering down the road for Santa.

She went past the mansion Spiro Spero built by Sir Homi and Lady Jerbai Mody in 1942 – which meant "While I breathe, I hope" in Latin, past H. F. Commissariat's bungalow Sylmoyne, before taking a shortcut to arrive beside Royal Stone, the residence of a Maharashtra minister, and finally the twisting, sloping lane to Peddar Road.

Where he was waiting.

It was a lonely lane with three residences, Madhusudan House, Alhambra and Sohrab Minar, and a BEST sub-station whose transformers hummed in the dark. A little further down outside the building Ajanta was a small Ganpati *pandal*, its loudspeakers silent at this hour.

People believed this lane was haunted on full moon nights.

If it wasn't, he chuckled, then after today it would certainly be!

"UMAIMA'S ACCOMPLICE!"

Ferraz was speechless. He forgot about his coffee and cigar.

"But why would Umaima… I don't get it, Sangeeta, wasn't she Haider's latest squeeze? The one who discovered the theft? I thought the Moplah woman Abida, the abandoned lover, was the accused who vanished with the paintings."

"That's what the art critic told me, sir. But I think Abida's innocent. She had nothing to do with the paintings. Or the murder. Her absence is bad timing and makes her look guilty. I think Umaima planned it. She cleaned out Haider's collection. There were several priceless artworks. Collectors would buy them without question. Gallerists sit on stolen paintings for years. Art appreciates. And old masters like Haider are always in demand. Umaima must have already had a buyer. But Haider had to be silenced first…"

"Before he confronted Abida?"

"… and also because the value of his paintings would skyrocket like crazy immediately after his death."

"Did Haider go to the Pydhonie police?"

"No, sir. He wasn't aware the collection was missing."

"*What are you saying! Where was it taken from?*"

"His home, sir. Haider stored his paintings on a loft."

"My God, he must have been mad! Were the paintings insured?"

"No idea, sir. But it's doubtful."

"Why didn't this Umaima go to the police?"

"The art critic said Umaima suspected Abida, but going to the police would mean a scandal and Haider's love affairs would become public, she wanted to save him the distress before his exhibition."

"She confided in the art critic, but not in Haider, isn't that fishy?"

"It was Eid-ul-Fitr the next day. Umaima was going home. She had no time. And she didn't want to upset Haider in the middle of his exhibition work. But she told the art critic that she would get Haider to tackle Abida later and threaten her with the police if she didn't return the paintings."

"She told the art critic that, but killed Haider before he–?"

"... before he found out about the theft and questioned Abida. The paintings are now gone. So is Abida. Umaima, on the other hand, comes across as distraught and concerned."

"Does the art critic think Haider was killed because of the paintings?"

"I don't know. He appears convinced Abida took them. He's a highly respected man in the art world. And, I'm sure, Umaima will get him to express his suspicion of Abida to us."

"So you only have his version of this alleged swindle?"

"I haven't been able to question Umaima or Abida, sir."

"Where was Umaima last evening?"

"She left for Mombasa on Monday, sir."

"*Mombasa!*"

Sangeeta couldn't help giggling this time.

"She's a Kenyan Muslim of Indian origin, sir. Mombasa's her hometown. The wealth management institute she works for said Umaima went on leave for Eid-ul-Fitr."

"Hmm, we have two fillies in the race... which is the dark horse?"

Sangeeta was amused at his analogy.

"Mombasa is two-and-half hours behind us. I will call Umaima at 10 am. Could you get the Kozhikode Crime Branch to visit Abida's home on Beypore River, sir? Her phone is switched off. The Rasheed family is well-known. If she is there, the Kerala police could question her for us."

"I'll do that," Ferraz said. "Call that art critic for questioning. I'm not convinced these paintings were stolen. But if they are missing, and they are worth crores as you say, then where the hell are they? Could they be the motive for the painter's murder? Get the Call Data Records (CDRs) of Abida, Umaima and this chap for June, July and August. What if he's in league with Umaima and they're playing us for fools?"

HE WAS waiting… the Rampuri open and ready.

A stone staircase from one of the upper bungalows descended to the narrow and twisting lane she was walking down, providing a niche in the rocky wall. He slipped into this, straining his ears for her footsteps. Any moment now.

A toilet flushed in one of the homes across.

It was still and dark, and eerie.

Where was she?

He peeped out and was startled to find himself face to face with her.

She gave a gasp and stepped back, the pug whining nervously.

"*Moryaa Re!*" he said, and the knife flashed.

But she had started to turn and was beginning to get away.

He reached for her in a panic, grabbing her by the hair and pulling her back against him, but she struggled wildly to free herself and flee.

They fought for a moment in silence.

Their dancing feet churning up the fallen leaves.

She dropped the dog's leash, and was scrabbling in a frenzy to reach behind and break the stranglehold that he now had around her neck, her back tight against his chest, both breathing hard.

But even with one hand, he managed to overpower her.

He pulled her head behind, driving his hip into her back…

… exposing her throat, tilting her face up, her eyes noticing with terror the gleaming knife that was reaching up for her and the maniacal expression on his cruelly grinning face.

He removed his arm and cut her with one transverse, brutal stroke.

The knife slashing her throat deep and wide.

Causing immediate and massive haemorrhage.

Then, violently, he shoved her away… gasping for breath.

She turned to face him and swayed weakly, on the edge of blackness, blood spattering the lane, narrowly missing him. He watched emotionlessly as she clutched at her throat in shock to stem the bleeding, bringing her bloodied hands up to her face in horror, before collapsing on her knees and falling facedown. A small and frail woman. Still struggling to crawl away from him, unable to scream. The life and soul of last night's party.

Now dying, choking on her blood, life ebbing out of her body.

He had no time to stand and watch, any moment somebody might…

The cell hung from a leather pouch around her neck. He reached for the strap and cut it with his knife, shuddering to find that her blood had already seeped into the pouch and was on the phone.

She stopped moving, her body was lying on its side, a thick rivulet of blood slowly snaking down the road, going after the dog that had fled with its tail between its hind legs.

5

BABURAO NAWALKAR had a disturbed night.

The painter's murder had shocked him profoundly.

The brutality of the crime was unimaginable. Just thinking of it gave the CP the creeps. Socialites and celebrities in Mumbai didn't get murdered at home.

Not like this, the killer had to be a fucking psychopath?

For his birthday somebody had presented Nawalkar with a book titled *Killers At Large*. It was a compilation of the greatest unsolved serial murders in the world. The killers in the stories were all psychopaths, violent and disturbed men who sometimes also sexually assaulted their victims before killing and mutilating their bodies. He had read a story every night until the psychos began to haunt him in nightmares.

Now the book lay untouched by his bedside.

The CP had not slept a wink.

He had an ominous feeling about this murder.

Why had the killer called him?

People who committed murder did it quietly and ran. Hoping they hadn't left any evidence behind. Who committed murder and then called the police?

That too *him* – the Police Commissioner!

Only somebody who had to be cracked.

Or somebody who was as mentally sick as Zodiac, the serial killer of San Francisco from *Killers At Large*. His body count was 49 and his specialty had been sending cryptic letters to newspaper editors and making haunting phone calls to the police after committing brutal murders. Like this fellow who had chillingly used the painter's phone to call him.

The savagery behind Haider's murder bothered Nawalkar.

Couldn't the killer have shot the painter dead? Country-made pistols, *chakris* or *kattas* they were called, could be bought for a thousand bucks. One bullet to the heart would have been it.

Instead, this bloodshed. Like a goddamn slaughterhouse.

Nawalkar had been repulsed by the blood in the studio. He could feel the anger behind the murder. He wondered why the killer had thrown Haider's decapitated head on Mohammed Ali Road. It spelled a sick mind.

This was no random killing, Nawalkar was certain. It was vendetta. Somebody had wanted the painter dead. But who? It wasn't the Hindu organization. This was not its style. Its leaders were demagogues who could stir the passions and prejudices in people for their own political ideology. Its activists were good at staging violent protests. This killing was more one person's rage. This was personal.

The painter's murder was big news on TV. Nawalkar wondered what the morning newspapers had on it. He had waited anxiously all night for the Crime Branch to tell him it had arrested the killer. Now he would have to face the press and reassure the Home Minister that the police were on top of the situation.

The clock in the hall chimed the half hour. It was 6.30 am. The Control Room would call any moment to inform him about all the major crimes and law and order incidents of the night. He was finishing a cup of tea when he heard the curtains rustle and the 'thud' of newspapers falling onto a mat in the hall. He was getting up when his cell phone beeped with an SMS notification. Nawalkar picked it up. He had one new message from an unknown number.

He put on his glasses and read:

'... I rule
this city at night
:Emperor of Darkness,
only I have the power
to switch on
the dawn... '

He stared at the screen blankly.

What the fuck was this? And who the hell had sent it?

Whose number was 9821018166?

He didn't recognize it, had to be some joker up at dawn.

Angrily he dumped the phone and was rising to get the newspapers.

When it suddenly rang.

With a startled grunt, Nawalkar reached for it again.

The same unknown number, 9821018166.

He felt a prick of *déjà vu*.

"Nawalkar."

"*Moryaa Re*!"

The CP nearly dropped the phone.

He recognized the voice immediately. He had heard it in his head all through that sleepless night. Now here the caller was again, like a messenger of doom. Had he sent that sinister SMS a minute ago? It had to be him!

"Yes!" he said apprehensively.

The dry chuckle made him wince.

"Expecting another murder?"

The voice was deadly, mocking.

"Who are–"

"I'm a KoBra..."

"Cobra?"

"... the Emperor of Darkness, didn't you read my SMS?"

"Why are you–"

"I'm making it easy for you."

"What?"

"You've got two murders now."

"*Two!*" Nawalkar was up on his feet.

"Why do you think I'm calling?" the man said contemptuously. "Will you attempt to solve these two murders or try and prevent the third? It's a challenge worthy of Scotland Yard."

"Who have..."

The dry chuckle sent icy fingers up and down Nawalkar's spine.

"This number will tell you... *Moryaa Re!*"

Nawalkar redialed the number at once.

The phone had been switched off.

Frantically, he called up his Joint CP (Crime).

"Arun! That *bhenchod* called me again!"

"Who, sir?"

"Last night's... the *madarchot* who called about the painter."

"*What!*"

"Yes!"

"What did he say?"

"Never fucking mind! He called from another number, take it down..."

Rathod had never heard the CP in such a flap.

"Give it to me, sir."

"9821018166... you know what–"

"Yes, sir... I will call you back."

Nawalkar sat down feeling suddenly exhausted.

His landline rang, making him jump.

It was the Control Room with its night report. He didn't pay attention to anything the operator was saying, his mind was on the call he had just received.

Two murders, he was thinking.

Who was the second victim?

And what had the caller meant by saying try and stop the third? Was he a serial killer? Why was he killing people? And calling him, the CP, like that? Was he telling the police something?

Rathod got back to Nawalkar in 13 minutes.

"Sir, I have bad news."

Nawalkar felt a constriction in his chest.

"The victim is the–"

"The person whose number… ?"

"Yes, sir," Rathod said impatiently, "it belongs to the wife of the British Deputy High Commissioner."

"*What!*"

"Yes, sir."

"And… ?"

"She was found murdered just now on ML Dahanukar Road."

"Where's that?"

"Opposite the Municipal Commissioner's bungalow."

"Altamont Road?"

"Yes, sir… the Gamdevi police are already there."

Nawalkar sucked in his breath.

"What's his name, this British chap?"

"The Deputy High Commissioner? Richard Nieves, sir."

"Has… has he been informed?"

"Yes, sir."

"This is bad. Who found her?"

"A milkman, her throat had been cut," replied Rathod. "He said nobody was around. It's a lonely spot. He rushed and informed the beat constable on Altamont Road. Some ladies who are regular walkers in the area identified the victim. Said she was Mrs. Esther Nieves… somebody who is… used to be… popular in the area. Just last night, they had a pa–"

"Is that number… ?"

"Yes, sir… it is Mrs. Nieves's number. The killer used the victim's phone to call you again. What did he tell you? And how did he get your number?"

"How did he get my... !"

Nawalkar was livid.

"You fucking convinced me to put it in those Police Helpline ads!"

"I know, sir," Rathod said smoothly. He remembered Nawalkar had been excited when he suggested this.

Now Rathod asked, "It was the same voice as last night?"

"Yes, yes... the same bastard. He called himself the Cobra this time and..."

"The Cobra!"

"... he also sent me an SMS calling himself the Emperor of Darkness! A fucking lunatic. And, listen Arun, he hinted there would be a third murder."

"A third!"

"What can we do to stop him?"

"We can't stop him. But we must tell the city," the Joint CP (Crime) said without hesitation. "It's our duty to warn the people."

"Yeah?"

"I suggest we hold a press conference."

"And... ?"

"Give the media the entire picture."

"That a mad man's on the prowl? He's killed twice? And has warned me he will kill again? But we don't know who, when and where? Or why? Think of the panic it will cause!"

"That's the truth, sir. Look at the sensation Haider's murder has caused. A decapitation on the front page. On prime time news. The Control Room has received hundreds of calls."

"The press will ask who's next," objected Nawalkar. "What connects a famous Indian painter to a British diplomat's unknown wife? We have no answers. No motives, no suspect. Not even a fucking theory!"

"True, sir. But it's just hours into the investigation. An aware city will lookout for itself. Not wait for explanations. We've got two big murders to investigate. The press will blame you if another person is killed. You knew and didn't say anything, it will accuse you. Hopefully, we'll arrest this son of a bitch before he commits the third."

"You think so?" Nawalkar asked doubtfully.

"I hope so, sir. Maybe Lord Ganesh will help us."

FERRAZ DIDN'T know what to think.

He was prepared to grab every lead and follow it to its logical conclusion. That's how police work was done. With dogged perseverance. They would investigate everything that didn't seem right. The police plodded along, nothing was too insignificant to check.

But Ferraz knew they were far from a breakthrough.

He didn't believe either of the painter's lovers was guilty.

Not of his killing, at least; the stolen art collection, maybe.

And the IM was an unreal suspect.

His friend in the Anti-Terrorism Squad of the Maharashtra Police, Sr. PI Virendra Wani, had dismissed the suggestion. Ferraz had called Wani late last night.

"The IM's war is against the state," Wani whispered. "It won't waste time on a single murder, that's not its style."

"Why are your whispering?" Ferraz asked.

Wani told Ferraz softly, "The Research & Analysis Wing (RAW) sent an alert that a Lashkar-e-Taiba *fidayeen* is holed up in Lokhandwala. He's a human bomb. He could enter a multiplex, a restaurant, a place of worship with a bomb around his waist – and boom!"

"He'll be on primetime news?"

The ATS didn't always receive specific information from a central intelligence agency. The warnings were vague. Not verified. Without the terrorist's name and description, the location of his hideout, the area of his operation, etc.

But after 26/11, no tip-offs were neglected. There had been 247 general terror notifications this year. They sent the ATS on a wild goose chase each time. Yet it was caught unawares by the blasts in Zaveri Bazar, Opera House and Dadar that killed 21 and injured 133 on July 13.

Now the ATS had quietly spread a dragnet for the LeT suicide bomber in Lokhandwala. They had kept it secret. Not even informing the local police at Oshiwara. And when Ferraz called Wani, the ATS was closing in on him.

"But he'd be blown up too," Ferraz said, "this suicide bomber."

"Think they care? To a *fidayeen*, death is preferable to life."

"He won't go to the Islamic Caliphate."

"Fuck that! Martyrdom promises 72 virgins waiting in heaven!"

Ferraz didn't believe there were any virgins in heaven.

But he struck out the IM.

Haider's killer was somebody the police didn't suspect at all.

He was to be proved right in less than a minute.

Ferraz struck another match to light his cigar stub…

… and his phone rang again.

He cursed and looked at it.

Joint CP (Crime) Arun Rathod! At 6.50 am!

"Sir?"

"Angelo… awake?"

Rathod seldom addressed him by anything but his first name.

"Quite, sir."

"Haider's killer has struck again," Rathod said without preamble.

"*What!*"

"He's just committed another murder."

"*Who got…*" Ferraz was blown away.

"The British Deputy High Commissioner's wife."

Ferraz grimaced.

A foreigner! Jesus, he thought.

"Her name's Esther Nieves."

"Where did he ki– when was the murder committed, sir?"

"A little while ago on Altamont Road, while people were out walking and jogging, can you believe it! He slit her throat."

"Any witnesses? And why her… any idea?"

"Why the painter last night? How the hell do I know!"

Ferraz knew when to keep his mouth shut.

"Get over there, Angelo. The Gamdevi police are at the scene. The body has been taken to JJ Hospital. Mugbe has sent the Additional CP South and DCP Zone II to the diplomat's house. I'm on my way. It's the same suspect. Gamdevi comes under Unit II. This investigation is ours. I'm clubbing both murders and transferring the investigation to Unit I under my supervision. You're in charge. Gamdevi police will handle the paperwork."

"Okay, sir."

"The CP and I and probably the Chief Secretary and also somebody from Delhi, the Joint Secretary from the External Affairs Ministry, I think, will call on the British Deputy High Commissioner later," Rathod said, adding, "you'll have to question him, but gently. Don't want a diplomatic row."

"How do we know it's the painter's killer again, sir?"

"The bastard called the CP to tell him."

Ferraz was aghast.

"From the victim's phone? He didn't use VoIP or anything?"

Voice over Internet Protocol (VoIP pronounced *voyp*, as in voice) enabled phone calls to be made anywhere in the world using a VoIP phone or a PC with a broadband Internet connection. They were difficult to trace because VoIP calls did not carry any particular number and were internationally routed through servers based in the Middle East or the Scandinavian countries. Criminals used it to avoid detection. The recipient's phone would show the call coming, for instance, from Syria, although it was made in the Philippines. It was confusing.

"Why VoIP?" demanded Rathod irritably, "He isn't a terrorist threatening a bomb attack or a gangster making an extortion call. This is his style."

"He used the victim's cell again, sir?"

"He wouldn't use his own now, *would* he?"

Rathod was elaborately sarcastic.

"But he must have one, sir," Ferraz said quietly.

"Who the hell doesn't have a cell phone!"

"Sir…"

"My son, who is only 17, has a BlackBerry Torch 9800. It's the leading smartphone this year and most expensive too! You were saying?"

"Sir, let's locate the cell towers on Altamont Road and Pydhonie closest to both crime scenes. And ask every mobile service provider for their dumps from these towers at time of the murders."

A cell tower dump was a mobile company's record of the calls, texts and data transmission of subscribers in the vicinity at a given time.

"I've asked Vodafone, which both Haider and Nieves used, for their CDRs. There are bound to be common contacts. Let's see who was in touch with both of them recently."

"Sir, the killer could have made or received a call on his cell before or after the murders. The chances of finding a common number in use at Pydhonie between 7.30 and 8 last night and at Altamont Road between 6 and 6.30 this morning are slim. But if we do…"

"… it puts that subscriber at both crime scenes when Haider and Nieves were being murdered," finished Rathod with awe in his voice. "Brilliant, Angelo! How did I not think of cell tower dumps?"

Ferraz heard him giving instructions on the landline to somebody.

Analyzing mobile phone data was easy only on TV cop shows.

"This will take time," Rathod said. "There are 13 cellular operators in Mumbai. We don't know what service the killer is using. So we'll have to check each one's tower dumps for Pydhonie and Altamont Road."

"Why is he calling the CP, sir?"

"I think he's a nut. This is his signature move. 'You-heard-it-here-first'. And he's enjoying the anonymity. It gives him power over us. This morning he told the CP he is the 'Cobra.'"

"Cobra!"

"Yeah, he sent the CP an SMS too."

"Something from some dark poem again, sir?"

"I wondered what that writing on Haider's wall meant. The SMS doesn't make sense, too. I'm forwarding it to you. Maybe both messages have deeper meaning. He's telling us something. Put someone to work on it."

"Yes, sir."

"And Angelo, he's threatened to kill again."

"Threatened? Has he made any demands? Is this extortion?"

"No, he hasn't."

"Then why tell us?"

"I think the sonofabitch's mocking us, he wants to be caught."

Dr. Yunus Miyasahib's warning, Ferraz remembered with a start.

"Calling the police is out of *The Silence of the Lambs.* Could he be a psychopath, sir? He's chillingly unreal."

"Yeah, it's creepy," Rathod admitted. "I don't know what to make of him. We've never caught a psychopath before. He sounds intelligent and could be somebody with a strong reason for murder who's now turned serial killer."

"It seems like revenge."

"Why not? Revenge is a motive."

"If he has suddenly decided to knock off some people who did him in, why tell us?"

"To get it off his chest, maybe. Unburdening his angst. Or he is boasting."

"How can we prevent the third murder, sir?"

"By detecting the first two cases."

"We have no clues to his identity, no witnesses. Our *khabris* have failed us."

"We have his calls, his message on the wall and today's SMS. And we also have the profiles of his victims. Forget the third murder. Let's concentrate on the two he's already committed."

"Profiles of the painter and diplomat's wife? How–"

"They're different, unrelated people. But *something* connected them."

"It's not obvious to us, sir."

"But the killer knew. That *something* provoked him to murder them. It cannot be their social prominence. It has to be more tangible. They were deliberately picked."

"The killer's linked to that *something*, sir?"

"It's what drew him to them. Find that *something*. It's the motive. Once we know the motive, our investigation will lead us to who wanted them dead. That *something* will also warn us who's next. Serial murder investigations hinge on *something* that's common in every killing. Some minute detail which the police missed, or the forensic experts overlooked, probably because nobody recognized its significance. Find that *something*, Angelo."

6

FERRAZ FINALLY lit his cigar.

He went to the door and got the *Newsday*.

'HAIDER HACKED TO DEATH!' the headline screamed.

Below it, a strapline ran across the page:

'Master painter brutally stabbed, beheaded; police clueless'

It had a gruesome five column picture of Haider's bloodied corpse and an inset of his decapitated head. Taken at the morgue. Ferraz controlled a shudder. Why had the editor let it pass? It was insensitive and offensive.

The report was disappointing.

The crime reporter complained that the police shared no information. He alleged that they had no leads. No suspect. The CP had said it was a "most bizarre case" in which "anybody could be the killer". The Joint CP (Crime) told the press that "there was no apparent motive" and "Haider could be a random victim".

That was last night; this morning the police knew better.

The story was sketchy. It was based on hearsay. Plus, the crime reporter's impression of what he thought had happened and an imaginative description of the crime scene based on what his sources told him. *Newsday* had cobbled together a companion piece of all major undetected homicides. Its editorial screamed about rising crime and police inefficiency. The newspaper's art critic Anant K. Rao had written a glowing obit on Haider taking tributes from the painter's contemporaries, gallerists and collectors.

Ferraz wondered if he was Sangeeta's source.

The 7 am TV news had no updates on the murder.

It still showed a hazy video of grim-faced policemen loading the corpse into a hearse in pouring rain. The newsreader gloomily said the police had no leads yet. The breakfast newsreaders had none of the zing of the chaps at night. Those guys were get-up-and-go. They read the news with energy and enthusiasm. This bulletin lacked the electricity and tension that the murder demanded. Ferraz tried to imagine the sensation Esther Nieves's murder would cause. His phone beeped to announce an SMS.

It was from Rathod. The killer's message to the CP this morning.

'... I rule
this city at night
:Emperor of Darkness,
only I have the power
to switch on
the dawn... '

Ferraz read it twice.

It made no sense to him. What the hell was the killer saying?

That he had committed a murder in the dark...

... and one at dawn.

Which the police already knew. Why make a song and dance about it?

What was it he had written on Haider's wall?

Ferraz scrolled through the photos on his phone, yes, here it was.

He zoomed in, lost detail, resized and read the grainy message:

'The flowers on the canvas have dried
Still life is never so still after all.'

Did 'flowers' mean the painter?

And was 'canvas' supposed to be Haider's life?

In which case, did 'dried' mean died?

He compared the messages, hopelessly struggling to read between the lines.

Ferraz had sucked at poetry in college. He never understood contemporary poems. Modern day poets were idiosyncratic. He didn't get their angst. Their poems were not fun. They had no meter, no rhyme and he found them taxing.

Flowers drying on the canvas and the Emperor of Darkness switching on the dawn, why would anybody write stuff like that? Was the killer also the poet of these dark verses?

HE CALLED Navroze Daruwala.

The phone rang and rang.

"Yeah?" Navroze's voice was gruff with sleep.

"Bawa?"

"Angelo! What's the fucking time?"

"We've got another murder."

"Another... what do you mean?"

"Same killer, this morning."

"Huh? What are you saying?" Navroze was properly awake now.

"Haider's killer has murdered again."

"Maara baap! Who?"

"The British Deputy High Commissioner's wife."

"Maa ki... !"

In the background Ferraz could hear Behroze, Navroze's wife, a large and placid woman, bustling about. The Daruwalas lived in a quaint, 105-year-old Parsi colony in Lalbaug called Navroze Baug. The Bombay Parsi Punchayet planned to redevelop it into a deluxe colony of luxury towers. Navroze was already angling for a penthouse flat.

Ferraz could also hear the music blaring from Ganesh Gully next to Navroze Baug, home to one of the largest Ganpatis in the city. It was just 7 am. How did Navroze sleep through this racket?

"Bol ni, dikra, who's the woman?" Navroze was asking impatiently.

"Oh sorry," said Ferraz. "Her name is Esther Nieves. She was found on Altamont Road half an hour ago with her throat slit."

"How do we know it's a related killing?"

"The killer called the CP again."

"That madarchot!"

"Yeah… he sent an SMS, too. Something about some Emperor of Darkness. He also called himself the Cobra."

"What's Emperor of Darkness?"

"No idea. Let's visit Altamont Road. This also is our case."

"Wasn't this woman covered by the SPU?"

"The Special Protection Unit?"

"Yeah, doesn't the Protection & Security Branch provide consul generals with security by the SPU?"

"The Israeli and American consuls for sure."

"This woman was obviously unprotected," Navroze said.

"Who's in charge of the SPU? Bapusaheb Thorat still?"

"No, Nandkishore Jamadar."

"What's happened to Thorat? Retired or transferred? Anyway, ask Jamadar whether the British envoy's wife had a Personal Security Officer (PSO)."

VIP security was a touchy subject.

The Mumbai Police, woefully short-staffed always, was saddled with the thankless job of protecting some 600 VIPs whose lives were in danger. In danger of what, Sr. PI Nandkishore Jamadar of the SPU, who provided them with security, never understood. He believed the threat was in the VIPs' minds.

Armed police guards were a status symbol.

Politicians, film stars, builders, businessmen, a variety of celebrities and even some former CPs flaunted them. The protection cost money. Unless the VIP was a public representative like a politician, judge, bureaucrat or even an ex-cop. For them it was free. The others paid rates decided by the Home Department. But many defaulted and the Protection & Security Branch was given a nice runaround for its money then.

The SPU cops were the cat's whiskers.

Like Black Cat commandos of the centre's National Security Guard, they were specially trained, carried sophisticated weapons, used advanced communication systems and were given fast vehicles. But no VIP was 100 per cent secure under Black Cat protection. National leaders had been assassinated by foreign mercenaries, abducted by Naxalites, and blown to pieces by Islamic *fidayeen.* Whereas Mumbai VIPs protected by the SPU never received threats again. Maybe Jamadar was right.

THE NIEVES murder reminded Ferraz of Percy Norris.

He was Richard Nieves's predecessor, 27 years ago.

The British Deputy High Commissioner was assassinated near Sachivalya on November 27, 1984. Two white men shot him from point-blank range near Cooperage Bandstand in peak morning traffic. He was in his car.

Mumbai was then Bombay.

And Mantralaya was Sachivalya.

The police were overwhelmed by the diplomat's murder.

It happened the day before David Gower's England was to play Sunil Gavaskar's India at Wankhede in the first Test of a home series. Norris had entertained the English team to dinner the night before. The match went ahead in tension. England lost. But with typical stiff upper lip fortitude it recovered and won the five-Test series 2-1 and the five ODIs 4-1.

Like Gavaskar's XI, the Bombay Police also took a beating.

The killing had been ordered in the Middle East. An Arabic-speaking caller told news agencies in Paris and London that the Revolutionary Organization of Socialist Moslems, a splinter group of that ruthless Palestine terrorist Abu Nidal, was responsible. It had earlier killed Israeli Ambassador Shlomo Argov in London. Norris's assassination was meant to pressurize Britain into freeing the Arab gunmen arrested for Argov's killing.

Norris's killers remained unidentified.

The Bombay Police, after searching hotels in vain and sealing the airport, harbor and railroad stations in their hunt for them, swept the diplomat's murder under the carpet.

Ferraz remembered Norris's son saying, "I hate the men who killed my father. I feel an enormous rage. In a diplomatic family you know your parents are at risk and something like this could happen. But somehow I thought it was something that would never really happen to us."

Now it had happened again.

FERRAZ CALLED Salvi next.

The Encounter cop had been questioning Hindu right-wing activists about Haider through the night. But Salvi was awake. He had heard about Nieves's murder.

"Hullo Angelo," he said yawning, "I was about to call you."

"Uh-huh, got anything?"

"Tchah!"

"You must be the most hated cop in Mumbai."

"Yeah, I scared these fundamentalists out of a year's sleep."

"What did they say?"

"They didn't despise Haider so much that they wanted him dead, they said. And death by murder? *Deva! Parmeshwara! Panduranga! Vithala!* They would denounce anybody who was anti-national. But attack an Indian for creatively expressing himself – *nevah!*"

"Datta, what about Muslim fundamentalists?"

"What about them?"

"Like the Raza Academy..."

"It's not fundamentalist..."

"... yeah, it's a Sunni organization."

"... promoting Islamic Sufi culture."

"But the painter was what, an atheist?" asked Ferraz.

"He was certainly outspoken about some Islamic practices."

"Didn't he have Muslims hating his guts and gunning for him too?"

"Yeah, but Angelo... gunning for him, I don't know."

"What was he, Sunni or Shia?"

"Who knows!"

"They violently disagree in their beliefs and practices, don't they?"

"Isn't this sectarian divide more in West Asia?"

"Hmnn, okay. What about the Deobandis and Barelvis?"

"Who are they?"

"Different schools of thought in Islam. We've had cases of violence in their fight for control over the *madrassas, dargahs* and *kabaristans* in Mumbai."

"Yeah, but the painter kept away from politics and religion."

Ferraz sighed.

"I'm striking out all options," he admitted.

Salvi understood Ferraz's frustration.

It was easier to encounter criminals than investigate murder. Salvi had packed off 32 of Mumbai's most wanted to that big gangland in the sky. The media called him an Encounter Specialist. But Salvi didn't enjoy killing; he was following orders.

The *Esquire* of London once did a story on Mumbai's gang wars. Its correspondent interviewed Salvi. The Encounter Specialist began by coolly placing his 9 mm Browning on the desk between them.

The *Esquire* man asked in awe, "Aren't you scared of death threats?"

Salvi told him, "This gun's magazine holds 13 bullets. If I can't protect myself with 13 bullets, then I deserve to be killed!"

But human rights organizations began filing Public Interest Litigations (PILs) in court alleging that the Encounter Specialists were undertaking "contract killings" to settle scores between rival gangs. The cops had become executioners for whichever gang bid the highest.

This was not untrue.

The Mumbai Police was forced to put a stop to encounters.

Salvi missed the thrill of the hunt.

The gangster marked for death was usually in hiding. He changed hideouts, always staying in rented apartments, moving overnight, using fake number plates on his car. The cops kept tabs on him, gathering information, breaking down his habits, and a plan was made. The gangster was taken down one night.

Bang! Bang! Bang!

They could have made the arrest, because Mumbai's gangsters didn't have the balls to shoot it out with the police, but they didn't want endless rounds of the court and an acquittal. So they encountered their man, sending him to the morgue instead of for trial.

Salvi hadn't killed anyone in two years.

Ferraz wished he had a suspect for him to encounter now.

He said, "Datta, remember British Deputy High Commissioner Percy Norris who was assassinated in November 1984?"

"Only what I read in the Crime Index Bureau."

"Okay, the threat from terrorists to British consular corps overseas..."

"Today? It's worse than ever before!"

"... exactly, and it's more widespread geographically."

"Also far more deadly, the threat level is substantial."

"Datta, the biggest threat to Britain today is..."

"From the Al-Qaeda, undoubtedly."

"... and other groups with common ideology."

"What's on your mind, Angelo?"

"Terrorists are searching for new cities."

"To plan and execute attacks?"

"Yes!"

"Uh-huh… like Mumbai, you mean?"

"Why not?"

"Terror organizations are now sharing information and expertise, they are coordinating their actions online and offline," Salvi said.

"And diplomats are facing threats from terrorists, religious and political extremists in the Middle East and North Africa," Ferraz said, adding, "many nations are shutting down their consulates and relocating staff."

"Hmm, so what?"

"Was Nieves under any kind of threat?"

"From the Al-Qaeda, you mean?"

"Yes, was there an Intelligence Bureau alert about a possible Al-Qaeda attack on the British Deputy High Commission in Mumbai?"

"I don't know, but–"

"Let's get this possibility out of the way, too."

"But Angelo… his wife was targeted, not him. And her throat was slit. Terrorists use AK-47 assault rifles and M-60 machine guns. They have Semtex, RDX, PETN, C4 and TNT to blow up buildings, they use rocket propelled grenades and shoulder to air missiles like…"

"Like in the *Die Hard* movies?"

"… the RPG-7 and SAM to shoot down aircraft; they arm cars, trucks and bikes with improvised explosive devises (IEDs) to assassinate people. I've never heard of them stabbing anyone."

"I know all that… so you're saying our killer is no terrorist."

"I'm saying the *madarchot's* a fucking psycho."

FERRAZ HAD three more calls to make.

Retired DCP Sanjay Parande answered immediately.

"Angelo," he said cheerily, "so early, you rascal, what's up?"

"Sir, sorry… but I knew you'd be up."

Ferraz had deep respect and much affection for Parande.

He was a highly decorated officer who had done outstanding work in the Crime Branch and Anti-Corruption Bureau. His knowledge of Mumbai's underworld was encyclopedic. And he had a thorough understanding of criminal law. Parande was still unofficially serving the Mumbai Police by helping its Detection officers whenever they got stuck.

"You're investigating Haider's murder, huh?"

"For my sins!"

"So, what's up?"

"The suspect's going by the alias Cobra."

"Cobra?" said Parande, surprised. "Like in the Cobra Gang of the 70s?"

"I don't know. Think there's a connection?"

"To what? Or to whom?"

"Some survivor from the gang… to the killer?"

"*Arre baap re!* The gang wound up with the murder of its leader."

It's leader was the notorious *goonda* Shashi Rasam.

In those days, they weren't known as gangsters. Rasam was the son of a police constable. The members of his gang were identified by tattoos of a hooded snake on their forearms. As their leader, Rasam called himself King Cobra. He was dreaded in Bombay Central where the gang ran bootlegging operations and *matka* dens. Rasam had wanted to be a cop, like his father, but ran foul of the law after he assaulted a *dhobi* and was booked. Amazing how one small incident can change the destiny of a man. He took to crime easily. Street-fights for territorial supremacy led to the murder of a rival gang leader. He was in and out of prison after that. But the difference between Rasam and other goons was that he was a *swadeshi*. He was strictly against smuggling. And he waged a war against the syndicates engaged in that kind of crime. His end came on Bombay Central Bridge where he was stabbed to death one night in 1978.

"That's 30 years ago," Parande said, "where's the connect?"

"I'm just going by the alias… why call himself the Cobra?"

"Why not? If he doesn't give himself a name…"

"Then the media or police will?"

"… exactly, and the gangs of the 70s and 80s, while they all had names like the Cobra Gang, Byculla Company, S-Bridge Gang and Golden Gang, those names didn't mean anything. They were expressions of bravado."

"Like the D-Company today?"

"No, no… the D-Company is one man's crime empire."

"You don't think the alias 'Cobra' is masking some criminal's identity?"

"No, I'm sure it isn't. But one thing comes to mind, Angelo."

"What's that, sir?"

"Aliases are associated with criminals of notoriety."

"Somebody with a long history?"

"Who's cut his teeth doing this sort of thing."

"And this killer is?"

"This killer, from what I hear, appears to be no criminal or gangster."

"You're saying he's got no record, sir?"

"I'm saying before last night, I doubt he's killed before."

THE SECOND call Ferraz made was to PSI Sangeeta Kadam.

"Hullo, sir!"

Breathless, an urgency in her voice, Ferraz felt guilty again.

"Sangeeta, know anything about poetry?" he asked, surprising her.

"Poetry? A lot! Are you interested, sir?"

"Do I look the type?"

"Actually, no sir. I'm an English Honors student, sir, I studied literature, prose and poetry at Mumbai University."

"Um, that's good. Okay, does Emperor of Darkness mean anything?"

"Emperor of Darkness? No, who's the poet? An Indian?"

"Don't know."

"Is that the name of a poem?"

"Well, I don't know."

What *do* you know, Sangeeta felt like asking her boss.

Instead she said, "Give me a reference point, sir."

"Okay, try this…

'*… I rule*
this city at night:
Emperor of Darkness,
only I have the power
to switch on
the dawn…'

… it came to the CP from our suspect as an SMS."

"Wow, that's heavy stuff. Like the message in the painter's room."

"That's poetry, right?"

"Well, sir, what is poetry? It's a literary work in which special intensity is given to the expression of feelings and ideas by the use of a distinctive style and rhythm. It's an art form in which the language is used for its aesthetic qualities in addition to, or instead of, its notional and semantic content."

"Sangeeta," said Ferraz wearily.

"But prose poems don't have verses, like what was written on the painter's wall, or even this SMS. Yet they can be visual."

"*Sangeeta!*"

"Sorry, sir… I'm just saying."

"*Don't try me… I've had quite a night.*"

"What is it you want to know, sir? The name of the poet?"

"I want to know what Emperor of Darkness means."

"Maybe I'll find it on the Net," she said.

"You think the poet is–"

"Connected with the murders? He's probably dead for centuries, sir!"

"Oh, I didn't think of that!"

"Are there any Indian poets, um, alive?"

Sangeeta giggled.

She was finding Ferraz's innocence and bewilderment cute.

"Plenty, sir! They are as young as 16."

"What! People are inspired to write poetry at that age?"

"And they win international prizes," Sangeeta said. "Let's find out how old this Emperor of Darkness poem is. And if it was written by an Indian poet."

"How will you do that?"

"I'll contact the Mumbai chapter of the Poetry Society of India."

"A society of poets, how quaint is that!"

"It was started in the 1980s to promote Indian poetry and look after the interests of Indian poets. It holds a poetry competition. I think the Poetry Society is Delhi-based. But there will be members in Mumbai."

"It's a long shot, but give it a try," Ferraz said.

IT WASN'T Sangeeta who got back to Ferraz.

But Sub-Inspector Sanjay Chhabria, the Crime Branch's Sindhi cop.

"Sir, about this Emperor of Darkness..."

Chhabria never ceased to surprise Ferraz.

He looked what he was – a shrewd, enterprising Sindhi cop. He was burly, had sparse hair, a handsome moustache, the broad forehead, bulbous nose, lustrous eyes and comically happy expression of his people, but lacked their trademark and sometimes harsh Sindhi nasal twang and the community's tight-fistedness which was legendary. Chhabria was husky and soft-spoken, he was mild-mannered and gentle, and generous to a fault.

He lived in a swanky apartment block on Khar's 15th Road. He drove a Honda City to work. His family was into home electronics and automations and had a showroom in Mahim. Chhabria was a gizmo freak. His other big thrills were movies, driving fast cars and eating out. He could have led the good life by joining his father's business. Instead, Chhabria had become a cop. Ferraz never figured out why.

Now Chhabria was excitedly saying, "He's a tyrannical deity, sir, a giant flaming entity of the Mycenae Empire. A cruel, maniacal tyrant."

"Who the fuck are you talking about!"

"The Emperor of Darkness, sir."

"Huh? He's a person, you mean!"

"He's the leader of that demonic tribe from the World of Chaos."

"Which fucking tribe from what fucking world!"

"You wanted to know, sir… I'm telling you, the Emperor of Darkness will open the Gate of Darkness to the World of Chaos thereby inheriting power to rule the world and kill anyone with immortal bloodline."

"Have you lost it?"

Ferraz was longing to relight his cigar stub.

First Sangeeta with her poetry, then Chhabria with this bullshit!

"No sir… the Emperor of Darkness is a Ninja Gaiden character."

"Ninja character?"

"Yes sir, from a video game. You know, like FIFA, Call of Duty, Battlefield, Assassin's Creed 3, Titan Fall… on Microsoft's Xbox and Sony's PS3."

"Are you serious?"

"Really, what to tell you sir, these electronic games are very popular."

"With kids, right… not killers!"

"Killers… oh no, the Emperor of Darkness is for kids."

Chhabria was sounding hurt.

"I figured," Ferraz said dryly.

"Another thing, sir…"

He was beaming again, Ferraz could hear it in his voice.

"Sylvester Stallone made a movie called *Cobra* in 1986."

"Uh-huh."

"He plays a cop on the LAPD's Zombie Squad."

"Uh-huh."

"The 'Cobra' in this case is Stallone himself, his name in the movie is Marion Cobretti, codenamed Cobra."

"Uh-huh."

Chhabria knew what that "Uh-huh" meant.

It meant, keep talking *choothiya,* I'm listening, but I have nothing to say.

Regardless, he happily continued, "He's after a New Order that despises modern society and believes in killing the weak, leaving only the strongest and smartest to rule the world."

"Who is?"

"Stallone, the Cobra, in this movie."

"And who are the members of the New Order," Ferraz asked.

"Psychopaths!"

AFTER HESITATING, Ferraz made the third call.

"Angelo!" cried Dr. Yunus A Miyasahib exuberantly.

Like he was happy to be hearing from Ferraz again.

"Doc, you were right – he's killed again."

"So soon!"

"An early morning stabbing, in the open, a British–"

"Nako re baba, just tell me, same modus operandi as in Haider's killing?"

"A phone call to the CP? Yes, from the victim's cell again. Preceded by another sinister verse this time in an SMS about being the Emperor of the Dark or something."

"He wants the police to know, Angelo."

"Know what, Doc? That the murders are his doing?"

"Yes, he's bragging. Not waiting for you to discover the murders."

"What's his game, Doc?"

"I can't even guess!" confessed Dr. Yunus. "But the murders appear to be just a sideshow, his game is something else. He won't stop. And he's cockily telling you that."

7

JACKIE AND Ferraz were having an argument.

This wasn't unusual. Not even at 7.30 am, at the dining table, which is where their liveliest discussions took place. Ferraz figured they had one every three days.

One spirited debate, past which they had now gone – *thankfully*, was over what he should eat for breakfast. Ferraz, in the carefree days before Jackie came along, was content with a mug of black coffee. And then he ordered a greasy meal from the police canteen once he reached work.

She was appalled.

"That's no way to start your morning," she admonished him. "What you're putting into yourself is… is utter *kachra!* Breakfast is the main meal of the day. Haven't you heard that you should breakfast like a king, lunch like a prince and dine like a pauper? You get 25 per cent of your day's calories from breakfast alone."

He hadn't heard this dietary wisdom before. That didn't stop Ferraz from telling Jackie, wittily he thought, "But I'm not a king!"

She had given him the look.

And over his protests, she had taken to ordering oats and eggs, she bought brown bread from a local bakery. Now she made breakfast before dashing off to college, insisting he ate it in front of her. Breakfast was a big bowl of oatmeal porridge, eggs – the way *he* ordered; scrambled, poached, omelet, boiled, even fried, but only the whites (she used the yolks in her hair) – cooked in rice bran oil. With two slices of toast. She kept only white butter at home. Ferraz thought it tasted like nothing at all. No jam, marmalade and cheese. Weekends, Jackie changed the menu. She served him pancakes with maple syrup last Sunday. He was not fond of pancakes with maple syrup. They didn't fill him, Ferraz grumbled.

"So what, you aren't working today," Jackie countered.

He had declined fruit, telling her – again, wittily he thought – that the only fruit he cared for was grapes, crushed and bottled, preferably as a crisp, dry and sweet late harvest Chenin Blanc wine.

She had given him another look, more withering.

Jackie didn't want him to go to work this morning.

She was complaining, "... it's Ganeshotsav, why do you have to go?"

Ferraz hadn't told her about the murders yet.

She wasn't faint-hearted. A murder was just another investigation. All part of his day. Though she wouldn't understand why these homicides had got the police in a flap. To her, all murder cases had to be investigated the same way, irrespective of who got killed; there was no distinction between bodies. A cop just had to dispassionately go about his job. Not emotionally get involved with the corpse, for God's sake!

He devoutly wished it was that way.

"Aren't there others?" Jackie demanded. "Why you? You promised to take me out today after college. And I've a surprise lined up for you."

Ferraz had showered and changed into khaki uniform trousers over which he wore a short sleeved, white cotton shirt. It hid the 9mm Smith & Wesson semi-automatic pistol in a holster clipped to his belt. He wore regulation tan police shoes.

Breakfast was over and Jackie was washing the dishes.

Ferraz went to the window.

A light rain was now falling. Carter Road was looking as pretty as a water color hung up to dry. Boys and girls were dawdling on their way to Rizvi College down the road, their umbrellas dotting the promenade.

Jackie came back, a cloudy expression on her lovely face. She had on black Nike tracks and an old, faded Mumbai Police T-shirt that came up to her knees.

"You mentioned a surprise," Ferraz said gaily.

"Yes, it's the Nativity of Our Lady next week… and the novenas at Mount Mary Basilica are going on," said Jackie, her anger forgotten. "I thought we ought to go to the church. And then to see the Ganpatis after that."

"That's your surprise!"

Ferraz never understood why people went to church. When he did, he came out feeling no different. There was no sensation of having being blessed. Jackie had asked him whether he expected God to reveal His divine presence with angels playing harps and doves flying around the church.

Sarcastically, but Ferraz had let it pass.

"Yeah… and *you're* not going to work today!"

She looked as if she was about to stamp her foot. He had to keep reminding himself that she was still a teenager, her Big City girl edge notwithstanding.

Ferraz sighed and pulled Jackie to a chair.

He regarded her hurt expression and softened.

"Listen sweetheart… there's a psycho on the prowl, he's killed twice since last evening, both the victims were big people, one a woman, and they were viciously stabbed to death. Now he threatens to kill again. Don't ask me why. The case has officially become mine. I'm sorry I have to go."

She frowned, so he hastily continued.

"But listen, I'll come to church after we arrest this sicko. Then," he added virtuously, "I'll really have something to thank God for, right?"

She pouted. He knew she was considering how to deal with his story.

"Okay, the condition is not that you will accompany me to church later… *that* is never conditional, understand? Instead, get me four tickets for Ram Gopal Varma's *Not a Love Story*… it released two weeks ago."

"That's a fuck–"

"*Angie!* How many times have I said I don't like you swearing!"

"People who swear tend to be more honest and trustworthy."

"Yeah, says who?"

"Honey, that movie sucks. This Ram Gopal chap is a fuck– *is* a weirdo, he has glamorized one of the ghastliest crimes committed in this city. That movie shouldn't have got past the Censor Board. And now he's making one on 26/11, can you believe his fuck– *his* bloody gumption!"

Jackie cut him short, "We aren't going for the entertainment value – of which, *I'm sure*, there's none. We are taking the clinical psychologist's approach to such a crime."

She was studying to be a clinical psychologist.

He thought she would have made a hell of a lawyer.

She frequently engaged him in fierce exchanges on criminal law, using reason or logic to justify and defend herself, telling Ferraz imperiously that he was as old fashioned as the law and like it must change.

"Who's we?" Ferraz asked suspiciously.

"We is the friends who are coming with me… there is Zeenia, Uncle Navroze's daughter who studies with me and I hope you remember, her brother Reyaz, and Damian."

"*Damian!*" he said, amazed.

"Yes!"

"As in the *Omen?*" he said, still amazed.

"*Angie…* I want four tickets for *Not a Love Story.*"

"Damian... why should I buy a ticket for this devil?"

She hustled him to the door, asking him mockingly, "Do cops actually buy tickets? Don't the black marketeers know you? Just send a constable to Globus and demand the best seats. Who will dare refuse Angelo Ferraz?"

As she closed the door, he stuck his tongue out at her.

FERRAZ REACHED Altamont Road at 8.14 am...

... two hours after Esther Nieves was murdered.

Navroze on his 1968 red Lambretta with cream detachable side panels, saddle seats and rear mounted stepney, put-putted up a minute later. The scooter had belonged to his father. It was Parsi-owned and an original Italian Lambretta, so it was in mint condition. With a smirk, Navroze parked alongside Ferraz's bike.

Ferraz's motorcycle was his pride and joy.

It was a 1962 BSA Gold Star, an iconic British motorcycle, with a powerful 500cc alloy engine and chrome-plated fuel tank bearing the famous red and gold BSA emblem. This wasn't a bike people used to get to work. It was a high-performance, sporty roadster that was noisy and fast and fun to ride. Ferraz had souped up its power and jazzed up its appeal. The motorcycle was now a sexy red, black and silver road machine that went like a streak and was capable of doing a roaring top speed of 120 kmph. It was fitted with a siren. And on its rear number plate 'POLICE' was written in red. Insurance against the Traffic cops towing it away from No-Parking Zones.

"This is where she got it?" Navroze asked, pointing to a spot on the slope zigzagging down to Peddar Road. A cold, hard drizzle had washed out the bloody traces of the murder that the posh neighborhood had woken up to.

A white Gypsy from Gamdevi Police Station was parked by the side. From its wireless inside a metallic voice squawked, *"Control calling Peter Colaba! Control calling Peter Colaba!"*

The Control Room had unusual callsigns. Peter Colaba was not the alias of some goon whose writ ran large over Colaba. Like Vinod Chembur was of the notorious bookie operating out of Chembur. Peter Colaba was the Sr. PI of Colaba Police Station. All Sr. PIs of police stations were called "Peter" for God knows what joy. Every cop in Mumbai knew who the Control Room meant when it called for "Peter Colaba".

Sitting next to the Gypsy was the milkman who had discovered Esther Nieves's body. He had been detained by the police. A silver-haired, elderly *bhaiya* dressed in a white *dhoti-kurta* looking sorry for himself. He was perched on a flower pot and was wringing his hands. His bicycle rested against empty milk cans. Apparently he was done with his milk round for the morning.

Cars crept past and motorists rolled down their windows. Some shot pictures on their cells. Navroze wanted to smack them. A motley crowd of domestic helps, watchmen, drivers, cabbies, newspaper boys, residents and lift men from the nearby buildings stood some distance away.

A Gamdevi sub-inspector came up.

"Do you want to question this man, sir?" he asked Ferraz, nodding at the scared and unhappy-looking milkman.

Ferraz grunted.

He walked down the slope to where devotional music was softly playing at a small Ganpati *pandal* outside a building called Ajanta. By the side was a taxi stand at which three cabs were parked with their meters down.

On the footpath opposite was a bunk-like bed. It was sheltered by a torn plastic sheet tied between trees. Alongside was a wooden trunk and on top of this, a photo-frame of some deity before a burning lamp. A clothesline stretched across the bordering wall on which hung a faded blue shirt and a pair of old, worn-out shorts. The home of some poor man, Ferraz thought. Across this shanty was Bungalow 8, designer Maithili Ahluwalia's concept store of unconventional Indian-inspired interior and fashion accessories.

Ferraz pointed out the shelter to the sub-inspector.

"Find out who lives there," he said, "and bring that person to me."

The crowd had swelled considerably when he returned to the murder spot. The elderly milkman waited nervously beside the police jeep.

"Tell me," Ferraz said addressing the old *bhaiya*, "what's your name and what exactly did you see when you reached here."

The milkman hesitated. He was a simple *doodhwala*, he was scared of the police, and he didn't like the steely look Ferraz was unintentionally giving him.

"Nothing, sir," he mumbled avoiding Ferraz's gaze, "I saw madam was lying in blood. I left my cycle and ran up the slope to the beat *chowki*. Everybody knows me here, I have been delivering milk for 17 years, they will all tell you they know me – Pandey Doodhwala."

"Where were you coming from, Pandeyji?" asked Navroze in a friendly voice.

"From Kamal Mahal on Altamont Road, I deliver milk from A-1 Dairy in Nanachowk to three homes in this building, then cycle down to Peddar Road and the building Vasant," said the old *bhaiya*. "I was doing that when… *when*, I saw the madam. I thought somebody had fainted. I got off my cycle. Then I saw the blood. I got scared."

"What did you do then?" asked Navroze kindly.

"I ran!" said the milkman.

"Did you see anybody on the slope?" asked Ferraz, "any stranger, or someone you see every morning, somebody from these buildings nearby?"

"There was nobody, sir," the milkman said miserably.

"Was the Nieves wo– was this madam alive?" Ferraz asked.

"I didn't wait to find out, I ran," repeated the milkman.

"You ran up *that* slope!" Ferraz snapped, looking at the old *bhaiya's* bow legs disbelievingly. To Navroze he said irritably, "Take his number, get the address of his dairy, and let him go. He's shit scared. Talk to him later."

A thin, unwashed youth in a pair of ragged shorts and a hand-me-down shirt came up. He was barefoot, had uncombed hair and a stubble, and stank of *desi daru*.

"You wanted me, sir?" he asked Ferraz, shuffling his feet and keeping his eyes on the ground. He had broken, *paan*-stained teeth and utterly foul breath.

Ferraz regarded him blankly.

"Who are you?" he asked.

"Sir, I am Sanjay Chavan," the youth replied, as if the name might ring some faraway bell in Ferraz's memory.

The Gamdevi cop interrupted, "Sir, he lives on the footpath opposite Bungalow 8… you wanted to speak to him."

"Ah yes," Ferraz said, remembering.

He regarded the youth. Just looking at him made Ferraz feel itchy and want to scratch himself. But there was honesty in his eyes, sadness in his face and the demeanor of somebody who had been shouted at all his life and put down for being nobody.

"Tell me Sanjay, what do you do?"

"I wash cars here, sir," the youth replied, swaying.

"Are you drunk?"

Sanjay Chavan giggled, surprising Ferraz.

His thin emancipated face lit up and he said, "Last night we got this Ganpati Bappa (he swept his hand down the slope) and had a little party. We always do this. I cannot afford to drink regularly… maybe I have a glass now and then, like when India wins a cricket match… but for Ganeshotsav and when we bring the Devi during Navratri, I get *fulltoo!* We buy *daru* from the donations people give. A bottle of DSP, Aristocrat, some good *maal*. We all drink then and dance on the road… late at night, nobody objects."

"You and who else, Sanjay?" Ferraz asked, amused.

"My friends… the boys of the area, Babban, Ankush, Bahadur…"

"Who are they?"

He giggled again, surprising Ferraz once more.

"They are nobody, sir, like me… Babban is a driver for a bank manager living in Ajanta, Ankush is the building watchman and Bahadur has a tailoring shop beneath the stairs of a building on Peddar Road," he said, proud of his friends.

"Hmnn, okay," Ferraz said, satisfied. "Did you know the woman who got murdered?"

"I didn't do it!" he said, suddenly terrified.

"Tch, I know you didn't," Ferraz said impatiently. "What did I ask you?"

"No sir… *how* would I know her! But I used to see her… always walking her dog. It's sad… what happened."

"Were you awake when it happened? Did you hear anything? Screams, the sounds of a struggle, anything? What time do you wake up to wash the cars?"

"I heard that… the *khoon*… happened around 6 am," Sanjay Chavan said. "I get up at 5 to wash cars. Every building has a tap at the back but the watchmen don't let me in for water when the *seths* are up. I wash five cars on this road. The *seths* pay me 500 rupees a car. I make a few thousands… enough for me… I live here alone. My wife left me. Did I tell you I was married?"

"You didn't," Ferraz told the youth. "Why did she leave you? And why are you living here – on the road?"

Sanjay Chavan's eyes welled up suddenly and his face crumpled.

"I don't know why… she left me," he said sniveling, large tears rolling down his thin, unshaven face. He wiped them away with the back of his sleeve. "She just went one day. I keep looking down the slope… hoping, hoping to see her come back, but… but… My father used to work here (he pointed towards Bungalow 8) and after he died, I just continued hanging around. Where else could I go? Sometimes… sometimes policemen come late at night and take money from me for sleeping on the footpath. They say it is for their *bada saheb*. If I don't have money, they abuse and slap me. They threaten to lock me up, they say robberies take place here because of people like me, cars are broken into and stereos get stolen, and they have cases they can drag me into."

Ferraz regarded him in silence.

"Tell me, Sanjay," he said in a softer voice, "did you see anyone, hear anything this morning, when the *khoon* took place?"

"No sir… how could I?"

"Didn't you say you wake up at 5 am to wash cars?"

"Not today, sir, today I was too drunk!"

Ferraz turned to Navroze in frustration.

"Hundreds of people around but not one saw the killer," he shouted, throwing his hands up in disgust.

Sanjay Chavan was still hanging around apologetically.

"Sir…," he muttered hesitantly.

"What is it?" Ferraz snapped.

"May I know your name? You know… when the constables come after me at night, when they harass me, I can, *I could* tell them I know you, and…"

Ferraz silenced him with a stare.

He turned to the Gamdevi sub-inspector and said, "Ask the beat *chowki* staff on Altamont Road to activate their sources, I want to know if any stranger was spotted here in the past two weeks."

8

THE MEDIA had laid siege to the Crime Branch.

It was only 9.30 am. But two big murders had been committed. And the city's bloodthirsty would be jumping for news. The announcement of Nawalkar's press conference had drawn crime reporters in numbers. Also the electronic media. Their OB vans, mobile Outside Broadcasting studios with their TV channels' logos emblazoned on the sides and powerful dish antennae bobbing on the roof, were parked all over in disorder. Brightly painted, they brought colour to the sombre Police Commissionerate.

Ferraz was surprised to see them.

After 26/11, a tight security blanket had been thrown around the Mumbai Police HQ with a barrier of screening machines installed at its entrance that were manned by armed policemen day and night. You had to have legitimate business and an appointment with the police, and valid identity proof, before they allowed you in.

But this morning it was open house.

The journos were outside the Police Press Room, a quaint bungalow adjacent the Crime Branch building, with a sloping tiled roof and large glass windows. Behind was the Police Canteen serving them *cutting chai* and *batata wada* for breakfast.

Ferraz could hear their excited voices.

Sensational murders, gang-rapes and kidnappings gave crime reporters an adrenaline rush. They lived for these stories. And he knew, like dogs with a bone, they would chew and worry the

Haider and Nieves murders until all the meat and juices had been drained out.

A number of them, Ferraz noticed, were young girls who looked like they were just out of college. They had attitude if not experience. They smoked and talked coarsely with the guys. Maybe it was hip to sound crass in order to appear cool in the media. In Mumbai, crime topped the news chart. And the police beat was as popular as covering cricket and Bollywood.

Ferraz always sought to dodge the press.

He parked his motorcycle in a patch of weak sunlight that was filtering through the trees and dancing on the cobbled courtyard. Leaping across a puddle of rainwater reflecting sepia toned images of the Victorian Gothic buildings, he was about to enter the Unit I office, when…

"Oh, Inspector!"

Ferraz recognized her at once.

Nahida Shaikh, the sultry correspondent of *Network Today*, lovely legs in blue jeans that ended in gumboots this morning, a white blouse unbuttoned at the neck but captured at the waist by a belt, an open flimsy sky blue raincoat on top, her raven black hair cut to frame a heart-shaped face, full sensuous lips open in a mocking smile that revealed perfectly shaped teeth, her lovely kohl-lined eyes smoldering with sensuousness, the body exciting enough to cause a Bishop to kick a hole in a stained glass window.

She was leading a TV crew this morning.

He gave her the swift head-to-toe, missing nothing.

"Inspector Ferraz… hello – d'you remember me?" she asked in a lazy drawl oozing sex appeal, swiveling towards him, one hand extended.

Most men would find it hard to forget her, he was willing to bet.

"I do, indeed," Ferraz replied with a cold wintry smile, ignoring her outstretched hand and remembering the time she had…

... this was soon after 26/11, he was investigating the sodomy and murder of a boy of six from the Geeta Nagar slums of Cuffe Parade. The kid's body was found in a creek that ran out to sea, savagely bitten and ravaged, and strangled with a metal coat hanger that still dangled around his neck.

Ferraz had been handling the case himself.

The investigation led the police to Varanasi. Where they arrested a homosexual *dhobi* who had gone missing from the slums after the crime had been discovered.

He might have got away had he stayed back.

Instead, he chose to run; to guilty minds fear lends wings.

He was trapped by his dental records. It was freaky. The Government Dental College, where the police learned the *dhobi* had gone recently, had his teeth impressions cast in a model of plaster and on x-ray film. It was a one in a million chance, but they matched the bite marks on the victim's body. The arrest was swiftly made. The police team was returning at night by the Varanasi-Mumbai LTT Super Fast Express when the *dhobi* asked for a cigarette and coolly told Ferraz about the murder.

This wasn't an interrogation into his bestiality.

He was just letting it out as the train galloped towards Mumbai, its compartments lurching and swaying, the wheels clattering as they changed tracks and went over points, the engine's mournful horn cutting through the darkness as the train passed level crossings with ringing alarm bells.

The *dhobi* then made a fatal mistake. Aware he would be produced in court, he asked if his was a bailable offence and how soon he would be out.

Ferraz was on him in a flash.

Hauling the *dhobi* roughly to his feet, he dragged him screaming loudly to the vestibule of the compartment. Before the accompanying cops could react, Ferraz had drawn his 9mm S&W and blown the *dhobi's* brains out.

The gun's magazine held 17 rounds. One bullet was all that it took. Ferraz had gently squeezed the trigger. Mercilessly allowing the man to stare death in the face... just as the little slum kid must have done when the *dhobi,* his lust satiated, was cold-bloodedly strangling him with the metal hanger.

The police put out the usual story.

That the accused was trying to escape after attacking the police party.

The press knew how it was. The *dhobi* deserved to die, anyway. What was one more encounter in a city where the cops were glorified in movies for killing gangsters in staged shootouts, ta-ra!

But one journalist thought Ferraz was going over the edge...

... because of what happened on 26/11.

Nahida Shaikh was reading the situation differently.

In a witch hunt against Ferraz, Nahida tore into the Mumbai Police with scathing articles in her channel's sister publication *Newsday.* She charged Ferraz with sadistically killing an accused who had no criminal record. And who should have faced trial. She went on TV and hammered the police some more in a blazing debate on the subject. Nothing came of it, the noise died down and the city soon forgot.

Then one Saturday night, months later...

... unable to sleep, Ferraz had stepped out at 2 am hoping the moonlight on the water and the calm sea breeze would...

... *uh-oh, but Carter Road was occupied.*

A bikers' gang was on the rampage.

He heard and smelled them first. They were drinking, smoking dope and looking for distraction after racing their bikes up and down Carter Road.

A girl and her younger brother provided it...

... they had chosen this unearthly hour to take a walk.

The gang pounced on them. They roughed up the boy, pinned him against a car and were forcibly pouring beer down his throat. He kept gagging. Each time they slapped him violently. He was overcome by fear.

Nahida Shaikh was the girl, being groped.

Unrecognizable without her mic and TV camera, stripped of the great sense of her own importance, she fought them silently, the authority and influence of her press card not protecting her now.

There was absolute terror in her eyes, tears streaked her face.

Ferraz took in this late night horror show with one startled glance.

Breaking up a law and order situation wasn't his obligation.

That's what the men in khaki were there for.

But where was a cop when you wanted one!

He could see lights on in the Additional Commissioner of Police's (West) office a 100 meters away, but the bikers cared a rat's ass for the cops. They were too zoned out to bother. This was Saturday night, baby, their time to howl.

Some situations you walked away from. But he was a cop.

The men pawing Nahida whirled around to confront him.

"Listen," Ferraz started saying, "you're..."

"Yeah," one said aggressively, "we are *what*, man?"

The others laughed, uproariously and drunkenly.

"You're making a mistake," Ferraz said, his heart pounding.

"Yeah, you think so, motherfucker?"

Slowly, wearily he said, "Look, I am from the police..."

He was in jeans and a T-shirt, wearing loafers.

But Nahida recognized him, hope was shining in her eyes.

"Hear that, Aditya," the hooligan shouted to the leader of this merry gang beating up Nahida's kid brother, "the cops are here, what do we do now!"

That brought more derisive laughter!

Ferraz was hoping a patrol vehicle would come by.

But that night they had Carter Road to themselves.

The men left the girl and ganged up on him.

"You're a cop?" one said disbelievingly, giving him a crack on the head.

"Don't," Ferraz started to say.

"Don't *what*, cop?" another challenged, pushing him hard.

"Look, I don't want trouble," he said.

"You don't want T-R-O-U-B-L-E?" Aditya was eyeball-to-eyeball with Ferraz now. "Then what you want? You want this?"

He grabbed his own crotch and shook it.

"Or *you* want this, prick?"

And he smashed the base of his beer bottle against a lamp post, converting it into an ugly and jagged weapon.

Ferraz raised his hands submissively.

"Hands up," Aditya shouted, laughing like mad. "Man, are you a cop or a fucking pussy! Like we saw on 26/11. Ten motherfucking Paki terrorists jerked off your entire force."

He spat on the promenade in contempt.

"Listen," Ferraz pleaded, "I don't want to…"

"You don't want to *what*, cop? Get killed?"

Aditya crisscrossed the air in front of Ferraz's eyes with the broken bottle, standing sideways like Zorro, laughing drunkenly all the time.

Ferraz continued to hold his hands up.

The others lost interest and turned on Nahida again, like savage beasts on *National Geographic* tearing into helpless prey, rough and ready hands grabbing, squeezing and hurting her.

She screamed.

Aditya turned to look…

… and one of the deadliest cops in Mumbai inched forward.

Nahida screamed once more, tearing the quiet of the night to shreds.

Aditya turned again…

… and Ferraz moved.

His hands came scything down, locking onto Aditya's wrist with frightening strength, knocking the bottle out. He yanked hard, so hard that he dislocated the hooligan's shoulder. Off balance, Aditya pitched forward helplessly. Ferraz sidestepped and smashed a powerful kick to his groin.

One down! The others stared, open-mouthed.

A second one charged him with an enraged roar.

Ferraz stopped him with a knife-like rigid hand to the throat.

The man staggered to a halt, coughing painfully and gasping for breath. Ferraz stiff-armed him with the heel of his palm to make space. And then kicked him, breaking three ribs and sending him cartwheeling into a parked car where he lay crumpled.

Yet one more tried to foolishly take him down.

The one who had slapped him on the back of the head. He swung a punch wildly at Ferraz, all the bluster gone out of him now, panic showing on his mean face.

Ferraz took the blow without batting an eye.

And then he hit back… all his pent up fury exploding in the uppercut that lifted the man off his feet, landing him with a thud several feet away, with a broken jaw and two teeth out.

The show was over. But the curtain hadn't gone down.

The hooligans were spoiled brats grown into adult bullies.

They came from rich and influential families.

There was a hue and cry. Complaints were lodged right up to Mantralaya. Accusations of police brutality were made against Ferraz. Pressure was brought for an inquiry. Demands were made for his arrest, suspension and dismissal.

But Ferraz had the people's sympathy…

… and this time led by the victim herself, the entire media's support. The Department stood by him and based on Nahida's complaint, booked the hooligans under Sections 354 and 509 of the IPC (for molestation and sexual harassment), Section 353 (for assault and criminal force to deter a public servant from discharge of his duty) and Section 323 (for voluntarily causing hurt).

He came out a hero. But he never spoke to Nahida Shaikh again.

Until today…

"Are you handling this case?" she asked.

"Which case would that be?" he replied innocently.

"These two murders, Haider and Nieves."

She still favored him with her wide, sexy smile.

"Me? Whatever gave you that idea!"

"Oh… but I heard you are."

She was finding his hard, impersonal stare distracting.

"Are you asking me or telling me, Miss?"

"It's *Nahida*. I thought you might help me."

"Me?" Ferraz asked again, incredulously, "How could I help you?"

"Well, the Crime Branch has taken over and – *no, don't say no* – you're the Investigating Officer. You must know something. C'mon Inspector… give me a break, *puh-lease*, I go on air soon after the CP's conference, there's no time to write a story, and I'd like to tell my viewers something different. Something exclusive, you know, this is big news… help me… tell me something about the murders that I don't know."

Crime reporters took that liberty with cops they knew. After seeing and hearing all the facts, gathering the information, if they were unable to find a story, they tried to dig out something from their police sources that the other reporters didn't have. It gave their reportage the edge.

Ferraz regarded her in unblinking silence.

She hesitated, then gave a false laugh and continued, "I understand both murders are being treated as one investigation. Why is that? What if they are unrelated and committed by different people? How can the police be sure it's the same killer?"

"You have a lot of questions."

"Give me some answers," she pleaded. "Are you close to an arrest? Is that why the CP has called for a press conference so early in the investigation?"

"If we knew who the killer is, we'd have him in here, don't you think?"

She chewed her lower lip then said, the words tumbling out in haste, "Right now it's all speculation. But I have, uh, a theory. You know, I… I have an American Master's degree in Criminology & Justice. Would you like to… *maybe*… share your thoughts with me… over, over a Cappuccino? Just have a friendly chat, off the record, tell me how the investigation is going… I'd really love that… and to…"

Ferraz interrupted her with a sunshine smile of his own.

"Thank you," he said, "but I hate Cappuccino."

UNIT I was in the Police Commissionerate.

The office was in an one-storey stone building between the colonial Crime Branch HQ with its wooden balconies, glass-paneled doors and quaint winding staircase and the grim Crime Branch lock-up that had accommodated corrupt politicians, scamster businessmen, dreaded gangsters, underworld dons and killer terrorists.

Its entrance had iron gates that had accommodated corrupt politicians, scamster businessmen, dreaded gangsters, underworld dons and killer terrorists. Beyond them, a flight of wooden stairs led to the first floor office. On the landing was the toilet outside which an old disused ladder stood propped against the wall. It had been there for years. The office was one large hall that had been ingeniously partitioned by cupboards containing case records, shelves with dusty files of convictions and steel trunks with the historic 13,000-pages chargesheet of the 1993 Bombay blasts case.

It wasn't a cheery room.

The barred windows gave Unit I an uncanny resemblance to the lock-up next door. From its high ceiling hung fans that provided little breeze. The sloping roof was asbestos. And it absorbed the cruel rays of the sun during summer and transferred the heat inside, making the room as hot as a furnace.

The DCB-CID cops thankfully didn't wear uniform.

But this wasn't like Friday Dressing – a trend wherein business executives celebrated a semi-reprieve from the constrictions of a formal dress code on Friday and dressed casually.

The cops here were unremarkable in their attire. No distracting prints and dazzling colors that would make them stand out. The freedom from uniform didn't mean they could throw etiquette to the wind and dress to look stylish or anything that conformed to what was currently in fashion.

An out-of-uniform cop was only a plainclothes policeman.

The large room had a conference table around which the cops sat on wooden benches and had lunch. Few official discussions took place here. They were held impromptu at the water cooler in a corner. Next to it was a dirty sink with a stained mirror reflecting unflattering images. The desks were old and solid and made of wood; they had glass tops beneath which some cops had proudly inserted press cuttings of the arrests they had made.

The first time Jackie came here, she had suppressed a shudder. After looking around the plain and shabby office in undisguised wonder, she hesitated to use the toilet and even accept a glass of water.

An interrogation was taking place.

Unit I was after a gang of auto thieves operating in Cuffe Parade. Its specialty was high-end SUVs. The Cuffe Parade police had registered 17 thefts of Mitsubishis, Hondas, Toyotas, Mercs and Land Rovers in two weeks. Enough to send the Colaba Cuffe Parade Residents' Association crying to the CP. It was a case for the Anti-Motor Vehicle Theft Cell. But the cell's detection rate was dismal. So Nawalkar gave the Cuffe Parade auto theft cases to Unit I to detect.

A *khabri* told Navroze that a gang from Pratapgadh in UP was behind them. Among its members in Mumbai were a computer engineer who broke the locking system codes of cars, an electrician who dismantled their alarms, a duplicate car key-maker, a mechanic and two taxi drivers. Once the stolen car reached Maharashtra's border, they changed its number plate, gave it a fresh coat of paint and drove it to UP.

Navroze's investigation led him to a petrol pump attendant in Sassoon Dock at Colaba who tipped the gang about all the high-end SUVs in the area after getting information from their unsuspecting drivers. The police picked him up. He was a Tamilian grease monkey nicknamed "Thambi". Which meant little brother in Tamil. Or dude.

Navroze was calling him "*Chootmarika*" when Jackie arrived.

Thambi had been remanded to four days' police custody. The cops had deprived him of sleep for 42 hours and questioned him without a break. He had been strung upside down, beaten with belts and canes on the soles of his feet, and given electric shocks to his private parts.

But Thambi hadn't broken.

Navroze's patience was running thin. His face had turned purple with the interrogation. He was threatening to arrest the mechanic's family next.

"They are in Tirunelveli," Thambi told Navroze with great dignity.

"They could be in Timbuktu, you *chooth*! I'll get them even if they are in Hell if you don't tell me what I want to know. I'll dip my *lathi* in red chili powder and shove it up your ass before them. And then I'll beat the fucking shit out of them one by one in front of you," Navroze shouted.

But Thambi was extraordinarily stubborn.

"I don't know what you want to know," he said quietly.

Navroze got up and slapped the mechanic hard.

Thambi somersaulted and landed on the floor with a thud.

Vishnu Shetty who was standing by, massively built, dark and with a thick moustache, looking ominously like Yamraj the God of Death, picked up the stunned petrol pump attendant and roughly shook him.

Navroze told Shetty, "Take this *madarchot* to Colaba Woods tonight and encounter him. He knows nothing about the stolen cars. Then throw his body in the sea near Badhwar Park. Don't let anyone see you."

Thambi gave a loud and anguished cry.

Jackie watched in wide-eyed, open-mouthed horror.

"Uncle Navroze!" she squeaked as Shetty led the blabbering mechanic away.

"Hiya sweetheart, you've come to join us?"

"Don't kill him, please," she implored, almost in tears.

Navroze roared with laughter and thumped the table.

"Arre nai, maari dikri. We'll just fire a couple of rounds under his ass. The bastard will shit *vada sambhar* and tell us everything," he assured her. "This is how we work. We aren't auditioning for *CID* here, you know."

People thought Crime Branch cops aped their TV counterparts.

That they too dressed in three-pieces, leather jackets and tight jeans. And wore make-up, frowns and fierce expressions. People also believed that like TV cops, the Crime Branch men were experts in forensic science, toxicology, ballistics, DNA testing and graphology. And that they conducted narcoanalysis, brain mapping and polygraph tests out of an office whose psychedelic lighting would have delighted a disco dancer. Not to forget attending post-mortems indelicately conducted under blue lights in a morgue resembling a beauty parlor with bottles and jars of colored products stacked on glass shelves. And like those geniuses, those super sleuths, those indefatigable crime busters on *CID*, the real cops also chased criminals around the world and had shootouts with them in London streets, outside Parisian cafes and on the Swiss Alps.

Ferraz was thinking about Nahida Shaikh.

His office was austere. It had an air-conditioner that the government wasn't supposed to know about. Also, a flat screen TV, a small refrigerator, steel and wooden cupboards, a large glass-topped desk and plastic bucket chairs for visitors. The Station House called, breaking into his thoughts.

All DCB-CID Units were required at the Police Club for the CP's monthly Crime Conference for August. Apparently Nawalkar had changed his mind and wasn't going to address the press. Ferraz wondered what would happen to Nahida Shaikh's big TV story.

There was a knock on his door. Sangeeta Kadam peeped in.

"Sir, we're all here," she told Ferraz.

SANGEETA was every criminal's fantasy…

… and most policemen's too.

She was 28, sensuously built, dusky and distracting with sharp features, smoky eyes, and a petulant, full-lipped mouth that made her look like that ravishing Bollywood diva Sonali Bendre.

When she wasn't fighting crime, Sangeeta was fighting the playful attacks on her virtue by her hot-blooded colleagues. Her father had been an ACP who got killed in the 1984 Bhiwandi communal riots. That explained why Sangeeta joined the Mumbai Police; but not her presence in the DCB-CID. It was seldom by default or chance that a police officer got inducted into the Crime Branch's elite squad of detectives. They had to be damn good cops to make the grade.

Sangeeta had been lucky.

She was posted at Airport Security. One winter night she

encountered an elusive armed gang that had been stopping taxis and cars on the Western Express Highway and robbing foreigners coming from abroad of laptops, sophisticated cell phones, expensive cameras, their foreign currency, and even imported liquor, watches, perfumes and chocolates.

These highwaymen were known as the Ghost Gang.

The police suspected it had operatives at the airport who selected victims when they landed and gave the gang descriptions of them. Registering the crime was difficult because the highway came under the jurisdiction of several police stations. The DCB-CID's Unit VIII, under which the airport fell, was also struggling to detect the robberies. And then PSI Sangeeta Kadam came along.

Her scooty had conked and she hitched a ride with a foreigner going to South Mumbai. A cold wind was blowing on the highway and Sangeeta had on a windcheater over her uniform. She looked like any other pretty face with a good pair of legs out late in Mumbai. When their taxi came to a screeching halt at a dark and desolate spot on the highway, Sangeeta who was chatting animatedly with the foreigner thought an accident had taken place and that somebody was hurt, people wanted help.

She got out, unsuspecting…

… and saw the men advancing, guns in hand.

She froze, eyes widening in fear, throat constricting, feeling her heart racing wildly and her limbs going weak as four armed men with dark sullen looks and sneaking gaits came up, but…

… seeing her khaki trousers and tan shoes, one hesitantly lifted his gun.

Sangeeta's hand dropped to the .38 Taurus holstered at her hip beneath the windcheater. She drew and fired in one movement, without taking aim, blowing him several feet away. Then…

… a second robber brought up his gun in panic.

Sangeeta was now in the classic policeman's crouch, her gun leveled and held out straight in front with both hands, her eyes squinting down the barrel. She fired without hesitation, just as the robber pulled his trigger, both explosions shattering the quiet of the night…

… killing the man on the spot.

The others fled.

Getting over her shock, Sangeeta hailed a patrolling Traffic Police jeep to take the injured robber to Cooper Hospital in Juhu. She then informed the Control Room and her ACP at the Airport Police about the shootout. Her prisoner died on the way. But not before Sangeeta and the Traffic cops interrogated him. Before dawn, she assisted DCB-CID officers from Units VIII, IX and X in busting the Ghost Gang.

Rathod got her transferred to the Crime Branch. Sangeeta brightened up the drab Unit I office with her vibrant sex appeal. She was a good cop. And also a sport. Navroze told her often to give up her gun for a bikini on the Kingfisher calendar.

"That's where the money is," he would say lewdly.

"More than the *hafta* here?" Sangeeta would ask teasingly.

Now she told Ferraz, "Sir, I spoke to Abida Ashraf Rasheed."

"The Moplah of Kozhikode?"

"Yes, sir," Sangeeta grinned sexily.

The other cops wondered what the joke was.

"Where did you catch her? Her phone was off, right?"

"She was on her way to Mumbai, sir."

"What! She's here?"

"Yes, sir. She saw Haider's murder on TV last night. And caught the 6.05 am Air India Express flight to Mumbai. She's heartbroken. I couldn't get a word out of her. I've scheduled an interview for later today."

"Won't she be at the painter's funeral? When is it anyway?"

"Women aren't allowed to attend funerals in Islam," Shadab told them. "It's at the Bada Qabrastan in Marine Lines this evening."

"Oh, okay. What about that Mombasa woman?" Ferraz asked Sangeeta.

"Umaima Mulla, no contact. I sent her an SMS and also an e-mail."

"We've had an eventful but disappointing time," said Ferraz ruefully after the officers had recapped their unfruitful experiences of the previous night.

Antone de Azavedo, the Detection officer working the door-to-door with cops from Pydhonie police station, had taken hours to talk to all the families in the building where Haider had spent his lifetime. He had worked through the night. Hoping somebody might have heard or seen something unusual. But nobody had anything useful to say. A search of all the garbage bins in the neighbourhood, which were overflowing and scavenged by stray dogs and cattle, had failed to turn up the murder weapon. No surprise. It had been used again this morning.

"And now we have another murder," Navroze reminded Ferraz.

"If this Cobra is our suspect," said Salvi, "and he has a motive, shouldn't we focus on finding the motive? Why spend time interrogating the neighbours, staking out underworld haunts, rounding up anti-socials, hassling the right wing guys, and arresting drug peddlers?"

"I agree," Ferraz said, "we have to find what linked the victims. But standard operation procedures have to be maintained. Questioning Haider's neighbors again might reveal something we didn't get last night. Maybe some resident saw the killer. And was petrified to tell us. But in daytime people get courage. Widen the search to the nearby buildings. Talk to the shopkeepers below. Don't ask if they saw anybody suspicious. They won't understand. Ask them if they noticed a stranger loitering around. The *khabris* might also turn up something. After we get the painter's phone records, we'll interrogate all those in frequent touch with him to find out who was friend and who was foe."

"He had no enemies in the art world," Salvi said.

"Nobody had a bad word to say," Sangeeta added, "we've been on the phone all night talking to gallerists, buyers, collectors, other artists."

"And the bugger had no laptop!" Navroze told them. "So there's no record of any hate mail."

"Hate mail would come by post," Khan said. "The cyber cops can track anything online. But there's no articles of post in the stuff we recovered from his house. God knows how he communicated with the world."

"Didn't he have a secretary?" Ferraz asked, surprised.

"I think Abida handled his work," Sangeeta said. "I'll find out. He wasn't on Facebook or Twitter. I think he was too old for that. And he has no website. Though there's unlimited content on him on the Internet."

"Pydhonie police picked up his *ganga bai* and *dhobi*."

Khan said, "They work in other houses in the building. Both saw Haider yesterday. He was painting and chased them away. They want to know who'll pay their August dues!"

9

"OKAY, WHAT have we got?"

They were at the Police Club in Azad Maidan. The brain and brawn of the Mumbai Police. Squashed into one big hall for the CP's Crime Conference. Nawalkar had blithely kicked it off by inquiring what progress had been made on the two murders.

Like they had been working the investigation for days.

We got two corpses, Ferraz wanted to say.

The morning was turning dark and gloomy.

Thunder crashed across the sky. St. Peter and St. Paul playing football in heaven, Ferraz thought, recalling a childhood legend. Minutes later, a slanting rain was glancing off the roofs of the police vehicles parked outside. The weatherman had gaily forecast clear skies today.

The Police Club was behind the Chief Metropolitan Magistrate's Court. At a pinch it took in the 250-plus cops who attended the Crime Conference. They were of the rank of Sr. PI and above. Mainly from the 93 police stations and 12 Units of the DCB-CID. Gathered to discuss crime trends. Murder was slightly up from July, sexual assaults too, so were suicides – punishable under Section 309 of the IPC; but street crime was down, and motoring offences also because the Traffic Police was asked to be lenient in the rains. The CP took special note of misdemeanors and felonies affecting the common man. Like chain-snatching, eve-teasing and house-breaking. He offered his advice on any major undetected crimes.

Then Nawalkar addressed the Haider and Nieves murders. He sat at a table under a halo of light from an overhead lamp. Flanked by Joint CP (Crime) Arun Rathod and Joint CP (L&O) Arvind Mugbe. Both in starched khaki. Looking like wooden bookends on a shelf. Nawalkar was sartorially elegant in comparison. He wore beige chinos and a navy blue Nina Ricci shirt.

Earlier, he had met both Joint CPs in his office. He wasn't in favour of clubbing the murders and transferring them as one investigation to Unit I of the DCB-CID. This was the sort of half-assed strategy an Indian paperback crime writer would use. Give both murders to a larger-than-life supercop who would challenge the enemy single-handedly. Nawalkar knew crime detection was not the breezy, exciting ride of pulp fiction.

Frederick Forsythe described it as 99 per cent routine work of unspectacular inquiry, checking and double checking facts, and laboriously building up a web of parts until the parts became a whole and the whole a net that enclosed the criminal with a case that didn't just make headlines but also stood up in court.

He was right, the arrest of an accused and his admission of the crime wasn't the end of the investigation; his conviction by the court was.

Thankfully, the DCB-CID had a decent conviction rate.

Its quality of investigation was always good. The Detection cops were diligent at paperwork and filing chargesheets, some specialized in legwork and field investigations, a few exclusively networked with *khabris,* others were skilful interrogators. And some were strong-arm enforcers.

"Why do we have to club the cases?" Nawalkar had asked, twirling his moustache and frowning at the Joint CP (Crime).

"Because it's the same killer, sir," Rathod told him patiently.

"That's not confirmed yet," Nawalkar countered. "Do we have DNA evidence from both murders to support this theory?"

"Forensics will take time, but– "

"So we have only the mysterious caller's word for it?"

"The modus operandi in both murders is similar," Rathod continued.

"How? He dumped Haider's head in plain sight, presenting it to us."

"And then he murdered the English woman in the open, in daylight, sir. Clearly he's a risk taker," argued Rathod.

"And *you* spoke to the same suspect both times, sir," Mugbe added.

"So you have decided there's a connection, then? Shouldn't we be open to all possibilities?"

"We have filed separate cases at Pydhonie and Gamdevi but will transfer them to the Crime Branch as one investigation and later file one chargesheet. The court can be asked to hear both cases together," Rathod explained.

"I don't like it at all," Nawalkar grumbled, "I was thinking of an all inclusive investigation…"

"Meaning?"

"… involving every available man in the force."

Used at they were to Nawalkar's out-of-the-box ideas, Mugbe and Rathod were unable to hide their surprise this time.

What the CP was suggesting was a manhunt for the sinister, arrogant killer using every cop in the 47,000-strong police force even while Unit I of the DCB-CID investigated both murders.

"But that would be a duplication of effort," Mugbe objected.

"On the contrary, the effort will be doubled," Nawalkar said, "if the Crime Branch fails, the sectional police may succeed. The DCB-CID is technically superior but restricted in terms of manpower. The sectional police has more force on the ground and better local intelligence."

He had a point there, they had to admit.

"The problem is that a higher-ranking sectional officer, or even a slightly older and more experienced Sr. PI, won't willingly cooperate with Ferraz who is heading this investigation," Rathod said doubtfully.

The police force was like any office, riddled with politics. There were ego hassles, manipulations, inter-department rivalry, seniority issues, backward class supersession, cronyism, bullying and backstabbing.

But Nawalkar wasn't having any of it.

"I don't want a game of one-upmanship," he told Rathod, "that's why I want you to be involved. Get your best Detection officers from all 12 DCB-CID Units to work with Ferraz. I want all hands on deck."

Nawalkar then revealed his plan.

"Create Special Investigation Teams (SITs) in all five regions headed by their Addl. CPs," he told Mugbe. "Each SIT should have competent officers and experienced staff from among the police stations in their region. You handpick the teams. The Sr. PIs of police stations are old bandicoots, they know the ground, take them into confidence."

He explained the SITs' roles next.

"They will boost the DCB-CID's investigation by increasing police presence on the road, tapping sources, conducting *nakabandis*, doing house searches, combing operations, gathering information of suspicious people and activities, and by identifying the VIPs in each police station's jurisdiction who might be the killer's third victim. We will provide them with security," the CP said. "The SITs will focus on this work while the police stations will continue with day-to-day policing."

Mugbe was relieved. He didn't fancy sending every uniformed cop from his 93 police stations chasing after a phantom serial killer. Law and order was the sectional police's daily headache. What if a riot suddenly flared up on Mohammed Ali Road? Or a stampede broke out at Siddhivinayak Temple? Who would handle it if every cop was working on a SIT?

Nawalkar told them, "Be hands-on, meet your Detection and SIT teams every day. Give them different assignments. Spell out tasks in the morning. Let them come back to you with feedback in the evening. Review the day's work. Change the teams. Make them work nights. I want the sectional police and Crime Branch to coordinate on this investigation. I don't mind healthy competition because the ultimate aim is to solve this case quickly."

Mugbe interrupted, "But there will be many verticals…"

"*Verticals?*"

"People relating to different levels in a hierarchy. Also silos…"

"What the hell are silos?" Nawalkar asked belligerently.

"Sir, it's a kind of attitude in organizations when several departments do not want to share information or knowledge with others in the same company," explained Mugbe mildly.

"Yeah," said Nawalkar sarcastically, "then silo mentality can take a fucking break here. This is the Mumbai Police, not Reliance or Tatas, and a police investigation needs teamwork. Not friendship. Make your Addl. CPs and DCPs ensure there is cooperation between all departments so that the investigation functions effectively."

Mugbe grunted morosely.

Having got that off his chest, Nawalkar stole a glance at the heavy gold Seiko on his wrist. It was getting to be 10 am. Time to leave for the Police Club and Crime Conference.

"What are we telling the press?" he asked.

Nawalkar hated crime reporters on sight. But he knew the importance of keeping the press on their side in an investigation like this. Passions would undoubtedly run high today. Two big murders. The press hadn't finished covering Haider's killing. And now it had the Nieves murder to report as well. The people would want to know what was happening. The police couldn't stall the press indefinitely.

The CP knew he would have to come up with something before the blood in both murders had dried.

Rathod wanted to hold the press conference.

"He's a serial predator who's threatened to kill again," he said. "Two murders haven't satisfied his lust. Who is he stalking? We don't know! We haven't understood why he killed Haider and Nieves. It wasn't for money or sex. But he took exceptional risks. He could be a psycho. If people are made aware they will take their own precautions."

"Psychopath? He could be as sane as you or me!"

"As sane as… ? Sir, would you or–"

"I get your point," Nawalkar cut in, "but publicity will bring out the crackpots, we're encouraging other criminals to act like this Cobra and mislead us. There could be copycat murders. The Control Room will be flooded by calls from anxious and frightened people."

Mugbe took the middle road.

He was as soft-spoken as Rathod was tough-talking. A short, podgy man with curly hair, rosy cheeks and horn-rimmed glasses, Mugbe looked like a family doctor with a good bedside manner.

"The suspect is unusually violent and he's vain," Mugbe said. "He may be mentally disturbed or he may just be motivated. Either way, he's exhibiting an unique pattern by calling you after his murders. We've never had a case like this. Murderers don't always get caught. Some have long careers. He's taunting us. Giving us a glimpse into his mind. That means he's not a criminal on our radar. And he's confident of not being detected either. So he's set to go on a killing spree. Sooner we realize we have a maniac on our hands, the better are our chances of stopping him. Rumors of the Cobra are bound to seize the public's imagination. By not giving them the facts, we are cutting ourselves off from any likely information."

"Information from whom?" Nawalkar demanded.

"The killer's family, friends, acquaintances, neighbors, somebody must know him… but isn't aware he's responsible for these brutal murders. Hopefully they'll recognize him from the info we put out."

"I agree in a standard murder case there is always someone who knows something, has heard or seen something, and this information helps our investigation," Nawalkar conceded, "but this is not that kind of case and he is not that kind of killer. He's cold-blooded and intelligent. He's committing murder for fun, it's a game for him, a challenge for us."

"Perhaps," Rathod said, "so people will now start paying attention to what's going on around them, they will ensure their neighbor's safety, they will start looking under their beds at night. A watchful public is the police's first line of defense."

"Okay," Nawalkar said grudgingly, "but aren't we jumping the gun by holding a press conference? A dedicated investigation must be kept a secret. The media will alert the killer. Why not get the Police PRO to issue a press release instead?"

It was true. CPs didn't address press conferences at the start of an investigation. No matter how monumental the crime. That was reserved for later. When the police had something to crow about. Like the arrest of an elusive or dangerous accused after some brilliant detection. Who they would parade before the media, handcuffed and hooded. Rathod and Mugbe reluctantly agreed to go with Nawalkar.

SOME CPS knew their senior policemen by name.

Nawalkar recognized faces. Ferraz, he liked. He thought Ferraz represented the good cop of every detective movie. He was meeting Navroze, Khan and Salvi for the first time. Crime Branch officers ran to type, he thought. And they were all packing heat!

In Hollywood, packing heat meant somebody was carrying a concealed weapon. Nawalkar believed sectional policemen didn't need to carry guns. The uniform was their authority. None of the Sr.

PIs from the 93 police stations at the Crime Conference were armed. But these chaps from the DCB-CID were. Like they were expecting a gunfight at the Police Club!

And then Nawalkar remembered 26/11...

... and the terrible memories it had for Ferraz.

For every cop, actually. They were on edge after that. Especially some IPS officers who enjoyed wining and dining at five star hotels. To be trapped in a hostage situation without his gun was every cop's nightmare. Caught with his pants down and his pistol not in, the CP thought, pleased with his joke.

Mugbe reviewed the case for the benefit of the sectional cops who would be working on the SITs and the DCB-CID officers who would cooperate with Ferraz's Unit I on the investigation.

The murders of the painter and diplomat's wife had been registered at Pydhonie and Gamdevi Police Stations respectively under Section 302 of the Indian Penal Code (IPC) and given Crime Register Numbers.

The Section said, *"Whosoever commits murder shall be punished with death, or imprisoned for life, and shall also be liable to fine."*

They had to catch *'Whosoever'* first.

There were no witnesses to either murder.

And there were no CCTV cameras at both crime scenes. Not at the chaotic Pydhonie junction on Mohammed Ali Road where the killer disposed of Haider's decapitated head. Altamont Road where Nieves was murdered, even the streetlights didn't work there sometimes, though the Municipal Commissioner's bungalow was just around the corner. The government's ambitious project post 26/11 for a surveillance web of 6,000 CCTV cameras across Mumbai at the cost of 1,200 crore rupees was stuck in red tape.

The police had provisional autopsy reports of both victims.

Haider had died of shock and massive hemorrhage. He had 17 stab wounds. Many were deep and severe, these were the fatal ones, they had ruptured the septuagenarian's vital organs and big blood vessels.

Looking at the breadth and depth of the painter's wounds, the forensic surgeon concluded that a pointed and sharp, single-edged knife like the Rampuri had been used. All the wounds were caused by one knife. The attack had been frenzied and messy. The painter had been stabbed by an inexperienced, unemotional but determined person. His tattered fingers and lacerated palms showed that Haider had put up a weak struggle.

The forensic surgeon said it required some violence to behead a human being. Or the skill of a butcher or surgeon. Such murders were seen in the districts, where every villager kept an axe, chopper and sickle at home. It was difficult to decapitate somebody with a Rampuri. But apparently it could be done.

They had lesser on the Nieves murder.

Again, there were no witnesses. The Gamdevi police questioned people in the area. The newspaper boys, the bread men, early risers who came out for a jog, boys who washed cars, people brought out for walks by their pedigreed dogs, residents of the buildings outside which the murder had been committed, their watchmen… but nobody knew anything. Countless people must have gone down that road to work and might have noticed the killer. The police hoped someone would come forward and volunteer information. The women walkers, all sharp-eyed bats who wouldn't have missed a stranger, had seen Nieves this morning. And one man had shouted "*Hari Om*" to her. But they hadn't seen any stranger or suspicious person following her.

Her autopsy revealed the cause of death as being shock, hemorrhage and asphyxia; the single cut on Nieves's throat that almost took off her head had caused her to choke on her own blood. The same single-edged knife had been used in this murder too. The transverse stroke had been from the left to right. And it had coursed obliquely downwards. The killer was right-handed, the forensic surgeon said.

No shit, Ferraz was thinking. The whole goddamn city was right-handed. Except Amitabh Bachchan and Sachin Tendulkar.

Nawalkar rose to address the Crime Conference.

He regarded the hall silently. Every cop looked at him expectantly but without expression. Their eyes boring into him like hundreds of double-barreled shotguns aimed at one target. His own flinty eyes swept the hall, head not moving an inch, taking in everything. If one man in the last row sneaked a look at his phone, Nawalkar would catch the movement.

"Let's call this investigation 'Operation Cobra,'" he began, surprising them. "I read somewhere that if you want to keep something secret, don't try to hide it, because the press will find out. So give it a name that will keep them busy trying to figure it out. The crime reporters will undoubtedly create a media persona for the Cobra. They enjoy creating bogeymen. Like they made Charles Sobhraj the Bikini Killer in the 1970s. And there was the Stoneman Killer in the 1980s and the Beerman Killer more recently. Hopefully, they'll get busy with the Cobra and leave us to find out who this killer is."

The cops shifted in their seats.

"Why 'Operation Cobra,'" Nawalkar continued, "is because this bastard called himself the 'Cobra' when talking to me. He also sent me an SMS referring to himself as the 'Emperor of Darkness'. I don't know why he called me. He wants to remain in the dark but can't help throwing light on himself. I will tell you what he said."

He gestured at Ferraz and his team, "I know 'Cobra' and 'Emperor of Darkness' mean nothing, these officers worked on both names, one belonged to a goonda murdered in the 1980s and the other is a teenager's video game. There's also a para unit in the Central Reserve Police Force (CRPF) called Commando Battalions for Resolute Action, or Cobra, trained in jungle warfare and meant for dealing with insurgents. I don't think he's a deserter from there. The killer left these names behind as his calling card. Every criminal thinks he's smarter than the police. But there's no such thing as a perfect murder. Okay, he's killed twice. In a society of millions, it's unlikely we could have prevented him. Even with information. To our knowledge, the Cobra has achieved nothing except the creation of fear. Maybe that's his game. There was unprecedented brutality in the killings. Criminologists say that 21st century stress has taken its toll on people, leading them to commit horrific crimes in a fit of rage even for trivial motives. But these murders were pre-meditated. The painter and the British diplomat's wife were not killed by a stranger over a dispute in a scuffle. They were murdered in cold blood. There was no attempt to destroy evidence. The killer brought both murders to our notice himself. He could be mentally deranged. Our investigation will find out. But I'm repeating, these weren't random, spur of the moment murders. They were committed for a deliberate reason. Now the same man's threatening to kill again."

The policemen were hearing this for the first time.

Every cop in the hall was listening to Nawalkar intently now.

"I want a good investigation, done quietly, without sensationalism. There's enough of that in the press already and we can't afford to be swayed by it," Nawalkar said. "So be unassuming. The people are watching. They will have their own theories. It doesn't matter. Good cops don't theorize, they go with open minds and collect clues along the way. There could be ten motives. Work on all ten. Be methodical and thorough. Check every bit of evidence. If there are witnesses, get their impressions no matter how cockeyed it might be. Then sift fact from fiction. Don't fit the investigation to suit your own pet theory of the motive. Don't collect evidence that way."

Nawalkar's gaze shifted to the IPS officers in the hall.

"Keep your working atmosphere friendly, indulge in a lot of one-to-ones, I want the Addl. CPs to have discussions with constables from the Crime Branch and police stations, they are the pulse of the police force," he said. "They have seen more crime than you, but they don't have your training, so they operate from a gut instinct. Allow everybody to participate in the investigation. A large number of constables live in slums and chawls from where most killers come too. And the constables often hear things and come up with information that bust cases. I want everybody to keep thinking of the murders. The crimes must grow on you. Like a puzzle. The Joint CPs are as good as their teams. The SITs have to come together and exchange ideas. What could connect the painter to the English woman? I don't know. But I need an answer. *Chalo,* even a theory will do. Give me leads, possible angles, suspects. The people might lose faith in us. The press will haul us over the coals. But it is the police that is hunting this mysterious killer. Not the citizens or the press. And he's trying to spread fear in the city. But from today the Cobra's going to be one man against an entire force."

Nawalkar sat down and reached for a glass of water.

The cops almost applauded.

A lot was now riding on Nawalkar's impression of the killer.

To the DCB-CID this information was vital. The CP getting calls from the killer – this was extraordinary. They needed to know every word that had been said. Rathod was hoping Nawalkar might give them a clue to the killer's identity. The Crime Conference was dismissed. Mugbe and Rathod retained only those cops working on the SITs and the DCB-CID's investigation.

"Tell us what the killer said, sir," Rathod urged the CP.

Nawalkar knew they would have been grilling any other man in his place, coming at him from all sides, hammering him with questions, but they were treating him like… like he was the fucking CP!

He got off to a shaky start.

"There's not much to tell. He said his name was Maria … or Mario… or something like that," he began, "but this morning he also said he was the Cobra and the Emperor of Darkness."

"Did he sound like a Catholic, sir?" Rathod asked immediately.

"No," Nawalkar said. He knew what the Joint CP (Crime) meant.

"And did he call himself Maria or Mario on both occasions?"

"Sounded like that. Yesterday he was calling from Mohammed Ali Road, there was such a bloody racket in the background, but this morning I heard him clearly."

"Did he repeat anything in his conversations, sir?"

"Yes, he asked if we were better than Scotland Yard!"

"Why, because he was planning to kill the British diplomat's wife and thought Scotland Yard might investigate the murder?" Mugbe asked.

"I don't think Scotland Yard will come," Nawalkar said. "But the joint secretary of the External Affairs Ministry wants us to share our information with the Research and Analysis Wing (RAW). It's the union government's primary foreign intelligence agency."

"We'll do that, sir," Rathod assured him.

"Both times the Cobra said he was making the investigation easy by informing us of the murders," Nawalkar recalled.

"How did he mention the third murder, sir?" asked Mugbe.

"He told me, 'You've got two murders… are you going to investigate those or try and prevent the third?' My first concern was for who had been killed after Haider. Not who is going to be his third victim."

"How did he sound, sir?" Mugbe asked.

"What do you mean?"

"Was he calm and controlled, or taunting and sarcastic, did he sound hysterical, was he raving like a lunatic, ranting like a fanatic?"

"No, he was damn polite, kept laughing."

"Laughing? Like a psycho?"

Nawalkar snapped, "How the hell do I know how a psycho laughs? How many psychos have you shared a laugh with, Arvind?"

"Did he sound the same both times?" Rathod cut in smoothly,

"You're absolutely certain it's the same man who called last night and this morning?"

"Yes," said Nawalkar without hesitation, "second time also he said his name was Maria… or Mario… or whatever. And – he asked me again whether we were as good as Scotland Yard."

"I wonder why," Mugbe said thoughtfully.

"Did he sound like a foreigner, sir?" Ferraz asked quietly.

"Not at all!"

"Did he give any indication why he had picked the painter and diplomat's wife as his victims?"

"None whatsoever, the calls lasted a few seconds."

"It's a mystery why he called you, sir," Rathod said.

Nawalkar was thinking the same thing.

"Let's go to the Mohalla Committees," he suggested.

Mohalla Committees were the city's watchdogs. They were started in 1994. After the riots and serial blasts. To bridge the gap between the agitating communities. And between them and the police. There were 13, located in sensitive areas where communities lived cheek by jowl. They quelled unrest and diffused tension, they promoted peace and tolerance by organizing events during religious festivals that reconciled people. They worked with the local police. By informing them, Nawalkar knew the police would be sensitizing the city to the serial killer's threat quicker than through any other means.

10

A VISIT from the police was always stressful.

People got agitated or defensive. Richard Nieves wasn't a suspect. But the police had his wife's killer to find. And presumably that's what Nieves wanted as well. Unless, *of course*, he was the killer himself. It was known to happen, such was life. Questioning a murder victim's next of kin was part of the investigation. But Nieves was guaranteed diplomatic immunity from criminal and civil proceedings of the state under rules set at the 1961 Vienna Convention on Diplomatic Relations.

All they could do was talk to the British diplomat.

His wife's body was with the undertaker. It would be embalmed and sealed in a casket. Then air-lifted to London. Like first class luggage on British Airways. St. Stephen's Church on Warden Road, where the Nieves's worshipped, had offered a mass for her soul. The cops wanted to catch Nieves before he left for the church.

It was 2 pm. As the Qualis swept down Marine Drive they could see black rain clouds above the horizon, gathering steam for another determined assault on the wet and bedraggled city. Navroze was driving like a man possessed. Stamping the accelerator and brake, clanking the gears, glaring through the windshield for gaps in the traffic. The other motorists kept out of their way. As they zigzagged down the road at 70 kmph, Ferraz struggled to read the Police PRO's press release.

It just said the DCB-CID was investigating the Haider-Nieves murders. The police suspected the same killer was involved in both crimes. His identity was unknown but the police were working on some leads. The murders were possibly linked. But no motive had been established. Police Commissioner Baburao Nawalkar appealed to the people not to panic or give in to rumors. Security had been beefed up across the city. However, because of Ganeshotsav, it wasn't possible to deploy police everywhere. The people were asked to be vigilant and call Police Control on 100 if they noticed any suspicious person or activity. The suspect was believed to be armed and dangerous. People were warned not to approach any such person on their own but to inform the police immediately.

Ferraz crumpled up the press release.

"A crock of crap, huh?" asked Navroze.

"Yeah, it sucks," agreed Ferraz. "There's no warning that he's threatened to kill again."

"Here we go," said Navroze swinging the Qualis into Altamont Road.

A stream of limousines led them to Nieves's building. It seemed as if the British Deputy High Commissioner was throwing another party. A high tea for Mumbai's swish set. They came fashionably dressed in black. Or white. Both the colors of mourning. Consulate cars with yellow CC number plates blocked the road. Their drivers knew condolence visits were brief. Their consul generals would be down soon. The number plate gave them immunity. No Traffic cop would ask them to move.

Nawalkar's car was also there. The CP had left the Police Club after the Crime Conference. Ferraz and Navroze were glad he was here. Nawalkar was a veteran Mumbai cop, he knew the pressure of investigating such a case, and he would go out and bat for them if push came to shove.

Navroze could find no place to park.

Altamont Road residents were finding it difficult to drive out of their buildings because of the traffic jam. They were furiously honking.

Many had stepped out to see what was happening. Pizza delivery boys from the local Smokin' Joe's were struggling to maneuver their red motorbikes through this chaos. The cops could smell the oven-baked pizzas in their carry boxes. To add to the drama a Bharat Petroleum gas cylinder cart had overturned, creating panic, and the delivery man was engaged in a fierce argument with a cabbie. An ambulance was trying to enter the rear exit of Jaslok Hospital and its siren merged with the cacophony of horns, policemen's whistles and angry, raised voices.

Gamdevi policemen struggled to control this situation.

Navroze squeezed the Qualis behind Nawalkar's car. A dark, heavily-built Traffic constable immediately walked up with a scowl. But Navroze flicked the siren on and off and he backed off.

The media waited on the road in anticipation.

They were prevented by the police from going upstairs to where Richard Nieves was waiting for the hearse bearing the mortal remains of his wife to arrive. That would be the photo-op of the day.

Amongst the crime reporters was the gorgeous Nahida Shaikh.

She was facing a camera, her back to the Nieves residence, making sure it would show up nicely behind her on TV screens. Spotting Ferraz and Navroze, Nahida indicated that the rolling camera pan off her and track the policemen, and she darted across and reached out an arm for Ferraz the second time that day.

"Hi," she said breathlessly, forgetting she was on air.

He paused and looked at her.

She had changed her white blouse from the morning for a baby blue sweater that swelled over her curves. She had also added a navy blue silk stole around her neck. Its ends were flapping in the breeze. He wondered when she had found time to change.

"Well, hello," he said nonchalantly, "fancy bumping into you here!"

She made a face.

"You *know* I have a job to do."

"And I can see… you're doing it!"

She placed a hand on his forearm, simultaneously making a slashing gesture with the hand-mic to the cameraman, telling him to stop rolling.

"Inspector… what's happening!"

"What do you mean?"

She took a deep breath and asked accusingly, "Did the police have information that Haider's killer was going to commit another murder?"

Surprised, Ferraz said, "I don't get you."

She looked at him in disbelief. He wasn't a dumb cop, she knew.

Angrily she felt like telling Ferraz, 'Read my lips!'

Instead, Nahida said patiently, "I'm asking, were the police aware–"

"Murders are committed daily. Who informs us?"

"Pre-planned murders of eminent citizens too? With a knife?" she asked scornfully. "My sources say the police knew a second murder was going to happen. But had no idea who the next victim might be."

"Your sources?"

"Look," she softened, "these are high-profile murders, both are connected, it's the same killer. I suspect you have a psychopathic killer on your hands."

"Could be a coincidence."

She pulled a droll face.

"You really believe the killer picked these two victims in passing? That he took a fancy to them and went to all that risk to murder them for nothing? Do you have evidence to prove the crimes weren't intentional? What if he kills another eminent Mumbaikar tomorrow? That'll make him a serial killer."

Ferraz and Navroze looked at each other.

Nahida continued, "Look Inspector, I've studied Criminology

at the University of Pennsylvania. Psychopathic serial killers are America's most elusive criminals. Nobody's safe from them. And they don't always get caught. In 2007, a study I did for the FBI's Behavioral Unit revealed that there were at least 500 psychos responsible for 6,000 murders that year. The FBI said serial killing had reached epidemic proportion."

"What's your point?" Navroze asked.

"These weren't accidental murders," Nahida said flatly. "If you think there's even a 0.01 per cent chance he might kill again, warn the people. They have the right to information. I sure as hell would want to know if there is a depraved creep tracking me with... *don't laugh!*"

Ferraz had smiled at the picture.

"Think *na baba*, won't it help your investigation to have several million people looking out for the same one person?" she asked him emphatically.

"I have no doubt," Ferraz murmured.

"My point is," Nahida hadn't finished, "something connects Haider and Nieves. You haven't found out yet. Look, you guys aren't masterminds. How many undetected cases got swept under A-Summary Closure Reports last year?"

The cops looked at one another again.

Some 20,000 cases were registered by the police last year. But not even 5,000 chargesheets got filed. An A-Summary Closure Report meant the police admitted their inability to solve a case in court after struggling with it for between six months to a year and sought permission to close the case.

They knew Nahida was right.

All crime reporters had sources. Some cop was bound to leak the story. That the Cobra had chillingly promised the CP he was going kill again. The news would create a stir. Like Chinese whispers it would get distorted and exaggerated, it would spread fear over the city.

Navroze whispered in Ferraz's ear, "She's right, you know. Withholding information isn't helping us at all."

"*Whaaat?*" asked Nahida curiously.

"Nothing," Ferraz told her.

He knew Rathod had wanted to take the press into confidence.

They weren't even close to understanding the motives behind the murders. They could bite their nails wondering who the Cobra was stalking next. Or they could take the media's help and hope for a breakthrough.

They reached Nieves's building.

The policemen at the gate let them in.

Ferraz turned to Nahida.

"Call me," he said, giving her a searching look. "I can't promise anything, I have to talk to the Joint CP (Crime) first… you have my number?"

She squeezed his bicep.

"I do," she said archly and winked, surprising him.

NOTHING COULD have prepared them for Richard Nieves.

The British Deputy High Commissioner, operating out of Bandra-Kurla Complex, looked after Gujarat, Madhya Pradesh and Goa in addition to Maharashtra – all states accounting for much UK-Indian investment. The main work of Nieves's staff of about 200 was trade and investment, entry clearance into the UK and bilateral relations.

To their surprise, Nieves was an Englishman with Indian blood.

His mother had been of Sussex Lane in Byculla where the Akres (that was her maiden name) were an old Anglo-Indian family before she married a "foreigner" and moved to London. Nieves understood Hindi, having spent some of his early years in Bombay, his father being in the diplomatic services as well and on the hop in and around the sub-continent.

He sat in the drawing room talking in a hushed voice to Nawalkar. The apartment was spilling over with people there to offer their condolences but more curious to know what had happened. Nieves's staff was dealing with them.

The policemen had the diplomat to themselves.

Nieves looked distinctly Indian, they thought.

The society press referred to him as a *bon vivant*. The cops didn't know what a *bon vivant* was. They never imagined it was someone with refined tastes, especially in food and drink.

"The only Diplomat I know is the whisky!" Navroze whispered.

Nieves's sartorial preferences were well-known. He wore Savile Row suits, custom-tailored shirts from Turnbull and Asser in London, and shoes from Ferragamo. Like plenty of Indians, he was a portly little fellow and nothing off the rack fitted him perfectly.

He was short and fat, also pink and totally bald. He looked like a bishop out of church, Ferraz thought, sitting limply in a deep leather armchair in black trousers and blue striped shirt, highly-polished slip-ons on his feet, a brandy goblet in his hand. He had just come from the morgue. Hence the fortification.

The home reflected his globe-trotting lifestyle.

All over were curios he had picked up on his postings, mementoes from his last ports of call. Japanese tatami mats, Italian sofas, Malacca chairs, tribal masks from Indonesia, a boy's surfboard from Australia. There were water colors on the walls, black-and-white posters of *Gone With The Wind* and *Dr. Zhivago*, exotic plants, a bookshelf with the philosophies of J. Krishnamurti and teachings of the Dalai Lama, an open bar crammed with bottles of single malt, a Samurai sword on a stand, a miniature red London double-decker bus, a record turntable with a stack of opera LPs.

And sitting grandly in the midst of all this…

... a medium-sized Ganpati on a flower-bedecked table. For whose homecoming the cocktail party had been held last night.

Nawalkar introduced them, mumbling under his breath, then sat back with his hands in his lap and his head down, as if he was not a part of this meeting.

There was the clap of thunder. Raindrops softly tapped the living room windows. Watching water snakes slithering down the glass panes, Ferraz felt a pang of pity for Nahida and the press corps on the road.

He cleared his throat, "Sir, we are sorry..."

"Yes, I know," Nieves said curtly cutting him off.

"It's a difficult time, but we have to ask you..."

"Yes," Nieves said again. "I understand... but I don't know what to say... I mean, who could have... who could have wanted Esther dead? And *why*?"

They were silent for a moment.

Then Nawalkar said, "It's early in the investigation, but we will look into all possibilities, that's why these policemen have come."

Nieves nodded, depressed.

"Ask what you want," he said shrugging helplessly.

"Do you have any reason to... suspect..." Ferraz hesitated.

"No."

"When was the last time you saw... you spoke to her?"

"Last night, after the party."

"And... ?"

"And what! We had just wound up this Ganpati party. They were clearing up, Esther hated waking up to an untidy kitchen; she was making sure the caterers left with all their stuff, and that everything was washed, every plate and glass was kept in its place, the cutlery in the drawers, the leftover food distributed among the staff, she generally didn't go to sleep until she had put the cat out."

"Put the cat out?"

"It's a manner of speaking. I said goodnight and turned in."

"What time was this?"

"*How does it matter?*" Nieves asked testily.

"We're trying to find out if anything happened after–"

"What could have happened in this house?" Nieves demanded, suddenly agitated, "she was murdered outside."

"Was there any friction with one of the guests, maybe between any of the guests, that could have–"

"Nothing that I can think of."

"We'd like a list of all the people who attended the party."

"To see if any of them had a problem with Esther?" he asked sarcastically. "And woke up and murdered her first thing this morning and informed you?"

Ferraz gave Nieves a steely look.

"No sir, to see if any of them noticed something that you missed."

Nieves blinked, the thought had never occurred to him.

"Where were you this morning when Mrs. Nieves stepped out?"

"Where was I – *you're kidding me!*"

Nieves was sitting up straight now, his back rigid with outrage, hands trembling on his knees, staring hard at them in frigid silence. They stared right back at him.

"I've seen crime shows on TV," he said, eyes flashing in barely concealed anger, "the husband's always the first suspect, right?"

"That's not what we said, sir," Nawalkar told him pacifically, thinking of the consequences of transgressing the 1962 Vienna Convention.

"I was at home. In bed. Where else would I be? What are you going to ask me next? If anybody saw me? And can give me an alibi?"

"Did she walk the dog every morning?" Navroze asked, changing tack.

"Yes."

"Same time every day?"

"Every single day, weekends too… there was no sleeping late for Esther. Like this morning… after last night's party… it got over pretty late, as I said. But she felt she had to walk the dog herself, and…"

The policemen were thinking the same thing. Anyone stalking Esther Nieves would know this morning routine of hers.

"Notice any suspicious-looking person outside recently?" Ferraz asked.

"What do you mean suspicious-looking?"

"Anyone out of place, who you felt didn't belong here?"

"No, I didn't. I wasn't looking," Nieves said. Tears welled up in his grey eyes suddenly and he asked, "Do you… do you think it was, it was… *difficult* for her?"

Esther Nieves's murder had been quiet, quick but messy.

"It was probably over in seconds," Ferraz said softly, thankful Nieves had not seen the crumpled, lifeless body of his wife lying in a pool of her own blood. The visit to the morgue must have been traumatic enough.

Nieves nodded silently. He looked with unseeing, wet eyes at a large picture of Esther riding the London Eye on the River Thames. She was gaily smiling into the camera.

"I know every man would like to believe his wife is… is popular… but the truth is I really don't know anybody who disliked Esther," he said, adding, "or disliked her so much to… to want her dead… to kill her… to…"

"Did she get along with everybody?" Navroze asked, "domestics, drivers, the cook, there was never any trouble there? You see, the reason we are asking is that most murder victims know their killer."

Nieves shook his head again.

Ferraz asked, "Do you have any enemies, sir?"

"Enemies?"

"Have you, through work, had to deal with any criminal types?"

"What the hell do you mean?"

It was Nawalkar who answered.

"What the Inspector is asking," the CP said apologetically, "is whether the British Deputy High Commission rejected anybody's visa... anybody whose plans for wanting to go to the UK may have been suspect... somebody who might have a grudge against you?"

"Me? I don't issue visas!"

"Yes, but your office..."

"Then ask my office," Nieves snapped.

"Well, we will get round to that."

"You *really* don't think this... what has happened to Esther... has got anything to do with me, *do you?* I mean... then why was I not killed instead?" he asked angrily.

He was beginning to bristle.

The policemen had no answer.

"What about the painter's murder?" Nieves asked suddenly, "it was the same killer, wasn't it? What was the motive there? Isn't it strange for somebody to go out and commit murder unless it's necessary? Isn't this what a psychopath would do?"

"A psychopath?" Nawalkar managed to sound surprised.

"Look... anybody who kills a gentle, peace-loving soul like Esther has to be crazy or sick. She was... it was done on the road, in broad daylight as press reports will undoubtedly say," he was being acidic, "and nothing was robbed except her cell phone. Would anybody risk committing murder for that? I don't think so! But Haider was murdered at home. Somebody entered his place, murdered and decapitated him, and robbed his cell phone. To call you. Like in Esther's case. There's a pattern. Yet where's the motive in both murders? They were also committed with hardly any time in between. You're dealing with a psychopath who needs no reason. Or there's something common between the painter and Esther that you've failed to recognize which triggered a murderous rage in this guy."

People always confused robbery with burglary, Ferraz was

thinking. Robbery was the crime of taking something of value by force; burglary was illegally breaking into a property with the intention of theft.

"We don't know if the killer's a psycho," Nawalkar said. "This is not a case where if the shoe fits..."

"No?" Nieves was mocking now. "You're saying a perfectly normal man killed my wife on her morning walk… *just* like that? And this murder makes sense?"

"That's what we are here to find out," Navroze said, "why anyone would want your wife or the painter… well, dead. We don't believe either of them was a chance victim."

"Was Haider a friend of your wife's?" asked Ferraz.

"No more than any of the guests who attended our party last night," the diplomat said. "In fact, we called Haider but he declined the invitation because of some exhibition he was working on. If he had come…"

"Did you patronize his art, socialize with him, was he doing any work for the British Deputy High Commission?" Navroze asked.

"Was your wife in touch with Haider?" asked Ferraz. "We don't have their CDRs yet… sorry, that's cell phone Call Data Records… so we don't know."

Nieves sighed deeply. His eyes were brimming with tears.

"I wish I could tell you something that would… that would not just help you but also bring some… some conclusion, some closure, to all the questions that will haunt me for the rest of my days. We have crime in London… there are muggings, there are murders and arson and hate crimes against Asians. But all committed for a reason. The perpetrators always cite a reason. However unacceptable it might be to the law. But here… I see no reason behind… behind what happened to Esther. Or Haider last night. It doesn't add up to anything. Nobody takes somebody else's life just like that."

The policemen looked at one another.

"Would your wife have told you if she was under threat?"

"Of course!"

"Have there been any kind of threats?"

"What do you mean?"

"On her phone, by email, anything…"

"Didn't I just tell you gentlemen, no."

"Are you under any kind of threat?"

Nieves stared at them unbelievingly, shaking his head.

"Do you have protection?"

"*You provided it yourself, thank you!*"

"Private bodyguards, besides the police?"

"No, I never felt the need."

"Was your wife covered?"

"No, she felt at home here."

"Did she have a secretary?" Ferraz asked.

"No, for what?"

"We need to create a timetable of her movements," Ferraz explained, "and for that somebody who worked closely with her would be of help."

"No, Esther handled all her own engagements."

"But we'd still like to question your staff."

"Go ahead."

"People store their contacts on their phones," Navroze said, "but is there a phone book that she maintained with names, postal and email addresses, birthdays, anniversaries, that kind of thing?"

"I'm sure there is," Nieves said, "I'll ask somebody to look."

"We'd like to take it with us, sir. Also her laptop if she had one."

He didn't say anything, just nodded glumly.

Ferraz turned to the Ganpati silently watching them.

"Esther always said if we got posted to India, she would keep a Ganpati at home. She is…" Nieves took a deep shuddering breath, "she was spiritual and interested in Eastern mythology. Read the Bhagwad

Gita, learned to play the sitar, she was studying Sanskrit. Well, people in the West are always fascinated by Indian culture. But Esther was developing a relationship with India that went beyond curiosity. She was planning to learn Bharatnatyam, had started doing Yoga, was taking Indian cooking lessons, reading about Ayurveda…"

"Where was she learning all this, with whom?"

"Not now, most of it she had already finished when I was posted elsewhere. As luck would have it, I got transferred here in 2008."

"And from the first year you've had a Ganpati at home?"

"Yes, from 2008."

"You keep it for the full ten days, sir?"

"No, just a day-and-half."

He paused, then asked, "Who's going to immerse it today?"

"Who does it every year?" Navroze asked.

"We have these boys from the office, they load the Ganpati in a car and take it to the sea. And there we sing and dance and celebrate the immersion."

"What about this party you had last night?"

"What about it?"

"A Ganpati party, isn't that unusual?"

"*Unusual?* No, why… what do you mean unusual? Aren't parties held for Diwali, where people drink and play cards? We have a traditional Christmas party as well every year. What's unusual about a Ganpati celebration? I don't understand."

"You've had it from the first year?"

"The party? Yes. The first time the British Council did the inviting, told people we were Indophiles, it was more a stepping out and meeting people kind of thing than a Ganpati party. People were bowled over by the Ganpati! Esther's going to miss the immersion…"

As the tears crept down his pink cheeks, they got up to leave.

Somewhere a clock struck 4 pm. And the chimes of the Big Ben filled the air, like in Westminster, London.

11

RETIRED ACP Nishant Bhuse was waiting for them.

Ferraz and Navroze were surprised to see him. They had missed lunch because from the Nieves residence they had gone to Gamdevi Police Station for the paperwork on the Altamont Road murder. Now they were hoping to catch a bite at Zaffran across the road.

"*Butter Chicken* and *roti*," Navroze said with relish.

But there was no time for that. They were informed that Joint CP (Crime) Arun Rathod wanted to see them in his office with Bhuse.

"Datta, ask the taximen's unions to round up all cabbies who picked up passengers from Altamont Road this morning around 6.30 am," Ferraz hurriedly told Salvi.

"There's a taxi stand near the crime scene," Navroze said.

"Next to the building Ajanta?" Ferraz asked.

"The same, but those cabbies have daily fares to Powai."

"What time do they come there?"

"Definitely not at 6.30 am. Maybe around 8.30 or 9."

"Too late," said Ferraz. He told Khan, "Send Dhananjay and Vishnu to Haider's building again in case Antone missed out anybody who works nights and left just before the murder. They might have passed the Cobra on the stairs, not knowing. And early tomorrow morning have them talk to the regular walkers on Altamont Road. People who knew Esther Nieves. I know the Gamdevi police did that unsuccessfully today. But maybe somebody noticed a stranger and thought nothing about it earlier. They will have time to think about it and discuss it with the other walkers. Tomorrow is a good time to meet them."

"Sir, have you noticed," pointed out Sangeeta, "the painter got killed on the eve of his controversial Ganpati exhibition and the British envoy's wife the morning after her popular Ganpati party. Isn't that weird?"

"What's weird?"

"Ganpati's like a witness to both murders."

"It's a coincidence," Navroze said dismissively, "Haider had done sexually explicit paintings of Hindu deities twice before, but nobody killed him."

"Yeah, and Nieves's party is being held since 2008," Ferraz said. "Nobody took violent exception to it three years, why would they now?"

Sangeeta appeared unconvinced.

"I just though the presence of Ganeshji–"

"Would the Modus Operandi Bureau have a file on Rampuri killers?" asked Salvi, interrupting her.

"Rampuri killers! This isn't organized crime," Navroze protested.

"The commonest murder weapon is the knife," Salvi told him. "When murders are committed at home, the weapon that comes to hand is the kitchen knife. It's easily available."

"Yeah, but who keeps a Rampuri at home?"

"Listen," Ferraz cut in, "criminals still use knives and choppers because guns aren't freely available. We've arrested most gunrunners and ended arms trafficking. Somebody took a Rampuri to kill Haider and Nieves. Check if MOB has a list of criminals still using it. Also if there are any criminals named Mario or Maria. We're getting the Nieves party guest list shortly. Everybody on it's a suspect, they are socialites, and all of them undoubtedly knew Haider as well. Sangeeta, look for people in that list who are possibly art patrons. The suspect has to be somebody who was closely connected to the painter and diplomat's wife, but didn't necessarily like them. Shadab, the domestic staff working at the Nieves residence have to be interviewed, see if anybody has a police record. Bawa, what about talking to all the Nieves woman's friends?"

The day was coming to a cold, grey and wet finish. The lampposts in the Police Commissionerate were glowing feebly in defiance of the fading evening light. The old stone buildings huddled together miserably against the rain's relentless onslaught.

Unit I was dank and gloomy. The place lacked the warmth and cheer of police squad rooms in Hollywood's LAPD movies. Where detectives like Clint Eastwood, Bruce Willis, Mel Gibson and Eddie Murphy sat around in civvies and shoulder holsters sharing sandwiches and coffee or pizza and coke over dirty jokes. Unit I was a grubby government office.

BUT Retd. ACP Nishant Bhuse was at home here.

He had been a Detection cop on the Crime Branch team that investigated the chilling Raman Raghav murders of the late 1960s. Raghav was India's most horrific psychopathic serial killer. He murdered 41 people in Bombay between 1965 and 1968.

Bhuse was gnarled and stooped at 86, with thinning white hair, feeble voice and shaking hands. His faded eyes restlessly darted around. He was wearing dark trousers, a crisp white buttoned-down shirt and leather sandals. Like a plainclothes cop of the 1970s. Breathing heavily through his thick bulbous nose, he gazed at them unblinkingly. Rathod and he were in conversation when the other policemen came in.

A constable brought a round of tea and biscuits.

Bhuse was saying, "Psychopaths have no moral compass, their motivation is psychological gratification. Sometimes there is sex. But that's absent in your two murders."

"According to the FBI," Rathod said, "the motives for a serial killer include anger, thrill, financial gain and attention. And if the modus operandi in the murders isn't the same, then the victims will have something in common. Like occupation, race, appearance, age."

"Yes, there will be a common thread," Bhuse said sipping his tea carefully, the cup and saucer clattering in his unsteady hands.

"The only thing common in our victims is that they were both socially prominent," said Ferraz. "But that's hardly a motive for their murders. How do we know the Cobra's a psychopath?"

"All psychopaths aren't criminals," Bhuse said. "They are extraordinarily ordinary people. Would you know if the man sitting next to you in church was a psycho? Not unless you knew his life history."

That's why I don't go to church, Ferraz was thinking.

Bhuse continued, "Psychopaths have a need for power and control, they enjoy the suffering of their victims, it makes them feel important. That's why they use personal methods like stabbing and strangulation. The murder is incidental. We did a lot of research on Raghav."

"What was he like?" Navroze asked.

"He was cold blooded, unfeeling, utterly ruthless, and *those* haunting, dead eyes – I will never forget," Bhuse said. "His victims were people living in hutments or on the pavements. The modus operandi was identical. They were killed at night in their sleep. Brutally hammered with an iron rod. And after murdering them, he... Raghav was... he was also necrophiliac."

"What's that mean?" asked Salvi suspiciously.

"Means he... he had sex with the corpses of some women."

"Oh God... why?"

"He desired to possess unresisting and un-rejecting women."

"Why did he kill?" asked Navroze. "What was his motive?"

"He claimed this was God's directive and that he could hear voices in his head," said Bhuse. "The murders were gruesome and motiveless.

He killed for things like an umbrella, a stove, a packet of *beedis*, a *kurta-pajama*, and once even for a 10 paisa coin. The violence he inflicted on his victims was disproportionate to the gains."

"Ramakant Kulkarni busted the case," Rathod said.

"Yes, he was DCP Crime," Bhuse said, "there was no post like Joint CP (Crime) then. Kulkarni took over the case in 1968. The murders spread terror across Bombay."

"You all must have been at your wits' ends," Rathod said.

"Fear gripped the city," Bhuse recalled. "People stayed indoors, the late night cinema shows were cancelled, nightclubs went empty. Nobody stepped out for evening walks. And beggars and the homeless who slept on pavements, the railways stations and in maidans, disappeared to God knows where. After sunset, nervous groups of people gathered at street corners. Housing society vigilantes would guard their buildings armed with hockey sticks. The fear was palpable. We had over 2,000 policemen patrolling the city at night."

"Weren't there supernatural rumors about Raghav?" Rathod asked.

"Yes, that he was a *sadhu* who turned into a fly, that's how he entered closed doors and killed people! And that he drank his victims' blood. Newspapers carried these stories and people believed them."

"Bombay must have heaved a sigh of relief at his arrest!"

"We got lucky," Bhuse said. "It was Ganeshotsav, like now, and Kulkarni *saheb* and the DCB-CID, we prayed to Lord Ganesh to help us catch this psychopathic serial killer."

Bhuse was chuckling at the memory.

"Ganpati heard our prayers. Sub-Inspector Alex Fialho on immersion day *bandobast* at Dongri suddenly noticed Raghav standing next to him in the crowd and recognized him from his description. He arrested him. Raghav came without a struggle."

"WHAT ABOUT the Stoneman?" asked Salvi. "Wasn't he a psychopath?"

"After my time," said Bhuse dismissively.

"And before mine," said Rathod diplomatically.

The Mumbai Police was loath to discuss the Stoneman killings.

They were the Crime Branch's shame because the psychopathic serial killer suspected of murdering 13 people in the early 1980s was never traced. He murdered 13 beggars and rag-pickers over two years starting in 1983. The killings were all in Sion and King's Circle. The modus operandi was similar. The killer struck in the dead of the night. He targeted homeless people sleeping alone in the open. He would crush their heads with a stone that weighed as much as 30 kg. The stone became grisly evidence in each murder; the police would find it covered with blood, the skull bones, hair and brains of the victims. As in Raman Raghav's time, Mumbai shivered in fear of the Stoneman.

But just as mysteriously as the killings started… they stopped.

Bollywood saw in the murders an opportunity 25 years later. Producer Bobby Bedi made *The Stoneman Murders* in 2009 based on the 13 serial killings. The film attempted to provide answers to the unexplained case.

Critics reviewed it favorably.

They praised its gripping story and taut performances. It was an edge of the seat thriller that sent viewers home spooked, but avoided the bloodshed and gore of the actual murders. One critic summed it up as "an honest portrayal of what could have been – but it's not as gripping as it should have been".

Every cop thought the film was worth a watch.

But here were Rathod and Bhuse dismissing the case.

"AND THE Beerman murders?" Salvi asked.

Another flashback. Of another psychopathic serial killer.

The murders began in October 2006 and stopped in January 2007. By then, seven people had been killed. In bylanes and on deserted foot over-bridges between Churchgate and Marine Lines Railway Stations. Bashed to death with a stone. Or stabbed. One victim was a cabbie, the rest were all homeless male vagabonds. Their bodies were discovered early morning, naked from the waist down, which suggested a gay sexual assault. The killer left a clue beside the victim's body each time. Two empty cans of Kingfisher Beer.

The case came to be known as the Beerman Murders.

The media thought the Beerman hated homosexuals. And that he took the blood of his victims to a cemetery near Marine Lines where a *tantrik* used it in black magic. All ghoulish and untrue. The police blamed the Beerman for three unexplained murders that had similarly been committed in the same area the previous year. Badly battered corpses had turned up early morning on Marine Drive in June, and outside the BHA Stadium and Wankhede Stadium in August and October respectively.

The CP then warned crime reporters, "People will take advantage of this hype to eliminate enemies and rivals and pass them off as murders by your Beerman."

Inadvertently giving the ungodly the idea.

The police psychiatrist said the Beerman was a homosexual suffering from a personality disorder. And the murders were his effort to make up for his inadequacies. He was a psychopathic serial killer, but he was also intelligent and a sadist and enjoyed watching his victims die. He was playing a game with the police. He knew their methods. Maybe he was a dissatisfied cop. And well off, too. He drank a premium brand of beer. Probably to get high and commit the murders.

That's when the police made an arrest.

They picked up a reformed extortionist and drug addict. He fitted the uncertain, hazy description of an eyewitness who saw a man leaving an unused foot over-bridge near Churchgate late at night where a body was found the next morning.

The suspect looked a killer all right.

He was menacing, he wore a skullcap, had a scruffy beard, shoulder-length hair, and a grim bony face. The police charged him with three murders in which they had solid evidence, the other four were left unmentioned. But the Sessions Court found him guilty of only one and sentenced him to life imprisonment.

Mumbai was relieved… the Beerman was put away!

Not for long. In 2009, the High Court overruled the sentence. It found the eyewitness' testimony and the narcoanalysis, brain mapping and polygraph test done on the suspect under duress inadmissible. He was declared not guilty and acquitted for lack of evidence.

The suspected walked free.

"The court acquitted me… but for the police I'm still the serial killer who got away," he told the media. Which was the truth.

Retired ACP Nishant Bhuse suddenly stiffened.

He tilted his head and cocked his ears, like an old hound. Then he was struggling to his feet, his old bent body standing as much to attention as the retired cop could push it.

Outside, a police bugler was sounding the *Retreat*.

It was sunset and the Mumbai Police's flag was being ceremonially lowered at the CP's office. When it was hoisted tomorrow morning at sunrise, the bugler would play the *Reveille*. The other cops also stood up respectfully as the bugler's sharp, plaintive note pierced the evening's stillness.

The day was over, Ferraz thought. Their investigation into the double homicide had yielded nothing. It was time to tell the Joint CP (Crime) about Nahida's suggestion.

AT THE same time, Haider Allarakha Khan's funeral was being held at the Bada Qabrastan in Marine Lines. There was no family to claim the body. No male relatives to handle it with respect, care and gentleness, and to bring it bathed and shrouded for the last rites, to participate in the *namaz-e-janaza*. A local Islamic organization made the arrangements.

This was a large Muslim cemetery, charming without grandeur; it was around 150 years old and managed by the Juma Masjid of Bombay Trust. Haider was interred at the Bagh-e-Rahmat or Garden of Mercy. A small, sturdy neem tree stood shivering over his grave in the rain-swept cemetery. There were few mourners. Several Muslims who were at the Bada Qabrastan for other funerals joined in the *namaz-e-janaza*. In Islam it was said if you participated in the funeral prayers of somebody you didn't know, you received blessings as big as a mountain.

The police were there, expecting a curious crowd.

But the funeral had gone without incident.

Abida Ashraf Rasheed, Haider's muse and the Moplah of Kozhikode, told Sangeeta Kadam who had summoned her for questioning, "The paintings of his exhibition are not yet dry and he's gone."

She was shockingly attractive, a buxom and stylish Malayali with large soulful eyes as jet black as her long, frizzy hair, and flawless skin the color of milk chocolate. There was no Arabian blood in her that Sangeeta could see. Abida had a huge *bindi* in the centre of her forehead whose design matched the ethnic border of her black silk *sari*. The Moplah beauty had hightailed it to Mumbai after learning about Haider's murder but still found time for makeup, Sangeeta was thinking.

Abida answered every question with Zen-like patience.

But now the investigation had taken a new direction.

It wasn't about Haider. Or Esther Nieves.

Somebody was executing well-known people connected to something. The police didn't know what it was. Or who was condemned to die next. Abida thought in vain for anything that would link Haider and Nieves, but was exasperated by her effort. She said they weren't socially close.

In despair, Sangeeta asked her about the missing paintings.

"Who said they are missing?" Abida wanted to know, surprised.

"Well, where are they then?" Sangeeta asked tactfully, not mentioning Umaima Mulla's alleged suspicion and the art critic as her source.

"At the National Gallery of Modern Art!"

"Here in Mumbai?" Sangeeta said, hiding her own surprise.

"Yes, it's a repository of art, like in Delhi and Bangalore."

"You mean a warehouse?"

"Not a warehouse, a museum. The NGMA is run by the Union Ministry of Culture. It's a premier institution and has the most significant collection of contemporary and modern Indian art. This Diwali, it plans to showcase the country's changing art forms over the last 150 years in a retrospective. Its director Sanjeev Mehta is a friend. He wanted Haider's collection. We were happy to lend it."

"By *we* you–"

"Haider and me!"

"Haider knew the paintings are with the NGMA?"

"What do you mean? He gave them. He was proud to be in the retrospective. The NGMA is like New York's Guggenheim Museum, a great place to see the works of legendary Indian artists."

"He didn't forget and think that the collection had been stolen?" asked Sangeeta carefully, looking into Abida's dark eyes.

"Stolen! By whom? Where are you getting these ideas from?"

So much for that, Sangeeta thought, feeling foolish. She was suddenly furious with the senile art critic for sending her on this wild goose chase.

Was he trying to cause trouble for Abida? Why? If Umaima didn't support his bullshit story when she returned, Sangeeta would kick the old duffer humpbacked so that he never stood upright and admired a painting again!

"When did you give the NGMA Haider's paintings?" she asked, dodging Abida's question for the second time and mentally making a note to check with the gallery's director that they had the collection.

"Two weeks ago," said Abida, her eyes suddenly shining with tears.

"I'm sorry, I have to ask, what was your relationship with Haider?"

"I was in love with him," Abida said sniffing, the tears quietly flowing.

"And Umaima Mulla?" Sangeeta asked gently. "What was she to him?"

"She was his financial consultant."

"Besides that?"

"And Haider was in love with her," Abida said, sobbing her heart out.

SATURDAY

12

FERRAZ WOKE up with a start.

It was early morning, a little after 5 am. He lay still in bed wondering what had disturbed his sleep. A gentle shower had crept in from the sea and was playfully running up and down Carter Road, rustling the trees, knocking on the windows. Almost apologetically, as if the rain knew that on Saturday some people liked to sleep late.

But it wasn't the rain that had disturbed his sleep.

And then he remembered.

He had been having a frightful nightmare.

A dark and sinister figure, in a black hood and cloak, and wearing a white grinning mask like the serial killer Ghostface from *Scream*, was chasing him across the Bandra-Worli Sealink. He had a wicked-looking knife with which he kept slashing furiously at Ferraz's back.

It was late night, the Sealink was dimly-lit and empty.

What they were doing there, how they had got there, he didn't know. The Sealink looked mysteriously disturbing. It stretched interminably under lampposts between which eerie shadows danced in the dark. No traffic zipped across. There was only Ferraz and this ghostly killer. And they were running like mad, which in itself was unusual, because nobody ran on the Sealink except during the Marathon. And maybe in their dreams.

But this was no dream – *this* was a frigging nightmare!

And the Figure of Death was getting closer.

Ferraz was running for his life. He could hear the thump-thump of the killer's feet, the ugly rasping of his breath over the sound of waves crashing against the Sealink's concrete legs rising out of the sea.

His feet felt leaden, his chest was heaving and he thought he would have a heart attack. It was only the swish of the knife as it missed his back and shoulders again and again that kept Ferraz going. He expected to feel the sharp pain of it plunging into him any moment and cringed in fear.

"F-E-R-R-A-Z!"

Suddenly the hoarse voice of the killer…

… calling out to him in the night!

He almost stopped running out of shock.

"F-E-R-R-A-Z!"

There it was again…

… a voice from the tomb.

Petrified, he picked up his pace. He wanted to glance behind to see how close… but was terrified of looking into those bloodless and hollow eyes of the white mask and seeing that unnaturally open grinning mouth. This was no ghost out of the movies, but a psychopath wanting to kill him.

On the Sealink of all places, *God*, how had they got here!

Ferraz looked down the curving carriageway. The toll booth on the 5.6 km Sealink was far off. If only he could reach it. He pounded on, his feet flying past the pylon towers of the cable-stayed bridge at the halfway stage, his eye suddenly catching a signpost that said, *"Speed thrills, but kills!"*

That's when he stumbled, his foot tripping on a cat's eye reflective safety device marking the centre of the road, and reached out in a panic to steady himself, his hands groping nothing but emptiness.

He fell on his shoulder, cracking his head painfully on the road, and at once rolled over in agony to face the tall evil figure coming to a panting halt over him. The mouth in the white mask was grinning grotesquely. The knife rising high for the kill.

But Ferraz twisted, rolling over and over, avoiding the first vicious thrust only just. On his back now, he watched in morbid fascination as the killer shuffled forward one spine-chilling step at a time, still grinning horribly, the knife searching for him.

Ferraz was desperately groping for the 9mm S&W tucked into his waist now. At the same time he brought his knees up protectively against his chest, curling himself into a small target and raised a hand up defensively against the knife that was descending…

… managing to parry the thrust with his forearm. Then lunging up he snatched the ghost mask away from this terrifying Sealink spook, the gun exploding into the black folds of the killer's robe, *crack-crack-crack,* three bullets booming in the night, sending his assailant crashing into the railing of the bridge, the knife spinning from his grip and disappearing over the edge.

That ought to have been that. But it wasn't over.

Bleeding now, the mysterious cloaked figure took a couple of staggering steps forward, arms outstretched. But Ferraz had gained his feet. He flung the ghost mask aside and held the 9mm S&W out with uncontrollably shaking hands, only to discover that he was looking into another grinning wraith-like face from Hell.

Ferraz's breath was coming in labored gasps.

He lowered the unsteady gun and stood rooted there, fearfully watching what was coming at him, incapable of running, thinking he recognized… *was* it, *yes* – in fact, he *knew* the evilly grinning face!

It was the Cobra…

… and that's when he woke up.

He lay in bed listening to the rain, disoriented and ashamed by his cowardly exhibition of fear. And also disturbed by his vulnerability in the nightmare. What had triggered these negative emotional responses? The two murders? A sense of *déjà vu* that more people were going to die because the police had failed to detect the Cobra?

Would somebody be murdered today?

The Cobra had said so, but dammit – *who*?

And *what* were the police doing about it?

What *could* they do!

He was unable to go back to sleep.

A line from Springsteen's 1985 hit *I'm On Fire* played in his mind…

… something about waking up at night with the sheets soaking wet and a freight train running through the middle of his head.

That's exactly how he felt.

He tossed in bed tormented by his thoughts. Then getting up, he tiptoed into the kitchen and made a mug of coffee. He took it to the window with the stub of yesterday's cigar. After hesitating, he went and got Jackie's copy of the *A to Z of Dreaming* from her bookshelf.

Carter Road was quietly sleeping.

All the restaurants, pizza houses, coffee shops, ice-cream parlors, frozen yogurt bars and donut places were shut. Stray dogs scavenged the road, snarling and snapping over leftovers. In the distance, he could see the twinkling lights of ships. A police van cruised by slowly, its dome light throwing orange bolts of lightning on either side of the road, the metallic chatter of the wireless coming faintly up. .

"Dreams can be bizarre, terrifying, joyful or confusing," the author wrote in the foreword, "we are able to have experiences in dreams that we could never expect to have in waking life."

You can say that again, Ferraz thought. Turning the pages uneasily, he searched through the Dream Dictionary section for 'Ghost'.

"Dreaming of a ghost could mean that you are in a state of confusion, or that you are concerned that the solution to a problem appears to be eluding you," the *A to Z of Dreaming* ominously warned.

With a shiver, Ferraz shut the book.

SHE HAD been the first to call him a psycho.

That was then, years ago; when actually he knew she was crazy.

They had accused each other of a lot of things. Half of which the police in that one-horse town didn't understand. They hadn't taken him seriously, they went against the law, because she was who she was. A Dalit with a powerful political background nurturing ambitions of her own. And he, an erudite Brahmin. Who nobody listened to. It was like talking to the air. He was made an example of. Humiliated, then boycotted and asked to go. Which he did. But he hadn't forgotten. That had been an eye-opener for him. A damning revelation. The incident had been like the slamming of the door by the outside world. Which led him to open the window to what he was feeling in his soul and seek escape. He ought to be grateful to her. But she would die. And because of her, others also.

Two were down already.

What a fuss was being made about their deaths. Well, their murders. That was not the point. Death was inevitable. Everybody had to die. Sooner or later. And that those who deserved to die – died the deaths they deserved. They got what was coming.

He saw to that.

But the public, the police and the press, oh my God, they were missing *that* point. Instead of trying to find out who he was, and why he was doing this, they should have been looking into what those two were guilty of – Haider and Nieves, the first two, they were guilty of blasphemy. All of them were answerable for impiety. Starting with her. But without a lead to his identity, without a clue to why he was ridding the city of these pseudo believers and fake worshippers, the police had called him a psychopath.

He was outraged, but also amused.

In this country, anybody acting abnormally, or indifferent to social norms and niceties, was simply classified as being mad. But mad meant different things. It meant insane, deranged, maniacal, demented if you were dangerously unbalanced… and absurd, foolish, daft, cracked if you were harmlessly idiotic. To the police, mad also meant psychopathic.

Which he wasn't, but… his mother had been bipolar.

Mad as a hatter, she came from an influential family and that family discovered she had the disorder in her early years. They put her on medication, not into the psychiatric ward. He didn't know much about all that. It wasn't exactly a secret. But like so many other areas of his life, it was murky. And he didn't want to go there. Closed doors didn't always reveal pleasant surprises. Why open them?

He had been exposed to his mother's madness, her mood swings.

Bipolar Disorder was like diabetes and heart disease, it had to be carefully managed throughout life. He realized that as long as she was taking her medicines, she behaved normally. When she stopped, which unfortunately she did when he was growing up – stubbornly refusing to accept treatment for an illness she never acknowledged, she gave them hell. Swinging from one emotion to the next. She went through various mood episodes, taking them on a dizzy, frightening ride that they never knew would end where and when. Her ups and downs were different from other people. Suddenly very joyful or overexcited, which was mania. Then extremely sad and hopeless, which was depression. And at times both – happy and depressed, when she was energetic, distractible, impulsive and reckless, a mood episode known as hypomania. Kept them guessing. Kept them on their toes.

It ended when she finally took her life… after innumerable threats.

Committing suicide by jumping into the village well.

Good riddance, but – the damage had been done.

He didn't know it then, he was unwilling to believe it now, but it was understood that Bipolar Disorder ran in the family. Researchers were still investigating genes that increased a person's chance of developing the mental illness. Genes were the building blocks of heredity. They helped control how the body and brain worked and grew. Genes were passed down from parent to child. And children of a bipolar parent were more likely to develop the disease than children whose family had no history of Bipolar Disorder.

He didn't care, really, but the thing was…

… he was vaguely conscious of being different.

And in his arrogance, which itself was a symptom of his disturbance, he took the distorted view that the world was abnormal and uncharacteristic. There was nothing wrong with him.

The Internet thought otherwise.

Going online made discovering yourself so easy.

Like taking an exam with objective questions and multi-choice answers, one of which was correct, which to click? It was an online lottery.

The Internet told him Bipolar Disorder was a brain disease that caused unusual shifts in mood, energy, activity levels and the ability to carry out daily tasks. The symptoms could be severe. In its mildest form, it made the bipolar feel energetic, excitable and highly productive. At a higher level, the disorder was associated with erratic and impulsive behavior and unrealistic ideas. The illness degenerated to psychosis. Which, simply put, was a loss of contact with reality. It meant having delusions about who one was or what was taking place. And hallucinations of seeing or hearing things that weren't there. When psychosis was accompanied by mania and depression, the diagnosis was described as manic depression.

That's what the Internet said, that network of networks.

Forty per cent of the world suffered symptoms of Bipolar Disorder at some stage in life. Genetics and environmental factors caused it. Doctors treated bipolars with mood stabilizers and psychotherapy. That he had seen. Some bipolars were a risk to society. Others were suicidal. Both of which also he had experienced. The Internet had asked him if he wanted help in managing his condition. He had logged out in anger.

All cock! Who, or what, was the Internet to ask him that?

Who owned the Internet, anyway? There was nobody, no organization, that controlled the Internet and could take responsibility for its bullshit!

But now the police were suggesting he was a psychopath.

In the newspapers this morning, and on TV last night, that's what they had insensitively and irresponsibly warned the people.

That a psychopathic serial killer was on the prowl.

Here in Mumbai.

He had murdered twice already.

And they had no way of telling who he would kill next.

Like that's what he wanted to do – kill just anybody.

Couldn't they see there was a… what was it that psychiatrist had said in one newspaper… yes, that there was a method to his madness? A pattern to his actions? Couldn't the police see that in the two bodies he had given them? What would it take for them to realize? That he was killing because he was displeased? Why was he informing that Police Commissioner what he was doing?

For them to spread panic by telling the people – *beware*, a psychopathic serial killer's around, his crimes baffle us, and we're sorry, we can't protect all 20 million of you. The Police Commissioner himself going on TV last night. Causing the fifth most populous city in the world to be gripped by unimaginable fear. Which is what he wanted, actually. It gave him a feeling of power, a sense of control.

And what had got into newspaper editors?

Turning to the resident shrink for answers. As if some medical stuffed shirt who specialized in clinical or counseling psychology, some psychiatrist who treated the illnesses of the minds of people rich and famous, some therapist who prescribed medication for those who were depressed …

… as if any of them could give the newspapers a line to him.

One had said that psychopaths are well aware their ill-advised or illegal actions are wrong in the eyes of society, but shrug off these concerns with startling nonchalance.

Got that off the Net, for sure!

Were his actions ill-advised? Or even illegal?

He certainly didn't think so.

They deserved what they got – Haider and that British woman.

And the eight others on his hit list who were going to get it next.

Yes, eight!

He hadn't told the Police Commissioner that. He had kept it from him. That after the third there would be a fourth and a fifth and a…

… the racehorse owner was next.

He would be the third, this evening, he couldn't wait.

He had warned the police about the third. They went and told the city!

What would they do if they learned there were altogether ten?

He was reading the newspapers, one ear cocked for the bread man who announced his arrival by ringing his cycle bell. It was 7 am. He couldn't make up his mind, *brun-maska* and *chai* for breakfast or *idli sambhar* and *sheera* from the Udipi down the road.

Decisions, decisions all the time.

Outside, it was classic Darjeeling tea weather.

The morning was dark and chilly. The paved lane outside his building was awash with mud beneath a large canopy of weepy gulmohars. It was deadly quiet. He could hear the gutters gurgling with rainwater from last night's showers. Overhead, an aircraft thunderously climbed the sky after takeoff. If he leaned out of his third floor window, he would be able to see the plane before the rain clouds swallowed it up.

Where was the bread man? Had he gone already? Couldn't be, he was up from 6 am. Waiting for the newspaper boy. He liked getting the papers before anybody else. He paid the local newsagent extra for that privilege.

He could hear the *put-put* of an auto entering the lane. And the watchman chatting over the wall with the neighboring building guy. Both *bhaiyas* from UP. Speaking Bhojpuri. Like most *autowallahs*. But they could be from Bihar or Jharkhand, too. Hard to tell. Bhojpuri was an amazing language. It was also spoken in Nepal and Mauritius. And it was one of the national languages of Guyana, Suriname and Fiji, he bet these *bhaiyas* didn't know!

Somebody rang the bell in the Ganpati temple down the lane.

How he loved that sound. It was auspicious. Like a reminder.

He loved Ganeshotsav. The biggest, grandest and most elaborate festival in the Hindu calendar. When Ganpati, the Remover of Obstacles and Lord of Beginnings, came down to Earth for ten days to bestow wisdom, prosperity and good fortune on His devotees. Millions welcomed Him into their homes. Giving Him a place of honor. And for the next few days, they treated Him like God, which He most certainly was. Feeding Him, performing *pujas* and singing *bhajans* to Him, proudly introducing Him to their neighbors. Which other God had such a friendly and informal relationship with His devotees?

But Gods, like human beings, were mortal. After their fixed time on earth they had to pass away. The city celebrated Ganpati's going away as well. That's why celebrants joyously shouted *"Ganpati Bappa Moryaa! Pudcha varshi lavkar ya!"* as they took their idols to the sea for immersion.

"Praise be Lord Ganesh! Hasten back next year!"

He had finished his worship already.

First thing in the morning, after a bath, the *Ganpati Atharvashirsha,* which was the most widely recited Sanskrit text among devotees of

Lord Ganesh. It was a tradition. He also performed the Ganpati *puja*, all Brahmins did that, and the house was now pleasantly blessed with the fragrance of incense. A *diya* burned before the orange and gold Ganpati idol he had installed on his bookshelf, its tiny yellow flame crackling and flickering. And then another ritual, the 100 *surya namaskars* – performed slowly facing east, non-stop.

He turned to the Sports pages for the cricket news.

India was beginning the five ODI NatWest Series against England at the Riverside Ground in Chester-le-Street, County Durham, today. He had no faith in this side. On Wednesday it lost the only T20 of this tour to England at Old Trafford. And before that, it had been shamefully obliterated in all four Tests for the Pataudi Trophy at Lord's, Trent Bridge, Edgbaston and the Oval. This was the same team that had won the ICC World Cup in April. Now the whole focus was on Sachin Tendulkar's 100th century.

The doorbell rang. It was the sweeper, grinning at him with stained teeth through the grille on the security door, but he had no *kachra* to give.

He returned to the papers. He was on Page 1, Tendulkar, Dhoni, Sehwag and Dravid were at the back, serves them right, the losers.

On TV last night, after the police had done their number, a news channel held a spirited panel discussion about people with an addiction for murder. The show's insufferable anchor wanted to know who was a psychopathic serial killer. One armchair guru informed the other experts that the term serial killer had been invented by the FBI to describe someone who killed repeatedly and obsessively.

"Before that, anyone who killed several people was referred to as a mass murderer," he had pompously added.

A theory justifiably rubbished in print this morning by a foreign neuro scientist – *what kind of expert was that* – who was in Mumbai for some highbrow literary festival.

"Mass murderers are whackos who suddenly and without reason

shoot dead 18-20 students on American campuses these days," he told the newspaper like this was the norm. "They aren't serial killers because the murders happen on the same occasion, not one after one."

The neuro scientist suggested that most people had the potential to be violent; everybody was born with the brain circuitry to become aggressive, impulsive and even psychopathic. What was different in people was the interaction between their genes and early life experiences.

"Morality, people are born with; ethics, they learn. Genetics loads the gun for the environment to pull the trigger," he said.

Just the rubbish people enjoyed reading on weekends.

This distinguished authority was an American expert in psychopathy, and he was certain that it was the lack of empathy that differentiated a serial killer from an aggressive or impulsive person. What sent a person's brain into a tizzy hinged on three factors: abnormal genetics, distorted brain function and early childhood abuse.

The doorbell rang again. It was the *dhobi*. With a bundle of ironed clothes under his arm. Where and how did the man dry his clothes in the rain, he wondered. He liked the smell of freshly-pressed clothes. The coal from the steam iron left them smelling of burnt matchsticks. Putting away the laundry, he returned to the papers.

What was it that American had said?

Something about early childhood abuse…

… and suddenly he was back home, in the attic, hiding in the old teak wardrobe whose doors wouldn't shut. He could smell the musty furniture under dusty covers outside, and the dampness on the green mossy walls, both familiar and comforting odors. And he could hear the rain rattling on the asbestos-tiled roof, it sounded like the time he threw handfuls of pebbles down from his tree house; but the howl of the wind as it sobbed among the mango and jackfruit trees was scary.

It frightened him. More frightening was Barve Mama that afternoon, his mother's brother, a tuition teacher who used to teach him Science and Math, now here dressed in blue and white striped pajamas with drawstrings, a thin cane in his hand, staggeringly drunk, his face flushed and eyes glazed and unfocussed, something disquieting and chilling about him today, his parents not at home.

"Nooooo, please!"

He had fled after the first shocking assault, out of his mind with fear, not knowing what was happening – only wanting to escape the horror, sickened by the taste of cheap alcohol on his lips, wanting to throw up, his mouth bleeding from the first brutal, rapacious kiss, Barve Mama's tongue plundering… his skin crawling from the sensation.

He had run upstairs in desperation and hid in the wardrobe. This was his refuge. The big green lizard that lived there didn't scare him anymore. And he was all of eight. But the polio he had since birth, it made his leg muscles weak.

Running was difficult. He couldn't escape.

Barve Mama followed him up slowly… he could hear the creak of the wooden sprung floorboards in this room where they once used to hold Ballroom dances, and he had stopped breathing, closed his mouth with his palm. And started praying. He wanted to shut his eyes but didn't dare to. There was silence outside. In which he could hear a dog howling somewhere eerily, the fragrant smell of September in the air.

And then suddenly his heart stopped and he was screaming in terror because Barve Mama had crouched and put his face against the crack of the wardrobe doors and laughed harshly. And something in that laugh told him everything he had to know about this uncle. A tall, fair and handsome man with the body of a Yogi, that's what Barve Mama always used to say about his physique, but after the first time when he had got him to… in the attic, made him… he couldn't forget Barve Mama's pink nipples and the mole on his pale chest, and how his grey-green eyes had shut in ecstasy as he lay back on the rickety planter's chair and put his feet up on the long armrests, Barve Mama's slender fingers guiding him to the drawstrings on his pajamas, his straight nose breathing hard, the thin lips parted, flecks of saliva dribbling out of the corner of his mouth, like his ejaculation later, and his own tears.

There were more assaults, further abuse…

… always in the attic where he used to hide.

This used to be his world before its privacy was invaded, its security ripped apart like his shorts and Mickey Mouse T-shirt, the peace and quiet of the afternoons shattered by the cries of the crows and his silent sobbing as he trembled in fear and in shame and in helplessness and suffered the daily molestation, while generations of forgotten ancestors frowned in silent disapproval from sepia toned portraits on the walls.

In years to come, he would realize that more boys than girls got sexually abused when they were young. And the crime was almost always committed by a family member or guardian, somebody like an uncle or a teacher.

He knew better than to tell his parents.

He didn't trust them to believe him. They had their own demons.

What? Barve Mama a pedophile? A sexual predator? Hahahahah!

What books have you been reading, child?

Dr. Jekyll and Mr. Hyde, eh?

There wasn't any such thing as a bogeyman in this world…

… only incestuous uncles who were supposed to be father figures and teachers, you bent to touch their feet and seek their blessings, but when you looked up, the drawstrings were dangling and the pajamas were open, and your small tousled head was being forcibly held and there was a pounding in your ears like waves crashing on the shore and a hoarse, ugly voice urging you to "Suck it, you little bastard"…

… ugh! He choked at the thought even today.

He didn't trust anybody…

… but Barve Mama, because what he did to him was real.

And what he threatened to do to him was unreal.

Until one stormy afternoon.

On his way out, Barve Mama stopped in the rain to relieve himself in the village well beneath the plantain trees, he was so drunk, he thought this was… God knows what Barve Mama had thought, because he didn't know what he was thinking until he heard the splash when Barve Mama hit the water, and immediately after that, a terrible thrashing, and realized he had shuffled and limped up from behind, under cover of the thunder and blinding rain lashing the leafy trees, arms outstretched.

Murder was childishly easy; he didn't feel a thing except a sudden hot flush when he had wet himself in excitement.

They found Barve Mama's umbrella by the side of the well and fished out the body next day. Peeping from behind the legs of the elders, he saw the blue and white striped pajamas one last time, the drawstrings open. And felt a surge of triumph. The same well his mother jumped into years later. He always wondered whether Barve Mama was responsible for that. A life for a life.

He bent and picked up the *Asian Age* that had slipped out of his fingers and lay all over the floor. Where was he, now? Ah, yes… an Indian professor of human behavior, who agreed that America had made the world aware of the serial killer, explained that psychopaths lacked the primary ability of empathy for fellow beings on a fundamental level.

"There are 20-odd genes in human beings related to violence," the profound Indian thinker said, "of which the MAO-A gene is most commonly found among psychopaths. It is called the Warrior Gene and behavioral economics show that it is linked to aggression. People with the high-risk version of this MAO-A gene are born killers."

He liked that line. When he spoke to that silly Police Commissioner again, he would tell him he wasn't a psychopathic serial killer, he was a Warrior.

Which would be later this evening, from the racecourse.

He needed another poem, perhaps a play of words and metaphors that the police would undoubtedly fail to understand. He would have to explain it to them. Again. Ah, he liked this one...

'This is the
sun
that breaks out
after the brisk drizzle.
This is the
storm
that turns in
after the thunderclap'

Yes, it was apt. If they calculated, he was giving them a 34-hour break between the murders, but not a day's respite. It was 25 hours since he had killed Nieves. And it would be nine hours before he struck again. He didn't want the police thinking they had scared him with last night's TV press conference.

There were eight more victims.

And eight days more in which to finish them. Tomorrow would be the fourth. Early morning. Before they got over this evening's surprise at the racecourse. No more long gaps in between.

Outside, it was raining again.

He loved this weather. Millions long for immortality who know not what to do with themselves on a lazy, rainy afternoon, one British writer had said. He chuckled to himself. Not him, he knew what he had to do this afternoon.

FERRAZ TIPTOED into the bedroom.

It was 7 am. Jackie was curled up in bed. And she was smiling in her sleep. Dreaming of things Ferraz knew she wouldn't be sharing with him. He felt a tug at his heartstrings. She always slept, even in summer, with the damn windows shut and the fan off. He could barely hear the murmur of the rain, it was so claustrophobic in here. She also wore socks to bed and covered herself with a thick duvet in all weather.

Initially he found this hilarious.

Till Dr. Yunus A Miyasahib, the police psychiatrist who had helped Ferraz deal with his own problems, told him that the duvet was a comforter. And Jackie's sleeping pattern was that of somebody who was insecure and vulnerable. Life had probably done worse things to her than Ferraz could imagine. Shutting herself in, hiding under the covers and curling herself up into a ball, was her defense against the world that gave her horrifying and vivid nightmares.

Ferraz had been dismayed; he didn't know what to do.

Dr. Yunus assured him that in time Jackie would come out of it.

Ferraz fervently hoped so. What was there to be afraid of, he couldn't imagine. He was always around. She had got used to his strength and authority by now. He knew she secretly loved the rock solid feeling of security he gave her. Not because he was a tough cop who commanded respect, but also because he treated her like a loving and caring…

… it was difficult for her to call him "Dad".

She wasn't uncomfortable, but shy. Her college friends made fun of her. Some of them had a teenage crush on Ferraz. It pissed her off. She called him "Hey Cop!", "Inspector Saheb" or "Oye Policewallah!" Like they were buddies. But most often she called him "Angie".

Ferraz didn't mind, it didn't matter, he told himself.

Now he gingerly plucked the edge of the duvet and stripped it off Jackie with a sudden jerk, shouting boisterously, "Saturday morning *s-u-r-p-r-i-s-e!* Wake up! WAKE UP! What's this, *what* the hell is this – what are things coming to in this house! A slip of a girl like you still in bed at 7? I can't believe my eyes… c'mon, rise and shine you lazy thing, shake that pretty ass of yours, what does a working man have to do to get breakfast here!"

Jackie rolled over and threw a pillow at him.

AT 8 am they were having breakfast.

Kheema parathas with yogurt and mint chutney, banana fritters with fresh cream, steaming mugs of fragrant Lipton Yellow Label Tea. Saturdays and Sundays, Jackie surprised him by tweaking the menu. Ferraz looked forward to the change. Outside, the morning was taking a pasting from the rain. He could hear the zing of raindrops ricocheting off people's air-conditioners and the dish antennae outside their windows.

"How different this breakfast is, and tastier too, from the healthy stuff you make me eat weekdays," Ferraz told Jackie enthusiastically, waving his tea mug. "Why can't we have this Lipton tea daily instead of that shitty Tulsi organic green tea!"

"Don't *lagav maska*," she said, "it's just for today, okay."

He pulled a face and asked, "Can I drop you anywhere, baby?"

"Never mind me," Jackie said, "what are you going to do with him?"

"Who the hell are you talking about?"

She jerked her head in the direction of the newspapers he had left scattered on the floor. He did that innocently on purpose to wind her up, she liked to keep a tidy house and it exasperated her to pick up after him.

"This Cobra you're hunting."

"Me? Kill him, what else!"

"Angie! You know what George Bernard Shaw said?"

"Isn't he dead?"

Jackie gave him a look.

She told Ferraz anyway, "He said, 'Criminals do not die by the hands of the law. They die by the hands of other men.'"

"That fucking storyteller!"

"How many times have…"

"You told me not to swear? Can't remember."

"… and GBS wasn't a storyteller. He was a playwright, an essayist and a novelist. The only man who got the Nobel Prize and an Academy Award for literature, did you know? Have you read his *Arms and The Man*?"

"Couldn't put it down!"

"You're such a liar!"

"I swear on all your saints!"

"Never mind, tell me about this killer, instead."

"What do you want to know? Whether he's read GBS? I doubt."

"Angie! How can you kill him?"

He was tempted to place the 9mm S&W on the table and tell her poker faced, 'With this – of course! How else?'

But she was a sensitive girl. Studying to be a Clinical Psychologist. Majoring in Psychology after which she would do an MA in the subject, then an M. Phil, which he didn't know was Masters of Philosophy in Psychology. Finally a Ph.D, because Jackie wanted to counsel people with behavioral issues and psychopathological conditions in schools, hospitals and the corporate world.

"Or should I do an elective course in Forensic Psychology?" she had asked him.

Ferraz hadn't a clue to what she was talking about.

"How does Dr. Jackie Ferraz sound?"

As a cop, he knew the name was immediately attractive. It had the kind of appeal that would draw all the weirdos to her with their emotional baggage. But Ferraz kept this information to himself.

Instead, he asked her, "Why would you want to do this?"

"Why did you become a cop?" she countered immediately.

She had him there.

Ferraz shrugged, unable to find a suitable reply.

"I want to help people who are unable to recognize the psychological problems in their lives," Jackie told him. "There's a lack of awareness in India. It's like OCD – Obsessive Compulsive Disorder – those that have it behave as if their actions are correct. People ignore or are unaware of the psychological and biological problems they face."

"*So they go around killing people?*"

"Angie, why are you sure the Cobra's a psychopath?"

"Darling, he's selecting and killing innocent and eminent people for absolutely no reason that we know of, so what do we call him?"

Angrily Jackie took the floor.

"Eminent, yes. But what do you mean innocent?" she demanded, hands on her hips. "And how do you know he has no reason for wanting to kill these people? Nobody commits murder just for the heck of it!"

"Agreed, unless you're mad – a psycho."

"The word 'psycho' doesn't exist in psychology."

"Oh, what do we call him then – Santa Claus?"

"*Angie!* Psycho's a harsh term, only the layman uses it. Clinically no patient is ever referred to as a 'psycho'. We call them mentally challenged."

Ferraz was speechless.

He regretted sharing the details of the investigation with her.

Then sarcastically, he asked, "What would you suggest we do with this mentally challenged patient, then?"

"I'm not saying he's not a killer…"

"*Hallelujah!*"

"… but what makes you certain he's a psychopath? Have you got his childhood history? Have you identified the underlying factor for his behavior? Found out why he isn't accepting social norms? Maybe he's got aggressive instincts suppressed in him..."

"*Yeah, and killing's the way to express them?*"

"... and if his needs are identified and the aggressive instinct is dealt with in an appropriate manner, his problem will be solved."

I'll solve that bastard's problem for good, Ferraz was thinking.

"How would you deal with him?" he asked, playing her along. "By kissing his ass till Kingdom come?"

She said, ignoring his sarcasm, "By building a comfort level. A relationship, I mean. And finding out the problems confronting him, the reasons why he's behaving this way. By showing him..."

"*Other ways of killing people?*"

"... what consequences his actions have on other people. He appears to be in a deep problematic state."

Ferraz sipped his tea quietly.

Jackie softened, "I know your intention isn't bad. At a larger level you're trying to eradicate a social problem. But maybe the Cobra's feeling helpless and frustrated. I'd communicate my support to him."

"*And what about me – trying to do a job?*"

"But the police have already described him as a psychopath..."

"Yeah, cold-blooded, vicious and extremely dangerous!"

"... without finding the reason for his behavior."

"Honey, I'm a cop... not a goddamn shrink!"

"Angie! I dislike you swearing!"

He blew out his cheeks, "Hoo boy, but you approve of this... this, what did you call him, this mentally challenged guy killing people, huh? Whose side are you on, girl?"

"I didn't say that! Sometimes I think *you* need psychiatric help," Jackie said and got up in a huff to clear the breakfast dishes. "If you kill a killer, the number of killers in the world remains the same."

She exited with this parting shot leaving Ferraz shaking his head.

13

SANGEETA KADAM couldn't stop giggling!

She was answering the Police Helpline set up for the serial killer. A much harried Nawalkar had announced it at the press conference last night before TV cameras, hoping…

Calls started coming in immediately.

Tushar Pandit, Arun Sawant and Dhananjay Gadkari answered them all through the night. The helpline had call hunting facility. All calls came to a dedicated number in the Control Room which searched for and connected them to the first cop who was free in the DCB-CID's Unit I.

No caller got a busy tone.

And no cop got a genuine caller.

Usually the Control Room handled this work. But Joint CP (Crime) Arun Rathod wanted Detection officers investigating the Haider-Nieves murders to take these calls. He believed people with sensitive information expected to talk to a cop, not a telephone operator.

The cops didn't have a dull moment.

Mumbai was full of strung out insomniacs. They worked off their anxiety by calling the helpline. Pandit, Sawant and Gadkari answered 256 calls between them. All false alarms.

Jittery people called to report that the serial killer was their neighbor who had been acting sinister lately. Men with harsh voices abused the cops with a string of expletives. Children phoned with vague stories of shadows going past their windows holding knives.

Hyper citizens dialed to say they suspected terrorists were in the neighborhood. Women phoned to complain about their cheating husbands, disrespectful children, interfering in-laws and gossipy neighbors. The old and lonely used the helpline because they wanted somebody to talk to.

The weary cops left a log of the calls for the relieving team.

Sangeeta, Sanjay Chhabria and Antone de Azavedo quickly got the hang of the helpline. They started at 8 am. In two hours they received 81 calls. Every single one a hoax played by pranksters who took over from last night's telephone pests. But they had to treat each call as a genuine one.

The city's Romeos made most of them. All hoping to get Sangeeta, the Crime Branch's sexy poster girl with the breathless voice, on the phone. They drove her nuts with their love talk.

Some asked to marry her straightaway.

Others wanted to go on a date.

A few engaged Sangeeta in lewd conversation.

These salacious callers knew they were being recorded. That the Control Room had Calling Line Identification software and cyber-backed satellite systems capable of tracking them to the corners of the earth. But they weren't making hoax calls about a bomb at the airport. Or threatening to assassinate the Prime Minister. They were just indulging in phone sex. Which also, these horny gentlemen knew, could get them arrested under Section 509 of the IPC for word, gesture or act intended to insult the modesty of a woman. A policewoman, no less.

Sangeeta knew about men's fantasies.

She knew men dreamed of doing it to a girl in uniform. Women cops were top of the lust list. The handcuffs were a turn on. Next came nurses, then airhostesses, teachers, waitresses and gym instructors. But as the city's heavy breathers continued to push their luck, Sangeeta tired of the game. Her next caller confessed to being the serial killer. He wanted to know in lascivious detail how Sangeeta would torture him after arrest.

She passed the call to Chhabria.

He had just finished talking to a garrulous old woman from Altamont Road who insisted that Esther Nieves' dog had seen the killer – so why wasn't the police doing something about it?

"After all, dogs are intelligent, you know," she said mysteriously.

Chhabria thanked her for the tip and finally managed to hang up.

Shaking his head in despair, he took on Sangeeta's caller.

By his side, Azavedo was struggling with a deaf old man who was asking over and over again if the news about Haider Allarakha Khan was true.

"But is he dead?" the old man repeated every time Azavedo said it was true.

"Yes?" Chhabria said in his gentle voice to Sangeeta's caller.

"What do you mean 'Yes'? Who the fuck are you?"

"Police Sub-Inspector Chhabria. You called, sir?"

"I did, how else would we be having this conversation?"

"Right. You have knowledge about the suspect wanted by the police?" Chhabria asked patiently, reaching for his notepad and pen.

"No, I don't! Who said I had?"

"Why are you calling then, sir, may I ask?"

"Who are you to ask! Where's the item?"

"I don't get you, sir. What item? If you didn't–"

"*Arre police ke bhadve*, put the girl back on the line!"

"She has left for the day. How may I help you, please?"

"By giving me her number."

"I'm afraid I–"

"What the fuck are you afraid of, man? You're a *policewallah, na?*"

"Yes, I told–"

"What's the item's name? Is she a senior officer?"

"May I have your name and address, please, sir?"

"For what? I'm not into men! Peddle your ass elsewhere, *gandu*."

"Sir, this is a Police Helpline, I assume–"

"Yeah, so help me, *na*. Give me that item's number, *yaar*."

"I'm sorry I can't do that. But you can talk to me. May I–"

"Keep wishing, *choothiya*."

Chhabria put down the phone and looked at Sangeeta.

"You set me up," he told her accusingly.

She burst into peals of laughter.

Azavedo began guffawing too.

Entering the office, Ferraz looked at them in surprise.

"What's the joke?" he asked, stopping at Sangeeta's desk.

Before she could reply, his cell phone buzzed.

Joint CP (Crime) Arun Rathod was calling.

"Here we go," Ferraz said entering his cabin and taking the call.

"ANY LUCK?" the Joint CP (Crime) asked.

Meaning with the new Police Helpline.

"All bogus calls, sir," Ferraz said regretfully.

"I thought the city would be buzzing with information!"

"There's a lot of speculation," Ferraz admitted, "but if we listen to what all's being said, we'll confuse the investigation."

"What have we achieved so far?"

"Nothing, sir. We visited both crime scenes again, last evening and this morning, around the time the murders were committed. Spoke to many people who knew Haider and Nieves and were familiar with their routines. But nobody could tell us anything unusual."

"How did he get away from Altamont Road at that hour?"

"No idea, sir. No cabbies picked up a fare there."

"That's bloody strange!" Rathod said. "Maybe he came by car or bike. If only there was CCTV, we'd have a video of him."

"We checked out every criminal in our records who is neither dead nor in prison and was earlier arrested for murder or assault by a Rampuri," Ferraz told the Joint CP (Crime). "All are in the clear. There's also no record of any goon by the name of Mario or Maria."

"What did the informers turn up?"

"The *khabris* gave us no leads, sir. In Nieves's case, that was expected. Until her murder, we hadn't heard of her. But Haider was a public figure. And he lived and was murdered on Mohammed Ali Road. Where it's impossible to be secretive about anything. Yet the *khabris* came up with nothing. We've not been able to establish a link between Haider and Nieves that could be the motive behind their murders."

"What about those curious verses? Flowers on the wall? Emperor of Darkness?" Rathod said. "The media is also talking about that."

"The Poetry Society couldn't shed any light there, sir," Ferraz replied. "A Google search for Emperor of Darkness only throws up information about the video game. Maybe these verses are his own work. The killer's a poet and he's unpublished. So nobody's heard about him. We're checking to see if any publishing house, or vanity publisher, has a book of poems in the making in which these verses feature."

"And the victims' CDRs?"

"Nothing so far, no subscriber was in touch with both Haider and Nieves. The service providers gave us their cell tower dumps from Mohammed Ali Road and Altamont Road. There were 13 networks operating with maximum cell usage being on Vodafone, Airtel, Idea, Loop and Aircel. Hundreds of thousands of calls were made or received at the time of the murders. It will take us time to find if a common number was in use at both locations."

"Any other line of action?" Rathod asked glumly.

"The guests from Nieves's Ganpati party were said without exception that it had been a wonderful night, the victim was an outstanding hostess. She had been the life and soul of the party. They didn't notice any tension about her. The staff at the residence also had no unusual activity to report. The lady was her usual self right till they bid her good night, chirpy and caring, thanking them for working overtime, making sure they took the leftovers. There was no shadow of tragedy hanging over her. But there's one thing…"

"What's that?" Rathod said sharply.

"We've questioned the British Deputy High Commission staff. Richard Nieves appears to be well liked. Since the time he joined in 2008, only three hands have changed there. Two retired. One was sacked. He was the driver, Porus Mistry, a Parsi living at Captain Colony in Tardeo. He had 18 years of service with them. But was reportedly an insolent, reckless speed fiend. He crashed the High Commission car in May when Nieves was in it. The BKC police said he was DUI. Nieves got rid of him. We're trying to locate Porus to see if he's carrying a grudge. The Captain Colony house has been locked for three months. Neighbors say Porus is a bachelor and a loner. Nobody knows where he might be. Our Navroze Daruwala has activated his contacts in all the Parsi *baugs* to try and find him."

The Joint CP (Crime) let out a deep sigh.

"But why would Porus murder Haider?" he asked.

RAJVEER SETH enjoyed his afternoon tea.

He had it at a table by one of the large bay windows in Gallops, that bijou eatery serving Indian and Continental food at the Mahalaxmi Racecourse. The racecourse had a bar, arguably the biggest in Mumbai, at Tote on The Turf. But Seth preferred tea over, say, a Pink Gin in the afternoon. He could have gone to any of the city's tea rooms. They offered flavors ranging from Darjeeling Orange Pekoe and English Earl Grey to Ceylon Breakfast Tea and Japanese Gyokuro.

But Seth owned racehorses, and Gallops was convenient.

Mornings during racing season, owners came to watch their horses being put through their paces while timekeepers sat in the stands and clocked them on sand tracks. Some owners visited the stables in the evenings. Others showed up only on race days. Often large syndicates owned a single horse. If their horse won a race, all 25 co-owners went to receive the cup.

Seth went before tea. He took a look at his thoroughbreds, had a word with the trainer, cracked a joke with the jockey, slipped the syces a couple of bucks, then made for Gallops. The racecourse was shut for the monsoon, but Gallops was open. Teatime was 4.30 pm. Seth's brew was Assam. It was served by deferential waiters who knew he wanted his space.

He was one of India's zillionaires – *Forbes* rated him among the Top 50, with blue chip companies in his pocket and partnerships in multinationals, his money lying in everything from pharmaceuticals and cement to steel and textiles. He was a bull in the stock market, a party animal at night, a regular man about town who had penthouses in New York and London and a beach house in Goa.

Seth owned 11 champion racehorses that ran at all seven racing centers in the country, he followed the F1 Grand Prix, enjoyed sailing and was a closet cook, a single malt and cigar aficionado, a bridge champion, a collector of vintage cars and he was now planning to invest in an IPL cricket team. He was married to a social butterfly now getting on in years. So Seth discreetly played the field. The couple's son and his heir was studying Business Management at Cornell in New York.

At 59, Seth was a lion in winter; a large and flaccid man with bad skin and soft effeminate features, long silver hair combed back, a thin moustache. When he was young, he used to play rugby for the Bombay Gym and beneath his corpulence he still had the frame of what he must have once been like in his prime.

Teatime was Seth's exclusive 'me' time.

Even on a rainy Saturday afternoon, he could follow his horses racing in Pune, Bangalore, Mysore, Hyderabad and Kolkata. The Turf Club had live telecasts and computerized tote betting. He sat lost in thought, the mind on some distant race, listening to the thunder of horse hooves, seeing in his mind's eye the animals' nostrils flaring as they came around the bend, hearing the *thwack* of the jockeys' whip, imagining the jocks bent in a crouch, the favorite a short head in front of the field, hearing the roar of members in their enclosure, the excitement of the crowds in the stands. Seth couldn't wait for November. When racing returned to Mumbai.

HE CAME from Haji Ali…

… entering the racecourse from a gate on the road to Mahalaxmi Railway Station and finding himself in the large car park. At this hour it was empty but for one car. He was expecting that. It wasn't raining just now and people would soon be coming. The walking and jogging track inside was as much a social hotspot as were the restaurant and bar. People walked their dogs in the car park, because dogs were not allowed inside.

The royal blue 1948 Jaguar Mark V saloon was parked beneath trees not far from the Members' Enclosure gate. It stood majestically like some great beast on spoked wheels that were fitted with classic Dunlop whitewall tires, its large chrome headlamps asleep, waiting for its master to come and stretch its legs. The leaping Jaguar radiator cap mascot above the upright chrome grille shone even in the poor light.

There was nobody around. Not even a watchman at the gate.

He knew Seth took pride in driving his cars. So there wasn't a uniformed chauffeur waiting beside the Jag. And the vintage automobile, priceless beauty though she was, was such a familiar sight here that it no longer attracted curiosity.

Young girls on horses, members of the Amateur Riders Club, trotted by giggling at some teenage joke, the horses whinnying and their hooves rhythmically going clip-clop on the asphalt.

Head down, listening to ODI commentary from the Riverside

Ground in Chester-le-Street, he headed boldly for the public track where people were jogging. A soar of black pariah kites, predators of the Mumbai skies, circled the track like there was a carcass below for them to pick. Beyond them, against the Worli skyline disappearing in misty monsoon clouds, he could see concrete towers coming up, construction booms jutting out from the upper stories, the hooks of gigantic cranes clawing the air.

He shuffled and limped past Gallops, resisting the temptation to look past the heavy ornate door with gleaming lamps at the large bay window where Seth would be sitting. From inside came the clatter of silverware against china and the titter of laughter.

He carried on past a garden of tall palms, past the Members' Enclosure, the Grandstand for members and their guests, and the new stand that had come up beyond the finish post. He went past the Members' Bookmakers Ring with its cages and blackboards on which the odds offered on every horse were scribbled on race days.

Here was the strangely named Badam Patti Lawn, where trophies were displayed, and the most popular spot of the racecourse, the Paddock, where horses were paraded before the race so members could admire them and then place their bets. Derby Day, there wouldn't be space to stand here.

Finally he came to the Public Enclosure, whose entry fee was 20 rupees, one-tenth the price of a movie ticket. Small punters laid their bets at the tote windows in the Bookmakers' Ring. Then dashed up the stands to witness the race and see whether they had picked a winner or a dud.

He wandered towards the 2,400 meters racetrack.

Opposite, on its northern curve, were the stables. He squinted at them in the dying light, barely able to make out the 30-odd stalls which accommodated 1,500 horses.

He looked at his watch, 5.15 pm. Time to get back to the car park. Where the Jag was waiting. He decided to wait with it.

The leather horse reins in his hands were looped to form a noose.

SETH STEPPED out of Gallops and sniffed the air.

The sky was overcast. He could hear the joggers, a young boy calling out jeeringly to someone who was lagging behind. Out in the west, a helicopter was flying low over the coast. The Governor returning to Raj Bhavan. The chopper looked like a giant dragon-fly in the sky. He could hear the whisper of its rotors slicing the air. He pulled a Montecristo tube out of his Burberry mackintosh and lit the cigar, taking a deep drag and blowing the smoke out strongly, savoring the aroma.

The tea and cigar put Seth in a good mood.

He walked buoyantly down the muddy pathway to the car park, puffing away, skirting small puddles of rain water. He met the gate watchman coming in who touched his forehead. Seth nodded civilly.

Reaching the gate, he paused and looked out, drawing on his cigar.

And it was then that he noticed the man in black. Leaning against the polished bonnet of the Jag, *damn him*, listening to a pocket transistor, one hand twisting what looked like a pair of reins.

Seth frowned. He didn't recognize the man; probably one of the syces of the Amateur Riders Club. He would have a word with the security to keep a closer watch on the Jag.

But… was this fellow waiting for him?

It certainly looked like it. Seth walked over briskly, searching in his trouser pocket for the car keys, and his cell phone rang.

It was R Srinivasan, his Man Friday.

"Yes Srini," he started to say, when the man pushed himself off the car, limped and sort of shuffled forward, and muttered something.

"What?" said Seth, "… not you, Srini."

"Moryaa Re!" the man repeated.

"What?" said Seth again, "… *dammit*, not you Srini!"

"*Moryaa Re!*"

Seth looked at him curiously, thinking the fellow had a bit… a bit of a baleful expression, there was something sinister about him, those reins… *was that*… it looked like a noose in his gloved hands, he was wearing rider's gloves, the transistor in his shirt pocket was relaying cricket commentary… and that silly lop-sided grin on his face.

He was about to tick him off for leaning against the Jag…

… when the man kicked him viciously in the groin, suddenly, but with expert precision, and with tremendous force.

With a startled grunt of agony, Seth dropped the cell phone and doubled over in pain, stumbling back against the car, reaching out to it for support, missing, and sprawled forward… the cigar falling from his mouth.

He was stunned by the impact of the hard ground and grasped fumblingly for his phone… groveling on his knees; the trauma of the pain in his crotch was agonizing, it spread to his abdomen, debilitating him. In a daze he realized he could hear Srinivasan hysterically asking him if he was all right.

He couldn't think… *Oh God*, but what… ?

Dizzy, the mind in shock, he tried to focus and ride the pain – as he used to when he was young and got injured playing rugby, and crawled shakily towards the footboard of the Jag.

Got one hand on it, was gasping painfully for breath and reaching up for the handle of the door…

… when the man stamped down savagely on his back, his right foot crushing Seth into the ground again, and holding onto the roof of the Jag for support, he continued stamping, like he was putting out a fire.

Numb with horror under the onslaught, feeling the man's foot crashing down on his back, his buttocks, the back of his head, unable to rise, Seth realized suddenly that the noose was around his neck.

He struggled to open his mouth and shout.

But his call for help was drowned by a terrible gargling that came from deep inside his lungs. The sudden and violent compression around his neck was unbearable, it was making him giddy, there was a ringing in his ears, and a sudden weakness in his muscles.

Blood was beginning to pound in his head. He couldn't breathe. His chest was on fire. But the tug on the reins was unrelenting, the foot on his back grinding him deeper into the ground, the leather biting into the thick flesh of his neck and constricting the air passage while hauling him up brutally.

He felt his upper body rising.

His hands dangled loosely by his side. Scratching the air, struggling to get a hold on the car, then reaching up frantically and trying to tear away the strap that was choking him. He tasted blood in his mouth, felt it oozing out of his ears and nostrils, and was shocked to discover that he had wet himself and soiled his trousers.

In a last and desperate move before he lost consciousness, Seth tried to get onto his knees, but it was too late, he had no strength left. The man removed his foot from Seth's back and dropped down on him with both knees, pulling the reins in tighter, causing Seth's eyes to roll up and his face to turn purple. His mouth fell open spitting out blood and saliva, his disgorged tongue stuck out, his body convulsed in its death throes.

Seth's last thought was of Srinivasan… who was on the phone, listening to him being strangled, waiting for instructions, for him to say that he wanted his thoroughbred Namasthetu prepared for the Pune racing season. First the classic Indian St. Leger on the last Sunday of September. Then the Pune Derby in the first week of October.

After that, Namasthetu would race in Mumbai from November.

Namasthetu was one of the 108 names of Lord Ganesh. It meant the Vanquisher of all Evils and Vices and Sins.

HE KICKED Seth's inert body aside and picked up his phone.

Somebody was on the line, a shrill and quavering voice full of anxiety.

"Hullo! Hullo! *Sir... are you all right?* Sir? Hullo? Sir, please? Hullo!"

Over and over again.

Srinivasan was going mad with worry, wondering what had happened to Seth. Eventually he would find out. And the realization that his master was being murdered even while he was listening on the phone would haunt Seth's Man Friday for the rest of his life.

With a chuckle he cut Srinivasan's call. It was time to move on.

He didn't know who Seth had been talking to when he stopped him in his tracks (he chuckled again, pleased with this pun), but that distressed caller would know something had gone terribly wrong for the racehorse owner and help might already be on the way.

They would find Seth with a noose around his neck!

Without hurry, and without another glance at the grotesque figure lying on its back with flies buzzing around the bloodied face and open, staring eyes, he shuffled and limped around the Jag and headed out, slipping the black leather riding gloves into his pocket.

Outside, he hesitated for a moment, looking left and right.

Right was towards Haji Ali. That's where they would come from, looking for Seth. Opposite was the Bal Mitra Mandal's Sarvajanik Ganpati. Large posters of Shiv Sena supremo Balasaheb Thackeray greeted devotees. There were saffron flags and streamers with the party's mascot, the roaring tiger, strung up between lampposts. He turned left and headed for Mahalaxmi Railway Station, his fingers punching out Nawalkar's number on Seth's phone, from which he sent the CP the poem.

NAWALKAR WAS having tea when his cell beeped.

He looked at it grumpily. It had been happening all day. People had been calling or texting to compliment him for boldly going on TV last night to tell the city about this… this bloody psycho who had got the police by the balls and was killing distinguished citizens one by one.

"Just two," he reminded them irritably.

They made it seem like the fucking holocaust.

"*So far two*," one society lady sniffed meaningfully. She asked him pathetically if she would require police protection.

Nawalkar wanted to tell her to drop dead.

The press conference had created a stir. He had not wanted to do it. When Joint CP (Crime) Arun Rathod came to his residence last evening, Nawalkar had been appalled by the suggestion.

"What?" he said disbelievingly. "Me, you want me to…"

"Yes, sir… go on TV and warn the city."

"… and admit that a psycho serial killer is around?"

"Yes, and we don't know who he might target next."

"How do you know this Cobra's a psycho?" Nawalkar asked. "What if he isn't a serial killer? What if he doesn't kill tomorrow? There's a difference between alerting the city and scaring the shit out of people."

They sat on his balcony sipping coffee.

Nawalkar with his arms crossed, shaking his legs, brooding.

Like many apartments in South Mumbai, his balcony offered the choice of sitting out in fresh air and natural light and enjoying the view and mild weather. He lived on one of the upper floors of the building Dilwara on Maharishi Karve Road in Nariman Point. Lots of IPS officers had flats here.

From the darkness came the long, eerie screech of an owl.

The balcony overlooked Cooperage.

The city's premier football stadium was under renovation.

Football was Kolkata's sport, Mumbai's was cricket. All the football greats visited Kolkata. Starting with Pele in 1977, to play a friendly against a local club at Eden Gardens. The great Diego Maradona came in 2008, blowing kisses and pumping the air with his fist, driving thousands of Bengalis mad at Salt Lake Stadium with his masterful juggling of the ball. Then just last night, yes, the Argentine superstar Lionel Messi led his home team against the Venezuelan national side in an exhibition match at the same ground.

The City of Joy, its cup overflowed.

Rathod was grateful Mumbai wasn't football crazy.

The police had enough on their hands without Messi.

Now he patiently told the CP, "Sir, we don't want him to kill anyone, that's why you should go on TV. If he doesn't, we can say our warning worked; but if he does commit murder, nobody can accuse us of not warning the city."

The two policemen regarded each other in silence.

Then Nawalkar said, "I don't see why we have to do this. What's the status of the investigation? Aren't we closer to finding out why he killed Haider and Nieves? What has the Crime Branch achieved?"

Rathod masked his exasperation and said, "I think we'll only know when we get there. But if the DCB-CID is to make any progress, which is looking difficult – let me admit, then I need you backing us all the way."

Nawalkar maintained a stony silence.

Undaunted, Rathod said, "Most people in Mumbai live their entire lives untouched by crime. But they fear it. Especially murder. It's at the back of their minds. The media keeps them informed, they see it happening – but to others. Their fingers are crossed. It's been the police's duty to assure the people they've got nothing to fear. Now suddenly we are being seen as helpless, undecided, useless… thanks to the Cobra, everybody in the city's feeling vulnerable and unsafe."

"So what are you saying?"

Rathod tirelessly went over the plan again.

"I'm saying I need you to go on TV, sir, and address a press conference, tell the people what has happened, express our condolence for the victims – but let it be known we couldn't prevent these murders, nor can we promise to stop this psycho from killing again, admit that the Mumbai Police has never been successful in tracking a serial predator..."

"The fucker's jerking us off, that madarchot!"

"... but say we'll do our best. Murders happen in Mumbai every day. This time it's the cold-blooded killing of VIPs. Then share with the city all the information we have, the modus operandi of the killings, the calls he made to you from the victims' phones, don't talk about his reference to the Cobra and his Emperor of Darkness SMS – that'll confuse people, but repeat his threat to kill again tomorrow..."

"And express our fucking helplessness?"

"... admit we are overburdened by Ganeshotsav, this is a city of 20 million people – anybody could be next, we can't protect everyone. We don't have a motive or suspect, no concrete leads, no clue to link the victims and detect who could be next. Ask the press and people to cooperate with us, suggest that somebody has to know the killer, it could be his wife, his children, a colleague at work, the neighbors, God knows who else – and it's their duty to inform the police, because even by innocently shielding him they could become an accessory. Announce a dedicated helpline..."

"A reward for information leading to an arrest?"

"... apologize that the police can't be everywhere, but we are taking his warning seriously, we have strengthened *bandobast,* increased *nakabandis,* formed SITs, yet the killer could strike anybody, anywhere, anytime. And the scariest thing is anybody could be the killer. So tell everybody to mind their own backs and be aware of what's happening around them, let them organize a neighborhood safety watch, look out for strangers..."

"An alert public is the city's first line of defence... your words!"

"... the city is full of famous faces, fortunately most have their own security, but there are others who don't. People might accuse you of spreading panic and causing fear..."

"They will, the fucking jackasses!"

"... you tell them – no, you are creating awareness, because the city's vulnerable to this kind of attack, it's like terrorism, he's terrorizing us."

"Isn't that what he wants?" the CP asked sourly. "To spread fear?"

"He wants publicity – so why not give him a splash?"

"Think the media will cooperate with us?"

"We've already taken them into confidence and sought their support – they will help us. I've said we won't reveal too much..."

Nawalkar snorted, "What's there to reveal?"

"... but we'll give them the facts. They will play along, they may criticize the Mumbai Police's lack of success in tackling the serial killer, but they can't write different from what you say."

"How long will the public remain alert?" Nawalkar asked. "Sooner or later the anxiety and watchfulness will wear off. People will stop looking under their beds. Then what? He'll kill again!"

"They'll remain alert until we arrest him."

"Why don't you go on TV?" Nawalkar craftily suggested.

Rathod had been expecting this. He played his trump card.

Sighing heavily, he said, "Two VIP murders, the killer calling the CP, this is no ordinary crime, the Home Minister might wonder why I went on the air and not you."

Nawalkar heroically conceded then.

It had been pandemonium at the press conference. Nawalkar had gone dressed in uniform, wearing all his medals and ribbons – *why not*, he was appearing on TV! And in the full glare of the media, he had fumblingly read a statement prepared for him by the Police PRO again.

"We have no definite leads, nothing on the suspect, not even a description, anybody could be the killer," he hinted darkly. "In a situation like this, it's hard to ask the people not to panic, but that is what is needed. It requires special precaution and awareness by everyone because the offender is at large and he has threatened to kill again."

When the crime reporters attacked him with questions, Nawalkar invited Rathod and Mugbe to join him. Which both Joint CPs were waiting for.

Together they delivered the message to the press…

… and unwittingly also spread fear across the city.

That a psychopathic killer was around. He had killed twice with impunity. And apparently for no reason. Now he was threatening to kill a third time. That would make him a serial killer. No, this wasn't an extortion racket by some gang. The suspect was working alone, the police were certain, he hadn't made any demands. There was no guarantee they would arrest him soon. The entire force was on the job. The people were advised to stay alert. The police had set up a special helpline for information that might lead to the suspect's arrest.

Nawalkar's phone had not stopped ringing since then.

He had enjoyed the first few calls last night. Now, on Saturday evening, he was tired of taking them. He had to be careful what he said, too. His phone was under surveillance. The Crime Branch wanted to record the Cobra if he called the CP again. That, too, Rathod convinced Nawalkar was absolutely necessary for the investigation.

"We have voice samples of many criminals in our data bank," Rathod had said somewhat apologetically. "There's always the chance that his voice will match one of them – like a fingerprint."

The CP had understood and reluctantly agreed.

"Even if we don't find a match, it's important that we record his voice. The recording can be used later as evidence. We'll match it with a voice sample taken after his arrest."

The police couldn't tap anybody's phone just like that. It amounted to violation of freedom and an infringement of fundamental rights. But for security reasons and law and order purposes, like to detect underworld activity and terrorist threats, or to prevent economic offences and tax evasion, the police could tap an offender's phone under provisions of lawful interception in the Indian Telegraph Act of 1885.

Sanction came from the Home Ministry.

The Additional Chief Secretary, Home, was the final authority.

In this case, the Crime Branch got a cloned SIM card for Nawalkar's number from the mobile service provider. It acted like a mute parallel line to his cell. They were able to listen to the CP's conversations and record his calls.

Nawalkar's cell beeped.

Somebody had sent another fucking SMS.

The whole city had him on speed dial today.

He put down his tea and snatched up the phone.

It was from Rajveer Seth.

He was among the 900-odd 'Contacts' on the CP's phone. The two men had been friends since Nawalkar's days at the State CID Headquarters in Pune, where Seth had introduced him to bridge and golf. Where was the time to play all that now!

Seth was probably texting to invite him for some big race.

He opened the SMS and read...

'This is the
sun
that breaks out
after the brisk drizzle.
This is the
storm
that turns in
after the thunderclap'

Nawalkar stared at it blankly.

What the fuck was Seth thinking–

Then his heart skipped a beat. He had just been complimenting himself. Saturday was drawing to a close. And there was no call from the Cobra. Maybe his going on TV last night had worked! There was no third murder.

But now this SMS from Seth's phone!

Nawalkar knew the racehorse owner and zillionaire industrialist was not given to forwarding dirty jokes and silly messages to friends. In a panic he remembered that the 'Emperor of Darkness' SMS had preceded the killer's call to him after the Nieves murder yesterday morning.

God! Was Seth safe?

His fingers trembling, the CP dialed Seth's number.

To his great relief, the phone rang. Then…

"Moryaa Re!"

Nawalkar gasped.

Then Seth's phone was abruptly switched off.

14

THE QUALIS howled down Marine Drive.

Navroze drove with one hand, splashing through potholes, jumping red lights, the other hand on the siren. He didn't slow down for speedbreakers. The Saturday evening traffic scattered in a hurry hearing him come.

Ferraz sat beside him, his heart in his mouth.

Navroze's driving always had this effect on him.

Tushar Pandit and Arun Sawant sat behind holding on for dear life, their eyes shut, feeling the fillings in their teeth shaking. Navroze always drove like they were in some high-speed chase. When he was excited or agitated, Navroze drove recklessly as well. They were rushing to Mahalaxmi Racecourse where Seth's body had just been found. Ferraz hoped they would get there in one piece.

The Tardeo police were there already. And the DCB-CID's Unit III under whose jurisdiction the racecourse fell. Also present was the slain racehorse owner's principal secretary, R Srinivasan.

They were all waiting for Ferraz & Co. to come.

"Bawa, slow down, red light ahead," Ferraz warned.

"I know," Navroze replied.

The Qualis hurtled towards Chowpatty at breakneck speed.

A small procession of Ganpati devotees was crossing the road, taking their idol to the sea for immersion, singing and dancing with gay abandon. There were children with them. And elders shuffling in between. This was one of those families that kept their Ganpati for three days. Two Traffic constables, hearing the siren and seeing the

Qualis approaching like a bolt of lightning, frantically waved them on and hurriedly got out of the way themselves.

We're going to mow them down, Ferraz thought.

But the processionists nimbly parted at the last heart-stopping moment and the Qualis swept past without incident, the wail of its siren rising above their exuberant cries of *"Ganpati Bappa!"*

'Morya,' thought Ferraz with a shudder.

He had asked for *nakabandis* to be set up for as far as five kilometres around Mahalaxmi. He had ordered all nearby DCB-CID Units to rush to Mahalaxmi Railway Station and the ones before and after it and help the Government Railway Police in conducting checks on suspicious passengers. He wanted BEST buses that had passed Mahalaxmi recently to be intercepted by mobile patrols and their conductors made to identify any passengers who had got on at the racecourse. Finally, Ferraz asked the Station House to send an alert to all cabbies who had picked up passengers outside the racecourse to report to the nearest police station.

Simultaneously, Sr. PI Dinesh Ahir of Tardeo Police Station sent plainclothesmen to Haji Ali Dargah and Mahalaxmi Temple to scan the crowds and zero in on anybody who aroused their suspicion. The Tardeo police and Unit III activated their *khabri* networks. All stops had been covered before Ferraz & Co. reached the racecourse.

SETH LOOKED lonely in death.

Srinivasan was in shock. He had rushed over from his Kemps Corner residence thinking Seth was having an asthma attack. Parking next to the Jaguar, Srinivasan got out, unsuspecting.

Next second he was fleeing, blabbering in horror.

After taking a few blind, faltering steps, Srinivasan stopped.

He was choking and couldn't continue. The battered and bloodied corpse, eyes staring glassily in death, tongue thick and protruding, had frightened him enormously. He recognized that Seth had been murdered. There was a noose around his neck biting into the skin. Srinivasan vomited on the grass. Then summoning courage, he made a hesitant second approach.

His body trembled with shock and revulsion.

He wanted to touch Seth, to make sure he was dead, unable to accept that this still, lifeless mass of flesh that was bleeding, smelling of shit and piss and buzzing with flies, had been his master 20 minutes ago.

The darkening sky made him uneasy.

He took another fearful look at the corpse and almost fled again. Then empathy, anger and a sense of loyalty set in. With an effort he composed himself. He had to take charge of the situation. The police had to be told. So Srinivasan dialed 100. He then called up Seth's company secretary and gave him the terrible news.

His duty done, Srinivasan moved away.

He didn't have to wait long. The Tardeo police, informed by the Control Room, came at once. From another gate a Bolero with Detection cops from Unit III slowly drove up. Ten minutes later, Navroze brought the Qualis to a jerking halt by the side of the Jaguar.

Ferraz heard the buzz before they got out. Everybody who had business at the racecourse was there, holding up a cell phone and taking photographs of the policemen huddled around the vintage car and its murdered owner. He knew Nawalkar, Rathod and Mugbe were on their way.

Not every murder drew the top brass of the Mumbai Police.

But this was no ordinary murder…

… it was the serial killer's third.

A sickening delivery of the Cobra's chilling promise.

The press, which had waited all day to break this story, started arriving. Newspaper and TV reporters got to work swiftly, talking to the police and Turf Club staff, mixing with the racecourse regulars, hoping to find a witness to the murder. The photographers fiddled with telescopic lenses, TV cameras began rolling and OB vans took the murder outside the racecourse and into people's homes.

AS a boy, R Srinivasan had wanted to be a policeman.

Now he watched in a daze how the cops went about their work. His eyes kept straying to Seth's body lying beyond the yellow and black plastic tape that said 'Police Line Do Not Cross'. Listening to the blare and static of the police wireless, he suddenly realized that Seth was the third victim of the deadly serial killer stalking Mumbai.

Ferraz told him, "We need to talk to you, give me ten minutes."

The DCB-CID's Sr. PI Shrikant Musale of Unit III was short, plump and jovial; he had soft brown eyes and a kindly, wizened face. Musale looked more like everybody's favorite uncle than a Detection cop. He had taken the Tardeo police's help and cordoned the area around the Jaguar where Seth's body lay. After that, he summoned the Investigation Van with forensic experts and advised them to bring arc lights and plastic sheets because the postcard monsoon sky was rapidly changing and rain appeared imminent. Finally, Musale put in a call to the Dog Squad.

"There are footprints," he pointed out to Ferraz.

It was true, there were muddy footprints near the Jaguar.

Remembering what little success the Dog Squad had at Haider's residence on Thursday night, Ferraz didn't say anything. He didn't want to dampen Musale's enthusiasm.

He looked at the ground around Seth's corpse.

There was no blood. Had the racehorse owner been strangled somewhere else and the body was dumped here later? The ground around the Jaguar was concrete. The muddy footprints could be Seth's or the killer's. The crime scene techs would undoubtedly match them with the bloody footprints picked up at Haider's residence.

"Shrikant, will you look after this?" he asked the Unit III head,

"We'll talk to the racehorse chap's secretary before the press grab him. He appears to be in a state of shock. He heard his employer being murdered. Must have been terrible for him."

"Of course."

"The noose… I wonder if it has any fingerprints," Navroze said.

"I'll tell forensics to check," Musale assured him.

Leaving Tushar Pandit and Arun Sawant to help Musale, Ferraz and Navroze walked Srinivasan over to Gallops where Seth had not long ago enjoyed his last cup of Assam tea. Navroze kept a friendly hand on the secretary's shoulder. He could feel tremors running through Srinivasan's body and felt sorry for the simple man.

As they went, Ferraz felt a strange tingling sensation running down his spine. He knew what that meant.

Somebody was watching them!

He turned, but saw nothing unusual.

Then he thought he did.

Somebody ducked into the crowd with a lurching movement. Somebody dressed in black. Who had stepped out to watch them go. And didn't want to be caught looking.

Ferraz hesitated.

Navroze and Srinivasan had gone ahead.

Once more, that itchy feeling on his back. He was positive somebody was watching them.

He turned again. Was he imagining a pair of eyes staring back at him evilly from between the crowd? Or was his mind playing tricks? The other two had reached the restaurant. Shrugging impatiently, Ferraz caught up with them. They took a table by the window. There was a hush in Gallops. The news of the murder had spread.

In funereal silence, they were served tea.

Srinivasan proved to be unexpectedly helpful.

Once he got over his shock, the secretary assumed his professional composure and took over the delicate task of completing all corporate formalities that followed the sudden death of one of the city's leading members of India Inc.

As it turned out, Seth's wife Malini was not at home. She was in Ithaca, New York, where the couple's only son was an undergrad at America's prestigious Cornell University.

"The Fall term begins in August," Srinivasan informed them. "Madam has gone to settle him in. She planned to return only in September. This will be heartbreaking for her. What's the time?"

"It must be early morning there," Ferraz said.

"Perhaps I should call later. What do I tell her?" Srinivasan asked with a catch in his voice. "Madam is going to ask questions but I have no answers to give her."

Ferraz cleared his throat. He didn't know what to say.

"I heard him being murdered," Srinivasan said hesitantly, giving the policemen the opening they were looking for.

"What did you hear?" Navroze asked.

"I had called him."

"Tell us from the start. What time was this?"

Srinivasan looked at his cell phone.

"It was 5.31 pm," he said.

"And he was… Seth was okay at that point?"

"Yes, he was."

"What did you hear?"

Srinivasan thought for a moment.

"I can't describe it," he said, sighing heavily. "But now, knowing what happened, I'm inclined to think that it sounded like a fight. Yet there was no shouting or anything. I could only hear Seth sir… and he sounded like he was… he was in a lot of pain."

"What sounds did you hear?"

"They were dull sounds, you know, muffled – like thuds, as if somebody was stamping his foot on the ground, or dropping something, and I heard Seth sir gasping. I thought he was having an asthma attack. He suffered from asthma, but yet he was a heavy smoker."

Both cops recalled the cigar butt by the side of the body.

"It sounded like he was struggling for breath," Srinivasan was saying, "or having a heart attack. I didn't know what to think. He was choking."

"Did he say anything or call out?" Navroze asked.

"Like what?"

"I don't know… like somebody's name, for instance."

"You mean the killer's name?"

"Yes," Navroze said, pleased with Srinivasan's grasp of the situation. "It could be that Seth recognized the killer. And you might have heard him addressing the killer by his name. Think about it."

"Noooo," the secretary said doubtfully.

"Wasn't there any conversation going on between them that your call interrupted?" Ferraz asked. "I mean, if Seth answered your call, he couldn't already be in a fight, right?"

"I don't know… when I called, Seth sir answered. He said, *'Yes, Srini'* and then *'Not you, Srini'* twice. I think he was talking to someone and I kept cutting in. I was confused. I heard the murmur of a voice once, that's all. It didn't sound like a conversation. Or an argument."

"What was that person saying?"

"He said something. But Seth sir didn't follow him, because he asked *'What?'* twice. I thought he was addressing me. But when I spoke up, he shouted *'Not you, Srini'*. Second time in irritation he said, *'Dammit, not you Srini!'* I think he was talking to the killer. And then he grunted and I heard the phone fall."

The policemen sipped their tea, Srinivasan hadn't touched his.

He paused and looked around wildly.

"Where's Seth sir's phone?" he asked suddenly.

"Never mind that for now," Navroze said, "what did you hear next?"

"After that came all those noises… it was horrible… I didn't realize they, they were sounds of him being… being murdered," Srinivasan reported, shivering at the memory.

"Do you know anybody who would want him dead?" Ferraz asked.

"No, but you do know that Seth sir was threatened by the underworld?" Srinivasan asked, surprising them.

The cops looked at each other.

"No, we don't," Navroze replied. "Was this reported to the police?"

"You are the police!"

"Yes, but all cases don't come to the Crime Branch. Why was Seth threatened – you're sure it was the underworld?"

Srinivasan shrugged, "Extortion, *what else!* They called him twice."

"When did this happen? Who called him?"

"If you're asking which gang, then I don't know who made the calls, but I answered them, the man didn't identify himself," Srinivasan recalled. "He asked to speak to Seth sir."

"He called on the landline?"

"Yes, at work. It came like a regular call. Sometimes shareholders who don't have the CMD's cell or personal number call the board and demand to speak to him. All outside calls, except what he got on his personal number, get routed through me."

"What's CMD?" asked Navroze.

"Chairman and Managing Director," Srini said blandly.

"When was this?"

"Oh, at least a year ago."

"What happened then?"

"Seth sir took the call, listened for a few minutes, then said, '*I don't know what the hell you mean*', and hung up."

"Then?"

"Then nothing happened for a while. But the man called again.

It was the same chap. I recognized the voice. He asked for sir once again…"

"And, *go on*, man… tell the story," Navroze said irritably.

"Seth sir didn't entertain the caller. He thought it was some crank. In fact, he asked the caller, '*Since when has the underworld started threatening horse owners instead of builders and film producers?*' That's how I knew where the call was coming from."

"He said that? What did the caller reply?"

"I don't think Seth sir gave the man a chance to say anything. He just laughed and disconnected."

"But you informed the police?"

"Yes," Srinivasan said, "I insisted… Seth sir didn't want to! He was dismissive about the entire thing."

"Why?"

"He imagined it was his friends having fun."

"What made him change his mind?"

"I think he started to believe that somebody wanted to discourage him from entering his champion thoroughbreds in racing. And later, he thought it was politics… somebody was trying to frighten him from standing for the post of Chairman in the Royal Western India Turf Club elections."

"Elections," Ferraz said at once, "for what did you say?"

"The RWITC was having its annual general body meeting preceded by elections for the Committee and Board of Appeals," Srinivasan explained, "it's a regular poll, voting takes place, but the main contest is for the chairman's post."

"You're saying an RWITC member may have threatened him?" Navroze asked, "Is there a list of the members?"

"You must be joking! There are 1,919 voting members!"

"Oh, and what about the Committee? Who contested against Seth?"

"Seth sir never stood for the elections. He had no time for politics, nor did he aspire for the chair, he thought the Committee was a set of jokers, all he cared about was his horses and racing."

"You said… he was to contest for the chairman's post."

"No, no, he wasn't going to contest. His club mates provoked him, it was their idea of fun, they used to tell Seth sir that he was chairman material and only he could save the RWITC from the mess it was in."

"What kind of mess?" Ferraz asked.

"Oh, it was running into losses over the years and the two camps contesting the chairman's election exchanged various charges against each other. The horse doping scandal was another hot issue among members… and, and come to think of it, there was a Crime Branch inquiry, I'm surprised you don't know," Srinivasan said sharply.

"We don't know everything at the Crime Branch," Ferraz said.

"What else was troubling the RWITC?" Navroze asked.

"There was the influenza epidemic that hit the stables."

"Anything else?" Navroze asked impatiently.

"Yes, the BMC threatened to cancel the racecourse's lease in 2013 because it had sub-let land to Gallops restaurant."

"Was Seth directly involved in any of this?"

"No, he wasn't."

"When did Seth's friends tell him to stand for elections?"

Srinivasan appeared surprised they were taking this seriously.

"This was all said in jest at the card table," he recalled. "After a round of drinks and a few hands of Bridge. But a lot of people were present. Seth sir imagined that somebody listening had got the mistaken impression he was going to stand for elections and was trying to discourage him. He found the situation hilarious."

"You mentioned his thoroughbreds…"

"Yes, Seth sir has… 11 champion racehorses. He entered them for all the classics. In Mumbai, Pune, Hyderabad, Chennai, Kolkata, Hyderabad, Bangalore, Mysore, Delhi and Udhagamandalam."

"Udha – what?" Navroze asked.

"Udhagamandalam – *Ooty*, you know."

"Oh, the hill station. It has a racecourse?"

"Yes, a charming one near the railway station in the heart of the town. Racing season is from mid-April to June, when people visit Ooty to escape the summer. The main event there is the Nilgiri Gold Cup."

"Okay... and how many jockeys did he have riding for him?"

"Quite a few," replied Srinivasan.

"Any rivalry between them?"

Srinivasan's eyebrows shot up.

"Why would they murder the man they were racing for?"

"We didn't say that – but you tell us."

"Every horse is a contender in a race. But the race is only about the horse, that's what Seth sir believed, he used to say the jockeys and the trainers are the side cast. It was the horse with better genetics that won."

"Any of his jocks were accused of throwing a race or had been suspended for malpractices?"

"No," said Srinivasan, "that's serious, the Stewards Committee nullifies such a race and suspends the jock – but it's never happened with us. Seth sir would never tolerate such an indignity."

"What was he doing here this evening? The racing season hasn't yet started in Mumbai, has it?" Ferraz asked curiously.

"Not in this rain," Srinivasan said. "He comes – Seth sir enjoyed a cup of tea here every afternoon. You can ask the waiters. He then checked his horses. His stallion Namasthetu is being prepared for the Indian St. Leger in Pune at the end of this month and then the Pune Derby in October. He was keen on entering Namasthetu in Mumbai from November."

"This was his daily routine?"

"The tea drinking habit here? Daily – everybody knew it."

In all three murders, Ferraz was thinking, the victims followed regular solitary habits that everybody knew. Especially the killer. Which made murdering them fairly easy.

"What was the outcome of the threatening calls?" he asked. "You said you lodged a police complaint, where?"

Srinivasan gave them a distasteful look.

"Your Department gave me a real runaround," he said, shaking his head.

They looked at him, saying nothing.

"I went to Malabar Hill Police Station, because Seth sir lives… he lived there. They sent me to Tardeo Police Station, because the racecourse comes under Tardeo, and the Malabar Hill cops thought the threatening calls were to do with betting."

"So the complaint was lodged at Tardeo?"

"No," said Srinivasan angrily, "from Tardeo, I was sent to Colaba Police Station… because our corporate office is in Colaba and that's where the calls were received."

"Well, that's how it is," Navroze said defensively.

"The Colaba police took down the complaint only after Seth sir had a word with your boss, Mr. Baburao Nawalkar, who is a family friend."

Navroze and Ferraz exchanged glances.

"Did the Colaba police speak to Seth?" asked Navroze.

"Yes, they did. But because Seth sir treated the whole thing as a joke, they didn't take the threats seriously. I wish Mr. Nawalkar had followed it up, he forgot or lost interest."

Ferraz asked, "Do you know what the calls were about? What did the underworld ask Seth for? Was it specifically extortion? Did they ask for money? Or was it about racing and betting and the elections?"

"I have no idea…"

"Was he offered protection by the police?"

"Seth sir declined it!"

"Why is that?"

"He told Mr. Nawalkar that all the security in the country couldn't prevent the assassination of a prime minister… what kind of protection would one armed police constable give him?"

"Then what… the calls just stopped?"

"Yes, the calls stopped."

"Or did Seth quietly pay them off and you didn't know?"

"No, I'm sure Seth sir didn't pay off anybody… he wasn't the kind of man to get intimidated or bullied."

"So you don't know what the calls were about?"

"I don't," repeated Srinivasan, "and that's what Seth sir told the police. Somebody was threatening him. But he had no idea why."

"You said it was extortion," Navroze reminded the secretary.

"I thought it was. But Seth sir laughed off the threats. He told the police he had no enemies, who would want to harm him?"

"The underworld doesn't target its enemies for extortion," Ferraz said.

"Anyway, the calls stopped after we went to the police. But somebody wanted him dead, and somebody killed him," Srinivasan said tearfully.

Before they left, Navroze questioned the waiters at Gallops.

They all said the same thing.

Seth had come alone this afternoon, as always.

He had not received any calls nor had he talked to anybody.

They hadn't noticed anybody suspicious lurking around.

Nobody had been asking questions about him.

They would miss him.

SUNDAY

15

HE LOVED Bandra Reclamation.

He knew the neighborhood fairly well. But he wanted to go over the ground. Make sure there were no surprises waiting for him. Not this morning. When he planned the mother of all surprises for her. The last one of her young life. The biggest of her meteoric career!

He chuckled to himself, yes, he liked this area.

It was so – he struggled for the word, yes – *unpretentious*.

Unlike Mount Mary and Pali Hill in Bandra. Where the living was, *well*, kind of uppity because the glam quotient was high over there. Those areas were strictly for the upper crust.

Bandra Reclamation was for the working class.

Not your wannabe actors, established designers and aspiring models, the snooty expats and social climbers, the fitness freaks and fashion trendsetters, the in-your-face lesbians and gays, the literati and glitterati, and the pseudo food and wine connoisseurs who haunted the pubs, gymkhanas and lounges of this Queen of the Suburbs – lo, that's what they called Bandra, these snobbish types.

They were two different classes of people.

At Reclamation, you had quarters for officers of public sector organizations like the Oil & Natural Gas Commission (ONGC), Unit Trust of India (UTI), Maharashtra Telephone Nigam Limited (MTNL) and General Insurance Corporation of India (GIC). And housing colonies by the Maharashtra Housing And Development Authority (MHADA) on land reclaimed from the Arabian Sea. That's why the name – Bandra Reclamation; just like you had Backbay Reclamation where skyscrapers housing South Mumbai's rich and famous frowned down upon old slums, chawls and the fishing village of Cuffe Parade.

Bandra Reclamation didn't have skyscrapers. But its public sector apartments were pleasant, modern high-rises in well-planned, tree-lined avenues. They were gaily painted in whites, beiges and greens and didn't have the wretched look of government colonies elsewhere.

This was once the boondocks of Mumbai.

Nothing but mosquitoes and mangroves.

That had changed, development had taken place. The Lilavati Hospital came up. Then Chhagan Bhujbal, a qualified engineer before he was overcome by the greed of politics, opened his Mumbai Educational Trust here. The Indian Education Society followed with its College of Architecture and Manik Vidyamandir. That brought in the youth. Banks opened, then corporate offices and eateries. And soon builders were buying land cheap and constructing middleclass cooperative housing societies. The BEST introduced bus routes and then set up a depot here as well.

Slowly the change happened.

But it took the Bandra-Worli Sealink, controversially named after former Prime Minister Rajiv Gandhi, to bring the entertainment, sophistication, society and custom of South Mumbai across.

Now look at the place.

As hip and happening as anywhere south of Mumbai.

With such cool hangouts as Chez Moi, Quench, IBar, Masala Zone, Turquoise, Zaza, Candies, Lancy's and Jamoji. Weekend nights, these bistros, cafes, restobars, pubs, restaurants and lounges rocked. Flashy neon signs, the sound of music and clinking glasses behind closed doors, snazzy cars and jazzy bikes outside with young people impatient for tables. It threw the traffic out of sync. God help you if you suffered a heart attack and had to be rushed to Lilavati in an emergency.

IT WAS different at 6.45 am on Sunday.

The shutters of these exciting places were down. The Saturday night vampires were back in their coffins. There was hardly a breath of life stirring. Bandra Reclamation was under the covers. But the sun was out, valiantly struggling to overcome the rain clouds and beam down familiarly on Mumbai once again.

He was at Dr. Jagdish Chandra Jain Chowk. Behind was Lilavati Hospital, looking more like an imposing five star hotel, with hundreds of east-facing windows reflecting the weak sunlight.

The signal at the junction blinked sleepily.

Opposite, a breakfast vendor with a samovar of hot tea and a vessel full of steaming *idlis* waited at the head of a lane for customers. An arrow pointed inwards to a Toyota service centre. At the end of the lane, devotional music was softly playing. The Ganesh Ekta Mitra Mandal was gently waking up its Nityanand Nagarcha Raja. It was the fourth day of Ganeshotsav.

He really liked this area.

Especially the trees, they were growing everywhere.

Lovely casuarinas, the fern leaf, tall ashokas and stately neems, the colorful laburnum and flaming gulmohar, and frangipanis, Christmas trees, weepy banyans and handsome rain trees, even jackfruit trees and fishtail palms. They were on either side of the road and in the centre, growing on the footpaths and in gardens of apartment blocks.

A naturalist, who had gone around Bandra Reclamation, blogged in excitement, "What a walk… saw a cactus which was actually a tree, a tree that is actually a plant, and bread growing out of trees…

also *jamun*, *chickoo*, banana, custard apple, wax apple, coconut..."

He wasn't a naturalist, he couldn't identify them at all.

But he liked the green cover the trees gave Bandra Reclamation. And how the road to the Sealink curved and disappeared among them. Reminding him of Robert Frost's...

The woods are lovely, dark, and deep,

But I have promises to keep.

He, too, had promises to keep.

He liked this area. He even liked *her.*

Too bad, she had to go. This morning...

SANGHAMITRA SARKAR burst out of the elevator.

The elderly night watchman waiting to be relieved in the lobby of this ONGC building knew she was coming. He didn't recognize her, popular though she was, but he knew she was a Bengali. And he liked the ebullient way she greeted the morning. They had the same look, these Bengali beauties, like Bollywood actresses. Oomph and intelligence... came from all that fish they ate.

This girl had that look in abundance.

It was there in her eyes... the eyes gave her away. They were classic Bengali eyes, large and eloquent, with a slight upward slant, blazing with intelligence and unspoken compassion, alternately smoldering with mischief and a hint of coquettishness. Put these eyes in a café latte dimpled face which had bow-shaped lips formed for kisses, a demure nose, and which was framed by dark, silky tresses that fell to elegant shoulders, and what you had was not some raging beauty, but a sensuous woman born to cause widespread heartache.

SHE WAS 24 and had the world at her feet.

Well, within her reach. And she intended to grab this world and clutch it to her soul. Being a pop artiste blessed with a sinfully gorgeous voice gave her the license to indulge in wild imagination and express crazy desires through music and dance.

Sanghamitra had been doing that since she was 21.

Singing at nightclubs of Park Street and the big Durga Puja celebrations in Kolkata, then for gigs in Delhi, Bangalore, Chennai and Mumbai. She was what the music world called an Indipop singer. Somebody who listened to folk and classical music with a western ear, then gave it a global twist by spinning what was traditionally Indian with modern beats from different parts of the world.

She wasn't the first, Indipop arrived in India in the 1980s. Critics said it was zingy, snippety snap and something other than soppy Bollywood love songs. The genre was all about narrating stories and over the top, exaggerated theatrics; it was western, jazzy and colorful.

By the 1990s, the country had her own Indipop divas for MTV.

Every bathroom singer came out from behind the shower curtain to use studio technology and sound like they were happening. But the magic fizzled out soon. In the 2000s, TV channels discovered reality shows. And record labels couldn't sell music that was now freely available online for downloading. Indipop artistes joined Bollywood as playback singers.

But a decade later the scene underwent change again.

A new wave of female rockers determined to climb the stairway to rock heaven emerged in India. They were all-girl bands with esoteric names like The Vinyl Records, Minute of Decay, The Hurricane Gals and Afflatus. Their guitarists, drummers and vocalists were talented musicians from the North-East, where freedom of creative expression knew no bounds, and they stormed this hitherto male bastion and made their presence felt.

Being accepted was difficult because it was unheard of for women to play rock in India. But good music will always find an audience.

And whether they played Indie Post-Punk Rock and New Wave at pubs and music festivals or Hardcore Punk and Garage Rock at college campuses and Tihar Jail, the new all-girl bands were finding supporters. From playing gigs they had gone to releasing albums.

SANGHAMITRA RESISTED Bollywood.

She made her debut with an Indipop single for a Hollywood musical called *Limelight* that was based on stardom in a reality show in Mumbai. *Slumdog Millionaire* had won eight Oscars, seven BAFTAs and four Golden Globes, Hollywood didn't want to reinvent the wheel. India was a lucky destination. Give an English film a Mumbai *tadka,* it worked wonders.

Sanghamitra's song was called *Oye Ganesh.*

It took *Limelight* to the top of Billboard 200, got it rave reviews in *Rolling Stone Magazine*, and excited the NRI and young Indian music geek to take a renewed look at the Indipop scene. The number was raunchy and full of *double entendre*, it was sexually explicit and set to foot-thumping music. But critics said *Oye Ganesh* paid as much obeisance to Lord Ganesh as Bryan Adams's *Reggae Christmas* did to Jesus Christ.

RJs loved it and spun it on their shows.

The music video made Sanghamitra an overnight sensation.

Shot on a set resembling Mumbai on immersion day, it had her scantily dressed and dancing with half-naked men and folk musicians while a gigantic Ganpati was led in colorful procession to the sea. The tempo was pulsating, the visuals erotic, and the entire effect spectacularly breathtaking. Like Shakira belly-dancing at the Colombian carnival to *Hips Don't Lie.* Sanghamitra was a trained dancer and a Yoga enthusiast and the gyrations of her sinuous body set viewers' fantasies on fire. *Oye Ganesh* soon became a Most Watched Video on YouTube.

She was happening.

Now she was in Mumbai for Ganeshotsav and in the news.

Limelight was to have a world premiere this month. An event manager, milking the popularity of the song, invited Sanghamitra to the big Ganpati *pandals* to perform *Oye Ganesh* for enthusiastic masses while TV showed it live to those who could not be there. She was also to do TV interviews, sing at the grand finale of a reality talent contest, and represent a leading designer label as its youth brand ambassadress in Asia.

It was too big an opportunity to be missed.

Not yet a big name and unused to throwing starry tantrums, the Indipop singer from Kolkata stayed with her elder brother who was an ONGC executive at his Bandra Reclamation flat instead of demanding a five star hotel suite. Sanghamitra immediately fell in love with Mumbai. She thought the Ganeshotsav celebrations here matched the dizzy heights Bengalis took their madness to during Puja in Kolkata.

What Sanghamitra missed was her workouts.

She was a fitness freak and in Kolkata there was not a day that went by without her playing squash or burning calories on the treadmill. She swam, did Zumba, practiced Yoga, attended Jazz-Ballet classes and on Sundays went for long bicycle rides with friends.

In Mumbai, she rose early and went for a jog every morning when it wasn't raining. She wished her brother was a member of Otter's Club or Bandra Gym, then she could have gone swimming as well.

She enjoyed running. It cleared her mind of all its idle chatter.

She ran for an hour, slipping through Bandra Reclamation while it was still asleep, taking a lonely bypass to the Western Express Highway, maintaining a pace that was smooth and easy. She returned to the ONGC complex to cool down and stretch in the children's park, her tracksuit soaking with sweat, feeling energized and positive and looking young and healthy.

HE KNEW the route she would take.

And he shuffled and limped there, listening to the racket the birds were making in the trees, like there was an aviary around the corner. An elderly couple were waiting at a bus-stop with a hoarding for Muthoot Fincorp. He went past the Reclamation Bus Depot, opposite the turn to the Sealink and Western Express Highway, crossing a building called Suman, and then he was on the lonely bypass that she took.

A wobbly old man was out taking the air, dressed in shorts and orange sweater, wearing kneecaps. And a milkman was cycling down the road, the cans on his bike rattling as the tires bounced on the uneven paver blocks that had been used to lay this stretch.

There was nobody else out at this hour.

The Maharashtra State Road Development Corporation's site office for the Sealink was here. Ahead was the Hindustan Construction Company's office, they had built the Sealink, and next to it a signboard announcing the spot for a Kamat Hotel of the future. The Deputy Chief Engineer (Mechanical & Electrical), Sewerage Project, Municipal Corporation of Greater Mumbai, also had his office here. It was an Effluent Pumping Station, ISO 9001:2000 certified. And right outside was an overflowing gutter.

He shuffled and limped past with a shudder.

Past a yard full of plastic pipes and broken traffic signals.

And a number of trucks parked by the side.

He was marking out a spot…

… when the paver blocks gave him the idea.

There was a heap of them next to a small public toilet.

He picked one up, hefting it in his hand.

It was amoeba-shaped; thick, flat, red in color and made of concrete.

He looked down the road where… *oh my God…* she was coming at a brisk pace, dressed in a grey tracksuit with its hood up, Nikes on her flying feet, the cell phone in one of her jersey's pockets... he had seen her taking calls while running when he did a recce for this fateful morning. It never crossed his mind to consider she might not come. That the weather might be bad.

He just knew she would be here.

He watched her jump over the wet patch of the overflowing gutter, coming closer with every step, her firm young breasts bouncing beneath the jersey that had '89 Varsity Pro Pitcher League' printed on the front, long legs flashing... she had good legs, last time she had been in shorts, they were sleek and clean legs, tanned, she had firm and fleshy thighs, and full calves tapering down to slender ankles.

With the paver block held behind his back he waited, overcome by a sense of elation and also terrible sadness, like a wildlife hunter pausing to admire the elegance and beauty of the gazelle through his telescopic sight before gently squeezing the trigger... she was so lovely and so young, so talented as well, pity he had to... *she was coming,* he stopped thinking, looked around once, and began licking his lips obscenely.

SANGHAMITRA RAN with her head down.

She knew the route. There was no traffic here but for the occasional water tanker or an MSRTC bus. And no residents, she could count the number of people she passed. There was the old man in kneecaps and the milkman on his cycle, nobody else was around, except a dim figure in black ahead by the side of a garbage heap.

She was thinking of the CNN-IBN interview she would do later today. A make-up man was coming to do her face and a renowned Bollywood stylist, her hair. She was excited by that. The interview was live. She was also nervous. She hoped she wouldn't fumble.

To entertain a live audience of 5,000 was a piece of cake.

But a live television interview...

What if they asked her to sing, impromptu?

A singer depended on musicians for back-up.

But… maybe, yes, she could do *Ekla Cholo Re* for them.

Rabindranath Tagore's patriotic Bengali song, it was like a poem.

'Jodi tor dak shune keu na ashe tobe ekla cholo re… '

'If nobody responds to your call, then go your own way alone… '

She liked to think of herself as… *what the*… what was this fellow in black doing in the center of the road, standing there with his hands behind his back and grinning at her in that… morbid… and his eyes, they looked… ugh!… reptilian and quite despiteful.

Where had he turned up from? And what was he waiting for?

She continued running, closing the gap.

And looked up to see if he had moved aside.

But he hadn't!

She was irritated. There was something not quite… about his stillness… it was disturbing and she didn't like the way… *God*, he looked possessed in a way she… she wouldn't come down this lonely road again, she would go past him and reach the highway where there would be traffic and people.

And she wouldn't look back at him, he unnerved her.

This city was full of weirdos, Kolkata was so…

She was five meters away and not wanting to look into his venomous eyes which she knew were on her…

… another two steps and she would be past him.

When he stepped into her path and said something.

Her step faltered and she looked up, directly into his face.

And that's when her blood ran cold and she stopped in her tracks.

She couldn't believe the malignant look in his eyes.

Suddenly she was more frightened than she had ever been in her life.

"Moryaa Re!" he said again.

"Listen, what's –" she started to ask.

When his right hand moved in a blur and the paver block exploded against her temple viciously and with all the force behind his arm, fracturing her skull immediately with the impact.

The suddenness of the blow more than the pain shocked her…

… and it rocked her on her feet, but she remained standing.

Her hand went up to her face, to find that the tracksuit hood had come off her head. Blood was spurting out of the deep gash, rolling down her cheek, blinding her, running into her nose and mouth, making her gag… the pain in her head was suddenly unbearable.

She took a staggering step, feeling faint, her body going into shock and becoming incapable of flight or fight, about to lose consciousness because of the concussion, and she opened her mouth to scream.

When he hit her again with the paver block…

… aiming for her face this time, closing his eyes when the stone savagely crushed the bridge of her nose and smashed into her finely-shaped arched eyebrows… breaking the nasal bone and delicate cartilage, almost dislodging her right eye out of its socket, the blood splashing down the front of her grey jersey now, a thick and bright red spurt.

She tottered like a punch-drunk boxer staggering around the ring in a bewildered and dazed manner before crashing down onto the canvas, arms outstretched blindly…

And she was opening her mouth to scream.

… when he hit her once more, catching her full in the face again, the stone breaking tooth and splintering bone, ripping her lips, sending a spittle of blood and broken teeth flying out of the corner of her shattered mouth, causing her to topple backward in slow motion.

He followed her body to the road…

… hitting the top of her head hard as she fell, cracking her skull and almost killing her, then moving aside to let her crash in an untidy heap by the side of the garbage dump.

Miraculously, she was still alive but barely when he squatted beside her. As he went to work on her again, cold-bloodedly and rhythmically raising the paver block up and bringing it down brutally on her upturned and unprotected face, he was humming.

Like a prisoner in a jail yard breaking stones, he struck her again and again about the face and forehead, mercilessly reducing her beauty to a bloody and unrecognizable pulp, the blood continuing to splatter with each strike, on his hands and on his face.

She couldn't feel the pain anymore, but she could hear the tune he was humming in that morbid, funereal way in the dark, vague recesses of her mind as she slipped into unconsciousness.

She thought it was familiar, and that she recognized it…

… it was, yes, she was… he was humming *Oye Ganesh.*

He went on hammering till her body stopped twitching and jerking beneath the uncontrolled assault and there was no life in her. Later, the autopsy would reveal that Sanghamitra was alive when she suffered the horrendous facial injuries. In her dying breaths, she inhaled blood and teeth fragments.

When it was over he stood up jerkily and looked around.

No witnesses again, he chuckled to himself.

Except the birds in the trees which were suddenly quiet.

There was silence all around. He tossed the paver block into the gutter. It disappeared in the murky depths with a soft, rippling *'kerplunk!'* Bending, he reached into the pocket of her jersey for the phone, humming to himself, not seeing the bloody mess already buzzing with flies and red ants.

He took off, shuffle-limp, shuffle-limp, without a backward glance. Ahead was a parked water tanker. He went behind it and twisted open the tap to release a gush of water. He rinsed his hands and washed his face. There was blood on his shirt. He dabbed water on it with wet hands.

Not going!

He kept on at it, until the stains grew fainter.

He didn't like blood on his hands. It repulsed him.

Closing the tap he moved on, sticking to the sidewalk, approaching the bus depot. On its fence was a small sign saying, 'JESUS SAVES'.

Not always, he chucked to himself.

Ahead was another sign telling people to 'Beware of Bogus Police'. What kind of warning was that? Where was the police, bogus or real, and how was the citizen to identify one from the other?

Talking of the police… what should he do?

Just send an SMS to that Police Commissioner? Or also call?

They weren't expecting this, the fourth murder.

He chuckled to imagine their reaction.

Hers was sure to be a Kolkata number. Would the police trace it in real time and locate her body? He didn't want somebody stumbling over her and dialing 100 in terror. Not before he staked the claim. This was his work and letting them know was like putting his signature across it.

He stopped at a bus-stop outside UTI Quarters. This one had a Lakmé hoarding. Nobody was waiting for a bus here. It was quiet, the bus-stop was close to the bordering wall of the housing colony and it was protected by a thick canopy of low trees.

He slipped into it and looked at Sanghamitra's phone. It was a Samsung Galaxy SIII touch phone. He swiped the screen to unlock the phone and lightly tapped on the messaging keypad with a bloody fingernail…

'Is it true that dawn
sometimes masquerades as dusk?'

Done, he sent the SMS to Nawalkar.

Gave the Police Commissioner two minutes to read it and wonder, then opened the keypad and tapped out Nawalkar's number. As the phone began to ring, he saw with irritation that a single decker BEST bus was making a rumbling approach to the bus-stop.

"Moryaa Re!" he said as the bus halted with a jerk before him.

Nobody got off. The bus stood shuddering on its tires, dripping oil, reeking of diesel, he could hear the windows rattling. The conductor was looking at him inquiringly. He called out something and then impatiently gave a double tug on the bell.

With a growl of protest, the bus got going again.

But the moment was lost. Angrily he switched off the phone. Stepping out, he went towards Lilavati Hospital without looking back. At the bus-stop, sheltered by thick burgundy bougainvillea bushes against the wall, a dirty old rag-picker sat curiously watching him shuffle and limp away.

"NAWALKAR."

"Moryaa Re!"

The CP dropped his phone.

It hit the dining table, bounced off his knee and crashed to the floor.

Picking it up feverishly, Nawalkar was in time to hear in the background the sound of a large vehicle grinding to a halt with a sharp squeal of brakes. He strained his ears. There was a pause during which he could hear the vehicle's engine loudly panting. Then a man called out something in Marathi. There came the abrupt double ring of a bell, the harsh metallic grunt of gears being roughly engaged, and the sound of the vehicle lurching to life and roaring off again, its tires humming as they picked up speed.

Nawalkar knew it was a BEST bus, without doubt.

"Hullo," he shouted into the phone.

No reply. He saw that the call had been disconnected.

He hit redial, but the phone had been switched off.

Nawalkar had been reading the SMS when the call came.

Now, his heart racing, he called Joint CP (Crime) Arun Rathod.

"Arun," he said, "quickly take down this number..."

"What, he called again? Don't tell me it's another–"

"... yes, I fear it is, the fucking *madarchot*. But he didn't talk. I've no idea who... listen, you can track the location of the call immediately, right? I'm certain I heard a bus in the background."

"A bus? He was on a bus, sir?" Rathod asked incredulously.

Nawalkar tut-tutted irritably.

"No, he was... waiting at a bus-stop, I think... because I heard a bus stopping and the conductor ringing the bell. It's the commonest sound in Mumbai. Anybody would recognize it."

"Give me the number, sir."

"Check the bus-stops at the crime scene, the BEST will be able to tell us what bus passed by at, say, 7.05 am. Its conductor may recognize him. I heard him call out something before he rang the bell. Don't know who he was speaking to. There might be witnesses. Other passengers waiting or getting off that bus."

"I hope somebody saw him and can identify him."

"And Rathod, he sent another SMS!"

"Saying what?"

"Some shit about dawn and dusk!"

16

RATHOD ACTED swiftly.

He gave the Crime Branch's technical unit the number. Homicide made all wheels spin faster. It was an Airtel number. The network service provider identified its subscriber. Then pinpointed through its towers the location from where its last call had been made.

Who the hell was Sanghamitra Sarkar, Rathod wondered.

Was she related to Aveek Sarkar, the Bengali media baron of Kolkata's *Anandabazar Patrika* and *The Telegraph*? There would be hell to pay. He was a powerful man, known for his strong opinions. But Rathod had no time to worry about that now.

The call had come from Bandra Reclamation.

Nawalkar said he heard a bus in the background. Rathod hesitated. Should he ask the BEST what buses ran through Bandra Reclamation? What if the killer hadn't caught a bus? And he just happened to be near a bus-stop? What if he was still in the area? Or lived there? And somebody had seen him? Perhaps even witnessed the murder?

Rathod called Ferraz.

He knew Ferraz lived not far from Bandra Reclamation.

Four minutes later, Ferraz was gunning his bike.

Roaring down the narrow, twisting lanes of Bandra, giving early Sunday morning church-goers a fright and leaving one elderly padre furiously shaking his fist after him, Ferraz reached Reclamation in three minutes flat. When he slowed down outside Lilavati Hospital, it was 7.34 am. Bandra Reclamation was still not fully awake.

Ferraz also hadn't heard of Sanghamitra Sarkar.

He wasn't going to look for her body. This was a vast area with housing societies, slums, dumping grounds and the seafront. Let the Bandra police find it. The murder had been committed 25-30 minutes ago. Ferraz was surprised nobody had stumbled upon the body yet.

The Cobra was supposed to have called the CP from a bus-stop.

He spotted a bus-stop. There was one across the road too. It was empty. But at the bus-stop this side sat a dirty old rag-picker. Ferraz stopped the bike.

He looked at the lamp-posts.

No CCTV cameras!

He gave the rag-picker a searching look.

The man was filthy. Years of accumulated grime made him look of indeterminate age. He wore a baseball cap back to front. His grey hair was matted, his moustache and beard straggly, he had on dirty and holey black corduroy trousers, a shabby T-shirt that drooped off thin shoulders and almost reached his knees, and old shoes cracked at the toes and worn down at the heels. A blood-stained bandage was tied around his left ankle. He looked like he hadn't had a bath in years.

The rag-picker gazed back at Ferraz unblinkingly.

He had a thin, sad face and grey watery eyes. He was smoking a *beedi* and pretending to read an old newspaper that he held upside down. He had a runny nose that he wiped frequently with the back of a dirty hand. Next to him were all the pitiful possessions he had in this world. These included the tattered polythene sack of his trade full of rubbish, a torn and dirty blanket rolled up, a stack of old newspapers, a plastic bag filled with God knows what, a dented plastic mineral water bottle and an umbrella that had lost its handle and most of its ribs.

There was nobody else on the road.

Ferraz called the Bandra Police Station. Beat constables were on their way, he was told, and a mobile patrol van was following. Almost immediately two constables arrived on a motorcycle, a walkie-talkie chattering on the pillion rider's neck. They leaped off and saluted Ferraz.

Together, the policemen approached the bus-stop.

The rag-picker spoke to them willingly.

He immediately told Ferraz he had been a Lance Naik in the Indian Army and had been posted in Meghalaya during the Indo-Pak war of 1971. Ferraz wasn't interested. He wanted to know if the rag-picker had seen anybody making a phone call from the bus-stop.

"About half an hour ago," he said, looking at the massive Sanda sports watch on his wrist.

"Let me see that watch," the rag-picker said, reaching for Ferraz's wrist.

"Never mind the watch… answer the Inspector," one of the Bandra police constables shouted, roughly pushing him back.

The rag-picker looked sulky.

A Maruti Gypsy pulled up with a sub-inspector and three more constables. Seeing the arrival of additional forces, the rag-picker shrank back in fear. Aware that he could be a potential witness, Ferraz waved the other cops back. He looked at the cowering rag-picker closely.

"What's your name?" he asked.

"It was Ghanshyam Yadav. What's yours?"

"*It was?*"

"Now people abuse me by any name," the rag-picker said and cackled.

"Okay Yadav, listen to me," Ferraz said. "Did you see anybody making a phone call from this bus-stop some time ago?"

The cops waited breathlessly while the rag-picker considered the question gravely with his head tilted to one side, as if he was answering Amitabh Bachchan's jackpot question on *Kaun Banega Crorepati.*

"*Why?*" he asked shrewdly, "What did he do?"

"*He* – you saw a man talking on the phone?" Ferraz asked softly.

The rag-picker nodded and grinned, showing horrible teeth.

"Did he catch a bus after that?" Ferraz asked, noting that the 1 Ltd., 86, 212 and 215 halted here. If the rag-picker said "Yes" and remembered what bus it was – they were off to the races!

Ferraz would ask the Control Room to put an alert out for that bus. Then try and chase it down. If the killer was onboard, the rag-picker could point him out. But too much of time had passed. He feared the bus may have reached its depot by now.

The rag-picker shook his head sadly and said, "No."

The caller had not taken a bus. He had walked off.

He pointed down the road towards Lilavati Hospital.

Ferraz knew he was telling the truth. But maybe there was still hope.

He hustled the rag-picker into the front of the police jeep and took the wheel himself. The sub-inspector and three constables hastily got into the back. And followed by the beat cops, the police party swiftly and silently zipped through Bandra Reclamation. But the rag-picker, who immensely enjoyed the drive, kept muttering and shaking his head at everyone they passed.

Ferraz was not surprised.

The wireless in the police jeep crackled.

And Ferraz's phone rang at the same time.

Both to say that…

… *Sanghamitra Sarkar's body had been found!*

They headed back to Bandra Reclamation.

A police van was slowly making its way down the bypass to the Sealink. On its side ironically was written, "Crime against Women,

Children & Senior Citizens – Call on 103". Two police jeeps were at the crime scene. Only the Investigation Van was missing.

Bandra Reclamation was playing to a full house.

Like magic, people had appeared on the road; they were also opening windows and peering out, standing on their balconies, coming out of their housing society gates. This was like *Crime Patrol* in real time. Uniformed policemen pushed them back.

Nothing like a murder… Ferraz was thinking.

He went up the bypass to a huddle of khaki. He could hear the wail of an approaching ambulance. Must be coming from Bhabha Hospital near Bandra Police Station, he thought, where the bodies of a great number of accident victims turned up.

He made his way through the assembled policemen…

… looked down and blinked in horror.

Oh God, he thought, this was worse than Haider's murder.

He looked at the bloody and broken mess of what was once Sanghamitra, now reduced to shards of flesh and splintered bone and felt a sudden, sharp stab of pain behind his eyes. No cop in the world dealing with homicide could prepare himself for this.

Ferraz turned away, his eyes sweeping the sordid surroundings, the gutter that belched rotten and acidic fumes… and he was suddenly depressed by life, by the nature of his work, by the cruelty of man… for a young and promising life to end this way. What was this city coming to?

"Any witnesses?" he gruffly asked a sub-inspector standing nearby.

"None, sir… but people may have passed her on the road. She came from the ONGC Colony (he pointed behind) and was jogging. The accused must have come earlier and was waiting at this spot. It's lonely here."

Ferraz nodded.

"Get the rag-picker from the Gypsy," he said.

The sub-inspector hurried away. Ferraz dug out his phone.

In a hushed voice he made his report to Rathod.

He told the Joint CP (Crime), "She's barely out of her teens. Why would anybody want her dead? A rag-picker was at the bus-stop when the Cobra called the CP… he saw our man. I'm bringing him in, sir. Let's get the police artist to do a sketch based on his description. We shouldn't waste any time interrogating this neighborhood. Nobody will know anything. The killer would have fled like a ghost again, nobody would have seen him."

"Okay, Angelo," Rathod said. "The girl's name is Sanghamitra Sarkar, that's what we got from her SDR, she's a resident of Kolkata. Don't know what she's doing here. And why she's his fourth victim. We'll find out soon. I've asked Unit IX to help you there."

Unit IX of the DCB-CID was based in Bandra.

"You rush over," Rathod continued. "I must inform the CP that we have a witness. He's been summoned Home… the Monsoon Session is starting tomorrow. We recorded the calls this bugger made to the CP this morning and last evening. And we got another SMS from him. I want the police psychiatrist to hear this recording."

The sub-inspector and two constables came up with the rag-picker.

Ferraz glanced at the cop's nameplate.

He started to say, "Patil, will you–"

And the rag-picker broke free.

He took off in a shambling run, dragging one foot, taking the constables holding him by surprise and sending them staggering.

Ferraz stepped forward, tripped him and brought him down.

He grabbed the rag-picker by the scruff of the neck.

Hauling him up, Ferraz slapped him sharply.

"What the fuck are you running for?" he shouted furiously, "We are not blaming you for the murder, you bloody fool – we only want your help to catch the killer. All we want you to do is tell us what he looks like. Is that so fucking difficult? Now, am I going to get your cooperation or…"

He dropped his hand to the 9mm S&W holstered at his hip.

The threat was implicit. The rag-picker trembled in fear. He had never seen such blazing rage in anybody's eyes. There was a tightness in the cop's face and tension in his body. He nodded in resignation, all the fight had left him, and tears began rolling down his cheeks. He hung his head, afraid for his own life. Ferraz led him by the elbow to the corpse.

The ambulance had arrived.

Two interns were coming up with a stretcher.

"Don't touch the body till the forensic guys get here," Ferraz told them.

The rag-picker came reluctantly, dragging his feet, his eyes rolling.

"Look, Yadav," Ferraz said, "look what that *madarchot* you saw did to this girl. She was young, full of life, just an hour ago… look at her now. And tell me who you saw. I want to know everything. Every small fucking detail is important. You've got nothing to be afraid of. You're helping the police… you're an ex-Army man, you'll be a hero after this, come on."

The rag-picker gingerly stepped forward.

He looked at the body. His legs gave way, his eyes turned back and he promptly collapsed onto the ground in a dead faint.

Ferraz cursed.

"Pick him up," he harshly told the constables. "Patil, have him handcuffed and sent to the Crime Branch. He's an important witness. We'll use your jeep. Sr. PI Kisan Savde of the DCB-CID's Unit IX will be here soon. The case will be registered by you at Bandra Police Station, okay? Secure the area. Only after the forensic team is done can the body be moved. Any idea where it will be taken for post-mortem?"

"Cooper Hospital, sir."

As Ferraz walked away, a loud sigh went up from the onlookers.

He returned to the bus-stop where his bike was parked. He paused by the police jeep. The unconscious rag-picker was lying handcuffed at the back. Ferraz ordered the driver to follow him. He was about to start the bike when a thought came to his mind. He pulled out his cell again and hit the keys.

"Jackie! You're awake, honey?" Ferraz asked.

"What do you think! It's 8 am and I'm late for church," she said sounding like she was in a flap. "But *where* are you? How dare you sneak off without saying goodbye? And, *and...* you left without breakfast? *Again!* How many times have I told you that–"

Ferraz cut in, "Okay, sorry I rushed out without waking you up. We got another murder on our hands... right here near Lilavati, yeah, the same psycho... that's why I left in a hurry. Yeah, I'm okay – *why* wouldn't I be? Listen *jaan*, I want to ask–"

"Why didn't you wake me up?" she demanded. "I would have made breakfast. You know I don't like you eating at that police canteen."

Ferraz sighed.

Jackie was a Scorpio – a zodiac sign of extremes and intensity.

Only she would worry if he had breakfast at a time like this.

"I won't eat at the police canteen – I promise," he said, "I'll go to the Taj and call you. You instruct the chef what you would like me to have for breakfast and how he should prepare it, in olive oil, peanut butter or whatever, fine? Now listen, sweetie –"

"Don't sweetie me, Mister!"

"Jackie, I need your help... listen please, it's police work."

"Oh, really!"

"Come on, honey... the girl who got murdered – yes, the victim is a girl, *didn't I tell you* – anyway, listen to me and for God's sake stop interrupting! She was young... very young and not from here. I think she came from Kolkata..."

"How do you know?"

"What do you mean how do I know! We're the fucking police!"

"Angie!"

"All right, I won't swear. But don't interrupt. We know nothing about her yet. I mean, *why* her? This psycho has murdered recognized people so far. She appears to be nobody. But she's his fourth victim. She could be some rich and famous man's daughter from Kolkata. Will you run a Google search and find out? I mean... she might be on Facebook, Twitter or Linkedin, you know how to find out."

"Why should I – *you are the police*, you just said!"

"You'll save me time, honey. We will find out eventually, the Bandra cops are already inquiring, she was staying with somebody at Reclamation... but I can't wait. I'm rushing to office. Any info you pass on will be helpful. Her name is... she was Sanghamitra Sarkar."

"Pretty please with sugar on top?"

"*What?* Oh yeah, whatever you say!"

"Okay... wait, I'll do it now," Jackie said.

"Noooo," Ferraz said, "you call me in, say, 20 minutes, got it?"

"Angie..."

"Yeah, now what? I'll eat breakfast, cross my heart."

"I'm not talking about your breakfast!"

"Then what?"

"Your phone!"

"What about it? It's working..."

"Angie!"

He sighed, "Okay, say... what about my phone?"

"I have been saying all along," she reminded him, "but you've got only a policeman's brain, what to do! If you had changed that disgraceful *dabba* and got yourself a smartphone... you could have Googled this girl yourself. Or I could send you her picture on BBM."

Ferraz's grip tightened on his battered Nokia 6233.

He had been using the phone since 2006. It was falling apart, literally. The cover was loose from the many times he had dropped it. And now when it fell, the phone split in four: the body, cover and battery, and the SIM card. The screen was horribly scratched. The keypad was worn out. The soft red and blue rubber buttons to take and make calls had lost their color; they were now a dirty grey. The phone itself had lost its original gunmetal sheen and was now a dull and sticky black.

Jackie thought it was abominable.

But the phone was full of fading memories.

And Ferraz intended to hold onto them as long as he could.

"There's nothing wrong with my phone," he told Jackie, adding haughtily, "may I remind you it's even got Bluetooth!"

"*Bluetooth*," she exploded, "really, I…"

"Isn't Sunday meant to be a day of rest?"

"What do you mean?" she asked suspiciously.

"You don't give your arguments, contentions and disagreements a rest."

"*My arguments, contentions, and disagreements…*"

"Yeah, you're spoiling for a fight all the time," he needled her.

"*Me! Are you saying that…*"

"Sunday, at least, take a break. Isn't that what the Bible says?"

"*Don't teach me what the Bible says!*"

"I'm not trying to… but didn't God say, '*Sunday is my favorite day, so remember to keep things light*' … or something like that?"

"*Angie*, don't be blasphemous! The Fourth Commandment is, 'Remember the Sabbath day, to keep it holy.'"

"There you are!"

"That's not what you said…"

"What I meant–"

"According to Pope Benedict…"

"*Who?*"

"... the demands of work can't bully people out of needed time off," Jackie continued. "Going to work on Sunday is not sinful, but God commanded that this activity should be done on the other days of the week."

"Pope Benedict can eat cake!" Ferraz cut her short, "I've got to go."

"Angie!"

He sighed again, "Now what, girl?"

"Go carefully," Jackie said and blew him a kiss down the phone.

THE HOME Minister was in a shitty mood.

The Monsoon Session of the Maharashtra Legislative Assembly was beginning tomorrow. And the Opposition was waiting to haul him over the coals. It had been gunning for him since the Budget Session in March. Its MLAs, a group of ugly rowdies, were planning to attack the government fang and claw. Several contentious issues presented themselves. All police related. Like crime against women, the increase in Naxalite activities, no progress on the CCTVs, anti-terror squads and coastal police after 26/11, the unchecked law and order situation in the state.

The Home Minister was in charge of the Maharashtra Police.

But what was he to do? Crime happened. Especially in Mumbai. Which city in the world didn't have crime? With this crazily burgeoning population and unrestricted migration happening from other states, you didn't need a reason for law and order issues to flare up – they just did. What mattered was how the police responded to them. Often they ended up fanning the fires instead of dousing the flames.

At the top of the Opposition's list would be the Mumbai murders.

The Home Minister was wondering how to explain them. He should have stepped in on Thursday itself when that painter chap had got killed. Instead, he had got busy judging this Sarvajanik Ganeshotsav Mandal contest for that media house in Nashik, Pune,

Aurangabad and Kolhapur. He had been away when the murders took place.

He was sure to get it in the neck now.

Four murders?

By a psychopathic serial killer?

What was the Mumbai Police doing?

The Home Minister intended to find out.

So he had called Nawalkar to his residence this morning.

They were engaged in conversation.

"Some crackpot's killing our people?" the Home Minister said. He got his information from the Additional Chief Secretary, Home. Whose official source was the CP himself.

"I don't know whether he–"

"Don't know! He wasn't dancing with his victims. Do you think your killer is a disco dancer, Nawalkar? You want to invite him to the Police Party at Diwali, is that it?"

"No sir, I don't–"

The Home Minister nodded.

"What's this bullshit about him phoning you?" he asked. "You *know* the fellow well, do you?"

"No sir," said Nawalkar, appalled by the insinuation.

"Then why is he calling you?"

"Every time he kills, he calls or texts to tell us. I don't know why."

"You don't say!"

"He calls on my cell phone and–"

"Where'd he get your number from?"

"Everybody knows it, sir," Nawalkar replied patiently.

"I don't," the Home Minister said shaking his head.

"Your PA and police bodyguards have–"

"So, what's the story?"

"Well, he killed the painter Haider Allarakha Khan first."

"Stabbed him, huh?"

"Brutally, sir."

"And then chopped off his head? Gross!"

"Yes, on Thursday evening, and then he called me."

"What'd he say?" the Home Minister asked. "He wanted to tell you why he'd killed Haider? Chatty fellow… doesn't sound like a psycho. Is somebody fingering you or what?"

"No… he didn't say why… but subsequently, after the British woman's murder, he said that he would kill again, sir."

"*Why* – did you ask?"

"*Why* he wants to kill again… or *why* was he calling me, sir?"

"Both!" shouted the Home Minister.

"He said we would find out, sir."

"And, well, have you… found out anything?"

"Not yet, sir. The Crime Branch is–"

"Is what?"

"The DCB-CID is working on this case, sir."

"Oh really, I thought they were on leave for Ganpati!"

"No, sir."

"I wouldn't put it past… *what* the hell are you grinning for!"

Nawalkar, who had rashly smiled at the Home Minister's sarcasm, quickly wiped off the jovial expression that had lit up his sullen face.

"What's with the delay then?" the Home Minister said, "Four stabbings of known people, what's the Crime Branch waiting for, huh? When will they shake their asses to get a lead on this… this psychopath, you're *sure* he's a psychopathic serial killer, Nawalkar?"

"I've got every cop on the job, sir," Nawalkar mumbled.

"That's apparently not enough! And now I'm hearing that the killer warned you again and again about his next victims…"

"He didn't exactly give us names, sir."

"… and yet the police were unable to prevent the stabbings. I don't like the sound of this at all, I can tell you that."

"All the victims weren't stabbed."

"What do you mean?"

"This morning's victim was bludgeoned to death."

"*Was what?*" the Home Minister asked.

"And the racehorse owner was found hanging by–"

"*Hanging?*" the Home Minister said. "Where? I thought you said he had been stabbed to death. Who was hanged? This murder is news to me."

"That was Haider," Nawalkar reminded him.

The Home Minister wearily passed a hand over his face.

"What do you mean *that* was Haider?" he asked irritably. "Who the hell was Haider? The painter fellow was Haider – *wasn't he*, unless you've confused the victims' names!"

"Haider was stabbed, I meant," Nawalkar hastily clarified, seeing that the Home Minister had got it all wrong, "and Seth was found strangled."

"*Then who was found hanging?*"

"Nobody… Seth was found with a noose around his neck, not hanging, but he had been garroted at the racecourse…"

"*Garroted!*"

"… with a pair of horse reins."

"Oh," said the Home Minister shaking his head, "I don't like that… he stabs some, he strangles others, eh? That's his modus operandi? But why horse reins, never heard anything like this."

"The girl just now, he crushed to death."

The Home Minister clenched his fists behind his back.

"Which girl?" he asked with exaggerated politeness.

"This morning's-"

"Crushed to death? Like in a hit and run? The killer has a car? He ran over her? Nobody told me! Who was she? Weren't there witnesses… we got the number?"

"Not by a car, sir, but crushed with a stone."

"*What!*"

"Yes, sir… but he was spotted near the crime scene. By a witness who could identify him if we make an arrest. We are getting the police artist to prepare a sketch of the suspect based on his description."

"Good work," the Home Minister said appreciatively. "Who's this witness?"

"Er, a rag-picker, sir."

"A rag-picker!"

The Home Minister snorted.

He didn't know what the Opposition was going to say.

Thank God the victims of this psychopath were of all communities. Last thing he wanted was for these serial murders to have a communal twist.

"How come the media is on our side?" he asked.

Nawalkar beamed.

"I put our cards on the table," he lied. "I told them, 'Look – don't tell us your problems, we got our own.' I put out the news that a psycho was stalking Mumbai, because that's the truth, and we really don't know who this *choothiy* – this bugger is going to stick next. It could be you, it could be me, it could be the Governor. You and I and His Excellency can take care of ourselves. But what about our duty towards the people? I thought, if we warned the city through the press, the people would start watching their own backs and get off ours!"

"Good work," the Home Minister said again. "Crack this case soon, Nawalkar. Four murders and we haven't a clue, shameful. Yeah, yeah… you have the rag-picker as a witness. Imagine producing him in court! The kind of tangle this is turning out to be… I'm giving you until the weekend to arrest the killer."

Nawalkar wisely said nothing.

FERRAZ COULDN'T wait to interrogate the rag-picker.

But he knew Rathod would want to be present. Every cop fancied he was a top notch interrogator with insight into the criminal mind when it came to important cases that attracted media attention.

"What's this," Navroze asked in surprise when Ferraz and the rag-picker walked in at 9 am. "You didn't tell me you were bringing your old man dressed in his Sunday best."

Navroze had been reading the morning newspapers.

The Seth murder made screaming headlines.

'SERIAL KILLER STRIKES AGAIN'

And below it, an embarrassing strapline.

'Clueless police also admit they are helpless'

The newspapers were full of nothing else.

"You don't want to know what they are saying," Navroze told Ferraz, tossing the newspapers aside. He wrinkled his nose at the rag-picker and said, "Pooh, open the windows, this place stinks!"

The rag-picker, who stank of all the gutters and garbage dumps in Mumbai and looked like he had rolled in them, agreed.

"Yes it does!" he said, shaking his head reproachfully. "Why don't you light some *agarbattis* in here? Or use those *dhoop* sticks?"

He plonked himself on the floor and looked around with interest.

"First time I'm inside a police station," he lied.

"This isn't a police station," Navroze corrected him.

"Oh, then what is it?"

"It's a Unit of the Crime Branch."

"What's that? Is it like the Army? We had Units in the Army." He pointed at Ferraz, "Did he tell you I was a Lance Naik in the Indian Army?"

"We are policemen who... *oh*, never mind," Navroze gave up. He whispered to Ferraz, "Who's this... and why have you brought him here!"

"I'm Yadav," the rag-picker told Navroze. "What's your name?"

"Inspector Daruwala."

"Daruwala," the rag-picker cackled in amusement. "You sell *daru*? What's that you're drinking? *Country*?"

Navroze looked around the room helplessly.

He needed *this* to liven his day, he was thinking.

His red, blustery face was lined with fatigue. And he looked deflated; his tall, angular body drooped lifelessly in the chair, as if all the air had been let out of him with a whoosh. He was on his third mug of green tea. And it was not yet 10 am.

Navroze drank only green tea.

It was an English custom, he told the others. His mug said 'World's Best Dad' on the side. The English drank Earl Grey. But who was going to tell Navroze that? Especially when he was claiming green tea had antioxidants, polyphenols, flavonoids, epigallocatechin gallate, theophylline and L-theanine, which were damn good for health.

Ferraz hated green tea.

Jackie insisted it was good for his heart.

"What's wrong with my heart?" he had protested.

"Nothing," she had told him, "but green tea also fights cancer, lowers cholesterol, burns fat, prevents diabetes, staves off dementia, reduces high blood pressure, alleviates depression, delays Parkinson's and Alzheimer's, undoes skin damage!"

"None of which I have," he had argued.

"But *Angie*, it reduces stress, strengthens the immune system, boosts stamina, uplifts the mood and is anti-jet lag," she had persisted.

"Anti-jet lag!"

"Yes, so enjoy it."

"I would," he had said bitterly, "if it didn't taste like *piss!*"

Jackie had rewarded him with one of her special looks.

Now Ferraz called for two *cutting chais*.

He leaned against Navroze's desk and looked at him sympathetically.

"Bad night?" he asked.

"Bad enough," sighed Navroze sorrowfully.

They had not known how to go about investigating Seth's murder. How many people could they talk to at the RWITC? And at Seth's many offices? His club? All of whom would have wanted to be part of the investigation but not have anything significant to contribute to the police's manhunt for the elusive serial killer. They were still doing the rounds of Pydhonie and Altamont Road. Questioning people there about Haider and Nieves. Hoping for leads, looking for some new twist that would shed light on the motives behind their murders. But their investigation had yielded nothing.

And now they had Seth's killing to add to it.

An enraged Nawalkar had taken them to task last night. Seth had been his friend. And the CP couldn't get over his murder.

"We are running around like headless chickens," he had yelled. "Chasing a fucking shadowy serial killer who has no name, no face, no predictable behavior."

But Nawalkar's fury had been impotent, he knew it wasn't the police's fault, he was just letting out steam. After that the Joint CP (Crime) went over the investigation with Ferraz's team.

They knew it was the same killer.

The Cobra, the Emperor of Darkness. Though his modus operandi was different. He had used a pair of horse reins to ruthlessly strangle Seth. Not stabbed the racehorse owner with the Rampuri. They wondered why. The reins seemed more vindictive, somehow. A personal touch.

"Why is he doing this?" Rathod asked in frustration. "Is he really a whacko or is there some rational thought behind these murders? And how does he select his victim? Randomly or precisely? How do we stop him when we don't know where he is going to strike next, or when and whom?"

Again, the Cobra had taken away his victim's cell phone.

From which he sent the CP that poem about the sun breaking out after the brisk drizzle. Incriminating himself in the murder, revealing his hand. They had no idea why he was doing that, too.

And why he kept calling the CP.

Was he getting his kicks more from the publicity surrounding the killings rather than the killings themselves? What happened to the missing cell phones? They had been switched off. There was no activity on them. Their IMEI numbers were under constant watch. The police had gone after all the notorious cell phone thieves in the city. Those who operated on railway stations and in trains, at bus-stops, in crowded shopping malls, multiplexes and other public places. They went to all fences who bought stolen goods. But nobody had come into possession of any of the victims' phones.

Like Haider and Nieves, Seth was a well-known socialite.

That was the only thing common among all three victims. But not reason enough, they agreed, for such ritualistic, cold-blooded murders. So Navroze, Tushar Pandit and Arun Sawant spent the night figuring out the mutual friends of the three victims. They came up with a long list of names. First they checked if any of these people had police records. Then they discreetly tried to find out if any of them had reason to dislike Haider, Nieves and Seth. Finally, they began inquiring where each of these friends had been at the time of the murders and whether they had alibis. They didn't get anywhere. Nor did a follow up with the Colaba police reveal anything about the extortion threats Seth had received a year ago.

DATTA SALVI was also in office this morning.

Sangeeta Kadam, Dhananjay Gadkari and Sanjay Chhabria were crowded around his desk. Gadkari, who did a stint in the Special Branch and used to gather political intelligence for the Mumbai Police, was now reading the newspapers Navroze had chucked aside. The DCB-CID turned to him in any criminal investigation that was politically inclined.

Sangeeta, in a very casual feminine way, was comfortably perched at the edge of Salvi's desk with one khaki-clad shapely leg resting on the floor, the other swinging. For some reason Sangeeta always wore uniform trousers with a knife-edge crease. With tan police shoes. Over which today she had on a mustard-colored *kurti*. Beneath it Sangeeta packed heat, Navroze frequently reminded the others, like the FBI's female agents who were privately referred to as "chicks with dicks".

Sangeeta was outrageously sexy. But she was also a sport.

She flashed her middle finger at Navroze when he wickedly asked if her khakis were space pants "because your booty is out of this world, babe".

Chhabria was leaning against a wall cabinet. Salvi never tired of ribbing him about the legendary stinginess of the Sindhi community. Like Marwaris and Jews, who were historically tightfisted, the Sindhis were doomed to carry the cross of their sense of thrift till the end of the world.

Chhabria knew Sindhis were supposed to be miserly.

"*Sai*, for the love of Jhulelal don't behave like a *pukka* Sindhi if you're ever backing me in a shootout," Salvi told him now in mock seriousness. "Don't be *kanjoos* with your bullets. If you have to shoot at a gangster or a terrorist, empty your gun at them, don't be cheap and sparing. You're not paying for the ammo. And if you're aiming at two criminals, then *Lal Sai jee mehrbani* fire twice. Don't be a calculating Sindhi and selfishly believe you can get two for the price of one, *samjhan!*"

Chhabria, who secretly admired Salvi and considered it an honor to work with the Encounter cop, smiled good-naturedly and replied, "But Sindhis are not *kanjoos* – Marwaris are. Sindhis are ingenious and resourceful!"

Ferraz was thankful there weren't any Marwari cops on the team.

Salvi also had a Sindhi joke or riddle for Chhabria every day.

"What's a corrupt Sindhi cop called?" he asked Chhabria, winking lecherously at Sangeeta.

"I don't know – *what?*" Chhabria replied.

"He's called Inspector Chaipani," Salvi smugly replied.

"I didn't know," Chhabria said, playing along.

"And what's the same corrupt cop known as after he's made enough to be considered among the richest Indians?" Salvi asked, not quite done.

"What – Ambani?"

"No, he's called Inspector Malpani," Salvi said with a chortle.

Everybody laughed at the joke, the rag-picker loudest of all.

Chhabria glowered at him.

Ferraz was hoping Salvi wouldn't pick on Navroze next.

"*Oye Bawa*," Salvi yelled out to Navroze, "*moo'nkhe chaa'nhi'n jo hiku pyaalo khape.*"

"What the fuck do you mean?" Navroze shouted back.

"He's asking you for tea, sir," Chhabria translated, amazed at Salvi's grasp of the Sindhi language.

"It's English tea," said Navroze offended, "not from Ulhasnagar."

"Never mind, Bawa," Salvi continued pacifically, "tell me, what do you call a Parsi who's angry with God?"

"You tell me," said Navroze with a resigned sigh, because Salvi would have told him anyway. And if he wasn't going to listen to Salvi's dirty jokes, then who would entertain his?

"God-rage!"

Navroze looked at Ferraz, shaking his head.

"First this rag-picker, then him," he grumbled. "I tell you, life sucks here. *Arre* Angelo, forgot to mention, Jackie called before you came."

"Oh, what did she say?"

"Plenty! Too much to take down… you know how these girls like to yak once they get you on the phone. But she mailed me something. I got a printout made. *Oh Khodai*, have I lost it already?"

He rummaged among the papers on his desk and produced a printout.

In silence, the policemen read all the snippets on Sanghamitra Sarkar that Jackie had culled from the Internet and painstakingly copy-pasted to make one crisp and informative document.

"Your girl would make quite a cop," Navroze murmured.

They quickly came to the end of Jackie's mail.

It told them all they needed to know about the eventful life and exciting career of the murdered Bengali Indipop singer… bringing them up-to-date with the promising vocational move she had decided to make this month when she left Kolkata to come to Mumbai and promote her chartbusting Hollywood single *Oye Ganesh*.

They missed the significance, those intelligent cops.

The reason for her murder was staring them in the face.

This was the fourth time they were failing to make the link.

It was like trying to assemble a jigsaw puzzle. They were staring at the incomplete picture. Not concentrating on the pieces in hand.

"Dammed if I know why," said Ferraz in frustration.

17

CALLING THE police artist was a mistake.

She arrived while they were waiting for Joint CP (Crime) Arun Rathod to come and begin the interrogation of the rag-picker. By then, the rag-picker had consumed three glasses of *cutting chai*. He was wondering whether he ought to ask that Inspector Daruwala for a mug of whatever it was that he was drinking. He had got over his initial fear and was now enjoying all the attention the Crime Branch cops were giving him.

He took an instant dislike to the police artist.

She looked more like a policewoman than the dusky lady cop here. The attractive one with the sexy strut. Now standing by the window looking at the rain, her butt pushed back, the outline of a gun tucked into her waist visible beneath her top. She was well stacked too. The rag-picker looked away embarrassed.

The policeman who said he had a liquor distillery, Inspector Daruwala, the tall, red-faced, angry-looking cop, was wickedly telling her, "Sangeeta, your ass is so nice that it's a shame you have to sit on it!"

The sexy lady cop ignored him.

Shambhavi Ragnekar was not a policewoman.

She was a freelance illustrator. She had studied at the JJ College of Applied Art where Rudyard Kipling was born in 1865, his father being the college's first principal – that's how old the institute was. Shambhavi got her Bachelor of Fine Arts (BFA) degree by specializing in Illustration. She was studying Computer Graphics now. And she read books on Psychology.

Her father had been a cop.

He had persuaded Shambhavi to give him an artist's impression of a notorious chain snatcher operating in his jurisdiction whose specialty was mugging elderly women out for morning walks.

Naturally, the chain snatcher's victims were witnesses to these crimes. There were dozens of them. Shambhavi talked to all. After listening to their descriptions, she had sketched a remarkable likeness of the chain snatcher. Her father had photocopied the sketch and passed it around his police station and to informers in the neighborhood. The elusive chain snatcher was identified and arrested in an hour.

That was the first time. Eighteen years ago. Shambhavi's father had since passed away. But she continued to sketch suspects for the Mumbai Police. And her sketches, after narrowing down the police's search, had resulted in the positive identification and arrest of 218 criminals. Among them were rapists, killers, extortionists and armed robbers.

Which was an impressive record.

The work made her feel like a part-time cop.

Shambhavi didn't look like an artist. She was lean and wiry. Her shiny black hair was swept back and tied in a bouncy ponytail. She wore rimless glasses and was dressed in jeans and a white smock with the sleeves rolled up. Her appearance was severe. Maybe because Shambhavi seldom smiled when working with the police. She was always concentrating on the description of the suspect that the witness was giving. And her quizzical expression, her no-nonsense questions, made her resemble a hawk-eyed lady cop. That's what the rag-picker was thinking.

Shambhavi was looking at him in dismay.

He was not her idea of the perfect witness. He stank of stale sweat and piss. Like the public toilet on a railway station. But the cops here didn't seem to mind his contemptible odor. The rag-picker looked like a nutcase, too. And that bothered her. Getting witnesses to describe suspects was never easy. Sometimes they were disturbed and confused. And their descriptions tended to waver and be inaccurate.

"This is your witness," Ferraz said apologetically, confirming Shambhavi's fear. He had decided to get the sketch done. Rathod, Joint CP (L&O) Arvind Mugbe, Nawalkar and Maharashtra's Director General of Police Satish Pradhan had been summoned to the Chief Minister's residence.

This evening was to be the CM's tea party customarily held on the eve of the Assembly. It was just as customarily boycotted by the Opposition which was preparing to attack the CM on the floor of the house tomorrow. The CM wanted to be prepared as well. He asked the top cops to explain the rising crime in the city and the breakdown of law and order in the state.

"What's the criminal done?" Shambhavi asked, opening the leather satchel that contained the tools of her trade.

"Murder – you heard about this psychopathic serial killer, he's murdered four so far, and this guy saw him this morning," Ferraz replied, watching her lay out pencils of different leads, white sheets of A4 size paper, an eraser and a sketchpad. Shambhavi then produced a thick coffee table-sized hardcover book. Ferraz wondered what that was for.

"You mean he's *actually* witnessed a murder and come to assist you guys?" Shambhavi asked, looking at the rag-picker with new respect. Why not, she thought, even crackpots could make conscientious witnesses.

"No, no… nothing like that," Ferraz corrected her, "but this chap was hanging around a bus-stop near Lilavati Hospital when the killer stopped there after committing the murder. We have nothing to go forward with but his description and your sketch."

"Hmnn okay," Shambhavi said, "but I must warn you my sketches are only 60 per cent accurate. The last time I sketched a serial killer was for the Cuffe Parade and Colaba police. They were investigating the rapes and murders of those minors in the Macchimar Nagar slums, you remember?"

"Yeah, they never got that guy."

"No, but they made an arrest based on my sketch."

"And he wasn't the suspect."

"No," Shambhavi said shortly. She added defensively, "But they made three arrests on their own and had to discharge these suspects because their DNA tests turned out to be negative."

"I know," Ferraz said, "we worked on that case as well, Colaba and Cuffe Parade come under Unit I of the DCB-CID, and the police collected DNA samples of 1,016 suspects and sent them for forensic analysis."

"Oh, I didn't know. All the tests were negative?"

"That's right. We also put over 500 workers of Sassoon Dock through sustained interrogation – but no result again. And we compared the fingerprints of 325 listed sexual offenders with those collected from the crime scenes. Nothing matched. We even installed 45 CCTVs in the area and deployed 200 cops on day and night patrolling… but the rapist-killer is still out there somewhere, that bastard."

"Sorry," Shambhavi said gently, "don't take it to heart, huh."

She looked at Ferraz, noticing that beneath the tough look of the cop there was a softness in his face, a pain in his eyes, and she knew that he genuinely felt terrible about the rapes and murders of minors that went undetected in Colaba and Cuffe Parade. He was wearing the faded blue jeans and navy Lacoste jersey over tan police shoes that he hurriedly got into this morning when Rathod called, his gun tucked into his waist. Shambhavi thought Ferraz looked as sexy as hell though she couldn't exactly figure out why.

"Why do you do it?" he asked, "it can't be the money."

She actually laughed, "The money is *chillar*, the police pay me 500 a sketch, and the money takes forever to come. I'm doing it because… you knew my father, ACP Vijay Ragnekar, I did it first to help him, now the police has become like a family. My father, I know, would be proud that I'm working with you guys to nab criminal suspects and put them away."

"Haven't you–"

"Yes, I've got death threats," Shambhavi said, "isn't that what you wanted to ask? But I'm not on anybody's hit list. One criminal who came out on bail called to say, '*Kaat dalunga!*' That's about it."

Ferraz was concerned. Sketch artists were like informers, details of them were always kept a secret, because they automatically became the targets of those against whom they were working.

"You said your sketches are only 60 per cent accurate…"

"Can't help it," she shrugged, "sometimes I get five witnesses who saw the same suspect and give me five different descriptions. They expect a police artist's sketch to be like a photograph. Or a painting good enough to go up at the Jehangir Art Gallery. Which sucks and makes my job difficult. I try to take their descriptions, use my imagination and sketch a likeness of the suspect that hopefully somebody will identify for the police."

"I understand," Ferraz said soothingly.

And so Shambhavi and the rag-picker got down to it.

The cops gathered around curiously.

"I want you to visualize the suspect," Shambhavi said.

"Who's that?" the rag-picker asked at once.

"The man you saw."

"Which man are you talking about?" he asked insolently.

She turned around irritably and looked at the cops.

Ferraz took a meaningful step forward. He stood by the rag-picker's side, legs spread out in athletic nonchalance, big arms folded across his chest.

"You mean the *phonewallah* at the bus-stop?"

"Yes him," Ferraz said, "I want you to tell the lady about him."

"But I don't know him."

"Okay, okay, let's start again," Shambhavi said. "Tell me what he looked like? How old do you think he was?"

"He was like me!"

"What do you mean – like you? How old are you"

"I can't remember!"

"Then, why like you?"

"I think he was."

"Was he tall or short, thin or fat, dark or fair?"

"He was standing at the bus-stop. I was lying on the ground."

"So?"

"How would I know?"

Shambhavi crumpled up the paper on which she had been doodling.

"Listen Yadav – your name is Yadav, right?" she asked.

"It's Ghanshyam Yadav," he said with a great deal of hauteur.

"Okay, Ghanshyam… what was this man wearing?"

"Clothes!"

"Okay, we are getting somewhere. What was it? A shirt and pant? A *kurta* and *pajama*? Was he wearing jeans and a T-shirt? A tracksuit? A safari suit? Was he in any kind of uniform? You know, like a cabbie or auto driver? Or a watchman, a Lilavati Hospital ward boy?"

"He was wearing spectacles!"

"Oh, okay… never mind the clothes for now. What kind of face did this man have? Was it happy, sad, angry… did you notice?"

"He looked like the man in that poster."

"Which poster?"

"There on the road – the man in the poster."

"Inspector... would you know?" Shambhavi asked helplessly.

Ferraz was lost in thought.

He vaguely remembered seeing a poster on the road to the Sealink.

"Call Sr. PI Savde of Unit IX," he told Sangeeta. "Ask him to send a man to Bandra Reclamation to look out for posters, hoardings and banners around the bus-stop. Some political party has put something up for Ganeshotsav. I want to know whose face is on them."

Shambhavi had now picked up the hardcover book.

"It's useless asking him the questions I put to regular witnesses," she told Ferraz, "like what was the suspect's skin tone, the shape and color of his eyes, what kind of hair did he have, was he balding, what kind of health was he in, was he wearing jewelry... because your witness is going to lead me on a merry dance."

Ferraz looked at her in dismay.

"I don't know if he's faking ignorance or is really plain and simple dumb, but it takes all kinds," Shambhavi added comfortingly.

"So what do we do?" Ferraz asked.

She opened the book and showed him.

It was a book of sketches.

Pages after pages of square, oval and triangular shaped faces, differently shaped skulls, hairstyles, eyes, noses, ears, mouths, side profiles – of both, men and women, and plenty of moustaches and beards, thick bushy eyebrows.

"Look Ghanshyam," she said playing it simple, "which of these drawings is like the man you saw?"

The rag-picker picked up the book in fascination.

Forty-five minutes later, Shambhavi was still sketching the suspect, her pencil lightly flying over the paper, black lines darting from the top of the sheet to the bottom, shading and shadowing, then erasing the impression of the man the rag-picker was now struggling to describe.

The floor was littered with her earlier efforts.

"This doesn't look like him," the rag-picker was saying stubbornly.

"Okay," Shambhavi said patiently, "tell me what's wrong."

"I don't know…"

"Does he have too much hair in this sketch? Is his nose too long? What about the eyes? Have I got that right? Is his mouth wrong – is it smaller, wider, does he have thin lips, sunken cheeks, come on Ghanshyam, you've got to help me, describe the man to me again… tell me did he have a moustache, a beard, surely you noticed that, any scars?"

"He was like me."

"Okay, if you can't describe him… then imitate him for me, you know what that means, mimic his actions, act like him, show me how he was talking on the phone, how he walked."

"I told you, he was like me."

Sangeeta came up and told Ferraz, "Sir, the poster near the bus-stop in Bandra Reclamation is that of Anna Hazare."

"*Anna Hazare!* Do we have a picture of him?"

"I could open a Google image on–"

"Immediately – do it!"

"Sir," Sangeeta hurried back to her laptop.

Two minutes later, she had Anna Hazare on the screen.

Ferraz led the rag-picker over, holding his breath.

"Who's that?" the rag-picker asked, looking at the image.

"Your man in the poster," Ferraz reminded him sharply.

"I told you he was like me," the rag-picker said aggravatingly.

"Not like the man in this picture?"

"I don't know this man."

Ferraz wanted to shoot him dead.

He looked at Navroze in frustration.

"This is not getting us anywhere," he said angrily.

"Let's keep him in detention," Navroze suggested. "Put him in our lock-up, make sure he is comfortable, but keep him in isolation. Who knows, he may play a role in this investigation yet. I doubt anybody would really miss him or object."

"Don't we have to produce him in court and get his remand?"

"Sssshhh, don't tell anybody," Navroze warned.

"Okay," Ferraz agreed reluctantly, "let's interrogate him separately, get different people to do it, Sangeeta you try – maybe he will open up to you, then Salvi, scare the shit out of the fucker. Also Azavedo, who can charm information out of the hardest criminal. Remember he's our only lead. Don't beat him up. But slowly, gently break down his resistance. Alternate days deny him sleep and food. And let him see how we treat others in custody. He sees us beating the daylights out of some accused, he'll come around. Let's see if his statement varies and his description of the suspect changes."

Vishnu Shetty and Sanjay Chhabria led the rag-picker away.

He walked with a shuffle and limp. He had a blood-stained bandage around one ankle. Nobody thought of asking the rag-picker how he had got hurt. He had proved to be a lousy witness anyway.

The rag-picker was thinking differently.

He had said that the man he saw was like him.

He wasn't exaggerating.

That policewoman with the sketchpad, she was only asking for descriptions of the man's face, how would she ever be able to show that the man limped, the rag-picker wondered.

That's what he kept telling them…

… that the man was *like* him – they both limped.

Ferraz leaned against Navroze's table watching him go.

Four murders, he was thinking, all committed by one man. Each executed with deliberate planning and cold-blooded precision. And they hadn't a damn clue who he was. Or why he was killing. He was beginning to doubt the Cobra was a psychopath. Weren't they supposed to be mad? This chap was chillingly ruthless. The brutality of the murders indicated anger. And vengeance. But these weren't killings committed in a fit of rage, they were passionately pre-meditated. So what did they mean? The killer had a hate list of people he was coolly going after?

Ferraz thought he figured out a pattern behind the murders.

Pulling up a chair, he sat down.

"The first victim on Thursday night was Haider – a man. Friday morning was Esther Nieves – a woman. Last evening was Seth – a man. And this morning it's Sanghamitra Sarkar – a woman," he pointed out to Navroze.

"So what – man-woman, man-woman?"

"You don't see a pattern there?"

"Could be just a coincidence. Is he going to murder again? Should we expect the next victim to be a man, then?"

"I don't know," shrugged Ferraz, "it's just a thought."

Gadkari came up with an armful of newspapers.

He said, "Seth's last conversation was with his secretary, R Srinivasan, minutes before he was killed."

Navroze nodded, "Srinivasan called him, but it wasn't a conversation."

"To discuss entering Seth's thoroughbred in the St. Leger at Pune?"

"I think so. A colt named – what was its name? Something very Indian. Mogadishu? No, that was the horse my wife's cousin rode for Poonawala in the McDowell's Derby," Navroze recalled. "Was it Brahmastra that was a close runner to Fortune Hunter in the Indian Oaks? Or Meghnaad that won the Major A K Mehra Super Mile? No… it had some other Indian name, I think it was Indrayani. No, that's a filly, what am I saying! His colt Astapi was an outsider in the Dr. S C Jain Sprinter's Championship. And Seth was planning to enter Shivalik in the C D Daddy Trophy. But that's not the colt's name, it's something else, but Indian – he kept Indian names."

"I didn't know you were into horse racing!" Ferraz said, astonished.

"It's the sport of kings and Parsis," Navroze told him grandly.

"Is the horse's name Namasthetu?" asked Gadkari.

"Yeah, that's what Srinivasan told me – *Namasthetu!*" Navroze exclaimed.

"Sir, you know what Namasthetu means, don't you?"

"No, what's it supposed to mean?"

"Namasthetu is one of the 108 names of Ganpati."

"Yeah, how the devil would I know?"

"And Namasthetu means Vanquisher of all Evils, Vices and Sins."

"Really? How do these guys pick their horses' names? I've known one thoroughbred to be named Tiffin! Why on earth would–"

"Oh my God!" shouted Ferraz leaping to his feet.

His chair went over with a crash.

They turned to him in alarm.

Ferraz looked like he was suffering a heart attack.

"Angelo, what the–"

Salvi was by Ferraz's side, Sangeeta and Chhabria on his heels.

"What happened?" Salvi asked looking at the chair on the floor.

"It's Ganpati!" Ferraz said in a strangled voice, grabbing Salvi's arm.

"What's Ganpati, man?" Navroze asked bewildered.

"The link to the murders!"

"What do you mean?"

"It's Ganpati," Ferraz repeated stupidly.

He turned to Sangeeta and gave her a two finger salute.

"You were right," he told her with a crooked smile, "the clue was there all the while. Look, Haider was murdered on Thursday before his Ganpati exhibition. The Nieves woman's throat was slit on Friday morning, after her Ganpati party. Seth, who was strangled last evening, has a thoroughbred named Namasthetu – that's one of Ganpati's 108 names. And this Bengali singer Sanghamitra Sarkar, who got beaten to death this morning, she was here to promote her Indipop song *Oye Ganesh!* The only thing common among the victims is their affinity to Ganpati, isn't it?"

They looked at him in silence.

"Oh Khodai – it's Ganpati!" yelled Navroze in excitement, "the common link between all four victims, the motive, is Ganpati you mean?"

"Yes, Bawa!"

"And it's Ganeshotsav – therefore the serial murders, that *bhosirino!*"

Sangeeta was grinning. This was her 'I-told-you-so' moment.

Ferraz punched Gadkari on the shoulder.

"Thanks Dhananjay," he said beaming.

Salvi said thoughtfully, "The murders are related to Ganesh Chaturthi?"

"Yes Datta, don't you see?" Navroze was exuberant.

Like they had busted the case, only the arrest was left.

"I see that – but it's a ten-day festival."

"Ganpati Bappa Morya!"

"Ten days, ten murders," Salvi said slowly.

There was an ominous silence.

18

JOINT CP (Crime) Arun Rathod listened in silence.

He was being been apprised of the Ganpati angle to the serial murders. Nawalkar was at Varsha, the Chief Minister's residence. It was 2 pm. Rathod caught a working lunch while discussing the breakthrough with Ferraz and his team. He asked Addl. CP (Crime) Nandkumar Sonawane to join them.

Joint CP (L&O) Arvind Mugbe was also present.

He declined Rathod's invitation to join him for lunch. Mugbe had strict notions of etiquette. Wolfing sandwiches and gulping coffee before the rank was not his idea of lunch. This was a police meeting, not some social gathering.

Ferraz, Navroze, Khan and Salvi sat across Rathod. Also present were Kisan Savde of Unit IX, a veteran Crime Branch man, Shrikant Musale of Unit III and PIs Shankar Bhogwekar and Rajendra Wagh of Unit II. The murders had been committed in the jurisdictions of these policemen. Ferraz was heading the investigation, but they were all stakeholders in the case.

"Are we dealing with a fanatic?" Rathod asked.

"Certainly his victims were, er, somewhat godless," Ferraz said, picking his words carefully, "and perhaps they unknowingly exploited Ganpati."

"Making him, what, suddenly angry and vengeful? And you're saying he probably has six more victims in mind?" Rathod asked skeptically.

"I fear so, sir."

"Why now?"

"Sir?"

"Why is he targeting people now? Why not during earlier Ganeshotsavs?"

"Maybe he's from out of town," Mugbe suggested.

"And lost it after coming to Mumbai and reading about Haider's exhibition?" Rathod asked. "It's not possible for him to have drawn up a list of famous people who are anti-Ganpati in the short time since newspapers reported Haider's art show."

"True," Mugbe agreed, "his plan is ingenious, it must have taken some preparation. The British diplomat's Ganpati party is public knowledge. It's being held for years. So Nieves automatically got shortlisted for murder. Likewise Seth, because the newspapers have been reporting the victories of his racehorse named after Lord Ganesh. But this Bengali singer is a brand new star, her single *Oye Ganesh* is just out, we hadn't heard of her and the song or were aware she was in Mumbai. But the killer knew. Means he already has a shortlist of personalities known for their disrespect to Ganpati and he's seriously taking one out each day of the festival."

Rathod ordered Sonawane, "Tell the State Control to ask all police stations across Maharashtra if they had any Ganpati-related murders in the past that remain undetected even today."

"So what do we do now?" asked Savde. "Try and identify all people who have been faithlessly but famously associated with Ganpati and have pissed off the killer? Hundreds may have innocently dishonored Lord Ganesh. It's only when somebody like Haider defiles a God and outraged devotees threaten him do the police come to know."

He resembled a college lecturer, thin, tall, with graying hair kept as long as the Department would allow, a wispy moustache, horn-rimmed glasses, and a scholarly manner.

"What's your point?" Mugbe asked.

"Anybody could be his next victim," Savde replied. "We'd be

unsuccessful if we tried to identify them all. Instead, let's profile the killer."

"Hmnn, he has to be a fanatic," Rathod said. "Also somebody deeply intellectual and with a mythological bent of mind. Not many would associate a racehorse named Namasthetu with Lord Ganesh. He's also a pervert and a psychopath. He's playing with murder and drawing us into a cat-and-mouse game."

Ferraz said, "We have a database of religious fanatics."

"And records of bigots in police stations," Savde added.

"Our *khabris* know the rabble rousers in their areas," Khan suggested, "remember that Kurla pedophile? It was a *khabri's* tip-off about the local pervert that helped us make the arrest."

"All ardent Ganpati *bhakts* go to Siddhivinayak on Tuesday," Savde told them. "He's sure to be among them if our theory is right."

Tuesday was dedicated to Lord Ganesh. Siddhivinayak, at Prabhadevi in Mumbai, was the most popular Ganpati temple in the world. The holiest of holies. Millions converged on it from far and wide.

Sonawane had an idea.

"Let's get CCTV feed from Siddhivinayak for, say, the last three months," he said, sounding like Denzel Washington piecing together the evidence in *Bone Collector*, "maybe the rag-picker will spot the guy from the bus-stop in it. And we could set a trap for him at the temple on Tuesday."

"It's a long shot but certainly worth trying," said Rathod.

"I will organize the videos, sir," Savde told him.

"I like Ferraz's idea," Mugbe said. "Let's check the fanatics too."

"Yes," Rathod told Ferraz, "get their numbers, study their CDRs, see if any of them was in Pydhonie, Altamont Road, Mahalaxmi and Reclamation at the time of the murders. Or if they made calls to the victims earlier."

Salvi raised his hand and spoke for the first time.

"The Bombay Psychiatric Society could ask if any of its members is treating somebody who happens to be a Ganesh *bhakt,*" he suggested.

"Excellent idea, Datta," said Rathod with approval.

PI Rajendra Wagh of Unit II had another idea. He was a short, dark and thickset man with an ugly, pock-marked face, pugnacious by nature, but a good and determined cop.

Wagh was saying, "Our Detection staff should visit the doctors in their Zones, the GPs with small dispensaries in housing colonies. People confide in their family doctor. These chaps will know if a patient is a religious fanatic."

"Another good idea," said Rathod, pleased.

Navroze said, "The Sarvajanik Ganpati organizers can be relied upon to keep a watch for our guy. They know all that goes on in their localities."

Rathod shook his head. "That means revealing his targets are people associated with Ganpati," he said.

"Isn't that what we should be doing, sir?" asked Navroze mildly.

"I don't know," the Joint CP (Crime) said, doubtfully.

"The media will get wind of this Ganpati angle," Ferraz predicted.

"And they'll blow it out of proportion," Navroze declared.

Mugbe asked, "Why keep people in the dark? If our theory is right, the Cobra's anyway going to murder somebody connected with Ganpati tomorrow. Why not warn the city?"

"It's the CP's decision, not mine," Rathod said doggedly.

He sat thinking, rolling a pencil on his desk.

"I have another fear," Rathod said finally.

They looked at the Joint CP (Crime) expectantly.

"What if this Ganpati fanatic's a cop?"

They looked at him silently, startled by the idea.

"He appears to know exactly how we work, he could be an insider."

Mugbe said hesitantly, "Or maybe an ex-cop, he got dismissed for corruption or whatever and carries a grudge against the force."

"Yeah, that's a possibility," Rathod agreed.

"And he's chatting with former colleagues, that's how he's following the investigation and staying ahead of us," Mugbe added.

"With all due respect, sir," Ferraz told Mugbe apologetically, "why would a rogue cop look for victims loosely connected with Ganpati to start a series of imaginative but brutal murders just to get back at the force? He could pick anybody as his victims. Why be clever?"

"Maybe because he is intelligent and deceitful," Rathod said. He told Sonawane, "All cops who were dismissed for corruption and dereliction of duty, and those suspended and facing departmental inquiry, find out where they are and what they've been up to. Keep them under observation. But discreetly. If one of them is the Cobra, he'll be expecting us to do this."

PI Shanker Bhogwekar of Unit II got up. He was a small gawky man with untidy hair, soda bottle glasses and a thin moustache. He spoke softly. But Bhogwekar had an unbelievably sharp mind.

"I know a criminal who defines the suspect," he said quietly.

The other policemen looked at him in astonishment.

"You do?" Rathod said amazed, "Who?"

"Chhota Rajan."

"Chhota Rajan? That Chhota Rajan!"

"The same, sir. He's a well-known Ganesh devotee."

"Are you–"

"I'm serious, sir."

"But he's been gone… like ages!"

"He doesn't have to be here, sir. Dawood Ibrahim wasn't here when he bombed Bombay on March 12, 1993."

"Okay, let's hear it…"

"CHHOTA RAJAN!"

Sr. PI Tanaji Borkar of Unit VI was disbelieving.

"Whatever gave you the idea, Angelo?"

Ferraz could imagine him grinning at the other end.

He had called Borkar, his Chembur counterpart in the DCB-CID, to see if the fugitive underworld don could be involved in their serial killings.

Borkar's jurisdiction was vast. Ten police stations came under Unit VI. Among them was Tilak Nagar, in which area the don had grown up, a Dalit worker's son who began his career in crime as a petty thief, bootlegger and cinema ticket black marketeer, and rose to become one of Mumbai's top three mobsters.

Tilak Nagar used to be a colony of lower middle class chawls in the smokestack industries of North Mumbai. These had given way to high-rises and towers with lavish gardens, swimming pools and playgrounds. It wasn't among the most sought after addresses in Mumbai. But it was famous for its Sarvajanik Ganeshotsav organized by the Sahyadri Krida Mandal and allegedly financed by the don since 1977.

The don was a confirmed Ganpati *bhakt*.

Decades ago, he was supposed to have implored Lord Ganesh to fulfill an outstanding wish and in return vowed to hold a Sarvajanik Ganeshotsav at Tilak Nagar every year no matter which part of the world he was operating from.

That was the story.

The Tilak Nagar Ganpati was spectacular.

Each year it was built around a tableau that outdid the previous year's in size and grandeur. Leading Bollywood art directors created impressive replicas of Indian religious and historical monuments for it. Like the Red Fort, Ajanta and Ellora Caves, the Mysore Palace, Shaniwar Wada, the Vivekananda Rock Memorial of Kanyakumari, the Ranakpur Jain Temple of Rajasthan and the Dakshineshwar Kali Temple in Kolkata.

The Ganpati attracted huge crowds, including film stars, cricketers, gangsters and politicians. But its alleged patron could not get a *darshan*. He had been in hiding since 1988, reportedly in Thailand, Cambodia, Malaysia, Australia, even Iran, wanted by the police for murder, extortion, smuggling, arms and drug trafficking. Additionally, he was hunted by Dawood Ibrahim whose crime syndicate he had disagreeably left in 1993 after the former's involvement in the Bombay serial blasts.

That had been a turning point in his life, the 1993 blasts.

Enraged by the attack on Bombay by *deshdrohis* (traitors), the don gave up all pretence of being a key aide to Dawood and swore revenge. From an underworld gangster, he became a patriotic Hindu don, and in "national interest" started killing all D-Company men who were accused in the 1993 serial blasts trial.

But he missed his Tilak Nagar Ganpati.

So, the Sahyadri Krida Mandal created a Facebook page which offered live *darshan* to everybody who couldn't visit Tilak Nagar and seek the Ganpati's blessings. Earlier, the don had experimented with satellite channels using DTH (Direct to Home) technology to catch Tilak Nagar's *aarti* every day.

Now Ferraz told Borkar, "Our suspect is a Ganesh *bhakt* like your Tilak Nagar don. He's murdering people who have disrespected Ganpati."

Borkar said, "These serial killings would be petty change for him. He wouldn't do it. And if somebody displeased him, why would he wait for Ganeshotsav to take revenge? He would do it immediately."

"Hmnn, I thought so," said Ferraz.

"Come and see the Ganpati, Angelo. The tableau is a replica of the grand Swaminarayan Temple of Akshardham this year."

"The temple attacked by terrorists in 2002?"

"No, that's in Gandhinagar. This is the new Akshardham Temple of Delhi. Over 150 engineers, architects and carpenters worked on it from July."

"Entirely financed by him?"

"Well, his gang members approach builders, hoteliers, restaurateurs, businessmen and other well-wishers for donations. The Income Tax also finds donations in gold and silver made by *benami* (unnamed) sources. People wanting to get rid of black money."

"You think he'll try to sneak in for a *darshan*?"

"No chance," Borkar said. "But we're looking out."

DR. YUNUS A Miyasahib was a character.

When not practicing psychiatry, which was a grim medical specialty, he lifted weights in the gym, wrote atrocious poetry, and was the main celebrant at karaoke clubs to his wife Yasmin's horror.

Mumbai's doctors were insufferable highbrows.

But you would not find a more rambunctious companion at Bombay Gym than this genial shrink if you wanted to get up on the table on Bar Night after a few beers and do the Russian squat dance.

He was a roly-poly, cheerful and bombastic man. He had an angular and naughty boyish face. And sad droopy eyes that made him look like an ageing Sylvester Stallone rather than Mumbai's top drawer psychiatrist.

Dr. Yunus routinely got called in by the Mumbai Police.

He helped them to profile elusive serial rapists and pedophiles. And to deal with doped detainees who had built up a lifetime's dependence on drugs. Sometimes the court asked him to examine an accused who was pretending to be a schizophrenic. Dr. Yunus put the prisoner through psychometric evaluation, ran him through the polygraph lie detector test, narcoanalysis, and finally subjected him to hypnosis to see if he was faking.

Now he would be called to hunt for a psychopathic serial killer.

Nawalkar had returned from Varsha and brought the rain.

Grey sheets of water poured on the Police Commissionerate out of a dark forbidding sky, unnaturally darkening the afternoon and messing with the policemen's minds.

The Crime Branch's technical unit produced two high-definition sound recordings of the killer's voice out of the CP's phone. One call was made from Seth's phone. And the other from Sanghamitra's. Unfortunately, they weren't conversations. All they got the Cobra saying was *"Moryaa Re!"*

The first time after strangling Seth at the racecourse last evening…

"Moryaa Re!"

And then after hammering Sanghamitra to death this morning…

"Moryaa Re!"

In the second recording they could hear a bus in the background. And the conductor calling out to somebody in Marathi before he rang the bell and sent the bus on its way. The call was made from Bandra Reclamation.

Savde's Unit IX traced the bus to the R C Church bus depot in Colaba. It was a 1 Ltd. which started at Bandra Station and after 62 halts and 25 km, terminated at R C Church.

The conductor was having a cup of tea in the BEST canteen when Salvi and Sangeeta arrived. It was 9.30 am. Colaba came under Unit I. They rushed over as soon as Unit IX tipped them off about the bus' location.

The conductor was surprised to see them.

Putting down his tea he listened warily to what they were saying.

"You know how many stops that bus makes?" he asked.

"Yes, we do," Salvi assured him.

"But we're confident you'll remember the man," Sangeeta added falsely.

"You're mad," the conductor said indignantly. "I can't remember passengers who got off five minutes ago. And you're asking me about somebody who was waiting at Bandra Reclamation for God knows what bus at 7 am!"

The conductor sent them packing.

Now they listened to the recording.

"Moryaa Re!"... "Moryaa Re!"...

"The bastard is saying *'Moryaa Re!'* and not Mario or Maria," Nawalkar shouted in realization, thumping his desk. "He meant *'Ganpati Bappa Moryaa'* – that *'Moryaa Re!'* right?"

"Yes, sir," said Rathod, relieved the CP had finally got it. "He appears to be a devotee of Lord Ganesh. And what's common in the four murders is the victims' superficial fancy for Ganpati. That's the killer's motive."

"Superficial fancy?"

"Perhaps he thought they were being irreverent."

"So he killed them?"

"That's our theory, sir."

"Four high-profile murders, that fucking psycho!"

"Psycho's a general-public and popular-press explanation for any unsolved, motiveless murders," Mugbe said. "Are we convinced the Cobra is one?"

Nawalkar seized on the idea, "Yeah, what if he's just settling old scores with the victims? A clever killer hiding behind the psycho's mask?"

"And they all had a connect with Ganpati?" Rathod asked laconically.

"According to Hercule Poirot, if the fact doesn't fit the theory, throw out the theory," said Nawalkar, an Agatha Christie fan. "Our *theory* is the suspect's a psycho. But the *facts* suggest a self-righteous, deep-rooted hatred for the victims. A blood lust for revenge. Would a psychopath have such emotion?"

"Why not – if he's also a Ganpati fanatic?"

"If we keep aside the Ganesh angle?"

"I'm not getting your point, sir," said Rathod.

Nawalkar clicked his tongue impatiently.

"Criminals get caught when they don't have planning or organizational skills. These murders must have taken not just cold nerves but also faultless planning. And he intends to remain in hiding and go on killing. That indicates the Cobra's above average intelligence."

"Maybe he's a split personality."

"I'm saying the murders don't appear to be the work of a psychopath. Or a Ganesh fanatic. They have been committed by an experienced criminal."

"Why is he saying *'Moryaa Re!'* each time?"

"Who knows how his mind works! If a Sardarji was the killer and went around greeting his victims *'Sat sri akal!'* before plunging his *kirpan* in them, we wouldn't suspect every Sikh going into a gurudwara of being a psychopath or fanatic."

Rathod said, "I think *'Moryaa Re!' is* a clue for us."

"Why would he give us a clue?" Nawalkar demanded. "It's Ganesh Chaturthi, he's just saying what everybody else is shouting on the roads. He may not be a Ganesh *bhakt.* The motive for the murders is weak. Let's not give the city a fucking coronary."

Mugbe said, "There's a popular Ganpati temple in Morgaon, outside Pune, dedicated to Lord Ganesh. It's called Shri Moreshwar Mandir."

"You think the killer comes from there?" asked Rathod.

"Unlikely," Mugbe said, "*'Moryaa Re!'* is a simple invocation to Lord Ganesh. It means 'Come, guide us from the front'. Its origin is linked to the 14th century saint Morya Gosavi of Chinchwad near Pune who was a Ganesh devotee. Pleased with his adoration, Ganpati asked Morya what blessing he wanted. And Morya replied that he would like his name associated with Lord Ganesh. That's where the *'Ganpati Bappa Morya!'* came from."

"I don't think we should read too much in that," the CP said. "In order to isolate what's possible let's eliminate every motive that's impossible."

The Detection cops sat quietly.

They had no time for theory. Or cared if the suspect was a psycho. Fact was he was a killer. They wanted to cut to the chase.

So Ferraz suggested they call Dr. Yunus.

The good doctor came at once, all enthusiasm and tell-me-more.

They sent a police jeep to fetch him.

He strutted in wearing the standard disguise of all doctors. Black trousers and a white short-sleeved shirt. A stethoscope – another favorite toy of everyone in medicine from student to specialist – dangled around his neck. He ignored the chair they offered and buoyantly took the floor.

"Heard you're looking for a serial killer?" he cried, gleefully rubbing his palms and whizzing around the room at top speed.

The policemen had to swivel in their seats to follow him.

Nawalkar frowned at his ebullience.

"Is he a psychopath, that's what we want to know?" he said stiffly.

Dr. Yunus glared at the CP.

"What do you think?" he demanded, arms folded across his chest. "A serial killer is not a specific mental disorder. He isn't your stereotype Bollywood crazy with glazed eyes and drooling mouth, running around with a knife. How's it going to help your investigation to know he's a psychopath?"

Nawalkar looked at him like he was cracked.

"Is this a Dark of the Moon phase?" Dr. Yunus asked suddenly.

The CP was superstitious, he was immediately struck by the idea.

Dark of the Moon meant there was no moon in the sky. It was

Amavasya. A mystical and magical phase in the lunar cycle. A transition period between the death of the old and birth of the new. A time of fear and superstition. For centuries the full moon was rumored to be a cause of madness. And the term 'lunacy' came from Luna – the Roman Goddess of the Moon who famously rode her chariot across the sky at night.

But Rathod said shortly, "No it's not. The killings are happening now, during Ganeshotsav, and the victims all have an undevout link to Ganpati."

"Your suspect's a Ganesh devotee of exceptional faith?"

"He has to be, *na*, Doc."

"He could be a fundamentalist. Like the Taliban fighting a jihad," Dr. Yunus shouted. "A lot of people worship Ganpati, not just Hindus, but how many would take their faith to this extent?"

"So he isn't a psychopath?" Mugbe asked.

Dr. Yunus looked at him pityingly.

"I didn't say that," he sneered at Mugbe, "psychopaths don't care for God, and if your suspect is one, then he's committing murder for his own carnal pleasure. For instant gratification. Not religion."

The policemen looked at one another blankly.

Dr. Yunus stamped around the room, arms behind his back, peering at them from up close. Stopping beside Ferraz, he asked, "Remember Ayatollah Khomeini's *fatwa* in 1989 ordering Muslims to kill Salman Rushdie for blasphemy in his controversial novel *The Satanic Verses?*"

"Wasn't the *fatwa* revoked in 1998?" asked Ferraz.

"Not the point," Dr. Yunus said rudely. "The *point* is that it was a violent reaction by the supreme religious and political leader of Iran. But moderate Muslims around the world ignored it. Why do some people become Islamist terrorists and not all your Miyabhais from Bhendi Bazaar?"

"I don't know," Ferraz said, feeling like he was in school.

"Those people are suffering from mania," Dr. Yunus yelled.

"*Mania?*" said Nawalkar blankly, "What's that?"

"It's a mental illness marked by periods of great excitement and violent behavior," said Dr. Yunus. "Mania is a manifestation of bipolar disorder which is associated with extreme mood swings. From high to low. Mania to depression. Bipolars are easily agitated in mania. They have high energy, racing thoughts, impaired judgment, and unrealistic overconfidence."

Nawalkar stirred uneasily.

"What's this got to do with us?" he asked irritably.

"I think your killer's bipolar," Dr. Yunus told Nawalkar. "Someone can be bipolar and also a psychopath. He's risky and extremely dangerous. If he's in a manic phase, it could last for hours, days, weeks and even months."

Nawalkar was more confused than ever.

"What's bipolar?" he asked. "We've only dealt with schizophrenics."

Dr. Yunus puffed up his chest and put on his best lecturer's air.

"A schizo is unlikely to be your killer," he said. "Schizophrenia is a mental condition characterized by delusions of persecution, suspicion, jealousy and exaggerated self-importance."

"What do psychopaths suffer from?" Ferraz asked quietly.

"From an abnormality in their psychological personality. It's a conduct disorder that takes root in childhood," Dr. Yunus said. "Psychos have disturbed childhoods in which they hurt and harm people, torture animals, commit arson, and not for personal benefit – but because it gives them sadistic pleasure to see other people suffer. Psychopaths are venomous, violent and dangerous. They're creative in a destructive way. They have negative intelligence. They enjoy mutilating, raping and murdering people."

"And bipolars?" Savde asked Dr. Yunus.

"The world is full of bipolars. Several megalomaniacs, multi-millionaires, actors, scientists and politicians are bipolars," the psychiatrist said. "It's a mental illness that changes moods and energy. A bipolar is happy and excited when in mania. Low and dejected when in depression. When he is both, happy and dejected, the bipolar is in hypomania. He starts believing he has superpowers and can do anything – even commit murder. But otherwise bipolars are charming, confident people. Creatively brilliant and smart. Smarter than the police. That's why terrorists are hard to catch. Bipolars are also boastful. Like your killer. Like the Islamist terrorists and Naxalites. They want the world to know about their glory."

"Is that why he's sending us these cryptic verses?" Mugbe said.

"Maybe that's his high," Dr. Yunus replied. "Are the verses helping your investigation? Giving you clues to understand the murders? Helping you to identify the killer? No! So they are of no value to the investigation. He's jeering at you. Showing off his superior intelligence."

"But the verses seem to have been selected with the victims in mind."

"Forget them," Dr. Yunus said, "they will misdirect the investigation and lead you to a dead end."

Ferraz asked, "Can devotion and fanaticism go together?"

"You're asking if the killer can also be spiritually inclined?"

"Like a split personality," Rathod suggested again.

"Bipolars and psychopaths will do anything if they can justify the action to themselves. It doesn't matter how crazy it's to the outside world – it has to make sense to them. Your killer appears to be trying to right some perceived wrong. He's punishing the victims. These are well-planned, revenge murders. Violence is his means to achieve his end."

"How do we find him?" asked Rathod.

"I wish you had a decent sample of his voice," Dr. Yunus complained. "It would have given me or any psychoanalyst, criminologist or voice expert the opportunity to analyze this fellow. A lot of inferences can be made from a voice. Whether he is a North Indian or from the

South, a Catholic from Goa, a Bong from Kolkata or a Miyabhai from Hyderabad. Each has a typical way of talking. An expert would identify that."

"Really?" said Nawalkar in surprise, "I spoke to him briefly twice and I couldn't make out at all. He had a regular *Bambaiya* voice."

"I see," said Dr. Yunus staring at him. "I would have told you if he was suffering from mania or depression. I would have guessed his age. Known whether he's illiterate or educated. Single or a family man. Genuinely restless and irritable or just trying to taunt you. Such persons have DID. That's Dissociative Identity Disorder. They have two identities. One is the host, his original identity. The other is his alter identity, which triggers his deadly actions. In the alter identity, his voice will change, he will speak quickly, his aggression will show."

"You'd know just by listening to him?" the CP asked incredulously.

"Not just listening," Dr. Yunus corrected him, "but talking to him intelligently. I would try and find out what he's going to do next. How and what he has suffered in the past. Whether there is anything we can do to help him. I would figure out whether he's delusional, hallucinating or if he's a drug addict. I would try to understand his thoughts and moods which would give me an insight to make a judgment on the situation. He could be just depressed. Maximum suicides are committed by people unable to cope with daily anxieties. It's not just HIV and cancer that cause people to hang themselves or take the leap."

"Why did he choose these victims?" Ferraz asked.

"Can't tell," Dr. Yunus said. "He has treated his victims as inhuman objects to be violated for his own amusement. At first he was aggrieved, but now he's become the aggressor. He's mentally unbalanced and delusional, he wants to be in control of his victims, to decide where, when and how they will die. Go through your records for incidents where somebody has desecrated Ganpati. Or mocked the Lord through ads, cartoons, movies, TV shows, songs. Such people are potential victims."

"Are all psychopathic killers alike?" Rathod asked.

"No," said Dr. Yunus. "Your guy is control-oriented. But there are sadistic killers who get pleasure through inflicting pain. Hedonistic killers who murder for lust. Some are predatory killers, they hunt for victims and murder for sport. And you have the mission-oriented killers, they target those that are unworthy of living, like prostitutes. But are you sure you aren't dealing with a gang? Why are you convinced one person's behind these Ganpati killings?"

"A gang?" said Nawalkar in surprise.

"Yes, why not?" Dr. Yunus said mildly. "Your serial killer could be a gang performing black magic and conducting human sacrifices. Ah, don't look shocked! It's happening in West Bengal. There are fanatical religious groups carrying out barbaric and ritualistic assassinations, especially beheadings in temples, in the name of Goddess Kali."

"Human sacrifice!" said Rathod, aghast.

"I was called to Birbhum district where the blood-splattered, beheaded torso of a young man was found in a Kali temple. Post-mortem revealed he had been drugged and slaughtered. What was chilling were the articles of worship found with the body. Marigold flowers, burnt incense sticks, a bottle of *alta* – the red dye Bengali women use on their feet at the time of religious ceremonies, an earthen saucer smeared with blood kept before an idol of Kali, a lemon and a black voodoo doll with pins."

"Who was the killer?" asked Nawalkar curiously.

"The local priest," Dr. Yunus replied after a pause, "and the police were reluctant to arrest him because of an inbred fear of Kali. The goddess is a ferocious slayer of evil, according to Hindu mythology, and is believed to have an insatiable appetite for blood. Myth is that Kali looks after those who look after her."

Intrigued, Nawalkar asked, "The government can't stop this?"

"How, when an entire village chooses a victim and cuts off his head in secret ceremonies with his parents' consent?" Dr. Yunus said disparagingly.

"This grisly practice continues?" Nawalkar asked, disbelievingly.

"A Press Trust of India (PTI) report stated that in the last three years, more than 2,500 young boys and girls were sacrificed to Kali," Dr. Yunus replied.

"All in West Bengal?"

"No," Dr. Yunus said ominously, "it's also happening here in Maharashtra."

MONDAY

19

NICOLE RAJA came awake with a moan.

What in the hell was happening to her?

Her head was splitting. Bright neon flashes exploded behind her eyes every time she blinked. She could hear her heart pounding in her ears like surf on a beach. She could taste the bile rising in her throat. And her mouth felt like the bottom of a parrot's cage, as one veteran drinker had described the hangover symptoms.

She was tripping on last night's binge.

Her world was a purple haze. She was groping her way down a twisting passage that was illuminated by flickering candles in tiny niche-like windows. Behind, silk curtains billowed in a strong breeze. Her faltering steps were guided by dance music. It was coming from a door at the end of the passage. In a half-dream she stumbled on, blindly grabbing at the haunting strains of the violin that floated past her.

The door was the entrance to a restaurant.

A gigantic lizard, pompously dressed like the *maitre d'hôtel*, waited outside with a reservation list and an air of hauteur. Beyond, in the dark recesses, a six piece band of frogs was playing *The Blue Danube*. A pair of bandicoots was whirling about in a soulful waltz. And flitting between tables, taking orders from other creatures, were crows in waiters' uniforms with white gloves on their claws.

She was hallucinating like Alice in Wonderland!

She looked at the clock by her bedside. It was 1 pm.

Where had the morning gone!

With an effort Nicole sat up in bed.

The eiderdown slid off her slender arms and body and settled around her waist, exposing the immaculate sweep of her throat and the arch of her full breasts. Waves of shoulder-length auburn colored hair tumbled down in a blaze against the stark white pillows.

She was amazed to find herself in last night's clothes.

The salmon pink tank top and high-rise magenta skinny jeans picked off Colaba Causeway for that 'Copy Cat for Less' story in *Cosmo*. She hadn't known what kind of evening lay ahead when her friend Zahra coaxed her to join this rave party a friend was throwing in a Bandra nightclub. Expect a heterogeneous crowd, Zahra had said. Some models, cricketers, Bollywood stars, the expats frat. And the Candy Man!

The outfit hugged her in all the right places and made her look cool, graceful and trendy. Which she knew she was. Even at 40, which she had gracefully turned in February. The Big 4-O milestone birthday.

Nicole was strikingly attractive. She was a former Bangalore fashion model of mixed parentage, she had her Parsi mother's elegance and her Sikh father's handsomeness. She was stylish and radiated beauty. Her chiseled physique made her the envy of women half her age. But she worked twice as hard as them to stay in shape. She had no children to raise and after her modeling career ended, she was content to be a socialite.

Nicole Raja was always the flavor of the season.

In demand everywhere – from fashion parties at the Cavalli Club in Dubai and F1 celebrations in Singapore to Christmas dinners at the Dorchester in London and summer brunches on Phuket beaches.

Everybody important aspired to be her friend. She was bewitching to look at. And scintillating company, besides.

Last night, she vaguely remembered some stranger telling her that the light pink color of the tank top complemented her dewy complexion.

Dewy complexion!

The golden tan of Bali was just fading from… but after four drinks, well, it was not the man but the alcohol that was talking.

Served her right for partying with…

Gosh! The party! And the police raid!

It all came back to her now.

Fuck, why hadn't she called up Ashfaque!

Her husband Ashfaque Raja, the city's leading labor lawyer, was in Delhi representing a captain of industry in an Employees State Insurance Scheme fraud.

She would have called him… if the police had arrested her!

When the cops arrived, she was in the ladies' room with Zahra. They had taken their coke and straw, giggling like teenagers – and they weren't *sipping* cola; this was their fifth medium-size line of the night.

Just before that, Nicole had downed eight tequila shots. Licking the salt off the back of her hand first. Then tossing her head back and swallowing the 1.5 oz of raw Mexican spirit in one gulp. And following this by sucking a lemon wedge and banging the shot glass down. Eight fucking times!

The crowd screaming, *"One tequila, two tequila, three tequila, floor!"* But Nicole had not hit the floor. The tequila burned a fiery trail down her throat to her belly-button. It was like an orgasm centered in her gut!

Zahra and she had taken a few tokes on a joint after that.

Whatever got you through the night was okay, John Lennon said.

Coke was their scene, it was a bonding experience to be crammed in the lavatory with Zahra. Hearing the commotion outside, they had flushed the white dust before opening the door.

The cops were everywhere…

… but the rave party was just hotting up.

Euphoric couples were intimately dancing. The DJ spinning a track with a vodka bottle in hand, screaming incomprehensibly. But the seedy event manager who had brought the Russian prostitutes ("Bollywood extras") knew this was a bust. So did the arrogant cricketers who were loudly arguing with the policemen. The wannabe actresses were looking bored.

Everybody was being herded into police vans. They would be tested for drugs at Cooper Hospital and released. Later, if the tests proved positive, the police would file a chargesheet in the Narcotic Drugs and Psychotropic Substances Court and the "accused" would be issued summons.

Zahra and Nicole covered their faces and got ready.

At the same instant the nightclub owner who was on coke and alcohol, and had been distributing Ecstasy and Liquid Drops to his guests, made a break. He had been full of fight a minute ago. That's what the drug and booze did, it created a third substance called cocaethylene in the bloodstream that was even more lethal than cocaine and whisky on their own.

The cops figured he was the Candy Man…

… the drug peddler.

The nightclub owner bolted, two policemen giving chase. All three went headlong into the DJ's console in a cartwheeling tangle of arms and legs. The music system and speakers came crashing down. Immediately there was silence. That's when somebody switched off the lights. As all hell broke loose – Nicole and Zahra ran.

She wondered if she had been recognized.

She had covered her head and face with the shrug. But the athletic pink tank top exposed her cleavage and toned shoulders. And just below the nape of her neck, Nicole had a tattoo nobody was likely to forget.

She had got it done when she was 18.

After she lost her virginity – like a recommitment to purity.

The tattoo signified becoming an adult. A coming of age. The guys had been turned on. They took her fore and aft – *more aft*, she realized – kissing the tattoo, worshipping her sinfully gorgeous body. She found that hugely erotic.

Getting a tattoo symbolized rebellion and the prevalent rock and roll culture. Those were the disco go-go years, man! The stereotypes went in for hearts and the macho skull-and-daggers; Nicole was a rebel – she chose a religious symbol.

Buddha, Shiva and Sanskrit *shlokas* were popular tattoos.

Foreigners intrigued by Eastern mythology had started the trend. Indians were quick to follow. Many who had lost touch with their roots and felt the need to have something omnipotent with them welcomed the idea of a tattooed presence of God in their lives.

Nicole's tattoo was Ganpati!

It was done in green and red ink and had pink skin undertones.

The tattoo was vibrant and gave the ethereal deity a tactile appeal. She was proud of her tattoo. It had made Page 3 often, playing peek-a-boo from behind backless *cholis*, off-the-shoulder dresses and bikini straps. The Girl with the Ganesh Tattoo… that's how society writers described her.

Her Ganpati tattoo didn't represent religious beliefs, it was more for symbolic value. She believed it brought her good luck. For 22 years, the tattoo had worked like a charm.

But now Nicole was wondering…

… would the Ganpati tattoo be her undoing?

What if she was identified by it at the rave party?

Would the police show up and force her to do a medical

test? Would the coke and alcohol still be in her bloodstream ten hours later?

Should she call up Ashfaque?

She reached for the morning papers that the maid had kept at the foot of the bed. Tomorrow's editions would have the raid on the rave party. She was dying to know what had happened.

Idly, she looked at the front page…

… and dropped the paper with a stifled scream. Like a Bollywood heroine, Nicole clapped her hand dramatically to her throat.

'PSYCHO STRIKES AGAIN!' the headline screamed.

Below it a strap line said, **'Serial killer claims fourth victim.'**

Swiftly she read Sanghamitra Sarkar's murder report.

Then sat motionless, thinking.

Her heart was thumping violently.

Her hands were shaking, her body was trembling.

She knew why the Bengali singer had been murdered!

It was the song – the Ganpati song!

That explained the other murders.

She had been following the story. Something had been pricking her mind after Seth's killing. She hadn't been able to put a finger on it. It was like she knew something that was eluding the police. And now… it was her fear about the tattoo that made the picture shockingly clear.

Ganpati was the link between the victims.

Poor Haider first, their friend for years, stabbed and beheaded on the eve of his *Ganpati* exhibition. Then the British diplomat's wife, with whom Nicole had worked on Asian charities in London, her throat slit on the morning after her *Ganpati* party which Ashfaque and she attended. And Seth, who played golf with Ashfaque and invited them to Pune for the derby where his colt Namasthetu, named after *Ganpati*, was the favorite. Now this singer from Kolkata… here to promote her Indipop number on *Ganpati*.

Nicole was chilled by the realization.

HE KNEW she partied hard.

He disliked her taking Lord Ganesh along like an escort. To these drink, drug and sex orgies where the trip was not spiritual. That was disrespectful. It made him want to…

… but no getting blood on his hands today.

He didn't want the police to think he was like Tony Perkins from *Psycho*, holding the knife overhead. My, how much that one had bled yesterday! Not as much as the painter, though.

He was thinking about her tattoo.

Some people chose tattoos to represent their religious beliefs. It took resounding faith to get one done. A tattoo was like a touchstone of that person's devotion. When they lost their way in life, the tattoo reminded them to become spiritual again.

But it was still an abomination of the body.

And she had chosen Lord Ganesh!

Getting the tattoo done was an act of vilification.

Showing it off vulgarly was blasphemy.

Problem was Ganpati was the most popular religious tattoo in the world. Hundreds of Americans, Chinese and Germans who understood nothing about Hinduism got Ganpati tattoos done.

He was appalled at this – *this* creation of skin religion

Celebrities who made tattoos popular, had the least faith.

The beautiful Hollywood actress Alyssa Milano had a Rosary on her right shoulder blade, a Sacred Heart on her lower back and Buddhist tattoos on her wrist. She also had 'Om' tattooed on the base of her neck. Miley Cyrus, the sexually explicit pop star, also sported an 'Om' tattoo on her left wrist. And the S&M singer Rihanna had a verse from the Bhagavad Gita inked upside down on her hip. Bollywood stars tattooed the names of their girlfriends and children on their arms, chests and backs. He was okay with that.

He looked at the clock on Grant Road Railway Station.

It was 1 pm. He stepped onto Sleater Road in the west and with a shuffle and limp slowly made his way towards Nana Chowk. From there he would walk to Kemp's Corner. And then to Nepean Sea Road where she had a penthouse in Manek Abad on Setalvad Lane.

He pulled out his little transistor.

Pakistan was chasing 88 runs on the last day of the only Test against Zimbabwe at the Queens Sports Club in Bulawayo. The match was about to begin, India was three-and-half hours ahead of Zimbabwe.

NICOLE QUICKLY got over her fright.

She had to share her discovery with somebody.

Her cell rang. It was Ashfaque!

"*Jaan!*" she had never been more eager to talk to him.

"*Kya haal hai!*"

Ashfaque always said that.

"Listen, you know those murders?" she blurted out.

"Which murders? Haider's and Seth's..."

"The police suspect a psychopath. But they have no clue why he's murdering these people. You're following the news?"

"Yeah, I heard... And I *also* heard about the rave party!"

"Who told you!" Nicole demanded.

"Oh, I have my sources," he replied primly.

"You do, huh?" she said. "A lot of people got picked up."

"I know... and if it's proved they consumed drugs, *finito*!"

"What happens to them then?"

"It depends... they are charged under the Narcotic Drugs and Psychotropic Substances Act of 1985 and the punishment depends on the quantity of drugs involved."

"Like what, give me an example, Ash."

"I'm not a criminal lawyer, Nixie," he gently reminded her, "Ask Satish, he's forever defending film stars accused of drug abuse.

Possession and trafficking attract different sentences, I know. The court is harsher on the peddler than the user."

"*Jaan*... what if somebody identifies me?"

"What do you mean?"

"Zahra and me, we got out unnoticed."

"So – why are you worried? The cops can't... *wait a minute*, were there TV cameras at the raid? Did the police invite the media?"

"No, there was no television or press."

"Then what's there to worry about?"

"But what if somebody saw my Ganpati tattoo?"

"So what? How will they prove you were there?"

"*Jaan*, there's another thing," she said hesitantly. "You know this psychopathic serial killer?"

"Yeah, the police believe the same person killed Haider and Seth, that's what I'm hearing. Listen, are we on for dinner with the Mahimturas on Saturday? They're leaving for Colombo after that."

"He also killed Esther Nieves – remember we went for her party on Thursday? And some young Indipop singer from Kolkata yesterday."

"Wow, what's the city coming to!"

"What if I'm next?"

"*You!* Why would he want to kill you, Nixie? My God, what did you have last night? I'm glad the cops didn't arrest you!"

"I'm serious. Can't you see... there's a link to the murders?"

"What link? I can't see any link! Neither have the police so far."

"*Jaan,* the link is Ganpati," she said with a catch in her voice.

"*Ganpati!* Are you PMSing or what? Or are you playing *Criminal Case* on Facebook and testing your investigative skills in solving puzzling crimes?

"I've got a theory," she said in a scared voice.

"Listen Nixie, you're sounding stressed. Take a Crocin and lie down till this... *this* Ganpati feeling passes away. I've got to go, now.

My case is up on board after lunch. I heard about the rave party and called. Court gets over at 5.30. I'll give you a tinkle then on my way to the airport. I'm booked on the 8.20 Indigo tonight. Stay indoors and keep out of trouble."

And Ashfaque Raja disconnected.

DAMN ASHFAQUE, he hadn't heard her out.

Nicole looked at the papers again. There was a picture of Joint CP (Crime) Arun Rathod and another policeman with the story. Ashfaque and she knew the IPS officer well, they were members of the same club, and they had bumped into him just last week. Arun had promised to "catch up over coffee". Everybody said that – nobody meant it.

She could have called Arun. But what if he knew she had been at the rave party? Would he think she was calling for help and using the serial killings as an excuse? Or would he patiently listen to her hunch about this Ganpati killer? Why should he? Her own husband had laughed!

She looked at the papers again.

And this time her gaze fell on Ferraz. *Whoa!* Who was this guy? He was undoubtedly a cop. He had that expression. But he also had a tough and deliciously dangerous look. He was standing next to Arun with his arms folded, a picture of strength and controlled violence. She read the caption. And Ferraz's name registered.

Wasn't he the 26/11 cop whom Nahida Shaikh had featured?

Yes, she was sure he was!

The newspapers said Inspector Ferraz of the Crime Branch was the investigating officer of the serial murders. With a naughty smile, Nicole picked up her phone and located Nahida Shaikh's number.

Her finger on the dial key, she paused.

What would she tell the police? That she had an idea why the murders were taking place? Or that she had a premonition? Of what, they would ask.

"That I might be next – see my Ganpati tattoo!"

They would think she was acting like somebody in *Final Destination* where the villain was the entity Death itself and the protagonists had premonitions about their fates.

She hesitated, one long finger tapping the phone indecisively.

Then she texted Nahida: "Hi. Do you have Inspector Ferraz's number?"

NEPEAN SEA Road was being widened.

Work had stopped for lunch on the thoroughfare named after British Governor Sir Evan Nepean. The machines were idle. Excavators that dug trenches and laid foundations; bulldozers that collected soil and emptied it into dumpers; cement mixers, water tankers and a paver machine to lay the asphalt. All on standby. Sitting on its iron haunches amid drums of tar, sacks of cement and mounds of sand and broken stones was a bright green road roller waiting to rumble.

Of the workforce, there was no sign. After lunch, labor in India compulsorily laid down its tools and put up its feet. It had to have 40 winks.

He reached Setalvad Lane.

It ran perpendicular to Nepean Sea Road. At their junction was an old bungalow called Ila Kunj. He looked over his shoulder. In the distance over a green haze that would be Malabar Hill he spotted large birds circling the grey monsoon sky. Below would be the Tower of Silence. The final resting place for Zoroastrians in Mumbai. The birds… were they vultures come to feed on the bodies? No, Mumbai had no more vultures.

Turning, he entered Setalvad Lane unobserved.

It was 3 pm. Right on schedule. Manek Abad was at the end, a six-storied building with stilt parking and 'In' and 'Out' gates.

NICOLE LOOKED at Ferraz's number.

Nahida had texted it to her without question.

She didn't know what to do now.

How should she introduce herself to this cop?

Why not just text Arun Rathod, instead?

She needn't bring up the rave party. Just text her notion and leave it at that. This was murder, after all; she sure as hell didn't want to get involved.

Her phone rang.

It was Ela Kapoor, Delhi's inveterate socialite.

"*Dahlin*, will you be going for the NY Fashion Week?" Ela trilled. "I'm told Diane von Furstenberg has invited the maximum number of celebrities to attend her show. And she has chosen to show on Sunday so that the men can attend, have you heard?"

"Yup, and I'm trying to get Ash to join me," Nicole replied.

"Ashfaque? Why, are courts closed in September?"

"No… but last time at NYFW I bumped into Sarah Jessica Parker, she was chatting with Barry Diller – he's DVF's husband, you know, and the tattlers say he has the biggest sailboat in New York."

"I've been on it," Ela sniffed, "he docked it in the French Riviera during party season last year – and, my, what a blowout he had! Valentino was there but you won't believe who attracted more paparazzi? Oscar de la Renta! You were telling me about Ashfaque… and Sarah Jessica Parker popped into the picture. Why? I'm afraid I've lost you, *dahlin*."

"He's a big fan of Sarah's," Nicole said.

"Who, Ashfaque?" asked Ela in surprise. "But listen, come with me… I'm invited to Lorry Newhouse's tea party at her plush Central Park West apartment. She's showing her Spring-Summer collection."

"Her husband Mark is a bore. All he can talk about is his frigging newspaper business," Nicole grumbled.

"So what? Fern Mallis will be there."

"I know Fern, she introduced me to Calvin Klein and Donna Karan."

"*Dahlin*, I know Donna from Puff Daddy's 'White Party' of years ago. I'm hoping to bump into Philip Green in New York. I need an escort for the London Fashion Week and he invited me last year. Anyway, you let me know your POA by the EOD, *mwaah*!"

SETALVAD LANE was a picturesque mix of the old and new.

At its head was Bota Manzil looking like a Parsi fire temple. The 1916 mansion was yellow and had blue window grills, a white gate and pillars, with bamboo and bougainvillea in the garden and parrots singing in the trees. Attenborough had shot portions of *Gandhi* here.

The Rubans was also a nice building; it had blue window ledges and roof, impressive gateposts and palms swaying in the breeze. Madhav Vilas was another old-fashioned residence with a stone courtyard full of potted plants and a lamp-post near the gate. A fat ginger cat sat on the low garden wall and looked at him with green suspicious eyes.

He passed Manek Abad. A bored-looking watchman sat at the gate. No problem. The watchman would go to the pump-room behind the building soon. Setalvad Lane got its municipal water at this hour. And the watchman immediately pumped it up to the overhead tanks. It was his duty every afternoon. The gate was unattended for 10 minutes. He planned to make his entry then.

SHE DIALED Ferraz's number.

"Yes," he answered immediately.

"Er, Inspector Ferraz?" she said nervously.

"Who is this?" he asked sharply.

She cringed on hearing his cop voice. He seemed to be on the road. There was the sound of so much traffic behind him. She almost hung up.

"Um, this is Nicole Raja," she said, hesitating. If he showed signs of not recognizing her name, she would disconnect and give up.

"Yes?" he said again, curiously.

"I got your number from Nahida – *you know* Nahida Shaikh, the TV girl? I hope you don't mind my asking her… Er, I also know Arun Rathod, he's a family friend."

"I see," Ferraz said without enthusiasm.

"There's something I want to tell you," she said quickly.

"What is that?"

"Not like this… I'd like to… can we meet?"

"You want to meet me? Why?" asked Ferraz in surprise.

"It's about these serial murders you are investigating."

"Uh-huh… *what* about them?"

"I might have the missing piece to your puzzle!"

"Puzzle? Missing piece? I'm not getting you, ma'am."

"I think I know why the murders are being committed."

"You think!"

He was silent. She looked at his picture in the paper and visualized him digesting this hot potato she had just dropped in his lap.

"Inspector, are you there?"

"Have you discussed this with Mr. Rathod, ma'am?"

"Nicole – *my* name is Nicole."

"Um, ok… have you… has Mr. Rathod asked you to call me?"

"No! Surely I can speak to you without his permission?"

"What is it you want to tell me, ma'am?"

She thought she caught a smile in his voice.

"I'm not going to tell you if you keep addressing me as ma'am. It makes me feel like a school teacher! You can call me Nicole. Or Nixie, friends call me that. You won't be breaking any law."

"You said you had information," Ferraz reminded her.

"Yes… it might help you to, well, understand the link between the victims and maybe anticipate who's next."

"How do you know there's going to be another murder?"

"You're not listening… I said meet me!"

"Where are you calling from ma'am?"

"Home!"

"Where's that?"

"Nepean Sea Road," she replied, rolling her eyes. "Where are you, Inspector? Crawford Market? Can you come immediately?"

"Crawford Market? No, I'm on Altamont Road," he said.

Probably following the Nieves murder, she thought.

"Oh good… you're not far off. It should take you five minutes to get to Nepean Sea Road. Can you come – immediately?"

"Now? Um, okay," he said, sounding doubtful. "But I wish you'd tell me what you know on the phone. Time is running out."

"Are you in uniform?" she asked, surprising Ferraz.

"No ma'am."

"Are you carrying a gun?"

"But what's–"

"Okay listen, if I help you today, you've got to promise that you'll help me when I need a cop."

"Why would you need a cop with a gun?"

"Oh, it's got nothing to do with the gun," she chided him. "Suppose I get busted at a rave party? Could you fix it for me? Or if I'm arrested for drinking and driving?"

"But I'm not in Narcotics or Traffic."

"Yeah, but you're a cop… and they are cops."

"Why don't you ask Mr. Rathod?"

"And tell him I go to rave parties and drink and drive… thanks!"

"But you're telling me," he protested.

"Well... you're a different kind of cop," she said lamely.

"I am?" he sounded astonished, "How is that?"

"Never mind," she sighed in his ear.

"Listen, ma'am..."

"Nicole... *say* Nicole! Okay, what if my car gets towed away... that happens all the blinking time, your Traffic cops are greedy for money... will you get it back for me by making a call? I've been told you can fix anything in this city, even murder, if you know the police."

"Who told you that!"

"Never mind! Do you want my help... or not?"

"I thought you *wanted* police help," Ferraz said, confused.

"Only when I'm in a spot... do I have your promise?"

He hesitated, "I'll try, but there's no guarantee."

"*Phew!* Thanks... okay, get to Nepean Sea Road and call me."

She disconnected and took a deep breath.

Getting up, she rushed out of the bedroom. Josephine, her maid and cook, was out for the afternoon. She had prepared a light lunch for Nicole. Her driver Amarjit, she now remembered, would be waiting to take her to this new Thai salon in Breach Candy for a massage. She dashed into the kitchen and took a Bacardi Breezer out of the EuroCave. Humming, she stepped into the shower with the pint.

SETALVAD LANE came to a dead end.

He could hear the sea beyond the bordering wall with its coconut palms and smell the tang of the salt breeze. There was evidence that people performed their toilet here. He turned away in disgust.

He was standing outside Jeevan Jyot, an ugly yellow building with a troubled history behind whose closed gates he could hear reconstruction work. This was where, in April 1959, the cuckolded

Indian Navy Commander Kawas Maneckshaw Nanavati shot dead his English wife Sylvie's lover, the dashing Sindhi society playboy Prem Ahuja.

He wondered who lived in the Ahuja flat now.

Against the wall holding back the sea was a Sarvajanik Ganpati installed by the Rahiwasi Mandal. There was nobody around. He slipped in and bowed his head before the small idol. Stepping out, he switched on his transistor and shuffled and limped towards Manek Abad.

HER PHONE was ringing!

Just when she was in the shower – it never failed!

Naked, she dashed out and took the call.

"Hullo," she said breathlessly.

"This is Inspector Ferraz."

"I know," she said.

"I'm in Setalvad Lane."

"Oh… how did you detect I stay here?"

"I asked Mr. Rathod," Ferraz said.

"Inspector! You didn't need Arun's permission to visit me!"

"I didn't take it… Tell me which building, please."

"Smart cop like you can't figure that out?"

She was flirting with him now.

"Well, no," he said, not taking her bait.

"Okay, it's Manek Abad, 6th floor. Come on up…"

HE SIDLED into the driveway of Manek Abad.

Nobody around. He could hear the hum of an air-conditioner from a flat above. And the sound of somebody washing clothes. That *thwack!* of wet clothing hitting the floor was unmistakable. It was a middle class sound. Somebody's washing machine was bust and the maid was doing the dirty laundry by hand. From the back of the building came the buzz of a motor running in the pump-room and the high-pitched hum of water rushing up vibrating pipes to the overhead tanks.

The watchman was busy.

The building did not employ a liftman.

But there was always the risk of running into a resident.

And he didn't want to run into anybody here.

He paused at the steps to the lobby, his body taut with tension.

Was he imagining an ominous silence, suddenly?

The birds had stopped twittering in the trees.

He remembered Damien, the son of Satan in the *Omen,* driving the baboons to a frenzy when he visited the zoo. They recognized him as the Antichrist. Animals had a sixth sense. Maybe the birds here had a foreboding of what was going to happen.

He looked around uneasily.

What was that sound, now?

It was coming from the side of the building.

He retraced his steps and peered around a stilt cautiously.

A uniformed driver was lazily flicking a white Audi SUV with a dust cloth beneath the trees. He was whistling tunelessly. Her car! So she was planning to leave. Not by the Audi, he chuckled to himself.

THE RAJA residence would never make *GoodHomes.*

It wasn't showy, but it was comfy; understated luxury and simple elegance. Nicole had done it herself. The hall reflected personality and warmth. Full length sliding glass windows offered an unobstructed view of the outdoors. With so much natural light, Nicole had dispensed with overhead chandeliers. She had installed multiple small lights, spotlights and table lamps that could alternately be switched on creating spaces and moods that were cozy. Three large, hand-finished prints of MF Husain's Mother Teresa series took up one wall of the hall.

The furniture was modern, dark chocolate corner leather sofas and footstools to complement the cream walls, good enough for family lounging or formal entertaining. A solid oak dining table that could comfortably seat eight, ten at a squeeze, stood in one corner with a candelabrum in the centre. Indoor potted plants gave the hall a bright, funky look, lifting the spirits with their quiet, pleasing and unobtrusive presence.

Opening out from the hall were doors to the kitchen, Ashfaque's study, the master bedroom, two guest rooms, and Nicole's exercise studio. They had the entire sixth floor to themselves, two three-bedroom flats.

Nicole felt a hot flush of excitement.

She was wearing white Citizens of Humanity jeans and a black and white striped Mango T-shirt with no bra. The T-shirt easily slid of her shapely shoulders to expose the Ganpati tattoo. She wondered if Inspector Ferraz would want to see it.

She had sprayed a little Gardenia Passion on her wrists and elbows, the base of her throat, on her cleavage and in her navel – all the body's pulse points where blood vessels were closest to the skin. It reacted with body heat to emit scent. Fashion designer Coco Chanel had said that a woman should apply perfume in those areas where she would like to be kissed.

The doorbell rang.

20

FERRAZ PARKED near the 'Out' gate.

He looked at the building in surprise.

It was, he thought, pretty ordinary. Not what he expected Nicole and Ashfaque Raja to be putting up in on posh Nepean Sea Road.

He had informed Arun Rathod of her call.

The Joint CP (Crime), amused at the society hostess' play for his cop, had warned Ferraz with a laugh, "Beware Angelo, she's a man eater!"

"So I've heard, sir," Ferraz said, "maybe she has something worthwhile to say. Sometimes leads come from the unlikeliest sources. This woman has socialized with Haider, Seth and Nieves."

"I agree," Rathod said. "She gets around, *this woman* – as you say. No harm in meeting her. As a person, she is lovely. If she gets tricky, I'll handle her."

"Tricky?"

"Cherchez la femme!" said Rathod hanging up.

Ferraz, who didn't know any French, wondered what he meant.

He entered the lobby and called for the lift. It was 3.25 pm.

Nothing happened. He pressed the call button again. High up in the elevator shaft, he could hear a bell ringing. Somebody had left the lift door open. He waited a minute, then buzzed again. The lift remained where it was. Irritated, Ferraz took the stairs. Sixth floor, she had said.

He sighed and began climbing.

THE DOORBELL rang again.

Ferraz had made good time, Nicole was thinking. It was 3.25 pm. She opened the door with her sexiest smile.

"Hullo there," she said, one hip provocatively resting against the door frame, an eyebrow raised coquettishly, the voice soft and sensual, like hot chocolate sauce over melting vanilla ice-cream.

But the man at the door was not Inspector Ferraz.

She felt foolish.

Straightening, she regarded him with a puzzled expression.

He stood there silently, hands behind his back.

"Yes?" she said inquiringly, thinking he was a visitor for Josephine.

He smiled briefly in a disquieting manner…

… and just for that instant, a strange light came into his yellow eyes.

Nicole almost missed it.

She gasped and stepped back.

What she had seen in his eyes unsettled her.

She looked at him closely.

He was intimidating… his stillness and that expression, intensely evil and full of contempt. Like he hated her and wished to harm her. But *who* was he and *what* was he doing at her door?

His silent appraisal was beginning to irritate her.

"Excuse me," she said impatiently, and was about to slam the door.

When he stepped forward, forcing her back.

"Moryaa Re!" he said with a chuckle.

And suddenly she was overcome with fear.

She had a horrible feeling she knew who this was.

She caught her breath in a shuddering sob.

He advanced, smiling murderously.

She turned and ran for the bedroom, dropping her phone.

Behind her, she heard the door slam shut and the scuffle of feet.

Petrified, she glanced back.

He was reaching out for her with hooked fingers, his face a rictus of savage, animal fury, his teeth bared in a snarl that chilled her.

She screamed, but there was nobody to hear her.

The bedroom was six feet away. But there was no way she could reach its sanctuary and close the door on him.

The windows!

If she could open them and scream for help.

She swerved, but he anticipated the move and outflanked her.

Like sprinters they headed for the tape in a photo finish.

This can't be happening, her mind cried out!

His right hand clamped down on the nape of her neck with a terrible strength, almost knocking her down. She struggled to shake her head free, but he was holding her in a vise-like grip.

She couldn't even turn sideways to look at him.

Together they hurtled for the windows.

Her feet were moving of their own volition now. She was helpless in his grip. Dazed by the shocking realization of what was happening, she was too dumbstruck with horror to even scream now.

He ran with her, beside her, in a curious shuffling-limping stride, the hand on her neck guiding her to the large glass windows.

Two feet away, he stopped with an abrupt jerk.

His legs splayed out to get a better grip on the laminate flooring.

And like a shot putter he twisted his hips, pulling back his left arm and shoulder, the action building up power and momentum, and extending his right arm he released her with a powerful shove.

Head first, arms flailing wildly, she crashed into the full-length window in a flying, staggering run. The glass cracked and broke beneath the impact, sending a shower of splinters down. Unable to check her rush, Nicole went through the jagged edges that cruelly cut and slashed at her.

For a moment she teetered on the edge, her face a mask of blood, her hands frantically trying to grab the drapes, to hold onto the cane plant, and then in slow motion she overbalanced and fell out with a chilling wail of terror. As she went down, she heard the bamboo wind-chime on the window tinkling in the breeze serenely.

Her life didn't flash before her eyes.

Instead, she saw death rushing up to meet her.

He stood with his arm still extended, like he was seeing her off, the Pope blessing the faithful congregated at St. Peter's Square in Vatican City on Wednesday morning, *dominus vobiscum*…

And as she plunged six stories down, he murmured, "*Moryaa Re!*"

The fall broke her neck.

Nicole landed with a loud and sickening thud on the hard concrete. She rolled over sluggishly and lay on her side, unfeeling and unmoving, broken and bleeding and no longer beautiful.

He didn't bother looking down.

Quickly, he shuffled and limped to the door, picking up her phone. There was not a spot of blood on his person. He chuckled to himself. He looked at the clock. It was 3.27 pm.

Stepping out, he pulled the door shut. He had kept the lift gate open. As it began to descend, he switched on the transistor.

FERRAZ REACHED the third floor…

… when he heard the whine of the lift on its way down.

As it passed him on the landing with a click and a lurch, he glanced at the small glass window on the passage door. A crouching figure inside stared back at him. Then the lift was gone. But there was no mistaking the sound that came from inside as it sank out of sight.

It was cricket commentary on a transistor.

Must be a delivery boy, Ferraz thought…

… and continued climbing to the sixth floor.

He rang her doorbell and waited.

There was silence from beyond the closed door.

He rang again, impatiently giving the bell a double blast.

No sound of footsteps approaching.

What was happening, Ferraz wondered irritably. She was expecting him, she had been on the phone with him minutes ago, where was everybody, surely they had hired help at home.

He rang again. Then put his ear against the door.

He could hear nothing. Surely this wasn't her idea of a joke!

He suddenly remembered the phone and dialed her number.

It rang and rang.

Was she was chatting with somebody…

… and had forgotten he was coming?

Cursing, Ferraz decided to wait for a few minutes.

From the elevator shaft came the sound of the lift making a jerky start and then the whine of it beginning its slow upward journey. He wondered who was coming up now.

HE STOPPED the lift on the first floor.

And from there, he cautiously went down the stairs.

He didn't know who might be waiting in the lobby for the lift.

But there was nobody.

The ominous silence of before was absolute and palpable.

Stealthily, he crept between the cars of the stilted parking lot, heading for the 'Out' gate. He could see her now – or what was remaining of her – lying in a dark crimson patch near the 'In' gate. He knew she was dead. Her driver and the watchman, who had heard the sound of her falling and come running, were staring at the body in shock and disbelief. They appeared to be incapable of action. Then the driver began hitting his forehead with his palm and yammering incoherently.

He slipped into Setalvad Lane…

Elvis has left the building!

… and took out her cell.

It was a shiny white iPhone 4, flat and thin, with a glass face and stainless steel rim. It had the touch screen. He hated touch screens, they made texting difficult. But he had an SMS for the Police Commissioner. Fumbling with the touch-and-type keyboard, he wrote:

'*Why am I always on the edge?*
Why am I always looking down
and wondering if I can fly?
Shall I try?
Shall I try to go where nobody's ever gone?'

He was about to hit the send key when he saw the BSA Gold Star with its chrome-plated fuel tank bearing the famous red and gold emblem. 'POLICE' was written in red letters on the rear number plate, and a siren was fitted on the crash guard.

It hadn't been there when he arrived, he was sure of that.

What was the police doing here?

He started down Setalvad Lane when her phone rang, startling him.

Inspector Ferraz was calling!

He couldn't believe his eyes.

This was *that* cop…

… the fellow investigating the murders.

Were the police onto him? Did they know? How could they? Even if they figured out *why* – they would never guess *who* was next. Or they would have been waiting here for him.

But why was this cop calling her, then?

Was that big police bike his?

And then it struck him!

That's who he saw when the lift was going down.

The Inspector had been on his way up, in plainclothes.

That explained the blatant sexual invitation on her face when she opened the door, the come-into-my-parlor tone in her voice, that shameless bitch. She had been expecting the cop.

Instead, she had got him!

But had the Inspector seen him in the lift?

Would he put two and two together?

Now wasn't the time to wait and find out!

He ran out of Setalvad Lane, shuffling and limping with anxiety, looking over his shoulder. But nobody was chasing after him. He reached Nepean Sea Road and luck was on his side.

A BEST bus No. 104 was passing. It slowed down right where he was because construction workers were trundling a wheelbarrow of cement slowly in front.

Impatiently, the bus driver honked.

He stepped onto the footboard and was carried away.

As Setalvad Lane went out of sight, he looked back.

Nobody was coming in pursuit; he sighed with relief.

The bus was packed. The conductor had not seen him hop on board at this unscheduled halt. He bought a ticket for Grant Road Station.

He couldn't get over how – *and why* – Inspector Ferraz had suddenly arrived at Nicole Raja's residence. That had been close. He found he was trembling. But was that a coincidence? How much did this cop know? Maybe he ought to take him seriously. He looked at her phone thoughtfully. Maybe it was time to change the players in the game.

THE LIFT shuddered to a halt at the sixth floor.

Amarjit the driver fell out, trembling.

"*Madam... madam,*" he stammered.

He seemed unable to control his shaking body.

"What happened?" Ferraz snapped, "Who are you? Where's madam?"

The driver's face was ashen, his eyes were wide and staring, he swallowed several times but no words came from his mouth. He looked like he had seen a ghost and was about to faint.

Ferraz grabbed him by the shoulders.

But the driver kept shaking his head, moaning and pointing down.

He suddenly vomited in the passage.

Fuck, thought Ferraz and leaped for the lift.

He pulled the driver in with him.

As they went down, he got Rathod on speed dial.

"Sir, something's wrong," he said urgently.

"What do you mean?" asked Rathod in a tight voice.

"I think something has happened…"

"To the wom – to Nicole Raja, you mean?"

"Yes, sir. Give me a minute."

Rathod waited in suspense as Ferraz rushed around Manek Abad to where the driver was pointing. The watchman stood there in deathly silence.

Rathod heard a sharp intake of breath. And then Ferraz cursed.

"Sir…"

"What!"

"It's… she appears to have fallen out…"

"From her penthouse?"

"… we'll have to check upstairs–"

"Angelo, are you telling me… is she dead?"

"I think so, sir," Ferraz said feeling for a pulse on Nicole's neck.

Her T-shirt had slipped off her shoulder.

And then… he saw the Ganpati tattoo!

Ferraz squeezed his eyes tightly shut. He could not believe what he was seeing.

He took a deep shuddering breath. When he opened his eyes

Nicole was still there, lying like a broken and twisted Barbie doll. He looked at the tattoo.

"Sir, she's got a big Ganpati tattoo on her back," he said, choking.

"Oh my God!" Rathod sounded like he was having a heart attack.

"I think she suspected she was next."

"What! Is that why she called you? Was she pushed to her death?"

"I don't know, sir. She had a theory about the murders. But I now think she feared the killer might come after her… because of the tattoo," Ferraz said, hearing Nicole's teasing voice asking him to promise he'd be there if she required police help.

Some fucking help he had been!

"Goddamn… I wish she had just said it out!"

It was now clear to Ferraz.

Nicole had guessed the motive behind the murders. But had she also known who the killer was? Did she open the door to him thinking it was Ferraz?

He felt a shiver going down his spine at this thought.

Ferraz suddenly came out of his shock.

Rathod was saying, "Stay with her, I'm informing the Malabar Hill police. They'll join you in minutes. And I'm coming there myself."

"Sir, he's somewhere nearby," Ferraz said softly, looking around as if he was afraid the killer might overhear him. "She was on the phone with me a few minutes ago. I think he came on foot. I'm going after him."

"Okay," Rathod whispered back.

Ferraz knew he had lost valuable time.

But he had to talk to the driver and watchman first.

He looked up at the sixth floor. Must have been quite a fall.

Nicole had made an effort to protect her head. Her arm bones were broken and protruding and her shoulder joints were grotesquely dislocated. He shuddered to think what injuries her skull must have suffered. She would have broken her spine as well.

Few features of her strikingly attractive face were recognizable beneath all the blood because her facial bones were fractured and teeth broken.

Her legs were awry.

From what he knew of deaths caused by falling from great heights, she must have suffered compound fractures to her lower body; the fall would have shattered her pelvis as well and caused great multi-organ damage.

She had bled a lot in those few minutes. There was also cerebrospinal fluid mixed with gray matter and blood. The autopsy would reveal inhaled blood, fat embolism and hemorrhages around the injuries caused by the physical trauma, which meant that Nicole was still alive after she hit the ground.

He felt sick and looked away.

If only the police had warned the city yesterday…

The driver was standing by his side, still trembling violently, but the watchman appeared to be coming around slowly.

"You," Ferraz snapped at him, "who went up to the sixth floor?"

"Nobody *saab*."

"Nobody? Or you didn't see anybody?"

"I went to the pump room for 10 minutes."

"Is that your routine every day?"

"*Haan saab*, water comes now; I have to pump it up."

"So anybody could have gone up in your absence?"

"Possibly *saab*, but Amarjit was here… he would have seen."

"Is that right?" Ferraz asked the driver harshly.

With difficulty, Amarjit pulled his eyes away from the horror on the ground.

"Yes *saab*… I saw you," he stammered. "But nobody… I don't think anybody went up before you. I didn't see anyone."

"Somebody did… and you both missed him. Somebody also came

down the lift when I was going up the stairs. He must have slipped out a few minutes ago. Okay, stay here… don't let anybody touch the body. I'll be back."

He ran out and leaped for his bike…

… one hand feeling for the 9mm S&W reassuringly tucked at his waist.

He roared down Setalvad Lane, braking when he hit Nepean Sea Road, the bike skidding on loose sand and rubble and almost unseating Ferraz.

His heart was hammering. He struggled to get his breath back.

Immediately he looked up at the streetlights.

No fucking CCTV here too!

He looked around frantically for a man on a cell…

… possibly the Cobra calling the CP from Nicole's phone.

Nepean Sea Road had several – passersby going about their lives and businesses, all chatting animatedly on their cells.

Instinctively, he knew the killer was not among them.

Traffic moved slowly in both directions. Ferraz gritted his teeth. Which side to go? Left towards Kemps Corner? Or right towards Walkeshwar? But go and do what? He didn't know what the killer looked like. He had never felt so helpless. Or so responsible for…

His phone buzzed with an incoming SMS.

Impatiently Ferraz hit the 'Open' key.

'*Why am I always on the edge?*
Why am I always looking down
and wondering if I can fly?
Shall I try?
Shall I try to go where nobody's ever gone?'

He knew at once where it had come from.

He recognized the number.

He wanted to be sick, but his phone was ringing. He thought it was Rathod. But his heart did a flip-flop when he saw the number flashing on the screen, the same one from which the SMS had come.

It was Nicole Raja's!

HE HOPPED off the bus on Frere Bridge.

Taking the skywalk to Grant Road Station, he shuffled and limped onto Platform No. 1 and looked at the indicator. Even before he could register what was highlighted, a train rolled in.

It was the 4.23 pm Andheri local.

Just what he wanted!

He boarded the Handicapped Passengers compartment, which was empty, and took a window seat. As the train pulled out of the station, he took out Nicole Raja's phone.

In just over a minute the train reached Mumbai Central. The intercity rail terminus with its many platforms and large concourse was already ablaze with halogen lights because the evening was turning dark.

Two outstation trains were getting ready to leave.

A white WAP5 engine with orange stripes, the workhorse of the Indian Railways, was being coupled to the 12951 Dn Mumbai-Delhi Rajdhani Express. The superfast train with red coaches would depart at 4.40 pm. It would reach Delhi at 8.30 am tomorrow. He could hear the rumble of the engine as the Rajdhani prepared for departure. Beside it, the blue double decker 12921 Dn Mumbai-Surat Flying Ranee waited respectfully for the superior train to leave. It was scheduled to depart at 5.55 pm and would reach Surat at 10.30 tonight.

He looked at her phone…

… and went to the last missed call from Inspector Ferraz.

Slowly and deliberately he pressed Dial.

FERRAZ STARED at his phone, unbelievingly.

He knew who this was. First that chilling poem, now a call.

A shower was beginning to build up.

Raindrops plinked and plonked around but Ferraz was oblivious to the drizzle. Pile drivers and jackhammers were making the mother of all rackets, pneumatic drills were stuttering, bulldozers grinding back and forth in the struggle to move earth, workmen's sledge hammers pounded relentlessly against rock. He made a snap decision and took the call.

"Moryaa Re!"

Ferraz flinched.

In the background…

… another unmistakable racket.

He was on a train!

Ferraz recognized the sound immediately.

The train's wheels were humming as they went clickety-clack over joints and crossings. There came the sudden blast of a horn and the deafening whoosh of another train rattling past at great speed, its sparking wheels screeching, the pantographs howling on the roof. In seconds it was gone.

"Moryaa Re! Inspector," he said again, politely and pointedly.

"Madarchot!" Ferraz shouted, unable to contain his frustration anymore, and then was immediately furious with himself for this impotent reaction.

There came a reprimanding chuckle.

"Inspector… I take exception."

Where the fuck was he?

Almost on cue, Western Railway came up with the answer.

An automated announcement said, "*Pudcha* station, Lower Parel."

It repeated itself in Hindi – "*Aagla* station, Lower Parel."

And then in English – "Next station, Lower Parel."

The message was audible. Ferraz was surprised. On railway stations the announcements were so scratchy and hasty that passengers missed the message and consequently the train!

So, he was reaching Lower Parel!

He had to be on a Bandra, Andheri or Borivli slow train. All three would halt at Lower Parel and every station after that till they terminated. He could get off anywhere, switch off Nicole's phone and disappear. The cell towers wouldn't be able to locate him. And the city would swallow him and keep his secrets safe... until the next murder. Right now, he was just a voice among millions of unknown faces.

Ferraz gritted his teeth again. He could do nothing.

Not even record the conversation on his Nokia 6233.

He wondered if the Cobra knew that.

He cursed himself silently.

Dr. Yunus Miyasahib said that a criminal's voice, the language he spoke, his choice of words and turn of phrase, could give the police some clue about his background. Ferraz decided to listen.

"Why did you call me?" he asked quietly.

His answer was a dry and amused chuckle, then...

"I'm disappointed with society."

"You are, huh?"

"My actions are a consequence of society's unconventional behavior. Insignificant people are getting famous by being amoral, by having no restraints, standards or principles."

His voice was calm. And shockingly cultured.

No symptoms of mania.

"You sick bastard," Ferraz said.

The trilingual announcement came up.

His train was reaching Elphinstone Road.

"Charles Sobhraj murdered 12. You didn't call him sick. The police admired his skills at deception and evasion and the media nicknamed him the 'Bikini Killer.'"

"Sobhraj was also a psychopath."

"But the police made him a celebrity, Inspector."

"Committing murder was Sobhraj's means to sustain his adventurous lifestyle. What's your excuse?"

"Inspector – *you* amaze me. Wasn't Sobhraj before your time?"

"Yeah, lucky for him," Ferraz said dryly.

He chuckled, delighted at the way this conversation was going.

"You know, Inspector, all psychopaths are not criminals."

"Uh-huh."

"I see myself as the victim here."

"Not the perpetrator?" asked Ferraz in surprise.

"Definitely not!"

He sounded shocked.

"You're cold-blooded, you have no empathy, these are symptoms of a psychopath. You're also a narcissistic bastard, inflated with a sense of self and you're happy to talk about yourself. "

"Am I different from a cop? A surgeon? Or a lawyer? Isn't empathy a luxury we all can't afford? Aren't your Encounter Specialists without conscience? Isn't the surgeon's mind as cold as ice? But do you accuse him of being low on compassion when a patient dies on the operation table? And the lawyer, what about the innocent witnesses he ruthlessly crucifies in the courtroom, isn't this a travesty of justice though he is doing only what his client is paying him to do? The policeman, the surgeon, the lawyer… do they care about the criminal they shot dead, the patient they lost in the OT, the witness they killed in court?"

Ferraz was stunned by his argument.

This was no master criminal, but evil incarnate.

How could this man be a Ganpati *bhakt?*

"Why are you doing it?" Ferraz asked, hoping he would reveal his link to Lord Ganesh. "You feel special and important, like a big fucking shot, after maybe a lifetime of rejection?"

"I'm doing it for society," he said thinly.

"Yeah, that's what the Yorkshire Ripper said while he was murdering prostitutes – that he was cleaning the streets of human trash."

"So that made the Yorkshire Ripper, what – a bad man doing good things or a good man doing bad things, Inspector?"

On the train, Ferraz could hear a beggar singing for alms.

Then he asked, "Have you studied Psychology, Inspector?"

"No," Ferraz replied, "but I'm learning about psychos."

He chuckled again, amused.

"I'm like Van Damme."

"Who?"

"That Hollywood star," he said vaguely.

"Why?"

"He told the world, sometimes you're going to like me and sometimes you're going to hate me, but what can I do – I'm not perfect."

"Fuck him," Ferraz said vehemently.

"Psychopathy has a vast framework. All of us have our place at some point in the spectrum. If madness in people was like the rain, some of us would be a drizzle and some a hurricane, as the American author John Green had said in *Looking for Alaska*. Where's *your* point, Inspector?"

The train had reached Dadar.

In the background, another voice was crackling on a speaker. The Dadar station master. Ordering passengers to move away from the bank of Platform No. 3 because the Rajdhani Express was expected to pass by a great speed.

"I'll tell you what, Inspector, I like you…"

Ferraz kept quiet.

"… so I'll make it more challenging. I'm going to interact with you again. You will know who I am – but you won't know it's me, because you're looking out for me but don't know who I am."

Ferraz struggled to register this.

"What–"

"Moryaa Re!"

ARUN RATHOD broke the news to Ashfaque Raja.

All cops hated this duty. Sudden death was always a difficult announcement to make to the next of kin. But to tell a man his wife had been murdered...

Nobody thought *murder* when the police called.

They assumed it was an accident.

Dead did not mean *killed!*

It took time for *murder* to register.

People were always disbelieving, they asked for details and had questions, playing for time, because they knew this was going to be bad. And they didn't want to hear it.

To tell Raja that his wife had been thrown out of their penthouse by a psychopathic serial killer was giving Rathod the creeps. He was uncomfortably nervous about making this call. But he was thankful he did not have to look Raja in the eye. He could not imagine doing it face-to-face.

He caught the jet-setting labor lawyer at Delhi Airport.

There was nothing for Raja to do after court and so he had chosen to spend his evening at the Indira Gandhi International Airport waiting for the airline to announce his flight to Mumbai.

Raja was fascinated by airports.

This was South Asia's largest and India's busiest; he bought a box of Haldiram's Sohan Halwa for Nicole at the food court, browsed around the bookstore, and was now having a drink in the lounge.

Raja had a minor panic attack when Rathod called.

He guessed the call was about Nicole.

Rathod was calling about the rave party. The police had found out about Nicole. And Rathod was doing his club mate a favour by calling Raja to warn him about his wife's naughty ways.

But the call brought his world crashing down.

Something died in him when he heard what Rathod had to say.

He listened in shocked silence.

In the background, Jet Airways announced the departure of its flight SW354 to Mumbai, passengers were asked to proceed for the security check and report to Gate 9 for boarding.

He felt anger and fury. Then horror and heartbreak when he thought of what poor, defenseless Nicole must have undergone in her final moments. But this was nothing compared to the pity and sadness he would feel for himself on the long and lonely flight home.

He thought of his last call to her.

Eerily, Nicole had figured out the reason behind the murders.

He had jokingly accused her of playing *Criminal Case* on Facebook.

And had a presentiment that she might be next.

He had laughed at her, thought she was out of her mind.

She had said something about her Ganpati tattoo.

He thought she was PMSing.

"Ashfaque, you know Nicole got in touch with one of my officers this afternoon and wanted to discuss these serial murders?"

"She did?" said Raja in surprise.

"Yes," Rathod told him, "she said she had a clue that would help us understand why this psycho is killing people. A missing piece to the puzzle, that's what she said, something that linked the victims."

"I had no idea."

"Yeah, but she refused to tell him on the phone. Nor did she… she didn't indicate the next victim might be herself. Or that she was frightened. If she had we would have… you know… that cop was on his way to meet her when Nicole got… when she…"

"She thought she might be a victim," said Raja brokenly.

"She did?" said Rathod surprised. "Why didn't she tell us?"

"I'll never know."

"You too knew this and didn't tell me, why?"

"I came to know only this afternoon when we spoke."

"What did she tell you?"

"She said there was a link among the victims… and she fancied she might be the killer's next… I, I laughed at her, it sounded so… so fantastic, and so far-fetched. She was not, Nixie was never neurotic or, or giddy-headed… I should have taken her seriously. But I was busy, I told her to go to sleep…"

"She revealed this link to you?" Rathod asked anxiously.

"Yes, she said the link was Ganpati."

"Ganpati!"

Rathod let out his breath with a sigh.

So, Nicole Raja had known. How had she found out?

"I think… you know Nixie has, she got this big Ganpati tattoo done on her back when she was young, she feared this psycho would target her because of that…"

Rathod groaned in despair, "I didn't know. Did she have a reason for anticipating… were there any threatening calls, somebody stalking her, anything like that because of this tattoo?"

"No… I don't know why she felt… she's had the tattoo for ever."

Rathod wondered what Raja would say if he knew the police had withheld the killer's Ganpati motive information from the city. It might have saved Nicole's life. The Joint CP (Crime) felt shitty.

"I'm sorry," he told the labor lawyer.

But Ashfaque Raja was lost in his own misery.

"Poor Nixie… to die, to be killed like that…"

And he broke down crying.

21

FERRAZ COULDN'T get over Nicole Raja's murder.

He had been within a heartbeat of…

… saving her? Catching the killer? He would never know.

Why hadn't the silly bitch told him what she knew?

Why didn't she mention her Ganpati tattoo? Were the police expected to know every citizen whose body was tattooed or pierced or whatever?

But this was all self-reproach; he knew he was on a guilt trip.

He kept seeing her lying on the ground, bloodied and broken.

If *only* the police had warned the city about the Cobra's motive…

… they might not have had a fifth corpse.

Another celebrity who had cold-shouldered Lord Ganesh.

Lying in the morgue with a tag on her toe, now.

The killing game was getting deadlier.

But Ferraz decided to unburden his guilt tonight.

Now he listened to what his squad was saying.

"We talked to all the watchmen and many residents in Setalvad Lane," Navroze told Ferraz, "but nobody saw a stranger. This fucker moves around like a ghost. There aren't any shops. And no vendors call at that hour. So nobody saw him. Forensics is turning the Raja apartment out. It's spick and span. But hopefully they'll find a print that matches one taken from Haider's place. God knows when we'll get the report. We got nothing from the leather reins used to strangle Seth. Guess he was wearing gloves."

Ferraz nodded.

"He might have used the doorbell," he told Navroze, "but I pressed the switch after him, I must have erased his fingerprint, damn it!"

"How were you to know?" Navroze consoled him.

"There's a small Ganpati at the end of the lane," Salvi said, "he might have gone there. It's run by local boys. But, again, it was unattended at that hour."

Ferraz hadn't seen the Ganpati *pandal.*

"How did he reach Grant Road station so quickly?"

"Perhaps by bus. There's a 104 that goes down Nepean Sea Road around that time," Khan said. "No cabbie picked up a fare to the station from outside Setalvad Lane between 3.45 and 4 pm."

"Has the Control Room message gone to all police stations in the state asking for any unsolved murders related to Ganpati?"

"Yeah," Navroze said. "And our Detection staff are walking their legs off visiting the GPs in all our Zones to see if any of these family physicians have patients who are *bhakts* of Ganpati."

"There must be hundreds," Ferraz said.

"Thousands! We've come up with nothing so far."

"Datta, send a message to all police stations in Maharashtra asking for information of criminal cases involving Ganesh *bhakts*," Ferraz said. "Specify that the accused we are looking could be psychopathic."

"What did he tell you?" Navroze asked Ferraz.

Ferraz had already told Joint CP (Crime) Rathod about the killer's call.

"He blames society for the murders."

"How did he get your number?"

"She must have saved it on her phone. I tried calling her–"

"He's following the investigation," Khan said, "that's how he recognized your name and knew you were a cop. Or is he a cop himself?"

"He didn't sound like one. Besides, which cop would take such daring, daylight risks?"

"How did he address you?" Salvi asked curiously.

"He said, *'Moryaa Re! Inspector'*."

"Like in the CP's tapes?"

"That's what he said."

"How do you mean he blames society?"

"Bawa, he said his actions were a result of society's unconventional behavior," Ferraz recalled. "A lot of insignificant people were getting famous because of their amoral behavior."

"Insignificant people! He calls his victims insignificant?"

"How did he sound?" Salvi asked.

"Quiet, calm, in control. I got the impression that he's quite learned, we are dealing with an educated man, well-read too."

"But middle class… if he travels by train," Salvi suggested.

"Why do you say he's well-read?" Navroze wanted to know.

"Just a gut instinct. He referred to Charles Sobhraj. Knew exactly how many murders Sobhraj had committed. How many of us can say that?"

"He knew Sobhraj was a psycho?"

"Yeah, and he said the police had made Sobhraj a celebrity."

"But he didn't admit he was a psychopath himself?"

"No, he seemed to know a lot about psychopathy though."

"What do you mean?" Khan asked.

"He made some bizarre comparison between an encounter cop…"

"Majhe aiyee!" Salvi exclaimed.

"… a surgeon, a lawyer and himself, all lack empathy, he seemed to think."

There was silence.

"Who is Van Damme?" Ferraz asked suddenly.

He remembered the Cobra's reference to some Hollywood star.

"Jean Claude Van Damme?" asked Sanjay Chhabria, excitedly.

He looked like he was bursting to reveal a secret.

"I don't know. Who the hell's Jean Claude Van Damme?"

"He's a Belgian martial arts superstar known for his Hollywood action movies," said Chhabria. "Van Damme's been around since the 1980s. You know, he made *Bloodsport, Kickboxer, Timecop*… and just confirmed he's working with Sylvester Stallone in *Expendables 2*."

"*Timecop?*"

"Yes, sir. Van Damme plays a cop in many movies."

"A cop, hmnn… he compared himself to Van Damme."

"Why the reference to this actor?" Navroze asked.

"No idea, Bawa."

"Here it is, sir," Sangeeta Kadam cried excitedly.

They turned to look at her.

At the mention of Jean Claude Van Damme, Sangeeta had quietly left the group and gone to her laptop where her flying fingers Google searched for the Hollywood action star.

"Sir, the Cobra's bipolar!" Sangeeta said suddenly.

"How do you know?" asked Ferraz surprised.

"Dr. Miyasahib was right," Sangeeta declared, her eyes shining. "Jean Claude Van Damme was diagnosed with bipolar disorder in 1998. He recently went on British TV and said, 'Sometimes you're gonna like me, and sometimes you're gonna hate me. But what can I do? I'm not perfect. I'm an extreme bipolar. And I'm taking medication for this.'"

They looked at her in stunned silence.

"That's what this bugger told me!" Ferraz said in amazement.

"*O Khodai*, hopefully the Bombay Psychiatric Society can give us a list of all bipolars being treated by their members," Navroze exclaimed.

"Yes," said Ferraz, "good work, Sangeeta."

"Anything else he said, Angelo?" Khan asked.

"He's promised to contact me again."

"On the phone? Or in person?"

"Wish I knew," Ferraz said helplessly.

NAHIDA SHAIKH was surprised to get Ferraz's call.

She was in the TV studio, where the 6 pm news was opening with Nicole Raja's horrific death, adding her two bits on Mumbai's favorite socialite.

The media didn't know Nicole had been murdered.

It was presumed she had tragically fallen while watering the plants. The buzz was that Nicole had been at last night's rave party. The Social Service Branch, which busted the party, denied this rumor.

But the media knew about Nicole's party habits.

The speculation was that she was tripping on acid when she stepped off her penthouse on a flight of euphoria that ended in her death. Another story was that Nicole had committed suicide. That she was fighting depression with drinks and drugs.

Zahra Khan, the dead model's friend, shot them down. Aware that she was inviting trouble, Zahra told TV reporters shoving mics into her face that Nicole wasn't a drug addict. She did coke occasionally.

"It opened her up, got her mind out of the way, coke's the taste of the present," Zahra said to the media's delight. "Nicole was too smart to get addicted. She knew there was no such thing as a happiness pill. Coke's a sociable drug, we did a line or two. Nicole was a happy person already. She just went along for the ride. Only hippies seek spiritual enlightenment, the truth and fulfillment in drugs."

The media loved Zahra's outspokenness.

Nobody suspected Nicole was the serial killer's fifth victim.

Not even Zahra.

Someone who was allegedly at a rave party the previous night, meeting her death after an unexplained fall, it had to be a terrible accident. Not suicide. Nobody thought murder.

A police team whisked Ashfaque Raja away from the airport before reporters could get to him. The family driver Amarjit and Sharma, the watchman of Manek Abad, who knew the actual story, were also swiftly taken into protective custody and kept away from the media.

Ferraz didn't say much to Nahida.

He simply asked if she was free to catch "that coffee" tonight.

"Somewhere quiet and close to home," he requested.

He was sounding exhausted. Nahida could hear the tiredness in his voice. Yet Ferraz wanted to meet her. And have coffee. Why?

Was it to do with Nicole Raja's death?

Did Ferraz know she had given Nicole his number today? Was there more to Nicole's death than what the police were sharing?

Nahida felt a surge of excitement.

She knew Ferraz was calling for a reason, coffee was an excuse.

They met at the Bagel Shop, a buzzing hangout on Pali Hill. It had an outdoors section with an asbestos sloping roof, old cane furniture, potted plants, paintings on the walls, lamps throwing yellow and white light, and whirring ceiling fans.

The indoors was air-conditioned. With glass doors and wooden rafters. And free Wi-Fi. Young girls sat with laptops on high cane chairs against a bar-like counter. There were posters on the wall announcing art exhibitions, poetry readings, yoga workshops and homoeopathy camps.

The menu was on a blackboard.

A refrigerated counter had cheesecakes, brownies, breads made with banana, fig and almond, and blueberry and chocolate muffins. There was the aroma of fresh coffee. An espresso machine sat hissing in a corner.

Ferraz was going there for the first time.

He parked the BSA opposite and looked at the Bagel Shop curiously. It looked like a quaint eatery in Goa, he thought. A cool sea breeze raced up from Carter Road making his hair dance. It was 9.30 pm. Yellow lights gave the place a cozy ambience, the potted plants screened it from the road, and young people stood outside smoking and chatting.

Ferraz had showered and changed.

He was wearing khaki police trousers, a dark brown T-shirt and suede moccasins. Jackie had dabbed Eau de Cologne behind his ears.

"You don't want to smell like a cop, do you?" she tartly asked.

He wondered what she meant. Cops everywhere in the world had the same look, he knew. But he hadn't known they smelled the same, too!

Nahida was sitting out at a table for two.

She watched Ferraz give Bagel Shop the once-over.

And all at once, she thought she knew why he was here!

"Hullo Inspector," she said brightly as Ferraz pulled out a cane bucket seat.

Swiftly he looked over the eatery.

No cops. Even though the Additional Commissioner of Police's (West) office and the Regional Control Room were down the road. Maybe this place was too pricey for them. But the Bagel Shop had a lot of other patrons looking chilled out. Two teenage girls deep in conversation at one table. A couple lost in each other on a sofa. A young man reading a book and sipping a coffee sat subtly exchanging glances with a single woman playing with her phone at the adjoining table. A pair of dirty hippies eating hungrily. Another table of young people hunched over a laptop. Waiters languidly moved around carrying trays of bagels, steaming coffees and tall, chilled glasses. By their table was a window opening into the Bagel Shop through which he could see a packed room where a book reading was animatedly in progress.

His searching glance came to rest on her.

Nahida was wearing a pink tracksuit and Nike runners. She had been listening to music. A pair of headphones lay on the table connected to her phone. Beneath the track top she had on a white singlet straining against abundant breasts. The track bottoms, he guiltily noticed, were snug against her flaring hips, full thighs and long, tapering legs.

"Well, here we are," he said unnecessarily.

She had noticed Ferraz checking out the place…

… and quickly appraising her.

"Spotted any serial killers?" she teasingly asked.

"Serial killers?"

He regarded her carefully and realized she was pulling his leg.

"None, did you?"

"Not yet," Nahida gave an amused laugh.

"What are we having?" he asked, picking up a menu.

"I'm treating, and if you haven't eaten here before, I suggest you try the Goan Chorizo Bagel. It's got lettuce, tomatoes and cream cheese. I'm having the Goat Cheese Bagel with pesto tomato lettuce, honey and walnut. The desserts are to die for, they are gluten-free. Shall we split a Chocolate Fudge Cake…"

Desserts! Jackie would jump from the roof!

"… and have an Americano since you hate Cappuccino?"

He nodded, missing her jibe, feeling strangely uncomfortable.

She noticed his awkwardness and smiled.

"You'll like the food," she promised.

"What are bagels?"

"Doughnut-like bread, the Jews of Poland introduced them."

He nodded again.

She called a waiter over and placed their order.

Getting that out of the way, Nahida looked at Ferraz quizzically.

"Tell me, Inspector."

He cleared his throat, hedging.

"Nicole's death… you're upset?" she said, giving him the lead.

Ferraz nodded, not looking at her.

"She asked me for your number..."

"I know."

Nahida took a deep breath.

"... just before... she... got... she was she killed, wasn't she?"

Ferraz stiffened.

"What happened, you want to tell me?"

Ferraz looked out.

A young man with a guitar slung across his back was asking for directions.

"She was pushed to her death."

"Oh God... this is related to the serial killings, isn't it?"

He nodded.

"Nicole!" she said, too shocked to say anything else.

"He's killing people who have disrespected Ganpati."

"Ganpati? What do you mean disrespected?"

"Nicole had a Ganpati tattoo on her back..."

"I know!"

"... the Kolkata singer just released a raunchy Ganpati Indipop song, the racehorse owner's champion colt had one of Ganesha's 108 names, the diplomat's wife was a pseudo devotee who held a Ganpati cocktail party, Haider had just done a series of sexual paintings on Ganpati..."

"So they were murdered, why?" she whispered, disbelievingly.

"To the killer's mind they were being sacrilegious."

"How? You can't be serious!"

"That's what the evidence indicates."

"But there must be thousands like them," Nahida protested, "there's no copyright on Lord Ganesh that was being violated."

"How do you explain that to a psycho?"

"Why are you telling me this?"

He looked at her in surprise.

"You wanted a story," he said, "the Department won't reveal

this because it will cause panic during Ganeshotsav. But we think the killer's got five more victims in mind – one for each day of the festival."

"Did Nicole know?"

"That's the thing. She refused to tell me on the phone. Just said she perhaps knew why the murders were happening. And she would help the police only if I met her."

"She might have guessed the motive," Nahida said.

"Because of her Ganpati tattoo?"

"Yeah, Nicole was intelligent."

"Would she have been afraid?"

"Of becoming a victim? I doubt it crossed her mind. She wouldn't have thought she's offending Lord Ganesh with that tattoo, no matter what this freak believes. She was *bindaas*. And she would have asked for police protection if she feared for her life. Her husband Ashfaque is powerfully connected, you know."

"If she had told me, we would have protected her."

Nahida was struck by a sudden, dreadful thought.

"Where were you when, when… it happened?" she asked fearfully.

"Climbing up her stairs," Ferraz said painfully.

Nahida shut her eyes in horror.

"Minutes away? Didn't… didn't you–" she choked on the question.

"I had no idea why she called me. Or that she was already dead… the killer took the lift down while I was on my way up, we passed each other."

She shuddered involuntarily.

"What a horrible thing!"

Ferraz said nothing.

"How long have the police known about this Ganpati motive?"

"We stumbled upon it yesterday and…"

"And you're saying–"

"… if we had announced it, maybe Nicole would still be alive."

"You think everybody with a fetish for Ganpati will come running to the police? That's absurd. People like Nicole wouldn't even imagine they were abusing Lord Ganesh."

"But we're at least warning them. The police can't be everywhere."

She sniped at him viciously, "Why haven't you guys been able to stop this prick? A force of 47,000 can't find one man? What the fuck!"

Ferraz refused to be provoked.

"Nahida," he said quietly, "earlier criminals were illiterates. They were poor people with no education and took to crime to make a living. It was easy to catch them because they weren't savvy with the ways of the police. Or they were gangsters already on our radar. Now educated people are into crime. It's difficult to deal with them. Crime is corporatized. There are political personalities involved. In 1993 it was difficult to believe that stockbroker Harshad Mehta packed one crore rupees into a suitcase to bribe Prime Minister Narasimha Rao to let him off the securities scam. Nowadays political scams run into thousands of crores of rupees."

"I'm sorry," she said, feeling ashamed of herself.

"It's okay," he gave a sad smile, "I get this reaction all the time."

"I understand, I really do," she said, feeling really awful now.

"Five murders, the victims all strangers to one another, no witnesses, no suspects, his obsession to hurt people who he believes have hurt Lord Ganesh is all we have."

"He's hiding in plain sight, isn't he?" she asked drily.

Ferraz told her about his conversation with the killer.

She listened in fascination and fear.

"He doesn't sound normally insane," she said.

"He's certainly psychopathic, but not a fruitcake," Ferraz agreed. "I'm almost certain he lives an everyday life, working a steady job, hanging out with normal people."

"Are you sure the victims weren't linked to him in the past?"

"The only thing we are sure of is that anger is the motivation. Serial killers otherwise do it for sex, greed, money, the thrill of the kill and for want of attention. They hang around in the dark waiting for a potential victim. But he's going after specific people."

"Suppose I break the story?" Nahida asked, "What happens to the investigation?"

"What do you mean?"

"This is a big story. It will give Mumbai a nervous breakdown."

"On the contrary," Ferraz said.

"How is that? You're setting a cat among the pigeons."

"Look Nahida," Ferraz explained, "people are terrified of randomness. And serial killers are the embodiment of randomness. They kill a whole range of strangers. That scares the shit out of the city. Everybody imagines they could be next. They don't realize why it's happening, they can't see it coming, so they look under the bed before going to sleep at night, they peep behind the curtain when they get home."

"You're scaring me," she said biting her knuckles.

"But by breaking the story, you're assuring 20 million people that he's not after everyone, he's only looking for people who have been profane with Lord Ganesh."

She looked at him in silence.

A waiter arrived with their order.

The bagels looked big and messy, the cheese was oozing out of his Goan Chorizo Bagel, he was afraid of dropping food on his clothes. Jackie was forever complaining that it broke her back to get the stains out. He reached for a paper napkin. Nahida asked for a Green Apple Soda. She was cutting up her Goat Cheese Bagel to offer him a bite. His order contained pork. She might be offended if he offered it to her.

"You get me?" he asked impatiently. "The city stops jumping. Those that have violated the sanctity of Ganpati and fear for their lives will come to us for protection or start looking out for themselves."

"And then?" she asked.

"Then it will be the entire city against one man."

Nahida smiled at his optimism.

"What will you do if you get him?" she asked.

"Personally?"

"Yes."

"I'll kill him," said Ferraz savagely biting into his bagel.

"Do you always carry a gun?" she asked.

Surprised by her question, he nodded.

"Even when you're out for coffee, so close to home?"

A guarded look came into his eyes.

But Nahida wouldn't give up.

"Ever since 26/11?" she asked.

He looked away.

She reached across the table and placed her hand on his.

Ferraz froze at this intimacy.

Pretending to reach for another tissue, he freed his hand.

She appeared not to notice.

"Tell me what happened," Nahida said gently, "please..."

What had happened was that...

... 26/11 changed his life.

Three days of heart-stopping terror, a proud Mumbai Police force of 47,000 humbled to ignominy by ten Pakistani terrorists, the world watching with horror and sympathy on TV at home.

His wife and son were killed at the Taj Mahal Hotel & Towers where they were least expected to be, two among 33 innocents cut down by the ruthless gunfire of cowardly terrorists in the name of God and country.

Ferraz never learned what happened, never talked about it.

And every night he went to sleep with questions, the answers to which he didn't want to know. He had learned to deal with that awful pain by blocking it out, by pretending it had never happened.

Their bodies were found in the hotel lobby outside the bookstore.

Three days later.

A storybook clutched in the boy's hands. Shot through the back. His face caked with dried blood that had gushed out of the terrible gunshot his mother had taken directly in the heart. She must have bent to scoop up her son and run when Death marched in with cold blood, AK-47s and grenades.

When 26/11 was over, Mumbai mourned her dead.

Ferraz had gone to the morgue.

It was a grim, old stone building in JJ Hospital attached to the defunct Coroner's Court. Far away from the wards of healing and caring, hidden from the eyes of the world. A huge banyan tree stood guard outside, its creepers reaching down to hug the morgue and comfort the dead residents inside. Beside it, casting an eerie glow was a lamp-post with three bulbs, like the one at Walkeshwar from which Teen Batti got its name.

Ambulances were unloading the 26/11 corpses wrapped in white shrouds. The next of kin stood by; some weeping, others shocked and silent but screaming like him from within. Among them the consular corps, dignified in its grief, waiting to claim the bodies of 37 foreigners who had been killed in the terror attack across Mumbai.

He took in the scene, eyes darting left and right, picking up impressions of the frightening situation rather than specific details. Noting everything but recording nothing. Like a cop. There was no need to, actually, the crime hadn't taken place here.

Grisly autopsies were being hastily performed in the morgue on large, tilted stainless steel tables with channels for the blood to flow down and out.

Death robbed people of all dignity.

He knew what the bodies of murder victims looked like. He had seen the corpses of people stabbed or hacked to death, those shot from close range, drained of all blood, stiff with rigor mortis, the horror of their sudden and brutal end mirrored in their eyes. And those that had drowned, been burned, killed in accidents, had fallen or were pushed off many-storied buildings, been poisoned, strangulated, trampled in stampedes.

But he couldn't believe what he was seeing now – the bodies dumped on steel bunks, on tables, lying on the floor, too many to count… *and among them…* he wanted to shut his eyes and blank out the horror of seeing their corpses bloodied and bloated, discolored in death, their bullet wounds screaming…

… and take back with him more peaceful memories.

Like the sound of their voices.

Their laughter.

That he would carry in his heart forever and a day.

Not this terrible sight, their lifeless eyes staring at him, pleading, this unbearable stench of death, which also would stay with him forever. He touched them achingly, hoping for a sign that they were still inside.

Next day at the graveyard…

… he watched their coffins being lowered on canvas straps into the receptive earth, silently praying, "Angels east, angels west, north and south do your best, to watch over them while they rest."

A pair of grave diggers stood by impassively, leaning on their shovels, waiting to fill in the earth again. They had seen it all.

The Lord giveth and the Lord taketh away.

He did not want to leave their graves because he did not want to abandon them. When it was *they* that had left him and gone. Without warning. The most painful goodbyes are the ones that are never expected, never said, and never explained.

That night he stood by the window gazing at the Colaba lighthouse winking across the dark sea, but not seeing anything. Painfully going over memories. The mind playing happy images of good times in flashback.

And then… the floodgates opened.

Suddenly he was crying, tears streaming down his face – the tears he had not wanted to yield to as a cop, great racking sobs coming from the bottom of his tortured soul. He tried to stop them. Tried to fight the tears by wiping his eyes with the back of his sleeve, feeling his nose running, and with the unending tears came the gut-wrenching realization…

… that he would never see them again.

"I'm sorry," Nahida said, "I hadn't any…"

Strangely, she felt like crying for him.

There was a terrible sadness in his eyes that reached out and touched her, making her heart break. Ferraz gave her a crooked smile. He reached for her green apple soda and took a sip without asking. His throat was suddenly dry.

She found the action very childlike and honest.

"I'm sorry," he said. "I haven't talked about this before."

They kept silent for a while.

"You have a…" Nahida asked hesitantly. "A little girl–"

He nodded, "Jackie is, she's 18 – that's hardly little."

Nahida smiled, men never seemed to notice and realize when babies became little girls and teenagers became young ladies.

"Who is Jackie?" she asked, searching his face for answers.

"Jackie is…" Ferraz struggled for the right words.

A year after 26/11 when he was dreading Christmas…

… one morning in December, the Bangalore Police called. It was amazing how life cruelly expected him to continue suffering these slings and arrows of outrageous fortune.

A gritty-voiced Inspector Duncan Archer was on the line.

"Inspector Ferraz," he said, coming straight to the point, "you know somebody named Carl Ferraz?"

Ferraz had been stunned by the question.

Unable to speak, he remained silent.

Carl, his twin brother.

Both boys had been abandoned after birth by vagabond parents who separated and disappeared, leaving them to be raised by their maternal grandfather, a kindly British soldier who remained in Bombay after Independence with his Indian wife from Madras. The old man could have put the twins up for adoption, but he didn't. Heartbroken by his wife's death first, and then his daughter's callousness, he took up small lowly-paid jobs as a railway guard, a hostel warden and YMCA watchman, and struggled to bring his grandsons up as his own, putting them through public school and then college with his meager savings and dismal income, shifting them from one temporary address to another, once even sheltering them on a railway station where he worked nights.

But it was a sad and troubled childhood.

No mommy's kisses and daddy's smiles, as the song went.

By 18, Ferraz was earning enough to pay his college fees. He had boxed at school and learned karate in college. He pumped iron at the gym where he worked as an instructor during the day. At night he studied to put himself into the Maharashtra Police Academy.

His twin Carl had taken after their parents; going from lazy to being crooked. He lived by his wits and off women, recklessly playing cards and backing horses. He ran rackets for gamblers, delivered illicit liquor for bootleggers, carried contraband for smugglers, and peddled dope for drug dealers. There was nothing wrong or bad that he had not done. At 18 Carl left home, breaking their grandfather's heart this time for good, and was never heard of again.

Until this morning.

Carl, long presumed dead, had miraculously surfaced, and he was now dead for real – killed by a speeding truck while drunkenly weaving across the road before a pub. On his person, the police found a 26/11 press cutting on Ferraz's personal tragedy.

Inspector Archer was on the line, impatient.

"You there, sir?" he asked curtly.

But Ferraz was thinking.

Carl had known… but where was he all these years?

They were twins, supposed to be inseparable, closer than any two people in the world, blood was said to run thicker between twins.

So what had happened to Carl, then?

Inspector Archer told him bluntly, one cop to another.

Ferraz was required in Bangalore, but he didn't want to go.

Inspector Archer was quietly persistent.

He met Ferraz at the airport.

A grave Anglo-Indian, like himself, fair skinned and with light grey eyes that looked at Ferraz with startled surprise. He seized Ferraz's hand, pumped it up and down and said, "Bad business, huh, dingo?"

Why dingo, Ferraz wondered.

Dingos were predatory Australian wild dogs. Australia, with its sunshine, beer and beaches, was where most Anglo-Indians hopeful of a better life migrated to. Were they known as dingos there? He hadn't heard this nomenclature before.

Inspector Archer had wrapped up the case.

Ferraz took one look at the body, unable to accept that this naked corpse on a freezing bed of stainless steel was his twin, feeling no connection to the dead man whose life had been such a goddamn waste.

Then Inspector Archer coughed apologetically.

Carl had left behind a daughter, he said sorrowfully.

Her name was Jackie, she was 16, studying in a boarding school.

Carl dumped her there when she was little and disappeared. They found an inland letter in his purse from the school sent to his last known address. The school thought he was dead. Like his wife. The girl remained with them as a charity student, brought up by caring Belgian nuns who ran the institution, quietly accepting her fate with a fortitude that was rare to find among kids.

Ferraz wanted no part of this family drama.

But Inspector Archer was quietly forceful again.

"At least see the girl," he pleaded, avoiding Ferraz's furious gaze.

Jackie was waiting for them on a bench outside the school chapel, legs crossed, chin cupped in her hands. All of 16, petite and pretty. She got up with feminine grace, wearing blue jeans and a white blouse, lustrous brown hair pulled back and tied in a pony tail. She had a dimpled, heart-shaped face, thoughtful brown eyes that were full of unspoken secrets, bow-shaped lips clamped tightly shut, and a teenager's body bursting with energy and life. She held herself back with grown-up reserve.

The picture of an absolute sweetheart.

Inspector Archer led him forward by the elbow.

And then Ferraz stopped and caught his breath.

Sometimes it's easy to draw a family resemblance.

But this was some wicked joke of genetics.

The girl looked like him!

The likeness was breathtaking.

He stood there staring, not believing his eyes. He glanced at Inspector Archer, remembering the Bangalore cop's surprise when he saw Ferraz at the airport, and understood that look now.

Jackie also was struck by the resemblance.

She came over uncertainly and stood before him, her head level with his shoulders, giving him the same searching look he was giving her.

He was bracing himself, expecting she would fall into his arms weeping. When the girl surprised him by asking with wide-eyed curiosity, "Have you *ever* killed anyone?"

She had spotted the butt of the 9mm S&W peeping out of his waist.

Ferraz was taken aback. Cops were always asked about their guns. But this was bravado, he knew. The girl was nervous and didn't know what to say. He didn't know what to reply. He once read that if you look inside a girl's heart and see how much she cries, you'll find secrets, promises and lies. But what you'll see most is how hard she tries to stay strong when nothing is right and everything is wrong.

Jackie stared at him with appealing brown eyes.

And then she asked Ferraz in a soft, tremulous voice that belied her outwardly calm, "What are you going to do about me?"

And Ferraz melted like butter on hot toast.

NAHIDA WOULD sensationally break the story next morning…

… rattling the city that was already spooked by the serial murders and on edge. From living in fear of the unknown, people would now start to be in dread of the known.

It had been too late last night to do a story on the "Ganpati killer" for *Newsday*. The paper had gone to bed by the time Nahida finished dinner with Ferraz at the Bagel Shop. But she inserted a "Stop Press" on the front page. Chillingly warning readers of five more murders during Ganeshotsav by the vigilante-like serial killer who was after people who had messed around with Lord Ganesh.

On *Network Today* at 8 am, after informing shocked viewers that socialite Nicole Raja hadn't fallen to her death but was pushed, Nahida would disclose without any drama how being irreverent to Ganpati had cost the Page 3 girl, the master painter, British diplomat's wife, racehorse owner and Indipop singer their lives in the most horrible manner. The police feared the killer was going to strike again. In this city of 20 million that was celebrating Ganesh Chaturthi, anybody could be the next victim and anybody the killer.

As other TV channels picked up the story, the city went hysterical.

Everybody tried to reach everybody else in a panic, the surge in calls causing the city's mobile and landline services to jam as networks failed to handle the unprecedented traffic.

Cursing the media and especially Nahida Shaikh, Police Commissioner Baburao Nawalkar tried in vain to reach Joint CP (Crime) Arun Rathod to find out who had leaked the story. His efforts were met with recorded messages advising the CP that "All lines are busy" and "This subscriber cannot be reached".

When he got through, Nawalkar began angrily, "Arun, this Ganpati–"

"Yes, sir… the media has got wind of it."

"How?"

"All crime reporters have sources, sir."

"But it's going to hamper the investigation."

"No, sir… now the city is aware, people will be guarded, the Control Room is already flooded with calls, something's got to give. It narrows down our investigation."

"He will know we know."

"But every Mumbaikar also knows, sir. He's not going to find it easy to stalk his next victim."

"We will be flooded with requests for police protection."

"The people will learn to look after themselves, sir."

"I didn't want a panic situation. I wish the media–"

"But the media is only helping us, sir. It will be on the lookout for him, too. This is the story of the year. Every crime reporter is on it. The media has beaten us before in tracking elusive criminals."

"Instead of helping us," the CP said grumpily.

TUESDAY

22

IT WAS the damndest thing.

And ordinarily, he might have dismissed it as being funny…

… not the amusing, ha-ha *funny*, but the peculiar, strange *funny*.

After all, a name was a name; there was no more reason to fault the man's name than there was to pick holes in his own. Ditto his residence. What could the man do about the name of his building? And of his Cooperative Housing Society? He was a bona fide shareholder and a member of the Society. He had four flats in one of the three wings. His family had been living there forever. That ought to have been that.

But unfortunately for Ganesh Shetty – it wasn't to be.

It was sheer coincidence that he lived in Ganesh Bhuvan of Jai Ganesh Cooperative Housing Society at the junction of Tulsi Pipe Road and Miya Mohammed Chothani Marg opposite Mahim Railway Station.

The 'Ganesh-Ganesh-Ganesh' trinity was coincidental.

But Ganesh, 42, an Udipi restaurateur of the Bunt community of south-west Karnataka, with the wheatish complexion of his people, thick, oily black hair and a handlebar moustache that curled up to his sidelocks, sacrilegiously stretched the coincidence.

He made a handsome living out of fishing trawlers back home, his prawn farms, rice fields, coconut, areca nut and cashew plantations, and his Udipi restaurants and suburban Mumbai nightclub. But Ganesh was a rogue, he was into adult entertainment and cricket betting as well.

The nightclub was to be his undoing.

It was an inexcusable copy of the buddha-bars in Paris, Dubai, Manila, Washington, Sao Paolo, Monte Carlo, Budapest and other cities which were renowned for their fashionable ambience, outstanding Asian cuisine, and eclectic music. The buddha-bars resembled temples. They had a two-storey dining area and an upstairs bar. A monumental Buddha statue was their presiding deity. It serenely lent a spiritual ambience to the restobars that were otherwise exotic and intimate places with rich mahogany furniture, brocade fabrics, Chinese and Japanese art objects, chandeliers with warm lighting and chart music.

To Ganesh, buddha-bar embodied the art of living. The cuisine was a gastronomy trip to exotic lands where Pan-Asian spices married Western influences in a culinary fusion. And the music! He was amazed to learn that buddha-bar's DJs regularly roamed the world searching for something new and different to spin for patrons.

For years, Ganesh dreamed of a buddha-bar in Mumbai.

When the Parisian chain opened its doors to India, Ganesh was delighted. But the franchise had just burned its fingers in Jakarta. Indonesian Buddhists got the restobar shut in protest against the presence of the Buddha statue in a venue serving alcohol. India was also an emotionally volatile country. This is where the Buddha found enlightenment. What heights might the backlash here reach?

So, after much deliberation, a new brand was created for India. It was called the b-bar and would open in Delhi on a 20,000 square foot property at the Select Citywalk mall. The b-bar would be like a buddha-bar in every respect. Only it wouldn't have the gigantic Buddha statue. The centre piece would be a Samurai. After Delhi, the plan was to take b-bar to Bangalore, Goa and a heritage hotel in Rajasthan. They weren't interested in Mumbai.

Ganesh was furious. Fuck them, he thought.

He would create his own buddha-bar here first.

And he quickly did, spiritually naming it ashta-vinayaka.

The name was significant. He was a Ganpati *bhakt*. Ashtavinayaka in Sanskrit meant 'Eight Ganeshas'. It was a reference to eight ancient temples dedicated to Lord Ganesh across Maharashtra in which the idols were not sculpted but naturally formed. Each temple had its own history and was as distinct from the rest as were the Ganpatis in them.

Ganesh was also superstitious.

He was a No. 8 according to numerology, a number associated with business skills and the ability to handle money. His birthday was August 8, 1961. The eighth day of the eighth month and the year, when added up, also amounted to eight. Moreover, his restobar was at the start of NH 8 – the old National Highway 8 between Mumbai and Delhi.

Too much of a coincidence for him not to get the drift.

He rightly named his restobar ashta-vinayaka!

It was just ahead of the Dahisar toll *naka*, originally a cavernous automobile workshop that Ganesh bought and converted. Outside, a signboard pointed north and said 'Ahmedabad'. Like Ahmedabad was just down the highway, not 526 km away.

As nightclubs went, ashta-vinayaka wasn't honky-tonk like other joints in the area. Those were cheap and noisy bars where truckers went to get drunk and have a jolly good time. It was a garish version of a downscale Asian buddha-bar with PDRs (private dining rooms) for families. It would never win any awards for ambience. But its bar served imported spirits, Mojitos, Caipiroskas and Sangria. And its menu promised a fine dining experience by an enterprising chef imported from the Taj Mangalore. Families living along the highway drove over for dinner. But the single men took their custom to ashta-vinayaka because of its adult entertainment.

The Thane Rural Police, in whose jurisdiction ashta-vinayaka fell, knew all about Ganesh Shetty. Betting on IPL matches, which was a multi-million dollar syndicate worldwide, was one of his major interests. Indian bookies ran hundreds of illegal telephone exchanges. The underworld used its network of *hawala* operators to transfer huge amounts of betting money across the country. Ganesh had a betting exchange. The police ignored his activities because he paid them well.

In the trade he was known as 'Jhinga'.

The specialty at ashta-vinayaka was the *Jhinga Koliwada* made famous by Punjabi *dhabbas* in Mumbai during the 1970s. Just as buddha-bar was famous for its *Lobster Tagliolini, Monkfish Fillet* and *Smoked Swordfish Carpaccio*, ashta-vinayaka was known for its *Jhinga Koliwada.*

And its portly proprietor by the alias 'Jhinga'.

That's not all ashta-vinayaka was famous for; there were the girls.

In 2006, the Maharashtra government amended the Bombay Police Act of 1951, prohibiting dance performances in eating houses, permit rooms and bars because they were contravening the licensing terms meant for places of public amusement.

"The dance is not pernicious," a top cop said, "but this is the kind of place where a woman's dignity is at stake because under the garb of dance bars, full blown trafficking is going on."

A San Francisco writer described Mumbai's dance bars as a neon underworld of drugs, prostitution and organized crime; the dancers were teenagers with Bollywood beauty and Slumdog's acid wit who came from abusive childhoods and life with prostitutes, pimps and transsexuals.

In the US of A, strip clubs were outlets for salacious entertainment.

Erotic dancers went topless, bottomless and did the Full Monty, nobody objected.

That happened only here, in this fucking city.

Here there was no stripping, the dance bar girls only shimmied between tables to Bollywood music for money. The court called it a 'stripless tease'. It ordered the police to halt this moral slide. Forcing many jobless dance bar girls into full-time prostitution.

However, the business quickly found its feet again.

Disreputable dance bars, with the police's blessings, began clandestinely operating at night. During the day they were beer bars and restaurants. At midnight, the girls sneaked into smoke-filled, dimly-lit halls from hidden rooms through secret passages. They danced on colorfully-illuminated glass floors while men showered currency notes on them. The rights to admission were reserved. Not everybody knew the ban was being flouted. Until TV channels exposed the farce with sting operations.

Jhinga opened ashta-vinayaka with an ingenious plan.

He employed Bollywood chorus line dancers as waitresses. He paid them well, dressed them stylishly but scantily, and got them to entice customers. In the dining rooms, he had smartly attired waiters. Restaurants and permit rooms got liquor licenses and could employ waitresses only if they had no live orchestra. Jhinga used a DJ and house music.

While taking orders if the waitress moved with the music, thrust her pelvis at a customer, innocently brushed his face with her bust, and if she presented him with the bill tucked into her waist which he paid by sticking the money down her cleavage, who was to say this was not part of her job? But with no orchestra and bar girls dancing, ashta-vinayaka was not breaking any laws.

However, Jhinga committed a cardinal sin…

… he installed a gigantic idol of Lord Ganesh inside ashta-vinayaka.

The Ganpati impassively listened to *Marjani Marjani, Zara Zara Touch Me* and *Choli Ke Peeche* every night and curiously witnessed the business of drinks, drugs and sex flourish in this restobar named after Him.

HE WENT there one S*A*T*U*R*D*A*Y* N*I*G*H*T*.

At 10 pm, when he shuffled and limped in, all was quiet. At midnight it would be like New Year's Eve, jam-packed and noisy, people swinging from the chandeliers. The girls were dressed suggestively, they were pretending to sway to the music, while cynically sizing up the swelling crowd with hard and practiced eyes.

The men were middle-aged, the *Raat ka Rajahs*, all hoping to get laid. But that would happen later. After much alcohol had been downed. And the DJ had spun *Sheila Ki Jawani* and *Beedi Jalaile* for the girls swiveling their hips, thrusting their breasts and bouncing their butts as they went about their duties for the benefit of appreciative patrons.

When he came in, the scene had just entered the sly glances, suggestive winks and discreet smiles stage. The vibe was exciting. He ordered a rum and cola and the signature *Jhinga Koliwada* to blend in.

He needn't have bothered.

Nobody was interested in him. Every man's eyes were on the girls moving among tables, taking orders, serving food and drinks. The music was *Munni Badnam Hui.* But the waitresses weren't Malaika Arora Khan. They didn't have the choreographed moves of the Bollywood actress.

All abundantly oozed sex appeal, however.

A waiter accepted a stack of ten rupee notes from a diner and went to a girl standing against the bar. Standing over her with the cash on one palm, he performed the money shot or scratching – flicking the notes with his forefinger in her direction.

He watched in fascination, quite enjoying himself…

... until one girl dipped her finger in his drink and swirled it around, then drew it slowly across his lips. She was leaning across his table, wanton and willing, and he could see clear until Ahmedabad she had on so little beneath. Then their eyes met. She recoiled immediately, shocked by the knowledge of what she had seen, backing away until she could see him no more.

Jhinga came in then.

A girl on his arm and a cigarette dangling from his mouth. He did a soft-shoe shuffle, bowing before the 20-feet-tall Ganpati that was looking at what was happening in ashta-vinayaka disapprovingly.

That's when he decided to kill Jhinga.

HE WAS waiting outside Ganesh Bhuvan.

It was lunch time. The building's Ganesh would come home any moment. After his *naam ke vaaste* visit to Siddhivinayak Temple. Timing was critical. He had worked it down to a science after studying the man's movements. Like he had done with the others. He had no time to waste. He didn't want anybody missing him. And looking for him.

When alarmed people told him about this morning's TV news...

... he had almost laughed, amused it had taken the police so long.

He had been telling them from the start, right after he ticked off that blasphemous painter from his kill list, but he was telling the wrong man. That Police Commissioner was a twit.

But this other cop, Inspector Ferraz, he was sharp as a whip.

He had figured out at once. The development excited him.

They knew, so what? He'd like to see them stop him!

Today was going to be the sixth, he was Whispering Death!

Jhinga was a hypocrite.

He pretended to have religious beliefs he did not possess at all. He went to Siddhivinayak on Tuesday, because Tuesday was Lord

Ganesh's day. There was nothing bigger happening in Mumbai today.

Some things you just accepted. That's what faith was all about.

Like you went to St. Michael's Church in Mahim for the Novena to Our Lady of Perpetual Succor on Wednesday, you didn't wonder why. And if you wanted to visit the Mahim Dargah and seek the blessings of Baba Makhdoom Ali Mahimi, Friday was the day, no question about it.

But Jhinga couldn't bear the crowds at Siddhivinayak on Tuesday.

It was beneath his dignity to stand in serpentine queues to get a foot in. So what he did was drive past the temple on Veer Savarkar Road and stop across. The centuries old temple was now a magnificent and monolithic structure of granite and marble towering over Prabhadevi. It wasn't just a shrine of historical importance or archaeological significance. It was Lord Ganesh's address in Mumbai. And if you stood across and looked up, you would feel a spiritual tug when your gaze rested on the golden *kalash* – the pointed dome – with an orange flag fluttering next to it. It was like a blessing from above.

That's all Jhinga did every Tuesday.

The atmosphere outside Siddhivinayak was festive. The lane by the side was lined by little shops with friendly Maharashtrian salesmen selling everything you needed for the *puja* inside – flowers, coconut, small *diyas* and the *ghee* or camphor to light them up. People came for the first *aarti* on Tuesday at 3.15 am. They walked through the night from across Mumbai. Others stood in the queue all day and made it for the last *aarti* at 12.30 am.

He liked the sanctity of the temple.

The world stopped outside its gates. No sounds of traffic disturbed the prayers offered to the 19th century stone Ganpati that sat two-and-half feet high, surveying everything and missing nobody, its trunk unusually twisted to the right, shyly flanked by the peeping idols of Riddhi and Siddhi, the Goddesses of sanctity, success, riches and prosperity.

HE GAZED at Ganesh Bhuvan impatiently.

It was a squat, three-storied yellow building whose ground floor was occupied by all sorts of interesting businesses. There was a helmet shop, a skin specialist, a motor driving school, a hardware and electronics store. Royal Enfield had an authorized service centre, Axis Bank had an ATM, and Idea and Tata Docomo had outlets. Beneath trees, flower sellers stringed together marigold garlands. A medical store was located next to a general practitioner. There was a wine shop, an investments company and a *farsan* mart; a mattress seller, a bookstall and a watch repairer.

Ganesh Bhuvan also had the New India Bar & Restaurant, Gee Lee Chinese Restaurant with ghastly red decor, Rajendra Restaurant & Bar, and Café Noorani from which emerged tantalizing aromas. Residents needn't go out on Saturday. They could make a bar-hopping night of it right there.

He had come by bus, hopping off at St. Michael's Church on Lady Jamshedji Road. On Wednesday, the day of the Novena, this area was a *mela*. Wednesday to Mahim was what Tuesday was to Prabhadevi. A day of faith and miracles because Our Lady of Perpetual Succor was a sort of universal mom. Thousands attended the 16 half-hour Novenas held in English, Hindi, Marathi and Tamil, starting at 6 am and ending at 9.30 pm. He went down quiet, leafy lanes, passing an East Indian chapel dating back to 1934, and Catholic homes with Christmas stars in the windows and tapestry saying 'Peace Be With You' on the walls.

He cut across Soonawala Agiary Lane, which had a Parsi fire temple and housing colony called Contractor Baug, and a Dr. Jerry Braganza practicing medicine next to Dr. Uday Gaitonde's Imaging Centre and Dr. Wilson Menezes's Pathology Laboratory, shuffling and limping past a roadside mechanic repairing vintage English motorcycles and a dentist's clinic reassuringly named Gentle Dental Care. Here was the Allied Industrial Estate with its Jagat Ganeshotsav Mitra Mandal. Music was loudly playing. And a buffet lunch had been spread out to which everybody working and living, begging and hawking in Mahim was invited.

He slipped inside unnoticed and bowed to the Ganpati.

From a green-domed mosque at a Muslim *kabarastan* next door, came the muezzin's afternoon call for *namaz*. He shuffled and limped past a smelly open fish market outside a BMC office for Roads, Drains & Gardens. Cats and crows fought for discarded fish heads, tails and entrails. Just beyond this unhygienic spot was the Pikale Hospital with all kinds of operative facilities, with a yellow ambulance waiting outside.

He was hurrying past fruit sellers and vegetable vendors…

… when a shower of sparks and the scream of tortured steel stopped him.

A bicycle knife-sharpener with his grinding wheel!

Silently he offered the man his Rampuri.

It took less than a minute, but when he lightly ran his thumb against the cutting edge, he knew the knife was sharp enough to go through anything.

Now he didn't dawdle.

He shuffled and limped past a 1906 marble cross of Jesus Christ erected by the Victory Sports Club with candles burning in the wind at its base. And then he was there, fiddling with his transistor and hoping India would show some spark in the second ODI against England at the Rose Bowl in Southampton today.

JHINGA HAD arrived.

He watched the restobar owner's Verna awkwardly enter the narrow gate of Ganesh Bhuvan – almost sideways like a crab – and drive into the compound where children played cricket next to a small temple. He got ready to make his move.

And then he stood staring.

Who was that next to Jhinga in the car?

A girl… but she wasn't part of this script!

He stared flabbergasted, uncertain what to do. He had no back-up plan. It wasn't meant to be this way. But how could he… *with the girl there…* he had not anticipated this.

It was too late to change strategy.

He couldn't reshuffle the victims.

There was no going back to the drawing board.

Should he take out the girl as well?

No, Ganesha forbid!

She wasn't an actor in this ensemble cast of 10.

But time was ticking away; he might not get a second chance.

And just when he was struggling with these thoughts, wondering how to overcome the situation, he saw the couple pause on the sidewalk outside Ganesh Bhuvan. The girl said something and swept her hand towards the druggist in the building.

Jhinga nodded morosely. He was smoking, a packet of Marlboro Red and his cell phone in one hand. He looked at his watch and said something. The girl giggled, jostled him with her hip and walked away.

His eyes followed her, noticing her sexy, confident strut.

When he looked back – Jhinga had gone!

He had entered the building.

There was not a moment to be lost. The girl would be back. He went after Jhinga, shuffling and limping, but not so quickly as to attract attention.

The staircase of Ganesh Bhuvan was not one of its redeeming features. It was tiny and narrow and low, the sides crowded in on the stairwell. It was also dark. When he had done a recce here, he wondered how families had taken their furniture up.

Jhinga was lumbering up the first flight, huffing and puffing and blowing back clouds of smoke. He followed on silent feet like Whispering Death, the knife glittering in his hand, his eyes on the man's broad back. The owner of ashta-vinayaka was tall and heavy, and he had the advantage of being on a higher stair, the place to take him would be on the small landing coming up on the first floor. And hope nobody stepped out of one of the four flats at that moment. He couldn't get it wrong. But there was too much of a risk here, he hadn't planned it like this.

His heart was beating loudly…

… Jhinga reached the landing.

Nimbly, he went around him.

Hearing a scurrying sound, Jhinga looked over his right shoulder.

But he was already in front, coming up from the left.

Frowning, Jhinga turned to begin the next flight and was brought to an unexpected halt. An evilly grinning stranger had appeared without warning and was standing two steps above him with his hands behind his back.

Where had he come from, he wasn't there a second ago!

"Yes?" Jhinga said inquiringly, because the man was blocking his path and looked like he had business with him, grinning in that lopsided crazy way.

"Moryaa Re!" the man on the stairs said.

"What?" asked Jhinga puzzled.

It was the last word he uttered.

The man's hand flashed from behind his back, the wicked knife glittering in the dark stairwell, and Jhinga felt a sudden, sharp and lacerating pain as it viciously slashed his throat… ripping muscle, cartilage and soft tissue, rupturing the trachea and esophagus as easy as cutting through butter, wreaking havoc in its sharp and shiny wake.

Outside Ganesh Bhuvan, there was the soft threatening growl of thunder.

Like the sky had apologetically stifled a burp from exploding impolitely.

Then a bolt of forked lightning struggled and broke free. It streaked over Mahim Railway Station, taking a few thousandths of a second, with a crackling bang that rattled the old building.

The rain came just as suddenly.

Jhinga coughed the cigarette out…

… and dropped the cell phone and cigarette packet.

His head fell forward, the severed jugular pumping dark blood down his shirt front, and he groped the walls on either side for support.

He had no ability to raise his head.

But in his dying seconds he had the vitality to make one desperate lunge at the man before collapsing onto the landing with a crash that also shook Ganesh Bhuvan.

"Moryaa Re!" said the man softly again.

Stepping over the nightclub owner's body that was bleeding profusely, he picked up the cell phone and carefully threaded his way down the stairs avoiding the blood.

He emerged from Ganesh Bhuvan and silently moved away.

Everything had changed… outside and inside.

Black thunderclouds had gathered over Mahim and Tulsi Pipe Road was looking as dark as it did at dusk. He watched the oncoming traffic crawling with windshield wipers slapping and headlights on, the tires hissing on the wet and slick road.

From a pocket he pulled out a piece of paper.

Reading from it, he dialed a number from Jhinga's phone.

At the curb, where the doorman of New India Bar & Restaurant stood holding an umbrella, there was a signal and a zebra crossing to the station. He shuffled and limped there, walking in the rain, his head bent. The girl was still at the drug store, sheltering beneath its awning, and he briefly caught her eye as he waited for the lights to change. She anxiously looked at her watch.

He chuckled to himself, thinking what was her hurry…

… time had run out for Jhinga.

FERRAZ WAS having a glass of tea when the call came.

He had spent the morning reviewing all the interviews they had done of people somehow related to the five serial murders victims. They lead to nowhere.

"*Namaskar saheb,*" the Station House operator said. "I have Sr. PI Farooque Baig of Mahim Police Station on the line. He wants to talk to you."

Surprised, Ferraz took the call.

"*As-salaam-alaikum, Ferraz bhai,*" Baig said. "You know this Ganesh Shetty from Mahim, owner of ashta-vinayaka?"

"Hi Farooque! No, haven't heard of him. What's ashta-vinayaka?"

"A nightclub in Dahisar."

"Dahisar! That's way off my turf. What does he want?"

"He's dead! Killed on the staircase of his building."

"Oh, in Dahisar?"

"He was murdered 10-15 minutes ago. We got a call from somebody reporting the murder. It happened at Ganesh Bhuvan on Tulsi Pipe Road opposite Mahim station."

"Ganesh Bhuvan, that's the building's name? Like the victim's?"

"Yes, the caller told my duty officer to inform you."

"Me! About the murder? Why me?"

"Don't know. But here's the strange thing. The caller ID showed that the call had been made from this victim Ganesh Shetty's phone only! And it's now switched off and missing."

Ferraz's drew in his breath sharply.

"How was this chap killed?"

"Somebody slashed his throat."

"One cut only?" he asked.

"More than a cut, his throat has been ripped wide open."

"Did the caller say anything else?" Ferraz asked in a tight voice.

"He said '*Moryaa Re!*'"

WEDNESDAY

23

THE COBRA got upstaged that morning.

At 10.15 am a bomb exploded in the Delhi High Court. Killing 11 and injuring 91. The explosion rocked Parliament a kilometer away. TV images showed lawyers in black coats fleeing through the smoke as police and firemen struggled to remove the injured to nearby hospitals. Dismembered bodies covered in blood and shredded limbs lay around.

The Harkat-ul-Jihad al-Islami, an Islamist fundamental organization active in Pakistan, Bangladesh and India, claimed responsibility. So did the Indian Mujahideen. It didn't matter which terrorist organization had planted the explosive. Delhi had been the target of so many bomb attacks that it was emotionally numb to them now. Death had become a number. There was no more outrage and fear. The capital struggled back to its feet. Psychiatrists said this was a process of habituation.

Like Delhi, Mumbai too was vulnerable to terrorism.

And Mumbai was now celebrating Ganesh Chaturthi.

The preparations had begun weeks in advance. Idol-makers from small towns and remote villages had been sculpting and painting Ganpati idols out of mud and clay behind tarpaulin screens in dark and damp courtyards and passages of Mumbai's mill areas. Ganeshotsav was the common man's festival. The simple Maharashtrians living in old chawls put their heart and soul into it like no other Mumbaikars could.

The city's 130-odd textile mills were gone. Finished by a strike in 1982 that never got resolved. It left 300,000 workers jobless. The mill owners sold out to entrepreneurs in the late 1990s who put up gigantic shopping malls with designer boutiques, multiplex cinemas, fine dining restaurants, rocking night clubs, electronic stores, car and bike showrooms, bowling alleys and video gaming hubs. They retained the tall, stone chimneys of the textile mills. These were the last vestiges of Mumbai's proud industrial past. Like the mill workers' families living in rundown chawls nearby. It was in these humble dwellings that Lord Ganesh felt most welcome when he visited the city.

You got a real sense of Ganeshotsav here…

… this is where the heartbeat and faith was.

For ten days from dawn till midnight, soulful *bhakti-geet* competed with thumping Bollywood chartbusters to disturb people's sleep. But who was sleeping? Everybody was out. Musicians blowing trumpets, beating drums and clashing cymbals led joyous processions of Ganpatis for immersion. Every street, every home was illuminated with colored lights and flickering earthen *diyas.* Shops and market places came spectacularly alive with dazzling displays of their wares at attractive discounts.

Mumbai never stayed still during Ganeshotsav. There was a buzz and a bustle everywhere. The celebrations were by individual families and entire communities. Most homes had their own small Ganpatis. And there was one Sarvajanik Ganpati in the neighborhood for everybody to share and worship and for others to come and admire. The city was a slow moving sea of people hopping from one Sarvajanik Ganpati to the next.

The Mumbai Police were in a dilemma.

The Maharashtra Legislative Assembly, which interrupted its Monsoon Session to condemn the Delhi blasts, refused to discuss Mumbai's serial killer. The Harkat-ul-Jehadi or Indian Mujahideen were the immediate threat. They were massacring in large number. Not one person a day like the Ganpati killer. The Chief Minister said that the police were more urgently required to secure Mumbai. Instead of going on a wild goose chase after a publicity-seeking serial predator.

A red alert was sounded…

… and the police locked down Mumbai.

A slew of security measures went into place.

Armed policemen in bulletproof jackets were seen everywhere. The Quick Response Team's commandos were deployed at sensitive locations and vital installations. *Nakabandis* and combing operations to weed out troublemakers were started. Sniffer dogs were used to secure public areas. Consulates and embassies were fortified. Unprecedented *bandobast* was mounted at major Sarvajanik Ganpatis and immersion sites. Metal detectors and baggage scanners were operated there by policemen who also physically frisked devotees. Over 15,000 CCTVs were installed wherever Ganeshotsav was being celebrated. Plainclothes cops mingled with the crowds. The security at the airport was tightened. Explosive detecting devices were brought in. The weekly holidays of policemen were cancelled.

Nawalkar addressed the press for the second time in four days.

The CP said, "Terrorists cannot be allowed to hold Mumbai to ransom. We will not shut down the city. We will secure it. The police are making every possible effort to ensure that nothing untoward takes place."

Murder was also untoward. But could they stop him?

HE WAS not a soap opera man.

Canned TV shows turned viewers into zombies, he thought.

They altered human consciousness, shut down critical thinking and rewired the mind.

Any wonder TV was known as the idiot box. Or the boob tube. Which was more offensive. He thought a boob tube was a strapless, shapeless brassiere made of stretch material. Apparently also slang for TV. But couch potatoes loved sitcoms. They followed them like this was the stock market and they were trading in melodrama.

He didn't like TV too much.

Didn't care to even watch cricket telecast live.

So he was looking forward to killing Nikhil Sanyal. The small screen's leading actor who made young girls swoon and old women weep with his performance in the No. 1 prime time Hindi serial *Sapne, Apne Apne.* He was a household name. Famous also in Pakistan, the UK and US, Canada, parts of Europe, South Africa, Australia, South East Asia, and even China – where the *saas-bahu* yarns were dubbed in Mandarin.

Good, he thought. Half the world would mourn Sanyal's death.

He had an appointment with Sanyal this evening. The actor was expecting him, but not what was coming, he chuckled to himself.

Whispering Death was coming, that's what.

JACKIE WAS on her phone…

… impatiently wishing Ferraz would pick up *his* damn phone!

She was rarely antsy with him like this.

But she had called twice already, his phone only rang and rang.

What was he thinking of… not to take her call!

He had been unusually subdued this morning after reading the papers. One big banner headline screamed **"WHO'S NEXT?"** in a front page report of Ganesh Shetty's murder. Some criminal lawyers and an NGO had filed a Public Interest Litigation (PIL) in the Bombay High Court to have the serial killings' investigation transferred to the Central Bureau of Investigation (CBI). They alleged the Mumbai

Police wasn't able to detect the murders and was deliberately misleading the city and media with false breakthroughs.

Ferraz had been dismayed.

Fortunately, the judges of the division bench didn't see merit in the petition. They were aware that the entire force, from the CP to PC (Commissioner of Police to Police Constable), was trying to catch the killer. They allowed the police to continue with the investigation, but ordered the public prosecutor to keep the court updated on its progress.

Now Jackie looked at her watch. Was Ferraz on his bike?

SANYAL WAS the Ranbir Kapoor of TV.

Just like Ronit Roy was once the Amitabh Bachchan of the small screen.

His decision to quit *Sapne, Apne Apne* would break a million hearts and cause the serial's sponsors to rethink their support because Sanyal was synonymous with the show. Once before he had quit one of these tearjerkers midway and the channel had to yank it off the air because fans rejected the replacement the studio got for him and the serial's TRPs plunged.

Television Rating Points – that's what it was all about.

A Bollywood hero got only the Friday of his film's release to impress the audience, while a TV actor got a new chance every night to redeem himself. But the success of a serial and the popularity of an actor depended on the TRPs they drew every week. For which the actor had to lend his ass to the studio. Night after night, life sucked.

But Tellyland couldn't hope to compare with Bollywood.

The working conditions of TV stars were dreadful, the hours were arduous and unearthly, the sets were deplorable and lacked basic amenities, even the food provided by the studio was yuck! Worse, most studios lacked a script bank. They were making changes and introducing twists constantly. They were writing the serial and shooting at the same time. Actors didn't know what the fuck to expect when they reported the next day. They ended up working 14 to 16 hours on an episode.

The labor law of the land, the Industrial Disputes Act, was unsympathetic; though CINTAA, the Cine & TV Artists' Association, pushed studios not to ask for more than a 12-hour day. The problem was TV actors worked on a contractual basis and were paid by the hour, for the day, or per episode. And they were generally locked in a three-year agreement. Studios did not leave the door open for pay hike negotiations even if their shows became super hits and the actor got compared to the current Bollywood heartthrob.

JACKIE RARELY called Ferraz when he was at work.

There was no telling what he might be doing. But she had information for him that might be a breakthrough in this serial murders investigation.

Restlessly, she jiggled her feet.

Answer! she mentally commanded Ferraz.

Miraculously he did.

"Hi honey, where's the fire?"

"Angie! Where are you? Why weren't you taking my call?"

In the background she could hear traffic. The noise was deafening. Ferraz was shouting, "I'm on the–"

"Okay, okay, never mind," she cut in excitedly. "Listen Angie, I have something that ought to help you with these serial murders."

"Yeah, what do you mean?"

He was suddenly all cop, she heard it in his voice.

"Actually it's my professor who came up with it."

There was the cacophony of horns and the screech of brakes.

Ferraz appeared not to have heard her.

"What?" he shouted.

"I said it's my professor who–"

"I meant what do you... which professor?"

"Prof. Murti, my guide, he teaches Abnormal Psychology."

"Prof. Murthy? What did he say?"

"Er, Angie, Prof. Murti's beside me. He wants to tell you himself."

SANYAL WAS tickled to be compared to Ranbir.

The actors looked not unlike each other. And he had spent as many years in TV as Raj Kapoor's grandson had in Bollywood. But Sanyal's following was much bigger because TV's reach was wider. Ranbir had nine films in five years, Sanyal was on the air every night. Bollywood only provided escapism. Whereas teleserials were the common man's nightly fix. Their situations reflected his middle class experiences. They gave the ideals of the quintessential Indian family fanatical attention, they made references to the *Mahabharata* and *Ramayana,* and added sex, extramarital affairs, murders, conspiracies and kidnappings to shock the conservative viewer. That's what Wikipedia said of the great Indian soap opera.

Soap operas dominated Indian TV...

... and because women were their central characters, the actresses came with higher price tags and took home fatter pay checks than the male actors.

Sanyal was sick of acting under these circumstances.

He was the face of *Sapne, Apne Apne,* the reason behind its success, but the director was focusing more on the female lead now. Sanyal knew TV stars had a short shelf life. If they stuck to doing soaps, their stardom would be temporary, by appearing on screen every night they also risked audience fatigue. The industry was full of burned out actors.

But Sanyal was a bankable TV superstar.

And Bollywood actor and producer John Abraham thought of Sanyal when casting for *Vicky Donor*, his forthcoming rom-com with the sperm donation and infertility theme. He had signed Anu Kapoor,

Ayushmann Khurrana and Yami Gautam for the film already. Like Sanyal, they too had started their showbiz careers in TV.

Sanyal couldn't believe his luck.

But how could he accept a film role? It required minimum 40 days at a stretch for the shoot on location, then post production work, and two weeks after that for promotions. His commitment to *Sapne, Apne Apne* was like a millstone around his neck. He couldn't back out of his contract. And he didn't have a single day to spare. The serial was looking set to run forever.

Sanyal struggled for an answer… and came up with a brainwave.

FERRAZ WAITED impatiently.

There was a moment's hesitation, then a whispered conversation between Jackie and her professor, before he came on the line speaking softly.

"Inspector *saheb*…" an erudite and cultured voice.

"Sir, my girl tells me you have some information," Ferraz yelled.

"Yes, these serial murders – by a psychopathic killer, the press says? Somebody who might be a *bhakt* of Lord Ganesh? Is that right?"

"What do you have to tell me, sir?" Ferraz asked.

"The suspect's been leaving cryptic verses behind?"

Ferraz silently cursed the press.

"Well, yeah… he's a crazy," he said.

"How many has he left? One after each murder?"

"Well, yes."

"What do you make of them, Inspector?"

"Nothing! Psychos aren't known for making wise decisions."

"Why! You don't think the verses will lead you to the killer?"

Ferraz felt like kicking Prof. Murthy in the ass.

He had nothing to say. He was after information. Like everybody else. And he was using Jackie to get it with this bullshit story of helping the police.

"Sir, I'm afraid I can't really–"

"I read about the writing on the wall, wasn't that at the painter's house? Some newspaper carried a picture of it… '*The flowers on the canvas have dried, Still life is never so still after all*'… And there was one about the '*Emperor of Darkness…* ' that also got reported."

"That's right, it's some kind of dark poetry," Ferraz admitted, "but the verses don't make sense. They're just a publicity gimmick."

The professor tut-tutted disapprovingly.

"Inspector *saheb*, these days it's all contemporary poetry. Greek and Latin to the dispassionate. People only understand the 'There was a young lady named Bright' variety of limerick."

Sensing a reprimand, Ferraz asked, "Well, what do you have for me?"

"Have the police considered taking a mythologist's help?"

"Who's help?"

"A mythologist, Inspector *saheb*."

"What's that?"

There was a disbelieving pause, then the professor said kindly, "Somebody who is an expert in mythology. He would interpret the Ganesh motive in the murders and perhaps give you a lead."

"A lead to?"

"To the man you are seeking, Inspector *saheb*."

"I don't see–"

"A mythologist isn't a criminologist, mythology is the study of a subjective truth of people that is communicated through stories, symbols and rituals, Inspector *saheb*. Unlike fantasy that is nobody's truth, or history that seeks to be everybody's truth, mythology is somebody's truth. And a renowned mythologist like Devdutt Pattanaik would tell you that what's true for the insider is false for the outsider. He's just out with a book interestingly titled *99 Thoughts on Ganesha*."

Ferraz didn't know what the professor was talking about.

"Did you see the Hollywood film *Seven*?" the professor asked.

Surprised, Ferraz snapped, "No!"

"You should, *Seven* is about a smart and meticulous American serial killer whose murders represent the seven deadly sins."

"What seven deadly sins?"

"Inspector saheb! Surely you're joking? I'm talking of Gluttony, Greed, Sloth, Pride, Lust, Envy and Wrath, they are part of Christian ethics!"

"I'm a man of little faith, sir. Excuse me, you said you have–"

"He also leaves writings in blood on the wall, Inspector *saheb*."

Ferraz was silent.

A cyclist was ringing his bell loudly and incessantly for a taxi parked in front to move. The cabbie pretended not to hear the jingling and jangling.

Ferraz felt like kicking him in the ass also.

"And the killer in *Seven* is also ahead of the police at every step."

"Why are you telling me this, sir?"

"Your suspect's not a crazy, Inspector *saheb*. He's an intelligent man, educated and respectable too, not your everyday killer, I'm afraid."

"How do you know that?"

"Well, I'm a keen student of Abnormal Psychology."

"Even then… ?"

"I know who wrote the poems."

GANESHOTSAV WAS coming.

And it was a tradition with the Sanyal family to get a Ganpati home. His parents were devout *bhakts*. Sanyal wasn't. He had no time for religion. His work was his worship. TV was his God. He didn't believe in Lord Ganesh. He never attended the *aartis* at his parents' house. Nor did he participate in the *visarjan*, great photo-op though it was for the media and his fans.

Then, last year, his parents were killed in a car crash on the Mumbai-Pune Expressway. And Sanyal, who overcame his grief by getting immersed in work, had not thought of the Ganpati his parents brought home. But now his brainwave took shape.

When Sanyal leaked it out in the press that he wouldn't be able to shoot for *Sapne, Apne Apne* over 15 days in late August and early September, the studio head had a fit and threw his contract onto the table.

But Sanyal pleaded. He had to fulfill his parents' obligation to Lord Ganesh. As their only child, he had to continue the family tradition. To discontinue the practice would be irreverent. It would also not be proper for him to work during Ganeshotsav. He wanted to spend time in service and prayer to Lord Ganesh in memory of his parents.

The studio didn't know what to do.

It knew this was an eyewash. To deny the actor leave from the teleserial would amount to disrespect for Lord Ganesh, which the great TV watching public wouldn't tolerate. But to relieve Sanyal for half a month when they couldn't spare him for even a day was to bring the curtains down on *Sapne, Apne Apne*. So they worked out a face-saving exit that wouldn't kill the show.

What they did was kill Sanyal instead.

They introduced a twist in the plot that dramatically took him out; that was the only way the studio could release Sanyal from its 14 hours a day, six days a week schedule without disturbing the serial's continuity.

As it turned out, the decision sent the show's TRPs shooting through the roof because Sanyal milked his death sequence for all it was worth.

He truly was a good actor.

Meanwhile, he also had to act like a Ganpati *bhakt* now.

In his parents' old bungalow at Khar, away from the ritz and glitz of Tellyland, Sanyal installed a Ganpati and kept the rituals, customs and traditions of the festival like a true believer. The bungalow was illuminated by colored lights, soft devotional music played through the day, and *diyas* cast a warm glow inside. The Ganpati wore a red and yellow silk *dhoti*, gold ornaments and a pearl neckpiece. Sanyal performed the *aarti* every evening and kept an open house for fans to pay obeisance to the Lord and also worship Sanyal himself from up close.

This, again, was a brainwave – to use the Khar bungalow.

He could have got the Ganpati to his own home. But fans and the media had no access to Sanyal's starry Versova apartment complex where lots of film and TV personalities lived. The security there was snobbish. Visitors were screened, signed in and announced on the intercom. The *janta* was discouraged at the gates. How would Sanyal play this Ganpati gig to the gallery if the audience was conspicuous by its absence? It would have been a no-show. The Khar bungalow had only a caretaker-watchman who was a family retainer now well past his prime. His orders were to stop nobody. You didn't need a gate-pass to visit Lord Ganesh at Sanyal's bungalow on 20th Road. It was open house.

FERRAZ THOUGHT he heard wrong.

He had halted at Kalbadevi to take Jackie's call. All kinds of people lived and worked here. There were Hindu temples, Parsi *agiaries*, a buzzing Khau Gully of unpretentious roadside eateries, two wholesale cloth markets, the cotton exchange, and Zaveri Bazar that sold diamond and gold jewelry. A BEST bus driver honked in his ear. And a handcart puller, his tense muscles dripping sweat, yelled at him to get out of the way.

"Could you please speak up, sir?" Ferraz shouted. "I'm afraid I didn't get that, there's so much noise here."

"I know who wrote the poems," the professor repeated softer than before.

"You do! Who wrote them, sir?"

"Pritish Nandy."

"Pritish Nandy? The–"

"Yes, Pritish Nandy, a very profound poet of our generation."

"How do you know this, sir?"

"About the poet?"

"No, who wrote the poems."

"I have his book."

"Pritish Nandy's poems? You aren't saying–"

"No, no, Inspector *saheb*, I am not suggesting Mr. Nandy is the..."

"–that the poet has something to do with the murders?"

"... man you're looking for. I'm only bringing to your notice that the poems the police are breaking their heads over are taken from Mr. Nandy's book."

"Good, because we have no idea–"

"Come now, Inspector *saheb*, Mr. Nandy is a celebrated name, he's a Padma Shri and has been a Rajya Sabha MP for years. In 1981, he suddenly stopped writing poetry to begin a spectacular career in journalism and public life."

"Quite," said Ferraz.

"It's hard to label him. Is he the editor who changed the face of Indian journalism? The guy who set the trend of power-packed signature shows on national TV by interviewing the biggest and most powerful? The maker of cult movies, 28 in the last decade, many winning international–"

"Tell me about the poems, sir," Ferraz shouted in a strangled voice.

"Oh, yes. They have been taken from his book of 2010."

"Last year? I thought you said he stopped–"

"Yes, this is his first book since 1981."

"Are you sure they are his poems?"

"Well, I'm reading the book. I was there for its launch at Crossword. Aishwarya Rai Bachchan read a few poems. Then Gulzar, Shashi Tharoor, and–"

"What can you tell me about the poems, sir?" Ferraz asked edgily.

"Oh, Mr. Nandy's a master at playing with words and metaphors."

"I see," said Ferraz, not seeing anything at all.

"One thing I could have told you from that writing on the painter's wall."

"What's that?"

"That your man was going to kill again!"

"Where does he say that in those two lines?"

He felt ridiculous having this absurd conversation.

But the professor's reply chilled Ferraz.

"Not in the poem, Inspector *saheb*, but it's in the title of the book."

"What's the title?"

The professor paused, then said, "It's called *Again*."

A CHURCH bell was ringing in Khar Danda.

He switched off the transistor at once.

He was trying to raise commentary from the Sportpark Het Schootsveld in Deventer, the Netherlands. Where Netherlands was playing Kenya in the Intercontinental Cup, an international first class tournament between leading associate members of the ICC. They included Ireland, Canada, Scotland, Namibia, Afghanistan and the UAE. It was raining in Deventer. The captains hadn't even tossed for the match.

The bell was being rung in the old St. Vincent de Paul Church. He pictured a venerable sacristan with an experienced hand reverently leaning on the rope to spread God's message far and wide.

It was 7 pm. He was on 20th Road in Khar, just behind the church. Hiding beneath an umbrella, although there was no rain, because chances were he might be recognized.

This evening would be the seventh murder.

There were only three left.

My, how time flies when you're having fun.

The police had gone around the bend with the first six. This one would kill them! The media would make a big deal of it. Especially the TV channels, because the victim was a famous and popular TV actor. He was used to being on the air every night.

Tonight would be his curtain call.

He had visited the Sri Saibaba Mitra Mandal's Ganpati on 14th Road before coming here. Huge, illuminated archways welcomed him. And a dazzling display of colored lights, by some technical wizardry, raced up and down both sides of the road dizzily. Political banners jostled with hoardings of sponsors. A buffet dinner was laid out for the poor. A press photographer, barefoot and standing on the wet road, took pictures. This was old Khar with new buildings, the old structures had been razed and redeveloped into modern high-rises, but the roads still had no names and continued to go with numbers.

It was a dirty neighborhood.

Garbage dumps overflowed. There were slums with ugly and open public toilets. The shops and establishments looked tired and jaded. Like they could do with redevelopment too. But Bollywood superstar Shah Rukh Khan had his corporate office here. Beneath which all kinds of businesses operated, from a coconut-seller and undertaker to a butcher and *dosawallah*. He could hear bells ringing in temples dedicated to Hanuman, Lord Krishna and Ganpati, all within a whispered prayer of each other.

He could see Sanyal's bungalow, there were fairy lights on the gateposts and in the trees, and a black Honda CRV was parked on 20th Road. A colony of bats was noisily waking up in a tree above him. There was little traffic, mainly auto-rickshaws that went by in a yellow and black blur, some motorcyclists and the odd car. It was a cloudy night. The sun had set quietly without its song and dance. He could see the landing lights of planes probing the darkness as they made their approach from the west.

The church bell was ringing. Or pealing or chiming. What was the verb? It wasn't tolling. That was associated with death. A church bell rung to announce death was frightening. A deep, haunting and slow paced 'dong' that broadcast a feeling of sadness and marked an inexorable march to the grave, the silence of death hanging between each toll. This evening, it would have been appropriate.

He looked at his watch.

It was time to go to Sanyal's bungalow. He knew that after the *aarti,* there was only the old family retainer on the premises with the actor. No driver and no bodyguard. Slowly he shuffled and limped towards the bungalow gate.

IT WAS the seventh day of Ganeshotsav.

Sanyal had got plenty of TV coverage the first three days and fans faithfully made the pilgrimage to the bungalow; but the media presence trickled down to the occasional print reporter now, and only a few fans straggled in. Sanyal didn't mind. His whole focus was on Bollywood. He couldn't wait to give a press conference and announce that he had signed his first film. That would make his fans and the press sit up.

This evening, a journalist from *The Daily* fixed an appointment with his PR agent to interview Sanyal. The man appeared silently before the *aarti*, when Sanyal was busy arranging flowers around the Ganpati after smiling and posing for photographs and seeing off the last fans.

"Dnyaneshwar Wagh," he said, presenting the actor with a visiting card. It said *Special Correspondent – The Daily*. Sanyal regarded the man. He had not bothered to check who was coming. He was expecting somebody more with it. Like a young, smartphone-using GenNext TV reporter who was used to visiting the sets for gossip, preferably a girl and hopefully a fan.

Instead, *The Daily* sent him this…

"I don't know why," Sanyal said, "but I thought you would be…"

He left the sentence hanging.

The correspondent chuckled in amusement.

"You thought *what*… that I'd be younger and different?"

"No, I…"

Sanyal didn't know what to say, because that's exactly what crossed his mind, and this fellow looked like one of those Mantralaya reporters who were forever getting in the Chief Minister's hair.

"Haven't you brought a photographer?" he asked.

"He'll come along in due time," Wagh said and chuckled again.

"I… never mind… let's begin," Sanyal said dismissively, "I don't want to keep Ganpatiji waiting, shall we talk after the *aarti*?"

His eyes gleaming, the correspondent said, "I can hardly wait."

Sanyal, who was dressed in a cream silk *dhoti*, turned to the Ganpati, applied sandal paste and *kumkum* on its forehead, palms and feet, then placed a garland around the idol, picked up the *puja thali*, began ringing a bell and chanting:

"Sukhkarta dukhharta varta vighnachi
Nurvi purvi prem kripa jayachi…"

THE INTERVIEW was going badly.

This Wagh chap, *The Daily's* Special Correspondent, was turning out to be the kind of journalist Sanyal hated most. They were boorish, with the knack of getting under the interviewee's skin. Also aggravating. Asking all kinds of personal questions for which they knew there could be no answers, damn them. They took perverse pleasure in setting up traps for the unsuspecting interviewee. And they were prejudiced, the interview was just meant to fill in the blanks of whatever it was they had already made up their diseased minds to write.

Sanyal thought this interview would be on him.

Not on Lord Ganesh, that's all this Wagh chap wanted to talk about. He seemed to know nothing about TV. But, oh my, was he an authority on Ganpati or what!

Sanyal wished he hadn't agreed to the interview.

They were in the hall where the Ganpati sat in resplendent silence. The caretaker-watchman was outside, he had finished locking up for the night and was waiting by Sanyal's car; from the road came the sounds of traffic and snatches of conversation of people walking by.

Sensing his unhappiness, Wagh struck the professional note.

He asked, "Aren't you suffering withdrawal symptoms, I mean, you're off TV work for over a week already, isn't that unusual?

"*Tchah,*" Sanyal was scornfully dismissive.

"But you've been working pretty much without a break since you became a TV star," Wagh pointed out patronizingly.

"So what? I give up smoking and drinking also during Ganeshotsav," Sanyal replied untruthfully, "but I'm not missing all that. Now don't write that I'm a saint, because I'm not. Devotion to Ganpati doesn't mean I go to the temple. My work is my temple. I'm not an atheist. But I'm also not a hypocrite."

"Meaning… *who* is a hypocrite, then?"

"Meaning, I don't go to Siddhivinayak every Tuesday after informing the press… there are celebrities who do that," Sanyal hinted, "they won't step out of their car unless they see TV cameras."

"So what do you do?" Wagh asked innocently.

"*Arre baba*, if I am passing Prabhadevi on Tuesday, then I look at the Siddhivinayak Temple and do this (he joined his hands and bowed his head with eyes shut), I believe it's better to excel in my work... isn't that better utility of my time than standing 10 hours in a long queue to enter some temple?"

"No, I disagree," Wagh said.

Sanyal shrugged.

"I think it's more important to be good, simple and honest," he said, "can there be any better qualities in a human being?"

"Are you like that?" Wagh asked, a strange look on his face.

"*What do you mean!*"

Sanyal was beginning to get the measure of his interviewer.

"You claim to be a Ganpati *bhakt*, okay, what's the difference between Gyan Yoga, Bhakti Yoga and Karma Yoga, do you know?" Wagh asked.

"Huh, what do you mean?"

"Don't know... shocking! I will tell you. Ancient Hindus believed that wisdom must never be given, it has to be taken. And through Ganesha, his image, rituals and stories, they created a mythological puzzle that contained a profound truth which changed their understanding of the world and enabled them to lead a richer, fuller life. If we are willing to decode that puzzle, the answers to leading such a life are right there in front of us in the form of Ganesha. How we approach Ganesha is up to us. The intellectual approach is called Gyan Yoga, the emotional approach is Bhakti Yoga and the mechanical, ritualistic approach that you have chosen to take is known as Karma Yoga," said Wagh, in a mocking tone.

Sanyal shrugged again.

Where was this interview heading? He was irritated now.

But Wagh was not done.

"In the Mudgala Purana," he said, looking at Sanyal closely, "Ganesha takes eight forms to destroy the eight demons that represent the disruptive and emotional state in man. Do you know them?"

Sanyal didn't. He hadn't heard of the Mudgala Purana, the core scriptures for devotees of Ganesha, in fact, until this fellow who was beginning to bug him had brought it up. He was wondering whether he ought to slyly bring out his phone and Google it.

"Vakratunda, Ganesha rides a lion to kill Matsara – the demon of Jealousy," Wagh was saying, "Ekadanta rides a rat to kill Mada – the demon of Vanity, Vikata rides a peacock to overpower Kama – the lord of Lust, Vighnaraja rides a serpent to kill Mama – the demon of Self-indulgence, Dhumravarna..."

"Stop," said Sanyal, raising his hands up in defeat, "I'm not that kind of Ganesh *bhakt*."

"Oh, then what kind are you?" Wagh asked, pretending to be amazed, "the make-up, lights and camera kind?"

He gestured towards the Ganpati that was silently witnessing this face-off and said, "There is a phrase in Hindi meant to describe liars, hypocrites and pretenders. '*Hathi ke dant dekhane ke aur, khane ke aur*.'"

"But, but... why are you telling me this?" Sanyal demanded, "I thought you were a TV journalist here to–"

Wagh silenced him with a wave of the hand.

"Do you know Ganesha was once a scribe? And that he documented the *Mahabharata* for the sage Vyasa who had witnessed the events of this epic but could not put his thoughts down in words? And that this happened on the day we know as Akshaya Tritiya?"

Sanyal looked at him in silence.

"Do you know that legend says the Mongolian Emperor Kublai Khan was born to his childless father after the latter was advised to pray to Lord Ganesha to bless him with a son?" shouted Wagh angrily.

"I don't," admitted Sanyal, "but why are you–"

"What do you know then?" asked Wagh venomously. "Okay, next question Ganesh *bhakt*, is Ganpati married or single, *bolo*?"

Sanyal was silent.

The interview had taken an ugly turn that he could not understand, this bugger Wagh had resorted to a vicious cut-and-thrust inquisition that was leading to God knows where. One thing Sanyal knew for certain, it was not going into *The Daily*. For the man had given up the pretence of taking down notes. He had folded his notepad and put his pen away. And he was now…

Outside, a large Ganpati procession was noisily passing by.

Suddenly Sanyal rose and pointed to the door.

"Get out," he said coldly, trembling with fury.

He would deal with the consequences of being arrogant and hasty with the press later, *but what the fuck*, he was Nikhil Sanyal – the most recognized face of the Indian soap opera, how dare this two-bit hack question him like this. He was an actor, and across the world and all mediums of entertainment actors were known to take liberties with artistic expression. But this rat of a reporter was accusing him of blasphemy. This pathetic, unethical newshound was casting aspersions on his character, the muckraker, he would call up his editor and protest, he would take it up with *The Daily*, he would go to the fucking Press Council of India, but there was no way he would allow this tattler, this cheap newsmonger searching for a byline and a headline in his rag of a newspaper to ride on his name, oh no.

Annoyingly, the Ganpati procession stopped outside the bungalow. The beating of drums was loud and deafening. But nothing to match the frightful tuneless sounds coming out of speakers connected through an amplifier to the electronic keyboard.

Wagh stood up slowly, an insolent smile on his face.

"Aren't you afraid?" he asked Sanyal.

"Huh… afraid? Of what or who?"

"Of the Ganpati serial killer?"

"What Ganpati serial killer? That psycho… who murdered Sanghamitra, Nicole and the others because he thought they misrepresented Ganpati? That sick bastard! Hasn't he been arrested yet? Who is he to decide what is right or wrong for Lord Ganesh…

the police should encounter him."

"Yes him, aren't you afraid?" Wagh's eyes were glowing, "There is fear in the city, the police are clueless, nobody knows who he is and who will be his next victim."

"Who cares – fuck him! He is a creation of you people – the media."

"I think you should be afraid."

"Me? What is there to be afraid of... and *why* should I be?"

"You've done the same..."

"Done what!"

"Desecrated Lord Ganesh."

"I told you to get out!"

Outside, there was an uproar of voices.

The Ganpati processionists had got into a row with somebody who was blocking their way. You just couldn't go against Lord Ganesha today. Meanwhile, the music raucously tried to drown their fight.

"You aren't a Ganesh *bhakt*, are you? And you know nothing about Ganeshotsav. You used Ganpati as an excuse for your selfish and ulterior motives, as a means to an end, this is all a farce, and you are as false as your TV serials..."

"Are you getting out or should I–"

"What if this Ganpati serial killer were to target you next?"

"I would kill the bastard myself – get out!"

"You would kill him, how? By throwing a *modak* at him!"

"You're sick... no, I know how to deal with psychos."

And Sanyal strode purposefully to a desk and opened the top drawer. He drew out a snub-nosed revolver with a black wooden grip. He thumbed the hammer, broke open the cylinder and verified that it was loaded, then gave it a spin like Bollywood baddies did before playing Russian roulette. He flipped the cylinder shut with an expert flick of the wrist, hoping he had impressed or scared this blasted reporter.

Firecrackers replaced the agitated voices outside. The music picked up tempo and went into high gear. The dancing began again and the Ganpati procession began slowly moving.

"My personal .32 Webley Scott," Sanyal said proudly, "it's licensed – don't worry, just in case you think I've got an illegal gun and there's a story here. I keep it with me always. The chamber takes six bullets. I'm a good shot. One bullet should be enough for your Ganpati killer, what?"

Wagh was staring like he had never seen a gun before.

Sanyal hefted the revolver and sniffed the barrel lovingly.

"Yes, I know how I would deal with your Ganpati killer," he said grimly and turning his back on Wagh, returned the revolver to the drawer and slammed it shut.

"You really think so?" said a new disquieting voice behind him.

Startled, he began to turn.

And his blood froze. Wagh was right beside him, smiling cruelly, his right arm swinging up in a tight, swift arc of shiny steel.

"Moryaa Re!" he said, contemptuously.

Sanyal saw with terror the knife coming up, and realization dawned… but it was too late.

At that moment, all his bravado deserted him.

The knife struck the side of his neck just below the jaw with a terrible force. At the moment of impact it made a dull and sickening *thuunnnk*! The upward cutting motion, almost like a boxer's lethal uppercut, ripped Sanyal's throat to shreds, cleaving through and through and leaving a ragged and horribly gaping wound where his Adam's apple had been. The force of the assault made him gasp and sent him staggering into Wagh.

He felt himself being violently shoved back…

… and fell onto the desk into which he had just packed his gun, blood splattering the top and spilling onto the floor, pouring down his naked chest and staining his cream silk *dhoti*.

He lay sprawled there, his face resting in a thick pool of his own blood that was spreading rapidly, struggling to breathe, his body gone into shock, too weak to raise himself, his legs thrashing, tasting the blood bubbling through his lips as he underwent a spasm of coughing, knowing he was dying, his eyes focusing on the Ganpati that was fading away slowly as was the music outside the bungalow.

Dnyaneshwar Wagh picked up Sanyal's iPhone from the desk just as a snaking stream of blood reached it, and shuffled and limped to the door. There he paused, thought a moment, then returned to the body.

Carefully, so as not to topple the murdered actor, he pushed Sanyal aside and gently opened the drawer of the desk. The .32 Webley Scott lay there next to some homoeopathic medicines and the iPhone's charger.

With a moronic smile, his mouth drooling, he reached for it.

He had never wanted to do *it* with a gun. He didn't like guns. Didn't know how to handle them. They were noisy, they cost money. Besides, where would he get a gun from? A knife, anybody could lay his hand on. Knives inflicted more pain. That's what he wanted. To cause pain resulting in death.

But he was now thinking the last one was going to be difficult, because it was going to be done publicly, and he wanted to do it spectacularly, in full view of thousands. The problem was, there was bound to be a tight security cordon. Not in anticipation of him. Nobody knew he was coming. He was Whispering Death. But the security was always there. It might be difficult to breach. He might not be able to get close.

In which case the Rampuri would be useless.

He wiped it clean on the lifeless form of the actor now, then clicked it shut. He stuffed the revolver into the waist band of his trouser. Then with a final look around, he shuffled and limped out of the bungalow. He didn't want to linger here a moment longer. It was too dangerous. He would fire the SMS from outside.

Outside, the old caretaker-watchman waited impatiently beside the Honda CRV for his master to leave. His attention was on the tail end of the Ganpati procession just disappearing around the corner. He was hoping to touch Sanyal tonight, angling for Ganpati *baksheesh*.

Just then the *patrakar* chap came out with his umbrella open and stood beside him, appreciatively sniffing the clean monsoon air. He took out a pocket transistor and switched it on. The old man looked skywards puzzled. There wasn't even a hint of rain.

He cleared his throat and was about to ask the *patrakar*...

... when the man dug some money out of his pocket.

Slipping it to the old caretaker-watchman, he said, "*Moryaa Re!*"

The old man hardly noticed him go. He was looking at the currency note with disbelieving eyes. It was 500 rupees. What luck, he was thinking. The interview must have gone well.

THEY WERE having dinner when he got the SMS.

Jackie was telling Ferraz not to talk with his mouth full.

"It's impolite," she said fussily.

"*I'm not talking, I'm arguing*," Ferraz said, ruffling her further.

Dinner was Pasta Carbonara with bacon and Parmesan cheese. Jackie had also made a tangy tomato soup. And a pan of garlic rolls. Ferraz had no idea how she produced all this. But the meal brightened him. He was thinking of pouring himself a drink.

"No," Jackie warned him. "Are you done for the day?"

He knew she meant, 'What if you get called out for another murder?'

Ferraz made a face.

The police's guesstimate had been right.

After they stumbled upon the Ganpati motive for the serial killings on Sunday and figured the Cobra had one victim in mind for each day of Ganeshotsav, he had given them two more corpses. That of socialite Nicole Raja and restaurateur Ganesh Shetty.

Six days on the trot.

Must be a record of sorts, Ferraz was thinking.

The audacity of the daylight murder yesterday shocked him.

It came after the city had been warned that the serial killer was not just an intelligent, sadistic psychopath, but a Ganpati fanatic. And his victims had invited his wrath and revenge by being disrespectful to Lord Ganesh.

Ganesh Shetty was the sixth.

None of the first floor residents of Ganesh Bhuvan, where the restobar owner had been found by his girlfriend with his throat slit, had heard anything. The girl's bloodcurdling screams brought them out. She could tell the police nothing. She was an architect in her early 20s. She began seeing Ganesh Shetty seven months ago when he hired her to redesign his house. She didn't think he was in conflict with anybody. Nobody had objected to his restobar being named ashta-vinayaka. Or to the presence of the Ganpati idol on its premises. She couldn't imagine who would want him dead. The staff of the restobar, and the waitresses, said the same thing.

The Thane Rural Police, too, were of no help. Ganesh Shetty's business was suspect, yes, but they didn't think a rival had done him in. He had never complained about a threat to his life. They were secretly relieved he had been killed in Mahim, not Dahisar, that would have brought the bars in their jurisdiction to the government's attention all over again.

But there had been no murder so far today.

Ferraz had his fingers crossed.

Now he asked Jackie, "Did that professor give you the book?"

"No, he'll get it tomorrow."

Ferraz nodded, thoughtfully.

"What are you going to do about it?" she asked.

"I don't know. See if the verses sent by this crackpot are from that Pritish Nandy's book, to start with."

"If the professor said they are – then they are."

"Uh-huh, I'd still like to see the book."

"Will you be talking to Mr. Nandy?"

"He's not in the country. His office said he's in Australia. Doing a recce for some future film called *Shaadi Ke Side Effects*. It's the sequel to his–"

"His 2006 romantic comedy *Pyaar Ke Side Effects*? How cute!"

"Something like that. He's getting back on Saturday."

"Oh, you called already? That was quick!"

"This professor, he said he teaches Abnormal Psychology."

"Yes, my class," Jackie said brightly. "It's a branch of Psychology that studies unusual patterns of behavior, emotion and thought which may or may not be part of a larger mental illness."

"What's abnormal behavior," Ferraz innocently asked, "something like me talking with my mouth full?"

"I said that's impolite, not abnormal!"

"Same thing!"

"What rubbish you talk, Angie!" she moaned. "By abnormal behavior I meant depression, obsession, sexual deviation, even a temporary case of the blues, which a clinical psychologist assesses in a person and treats the psychological condition in a clinical practice."

"And this resident poet of yours, he–"

"The professor is distinguished in the study of Psychology!"

"Why isn't he in clinical practice, then? Instead of reading dirty limericks."

"Angie! He doesn't read dirty poems!"

"Not in class, maybe. But–"

"And not at home, either!"

"I'm saying, where does he get–"

"He doesn't get time. The professor's busy writing a paper on whether abnormalities caused by biological disorders and illnesses which are usually treated with drugs and surgery can now be dealt with by using hypnosis as a therapy. Poetry is his hobby."

"Hypnosis? You mean he's also a conjurer or magician?"

"He's just trying to help the police, I don't know why you–"

And that's when Ferraz got the SMS…

'*My friends are famous. My enemies too…*
And that's how I would like it to be.
I raise a toast to my anonymity'

… and the fun started.

THURSDAY

24

SHIVAJI PARK was lousy with cops.

And watching them curiously was an ex-cop. He was sitting on a stone bench at the northern end of the *maidan*, opposite Barista and Café Coffee Day, pretending to mind his own business. But once a cop, always a cop. Policemen never retired. They continued poking their noses. That was the curse of the job. This Thursday morning it was retired ACP Vithal Gosavi's moment in the sun again.

After he finished with the Mumbai Police, Gosavi became the security consultant of a conglomerate that had interests in real estate, financial services and power. He lived in one of the old buildings at Shivaji Park. At 63, he took five rounds of the *maidan* as exercise every morning. He was on his way home when the murder of Ajit Narkar, a former trustee of the Siddhivinayak Temple, had been discovered.

It was 6.30 am.

The man who washed cars in the neighborhood found Narkar slumped behind the wheel of his Honda City in a bylane off Shivaji Park, his throat slit and his head fallen forward. Narkar's white bush shirt was soaked with blood. The car cleaner dropped his bucket and ran screaming *"Khoon! Khoon!"* onto the main road. It was like a scene out of a movie.

Gosavi reached the silver grey sedan seconds later.

Grizzled and hawk-eyed, wearing baggy tracks and a sweaty T-shirt, dusty red Pumas on his feet, Gosavi's cop instincts took over immediately.

He saw through the retracted front window that Narkar had been murdered. There was blood on the dashboard. It was dripping thickly from the steering wheel which the dead man grimly held onto. There was blood on the front seat and the floor, and it was trickling onto the road through gaps in the car's bodywork. A small red bubble chillingly burst out of Narkar's lips.

He had just been murdered, Gosavi realized.

He looked around quickly. But there was nobody about. That's when he spotted the message on the windshield. Written in blood.

'I am my own assassin
My finger is always on the trigger'

The Honda City was parked in a quiet cul-de-sac leading to the sea. The small three and four storey buildings here had names like Sagar Tarang, Sushila Sadan, Navandeep, Amber Kutir, Raval Seaview, Steadfast – yes, and Vinay Kunj. Narkar lived in one of them. Residents were rushing out in their nightclothes. Narkar's son, daughter-in-law and wife, who collapsed beside the car in disbelief, among them.

Gosavi watched in silence.

News of the murder spread quickly. In minutes, the lane started filling. People came running up in alarm and fear, curiosity showing on their faces.

What? Narkar murdered! When? By whom? Right here?

The buzz went around quickly. They wanted to open the car and pull the dead man out, rush him to Hinduja Hospital that was two minutes away, hoping…

Gosavi warned the people not to touch the car.

He then called the Control Room from his cell. After identifying himself, he reported the murder. In seven minutes, a mobile patrol van from Shivaji Park Police Station came wailing into the lane and scattered the crowd. Gosavi greeted the cops who hurriedly got out and gave them a brief statement. Then reluctantly he returned to Shivaji Park and plonked himself on the bench, virtually on the periphery of the crime scene, to watch the morbid excitement building up. He witnessed the top brass of the Mumbai Police arriving and felt kind of left out. But he knew he had no role to play beyond that of the curious spectator here.

When Ferraz rode up, Gosavi wasn't surprised.

"Angelo, over here!" he hailed Ferraz.

FERRAZ WAS fatigued and sleepy.

Nikhil Sanyal's murder the night before had done him in. A false dawn had lit up the sky by the time he left the TV actor's bungalow. Early joggers were out on Carter Road, their voices carrying in the stillness of the morning. Ferraz had got home and let himself in quietly. Peeping into the bedroom, he saw Jackie was fast asleep.

Forty-five minutes later he was at the window gazing blankly out at the sea. He had showered and made himself a mug of coffee. But his frazzled mind kept returning to Sanyal's body lying in a congealed pool of blood, his eyes staring in vacant horror at the Ganpati in the room.

The actor's murder had unnerved the police.

The Ganpati serial killer was getting to be really scary.

The murders were so horrific and gut-wrenching that they psychologically disturbed the policemen. They were executed with such vicious and dispassionate cruelty, that there was no doubt in anybody's mind that the killings were revengeful in their intent. And the nonchalance with which the Cobra stalked his victims, it was chilling and inhuman.

The cops knew blood feuds happened in the city.

People cared a fuck about *dharma* and *karma.*

Nobody believed that actions in this life would determine a person's fate in the next. Some wrongdoings had to be avenged outside the legal system.

Right here and right now.

Like honor killings that happened in villages, quiet revenge murders in the city were considered altruistic. But only by the underworld. The cops didn't get the payback in the Ganpati serial killings.

Each of the seven murders had been different from the others in depravity. After the gruesome butchery of Haider last Thursday in his Mohammed Ali Road studio, it was the savage stabbing of Sanyal in his Khar bungalow last night that made screaming news. He was TV's biggest star. He had fans in the remotest corners of India. The news channels were extracting every bit of drama from the murder. Drop by bloody drop.

All of last night, the media waited outside Sanyal's bungalow in the rain, their mounted cameras and stationed OB vans blocking the road. The body had been taken to Cooper Hospital for post-mortem in a blaze of publicity, photographers chasing the hearse, like something out of the American TV crime dramas. And when the big cops arrived, the crime reporters and TV anchors had scrambled to corner Nawalkar, Rathod and Mugbe.

But the cops ducked the rain and dodged their questions.

Later, Nawalkar addressed the agitated press corps.

Somberly, the careworn CP admitted that the murder appeared to be the serial killer's doing. The evidence pointed in that direction. The police had swung into action. The investigation would be linked to the earlier murders committed by the same suspect.

Nawalkar didn't tell the press that the killer had come as a journo.

They found a visiting card. It said Dnyaneshwar Wagh – Special Correspondent, *The Daily*. That was their only lead.

The old caretaker-watchman confirmed that a *patrakar* was Sanyal's last visitor. He could not describe the man, his eyes were old and faded, and the *patrakar* had kept his face hidden beneath an umbrella. Guiltily, he didn't tell the police that the *patrakar* had given him 500 rupees. What if they took it away? He forgot to also inform the police that the poor *patrakar* limped. And that he carried a pocket transistor.

But the old caretaker-watchman gave them two vital pieces of information.

He was sure the *patrakar* had bid him *"Moryaa Re!"*

And he regretted Sanyal wasn't able to protect himself with his gun.

This was the first the police were hearing about a gun. They looked for it at once. They found Sanyal's arms license. It had been renewed in November 2009. Sanyal had possessed the .32 Webley Scott since 2004. Now it was stolen. This was serious business. The Control Room alerted all police stations. And the cops turned to their *khabris* hoping the stolen revolver would turn up for sale. But they knew the Cobra hadn't taken the .32 to sell it. They hoped he wouldn't use it.

A psychopathic serial killer with a gun…

… that changed things.

By the time Ferraz left Sanyal's bungalow, it was almost dawn.

The investigation at the crime scene had taken the night. Datta Salvi, Sanjay Chhabria, some officers of the Crime Branch's Unit IX from Bandra and cops of the Khar Police Station were still securing the area. The crime scene techs had collected all the evidence at the bungalow and would later try and reconstruct the crime.

Meanwhile, separate teams from local police stations and zonal DCB-CID Units had worked through the night making routine inquiries at Sanyal's home in Versova and the TV studios in Goregaon,

Naigaon, Saki Naka and Powai. Hoping for a lead.

Ferraz made a call to *The Daily* and spoke to the real Dnyaneshwar Wagh. The Special Correspondent was horrified. Ferraz apologetically asked him where he had been all evening. Wagh was attending the Chief Minister's briefing at Mantralaya of the day's business in the Assembly. The other journalists could confirm this. The CM would remember him too because Wagh had engaged him in a heated debate over the Ganpati serial killings! He had no idea how the killer got his visiting card. Wagh said he would present himself at the Crime Branch in the morning when the cops were questioning the old caretaker-watchman. The old retainer would tell them this wasn't the *patrakar* of last night.

When Ferraz stepped outside Sanyal's bungalow he was hit by the dazzling lights of TV cameras that spookily lit up 20th Road. His hand went up to shield his eyes. In the shadows he could see hundreds of people curiously waiting and watching. Nahida Shaikh was interviewing Sanyal's neighbors who were ghoulishly keen for two minutes of fame on TV.

Ferraz finished his coffee. He was preparing to grab an hour of sleep when his cell phone vibrated in his hip pocket. He looked at the time. It was 6.45 am. Wearily he dug out the phone.

"Angelo… Sameer Usgaonkar."

His friend, the Sr. PI of Shivaji Park Police Station.

"Hi Sameer… kind of early, what's up?"

"Listen, Ajit Narkar was murdered this morning."

"Who the hell is Ajit Narkar?" Ferraz asked irritably.

"That trustee, don't you remember the Siddhivinayak scam?" said Usgaonkar, sounding surprised.

Siddhivinayak Temple!

Ferraz closed his eyes.

"Murdered where? Not in the temple!"

"Shivaji Park, outside his home."

"Yeah, but Sameer..."

"Angelo, you're handling the Ganpati serial killings?"

"Don't tell me," said Ferraz suppressing a groan.

"Yeah... Narkar could be your eighth victim."

"I'm on my way," he told Usgaonkar in a resigned voice.

TRAFFIC COPS were at Shivaji Park.

Motorists were slowing down seeing the police cars. A massive jam was building up north and south. Ferraz spotted two white Indicas with orange beacons.

Arun Rathod and Arvind Mugbe were already here.

He hesitated for a moment, then joined Gosavi. A weak sunlight invaded the *maidan* from between the rain trees standing protectively around. A football camp was in progress on the green grass and young boys were warming up.

"Sir," Ferraz said managing a tired grin, "don't tell me they've dragged you out of retirement to help us with this bloody case?"

"This is one of yours?" Gosavi asked. "You know who he was, right?"

"I didn't - but I've been told," Ferraz admitted.

"I called in the murder," Gosavi said, shaking his head in disbelief. "He was killed right there, outside his residence, in his car."

"In the car?" said Ferraz, amazed. "What time was this, sir?"

"Must have happened around 6.15," Gosavi said looking at his watch. "His throat had been slit. Wasn't that the modus operandi in the–"

"Yes, in the murders of the British diplomat's wife, that Mahim restaurateur and the TV actor last evening," Ferraz confirmed. "One transverse cut?"

"Appeared to be," Gosavi said. "This is a dangerous, sick and crazy individual. No suspects too, right? Narkar's killing is going to... get you more flak."

"What can we do, sir?"

They were silent for a moment.

Around them, Shivaji Park's geriatrics were beginning their day. They were shuffling around the *maidan*, conservative women in *salwar-kameez* and shy old men in shorts and T-shirts. The really senior citizens sat on the stone benches lost in their thoughts. Some were reading newspapers. Others were practicing Yoga. Small groups discussed the murder. From the Shivaji Park Gymkhana came the *whack!* of leather on willow as budding cricketers practiced their strokes.

Ferraz asked, "Was Narkar going out? Or returning?"

"No idea, but you can find out," Gosavi told him. "The killer knew his routine and was waiting. Narkar was obviously murdered because of that..."

"Siddhivinayak Temple scam?" Ferraz asked curiously.

"... yes, what else?"

"What was the charge?"

"Political interference in the allocation of funds meant for charitable causes. He was one of the temple's trustees. Crores of rupees received in donations were allegedly misused by the trustees. All siphoned off to companies owned by ministers."

"Wasn't there a High Court inquiry by an ex-magistrate?"

"That's right," said Gosavi, "a resident using the Right to Information Act had filed a litigation accusing the trustees – all ruling party appointees – of giving away huge donations to organizations owned by politicians. The money was meant for maintaining the temple and the Ganpati idol and for providing facilities to devotees. The inquiry confirmed the fraud and exposed the corruption."

"I remember," said Ferraz.

"The ex-magistrate said that the temple trust had become a personal *jagir* for the ministers," recalled Gosavi with a chuckle.

"What happened after the enquiry report was tabled?"

"The High Court prohibited the trust from giving any further donations," said Gosavi, adding bitterly, "in spite of which several hundred donations were still indiscriminately made!"

"So you're saying?" Ferraz began.

"Narkar robbed Lord Ganesh," Gosavi said firmly.

"And so?"

"And so your suspect, a Ganpati *bhakt* I believe, executed him for his omission and commission of sin. End of story."

"I wish it was the end of the story, sir."

Ferraz got up to go.

The sound of temple bells distracted him.

"There," said Gosavi, pointing to the Shree Udyan Ganesh Mandir whose idol watched over the *maidan*. Next to it was a police *chowki*. And the grand statue of the legendary Maratha warrior king Chhatrapati Shivaji after which the *maidan* got its name. Shivaji Maharaj was majestically riding his horse, one arm outstretched, as if ordering the army to follow his charge.

Ferraz reached his bike and noticed the Shivaji Park Sarvajanik Ganeshotsav in the building by the side. He paused. Had the killer been here? Was there CCTV that might have captured him entering Narkar's lane?

Yes – there was on the main road!

Ferraz's heart leaped. Would they finally get a video of the Cobra?

A large and curious crowd had gathered at the head of the lane where a fast food joint advertised its chicken cheese and onion sausage. Ferraz pushed his way through and went to where Rathod and Mugbe stood talking quietly to the zonal DCP and divisional ACP. He saluted the group. A couple of feet away guarding the Honda City and looking distinctly uncomfortable was his old friend Sameer Usgaonkar of Shivaji Park Police Station.

Ferraz read the bloody message on the car's windshield…

… thankful that a shower of rain hadn't wiped out this evidence.

Was the message mockingly saying the victim invited his death?

Ajit Narkar was not a pretty sight.

Policemen were putting up crime scene tape across the narrow lane. The Honda City would be towed to the Forensic Science Laboratory in Kalina after the body was removed for post-mortem. The killer's prints were sure to be on the car. From windows, balconies and terraces of buildings, people peered down fearfully.

"Angelo," said Rathod in a resigned voice. "How do we protect everyone? There is unmitigated fear in the city, but nobody seriously thinks they could be the next target."

"Was Narkar's phone taken?" Mugbe asked Usgaonkar.

"No, sir. His phone is at home. Family says Narkar used to visit the Siddhivinayak Temple every morning at 6 am. He drove there himself. Generally returned by 6.45. Nobody realized the car was still here until his body was discovered," Usgaonkar replied.

That explained the message on the windshield, Ferraz was thinking. The Cobra had no access to Narkar's cell. Couldn't call the CP or send him an SMS. His claim to fame was this message left in blood for the police. Who would have guessed it was him, otherwise! But, my, the Cobra had to be the ballsiest killer in the world. Imagine dipping a finger in his victim's blood and scribbling this on the windshield. Anybody might have seen him. As it turned out, nobody had in the quiet bylane of Shivaji Park.

"What about CCTV grabs?" he asked.

Usgaonkar looked embarrassed.

"They aren't working," he said unhappily.

"Oh God!" Rathod threw his hands up in despair.

"Half the CCTVs are defunct because the government forgot to renew their maintenance contracts," Mugbe informed them. "And the BEST replaced old electric poles on which the BMC had installed cameras. It'll take months to reinstall them and cost the exchequer an additional 4 crore rupees."

Ferraz looked at Rathod and shrugged helplessly.

"Right," the Joint CP (Crime) said. "Angelo, I want a full report. Usgaonkar's doing the ground investigation. His officers are talking to Narkar's family and residents of the lane. Sr. PI Bala Mungekar of Unit V that looks after Dadar and Shivaji Park will come in. This appears to be the eighth murder. There's no point going off on a tangent on the investigation. Let the Shivaji Park police follow any leads. The DCB-CID will continue to pursue the Ganpati serial killer angle."

Ferraz and Usgaonkar walked to the end of the lane.

The sea was just a couple of meters away. It was high tide and the waves rushing in met their ends on the wicked rocks guarding the coastline. About two hundred meters away was the Sealink reflecting the sun on the windshields of morning traffic. A plane made a slow, sweeping turn high above as it charted a southern course. They were at one of Shivaji Park's immersion sites. Police watchtowers had been erected and BMC bulldozers were smoothening the path that led to the sea.

A telephone was ringing in long bursts in one of the buildings.

An outstation call, Ferraz was thinking, surprised that people still used MTNL landlines over their cell phones. Must be only old people in that home. Irritably, he wondered why nobody was taking the call.

"They are all on the terrace watching the show," said Usgaonkar with a slow smile, reading his mind.

Ferraz's respect for his old friend went up a notch.

"Tell me, Sameer," he said warmly, "all the stories about Narkar's involvement in the Siddhivinayak scam... are they on record and true?"

"On record, I can't say," Usgaonkar admitted, "you know how it is, and I have no idea what happened after that enquiry was commissioned, but the stories are true."

"Hmnn, so he had it coming," said Ferraz.

"Looks like, doesn't it," Usgaonkar said wryly.

IT WAS a question of faith.

You had to keep it. Or go back to it.

"Let's visit Baba Makhdoom Ali Mahimi," Shadab Khan suggested.

"Baba who?" asked Navroze with a frown.

"The Mahim Dargah, you know, where students giving difficult exams and policemen like us investigating challenging cases go?"

"Policemen? They go for what?"

"*Arre yaar*, Baba Makhdoom was a Sufi saint who lived between 1372 and 1431," Khan said touchily. "He was a preacher known for his knowledge of Islam and the Quran and also his liberal thoughts and humanist views. The Mahim Dargah is where he was buried. You know that 12-day *Urs* in December?"

"It begins from Mahim Police Station?" Ferraz asked.

"Yes! That's held in memory of the Baba. Millions of people of all faiths visit the *dargah* in that period. An *Urs* is a death anniversary. But this celebration is a *mela* with giant wheels, the merry-go-round, fun-n-game stalls, food, toy shops, a shooting gallery..." Khan shook his head.

"What does the Mahim police have to do with it?" Salvi asked.

"The police station's where the Baba used to live. His belongings which include a chair, a pair of sandals, and his hand-written Quran are preserved in a room there. It's like a museum and is opened once a year. The *Urs* begins with a procession from the police station to the *dargah*. Two cops from every police station represent the force's centuries-old association with the saint. It's led by the Sr. PI of Mahim who offers the first *chaddar* at the Baba's tomb."

"Wow, I didn't know that," said Salvi in awe.

"You want us to go today?" Navroze asked. "But the *Urs* is in December."

"Baba Makhdoom's the patron saint of the police," Khan said. "There's a belief that he used to miraculously assist Detection officers of the British Raj in cracking difficult cases. Cops have always sought his blessings. I know officers who visit the *dargah* for Baba's guidance with the case papers of challenging investigations."

Navroze said fervently, "God knows we need all the bloody help we can get with this case. I'd sleep with the devil if he would help us."

"Thursdays are special at the Mahim Dargah if you go with faith."

"So let's go," Ferraz told Khan, "and inform Sr. PI Farooque Baig of Mahim Police Station we are coming, he will be happy."

FRIDAY

25

POOR RUSI Batliwala.

He died whispering, "*Shree Ganeshaya Namah*"...

... appealing to Ganpati for deliverance.

But for the first time in the long and eventful life of the great Parsi astrologer and psychic, Lord Ganesh who was his anchor, protection and strength, failed to come to the condemned Batliwala's help.

Ganpati paintings by famous artists adorned the walls of his Churchgate flat. Idols in different sizes and forms, created by renowned sculptors in Italian marble, red clay, jade, black onyx and Prague crystal, sat on tables and shelves. Silently watching him being murdered.

The large ears of the benevolent, pot-bellied, elephant-headed God didn't hear Batliwala's dying "*Shree Ganeshaya Namah*"...

The murmur of rain came in faintly through the closed windows.

... they were listening in mystification to the "*Moryaa Re!*" being repeated by the man who pressed a large, soft pillow onto the face of the helpless old astrologer lying supine on his bed and smothered him to death.

When it was over, he stood silently over Batliwala.

Blood was oozing from the astrologer's mouth and nose. He had bitten his tongue and it was protruding. His face had turned blue. The man closed the astrologer's bloodshot eyes that were staring into nothingness with a gentle sweep of his hand. Giving Batliwala dignity in death, allowing him to rest in peace, because when the soul was taken away from a body the sight followed.

He then picked up Batliwala's cell phone. Smiling cruelly, he sent Angelo Ferraz an SMS from it saying:

"*Shall we call it quits then?*
You stop playing God
and I shall not chase Eternity…
You stop questioning me
about why I do everything wrong,
why I prefer Sin…"

Before he left the bedroom of the man Google rated among the 100 great astrologers of the world, he blew out the oil lamp burning before a solid brass Ganpati idol on a bedside table.

Vedic astrology is called *jyotishi* – which in Sanskrit means Light of God.

And he extinguished the light… like he did Batliwala's life itself.

He shuffled and limped out, leaving the front door ajar for the police, careful not to disturb Batliwala's attendant sleeping in the kitchen. He looked at his watch. Time for the third India-England ODI to begin at The Oval in London.

BATLIWALA DIDN'T see his end coming.

The astrologer otherwise had ominous clairvoyance for dreadful events related to sudden death. Like earthquakes and assassinations, air crashes, killer diseases, flash floods, bloody coups and wars.

He wasn't any ordinary crystal ball-gazing astrologer.

Batliwala was blessed with extraordinary ESP. He read the planets, combined the principles of Vedic and Western astrology, used Tarot cards, applied the I-Ching, Numerology, the Hebrew Kabbalah and

Palmistry. His predictions were based on knowledge and intuition, he made them after seeking Ganesha's blessings.

Batliwala began and ended everything with *"Shree Ganeshaya Namah."*

Ganesha was his Lord and Master, though he was a Parsi, he wore the Zoroastrian *sadra-kusti* and went to the *agiary*. The Parsis were a tolerant people. Batliwala's fascination for Ganesha they put down to the gentle eccentricity that was supposed to be inherent in every Zoroastrian.

In his time, Batliwala had famously predicted the successes of film stars and cricketers, the political fortunes of world leaders, the destinies of nations. He had forecast unimaginable breakthroughs in science and technology, space travel, genetics, communications. And he snubbed the Prophets of Doom predicting the end of the world by telling them imperiously that he saw a future that didn't have the cosmos shutting down with a clang and people going down fighting and screaming. All of which fetched Batliwala widespread recognition globally.

Sometimes his predictions failed.

Batliwala then told disbelievers, "I am as fallible as anyone. On the chessboard of life, fate is king. Nobody is wiser than destiny."

He didn't know, or care, whether astrology was a science or an art.

"Fact is it works. You can call it science or you can call it bullshit," Batliwala rudely told people. "But you must have it in your destiny to predict correctly."

After zipping around the world for half a century thrilling politicians and royalty, spiritual leaders, showbiz celebrities and sports personalities, when he turned 80 and was fitted with a pacemaker, Batliwala settled down in Mumbai. He accepted that his advancing years and failing health demanded a slowdown in lifestyle and change in business.

A website offering personalized and supposedly path-breaking astrological services asked him to come on board as its ambassador. Batliwala agreed, for a handsome fee and only when they named it after Lord Ganesh and gave him the reins.

The service was high on theatrics.

Speaking for Ganesha, the crafty old astrologer took questions from devotees online. He answered them with stock replies generously spiced with Vedic astrology and planetary mumbo jumbo. He ended the Q&A by blessing devotees "*Shree Ganeshaya Namah*" and assuring them that their wishes would come true.

It worked wonderfully well, but was to be Batliwala's death sentence.

In his online avatar as Lord Ganesh, Batliwala knew he was being wicked. But he believed that when people prayed to Ganpati, the Vighnaharta or Remover of Obstacles, then anything they wished for with a true heart would be fulfilled even in the virtual world. He was only interceding with Lord Ganesh for them.

Batliwala made a lot of money by peddling Ganesha as a commodity.

He was also seeing two clients a day at home.

His fee for each reading was 25,000 rupees.

During Ganeshotsav, Batliwala turned down all appointments…

… except this fateful one he accepted that led to his death.

THE man represented *International Astrologer*, the journal of the US-based International Society for Astrological Research (ISAR). It offered its vast readership a diverse selection of astrological articles ranging from the natal and mundane to political and celebrity analysis, research and financial astrology, book reviews, conference information, etc.

He said the journal was looking for new writers…

… Batliwala couldn't resist the temptation to see him.

"*Shree Ganeshaya Namah*," he greeted the man who was

admitted into his bedroom by his male nurse and attendant at 2 pm that Friday.

Batliwala was propped up in bed at his Swadhin Sadan flat on C Road in Churchgate, smoking a *beedi*. This was an affectation. With his health, he shouldn't have been smoking. His lungs had all but collapsed, he was asthmatic, relying on the Asthalin inhaler to relieve his wheezing.

His doctor had warned the astrologer that smoking could kill him. Especially *beedis* that were 18 rupees a pack of 30. Batliwala said at his age he would like to go smoking or die in bed with a girl of 19. The doctor advised him to stick to *beedis*. Batliwala had laughed.

But this was no ordinary *beedi*. He smoked Ganesh 501 from Mangalore, arguably the world's most popular *beedi*. It sold in the US, Germany, France, Switzerland, the Caribbean islands, Middle East, Singapore and Australia. He liked the familiar pink sachet with its yellow label of Lord Ganesh.

Swadhin Sadan was under reconstruction.

The building was dressed up with scaffoldings and waterproof blue tarpaulin. Inside, it was dark and damp, there were traces of cement, brick and sand on the passages of every floor. The noise couldn't be helped. Of workers chipping away the outside walls, cement mixers churning, the shrill whine like a dentist's drill of the marble cutting machine. It travelled up and down the elevator shaft. The doors and windows of the flats had to be kept shut while the work was on. Residents didn't know what was happening outside. Day and night were one.

Churchgate Station was across the road.

He came from there. Shuffling and limping among students of Sydenham, Jaihind and the Government Law College. He held a folded newspaper over his head to protect it from the rain. First he stopped at the Sarvajanik Ganeshotsav Mandal outside the Indian Merchants' Chamber put up by the Churchgate Hawkers' Association. Then he slipped into Swadhin Sadan when the workers were assembling after lunch. The watchmen failed to notice the stranger shuffling and limping to the lift.

Batliwala knew at once the man was a hoax.

He knew nothing about astrology. But he was a Ganpati *bhakt*. So in his kindness, after blasting the man for his act of duplicity, the old astrologer gave the man 10 minutes of his precious time for a chat.

"But don't ask me to read your horoscope," he warned.

Business was business and there were no free lunches.

The man gave up the pretence of representing the *International Astrologer*. With that awkwardness out of the way, the meeting proceeded amicably. Batliwala was telling him how he introduced Ganeshji to the Americans.

"I told them He was like Santa Claus," the astrologer boasted, "and they understood immediately. I was addressing students at the University of Washington. It's in Seattle. Don't confuse it with Washington University in St. Louis whose campus is a den of criminals! I said just like Santa at Christmas, Ganpati during Ganeshotsav is all about giving and loving without expecting anything in return."

The man listened, fascinated.

"And like Santa, our Ganeshji is also big and roly-poly," Batliwala said, unaware that the clock was slowly tick-tocking a deadly countdown to his death. "Size is important in life. Ganesha is truly big. People have extra faith and trust in Him. And because of His size, we feel secure with Him psychologically. Size is safety as the Americans say."

The man asked, "What's Ganeshji to you?"

"Great protection and mighty blessings," Batliwala replied. "I will tell you the secret of my love for Ganeshji. Pictures and images make the strongest impression on our mind. Therefore we go crazy over Bollywood films. Ganeshji is this picture of an elephant. It becomes easy for us to relate to Him. And we invite Ganeshji to our house every Ganesh Chaturthi and finally say a sweet goodbye to Him till the next year. By doing so our children understand naturally and effortlessly in their young minds that life is a cycle which deals with birth and death and rebirth. To me this is a wonderful and remarkable way of teaching them and the whole world that nothing is final in life except God."

"But why Ganpati?"

"*Arre baba*, because He chose me!"

Batliwala was getting crotchety now.

It was time for his nap.

On working days, he slotted appointments before 12 and after 5. He never saw anyone in the afternoon. But this fellow insisted on coming at this hour. Very uncivilized of him. Batliwala agreed, thinking he represented the *International Astrologer*. Now the man's 10 minutes were over and the old astrologer wanted him to go. But the bugger wasn't satisfied.

"What has Ganeshji to do with astrology?" he asked, "Why do you invoke his name before you make a prediction? I've seen you do it on TV also."

"I feel happy, it just comes out naturally," Batliwala said shortly.

"But why Ganpati?"

"*Arre*, why not? Ganeshji means different things to different people. He is kindness, wisdom, knowledge. Tomorrow if I write a book about the life of an astrologer featuring Ganeshji as a cartoon among aliens, a mad scientist, an invisible man, and a spiritual master, who's to tell me not to do it!"

"How does Ganeshji come online to answer people's problems?"

Batliwala was wondering if the man – *he never even asked his name* – was serious or just having fun. This was the first time he was meeting somebody who didn't tell him his birth date, show him his palm, or ask him to predict something.

The old astrologer was intrigued. Why was this fellow here, then?

"Ganesha is the epitome of mercy, love and compassion," he said. "All of us face problems in our lives. Ask Ganesha for a solution to your problems with a pure heart and mind and you will get an answer."

"How true are those answers?"

"You need to be a little patient for change to occur. Ganesha is always there. The greatest lesson of astrology is that you become aware that life itself is change. Accept it and enjoy it in every possible way," Batliwala philosophically said.

"You think it's enough to say *'Shree Ganeshaya Namah'* for everything?"

Batliwala reached for an ashtray because his Ganesh 501 *beedi* had died.

The man looked at him with sudden distaste.

There was a sort of evil, demonic gleam that came into his eyes and vanished just as suddenly. A naked hatred. Like somebody had flicked a switch on and off inside his face. He had curious eyes, almost yellow in color, Batliwala now noticed. He felt uneasy. He decided to answer this question and then ring for his attendant to show the man out.

"If I meet God, and I will go to Ganesha after my death, then I will accuse him of being a wicked God for harassing mankind. I will implore Him to pardon the world and start it again. Forgiveness is powerful," Batliwala said, sliding down in bed and lowering his voice to a murmur.

He was overcome by waves of drowsiness and closed his eyes.

"Worshipping Ganeshji has taught me to forgive people. I tell God, make the world happy or blow my heart to smithereens and finish me off. Even the anticipation of peace is so wonderful and elating. There is so much pain and suffering in the world, end my life, I will say to Lord Ganesh."

"Moryaa Re!"

The whisper was soft and deadly, close to his ear. Batliwala opened his eyes quickly. And was in time to see the pillow coming down on his upturned and unprotected face.

He was too frail and weak to put up a fight.

But the old astrologer struggled for life. Feebly he tried to pull away the pillow that was covering his nose and mouth, asphyxiating him, preventing the intake of air into his tortured lungs and snuffing the life out of him. He felt a tightness in his chest and knew he was getting a heart attack. He squirmed for several moments, his legs thrashing, feeling himself blacking out.

Before his body went limp, before darkness took over, Batliwala managed to open his mouth. With his dying breath the old astrologer said *"Shree Ganeshaya Namah"* one last time.

In the kitchen, the attendant slept on peacefully.

He had not given any attention to the man who came. The attendant hadn't even noticed that he walked with a curious shuffle and limp, because he had been leading the man into Batliwala's bedroom. He didn't know the old astrologer had been murdered. Suddenly the apartment was swarming with policemen. He woke up in alarm to discover the 'Sickbed Slaying' as one newspaper would describe it tomorrow.

UNIT I of the DCB-CID itself responded to the crime.

There wasn't any call. Just the SMS to Ferraz.

Another poem from Pritish Nandy's book. Sent by the Cobra from the astrologer's phone. Telling them he had killed.

Again! For the ninth time.

They had shamefully resigned themselves to his series of ritualistic murders. They knew this would be coming. But they didn't know who would be killed today. They were sitting with their thumbs up their asses.

Loop Mobile told them the SMS had come from Batliwala.

The cops were horrified. They knew the SMS spelt doom for the Parsi astrologer. The mobile service provider gave them his address and they set out at once. Ferraz stopped only to inform Rathod and the Station House. The Joint CP (Crime) listened in grim silence. Then picked up the phone to warn the CP. The cops reached Swadhin Sadan in 13 minutes.

The Marine Drive police were already there.

Navroze knew all about Batliwala. He told them about the astrologer's obsession with Lord Ganesh. And how he exploited people's faith in Ganpati to make a fraudulent living.

"This has to be the reason for his murder," Navroze said angrily.

Ferraz grunted. What else, he was thinking.

They parked the Qualis outside Swadhin Sadan. On either side of the entrance stood a Christmas tree. Two police jeeps and a mobile patrol van were on the scene. Policemen were clearing C Road on which cars were double parked. Rathod and Joint CP (L&O) Arvind Mugbe would be coming.

Uniformed cops were in a huddle with the building's secretary and some other members in the compound. A constable was on the walkie-talkie asking for a forensic team and an ambulance. Ferraz, Navroze and Salvi leaped across a gutter rushing with rain water to enter the building. The secretary volunteered to take them up to Batliwala's flat.

Ferraz noticed the workers hanging around uncertainly.

They looked back at him with fear and worry. He knew that look. A murder had been committed. They were afraid the police might not believe they hadn't seen the killer or know anything about it.

"Datta, handle them gently," Ferraz said, nodding at the workers.

The building's security in-charge stayed down to assist Salvi in the Q&A.

Navroze and Ferraz rode up the dusty elevator with the secretary.

The landing outside Batliwala's sixth floor flat was crowded with uniformed policemen, the Parsi astrologer's shocked neighbors and their curious male servants. Almost every flat employed young men from Kutch and other districts of Gujarat as domestics. At night, these servants slept in the passage. The housing society had installed ceiling fans for them. The cops could see their bedding stacked in a dark corner.

Batliwala lay exactly as the policemen from Marine Drive had found him.

Sprawled out at the astrologer's feet that were already turning grayish-blue was his attendant crying his heart out.

"Philip Varghese," one of the policemen said, nodding at him.

They took the blubbering attendant into the kitchen.

Lunch vessels still stood on the gas rings of a hotplate.

Varghese had been waiting for the astrologer's visitor to leave. He had put his head down and dozed off. That's how the cops found him.

He had a bewildered, frightened look on his thin face.

He was also dim-witted. They questioned him swiftly.

"Who came to see Batliwala?" Ferraz asked.

"I thinks it must have been a client, *sar*."

"You got this client's name?" Navroze asked.

"No *sar*, but must be Rusi *sar* he entered it in the diary."

He fetched a diary from the bedroom.

Navroze opened it to Friday, September 9. The page was blank.

"There's no appointment here," he told Varghese.

The attendant looked surprised.

"Rusi *sar* he usually take down the client's details," he told them.

"What details?" Ferraz asked.

Navroze flipped through the pages.

"Here it is," he said.

The last entry was for Wednesday, last week.

There were two appointments. At 11 am for a Jyoti Purswani. And at 5 pm for Parshu Desai. Beneath each person's name and telephone number, was their date, time and place of birth. Batliwala had calculated what number they added up to according to Numerology. And had made birth charts showing the positions of the sun, moon and other planets at the time of their birth based on Indian Vedic astrology.

"Why is there no appointment for today?" Ferraz asked Varghese, slapping the diary against his leg and looking at the attendant expectantly.

"There's nothing also for the last eight days," Navroze pointed out.

Varghese looked nonplussed. Then realization dawned.

"Ah, Rusi *sar* he take no appointments during the Ganesh festival."

"Okay," Ferraz said, "tell us who came. How did this man make the appointment? Was it for a reading or something else? What did people usually do? They called Batliwala? On his cell phone? Is there a landline in the house? An MTNL phone? Who took down the appointments? Batliwala or you? Since today's client is not mentioned in the diary, could he be a friend? Or a salesperson? Maybe somebody from the Ganpati website? Did you see this person before? When did Batliwala tell you he was expecting somebody? What exactly did the astrologer tell you? What did Batliwala do in the last eight days when he saw no clients? Did his clients pay him in cash? Where did he keep the money? Describe this morning's client, how did he look? What was he wearing? Did he introduce himself? What did he say?"

Varghese buried his head in his hands in despair.

They questioned him for 45 minutes. The attendant was an absolute duffer. He took his time answering them. At the end, they were not much wiser.

He knew nothing about the visitor. Batliwala had told him somebody was coming at 2 pm. He hadn't given a name. Batliwala handled all his calls personally. He advertised his astrological consultancy in the Parsi and Gujarati newspapers. Varghese showed them small classified ads in the *Parsi Times*, *Jam-E-Jamshed,* and *Mumbai Samachar*. They all gave Batliwala's numbers. He took his consultation fees in cash. It was kept in a Godrej safe in the almirah. During Ganeshotsav, Batliwala did no business. He stayed at home. Doing Ganeshji's *puja*. Why this man had come today, Varghese didn't know. He didn't pay attention to clients. Just opened the door, took them to Batliwala, then let them out.

It had been that way today too. Except he had fallen asleep.

Varghese was a little hard of hearing. That's why Batliwala had installed a bell to summon him. The attendant looked distraught when the cops asked him how he hadn't heard Batliwala crying out when being smothered.

Ferraz was frustrated.

When had the Cobra fixed this appointment? They would have to ask the phone companies for records of all incoming calls on Batliwala's cell and landline for the past week. See if they could find a client to match every call. The forensic experts would take the computer from which he did his online astro-activity and see what history there was on it. Nobody in Swadhin Sadan had seen a stranger entering the building. Normally one of the watchmen doubled as the liftman. But this afternoon, there was nobody. The security in-charge said the CCTV in the lobby and compound had been covered with plastic because of the reconstruction work.

Ferraz asked Varghese, "If you saw this man would you recognize him?"

"I thinks so maybe I would, *sar*," the attendant said, doubtfully.

Ferraz asked Swadhin Sadan's secretary, Rajiv Parikh, "Sir, if your car's parked in the building, may we use it for a few minutes, please?"

Mr. Parikh, it turned out, had the 2011 model Mercedes Benz C Class 220. It was parked below and under covers, he obligingly told the cops.

"Does it have dark glass?" Ferraz asked.

Mr. Parikh looked at the policemen uncertainly.

"We want to send Varghese out to see if he can spot the suspect in the vicinity. Killers sometimes hang around the crime scene to get second hand pleasure from the police activity," Ferraz explained.

Mr. Parikh caught on immediately.

"You don't want to use a police vehicle? That will alert the killer?" he asked. He volunteered to drive the Merc himself.

When he went to get the car keys, Varghese approached the policemen.

He was hesitantly holding out a business card.

"Batliwala *sar*, he said to call this man if anything happens."

Navroze took the card.

It said Sam Patel, Advocate, Bombay High Court.

He called the number on the card and was soon in conversation with the legal expert who was not only a friend of Rusi Batliwala's but also represented the astrologer in legal matters and drew up his will.

Sam Patel was distressed to hear about Batliwala's murder.

He listened to Navroze in sorrowful silence. He wanted to help. But was unable to contribute anything to the police investigation. He assured them he would look after Batliwala's last rites and execute his will. That was his final responsibility to his friend, he said tearfully. He asked for a copy of the death certificate, autopsy report, and the FIR that would be filed by the Marine Drive police.

"What's in the will, can you tell me?" Navroze asked hopefully.

"Nothing that should matter to the police," Sam Patel said forlornly, "except that Rusi expressed the wish to be cremated at Chandanwadi. He thought our Parsi system of disposal of the dead at the Tower of Silence was primitive and barbaric."

Navroze was appalled.

SATURDAY

26

THE PERSISTENT buzz of his phone awoke Ferraz.

Cursing, he snatched it up and looked at the time in one movement.

"Angelo? Are you awake?"

Dr. Yunus A Miyasahib at 3.20 am!

"No, I'm fast asleep!"

There was a cackle of laughter!

"You're a scream! Now you know what it's like to be woken up–"

"Surely you're not calling to return that favor!"

"What do you think?"

"Doc, I've got a big day."

"Yes, and I wanted to tell you…" Dr. Yunus hesitated.

"What?"

"This psychopath…"

"What about him?" asked Ferraz, now fully awake.

"Remember what happened in Raman Raghav's case?"

"Raman Raghav! That was fucking 1968!"

"The police couldn't prove he wasn't a psycho and fit for the noose. The state wasted lakhs of rupees and thousands of man hours trying."

"So?" Ferraz was confused.

"My gut tells me you'll get him today."

"Who?"

"Arre baba, your serial killer!"

"Your gut? What the fuck have you been eating, Doc!"

Dr. Yunus broke out into gales of laughter.

"Angelo… please, I have a feeling–"

"A feeling!"

"–and when you get him, save the state a trial."

"How?"

"You dumb cop!" Dr. Yunus shouted. "Nothing will come out of an arrest. If he's a psycho, you won't be able to interrogate him. I will have to assess him. But nothing he says will stand up in court. The criminal justice system here, it will meddle, it will fuddle, the defense hired at the state's expense will raise objections at every step of the trial. The prosecution will have to prove its case beyond all reasonable doubt. How will you establish proof of the murders? Do you have testimonies of witnesses, CCTV grabs, phone call records? Any conclusive forensic evidence? The human rights people will protest if you force a confession. The media will conduct its own trial. You surely remember Kasab…"

Ferraz took a deep breath.

"… and what a mockery of the trial the defense made? His counsel appointed by the state said Kasab had come from Pakistan to join Bollywood and was strolling on Juhu Beach when the Crime Branch arrested him on 26/11–"

"I know all that, Doc."

Dr. Yunus sighed in exasperation.

"Angelo," he said, "a trial like this could go on forever and then run into appeal. He will be declared unsound and locked up in a psychiatric ward. The case will play on your conscience. Do you want that? You must know when to turn the page and when to close the book."

And Dr. Yunus hung up, leaving Ferraz wondering.

ANANT CHATURDASHI came with a beaming sunrise.

At 6.45 that Saturday morning, the sea off Girgaum Chowpatty waited placidly for the arrival of the big Ganpatis later in the day. It was a dirty grey sea. Fishing boats with gaily painted flags bobbed on the water. Across the bay, exhausted by its night vigil, the Colaba lighthouse dozed motionlessly and waited for the dark.

All roads would lead to Chowpatty this evening.

The beach wasn't besieged by public yet, so all was calm and quiet, the dawn's peace was undisturbed. There were only the morning joggers and sleepy policemen around. A family of seven was performing a *puja* at the water's edge before immersing their small Ganpati.

This would be the first one of the day.

He stood beside the Girgaum Chowpatty Police Chowki.

The Anti-Terrorism Squad had put up posters of 'WANTED' criminals hoping people might identify them if they were on the beach. Behind him, the rising sun peeped over high-rise apartments. Early morning traffic zipped by. A woman learner with an ill-fitting helmet shakily rode her scooter with an impatient-looking man sitting pillion. He watched her zigzag progress. The traffic would be madness later. But the Traffic Police had got the hang of it. They would stay on till the last Ganpati came. With entire streets and full chawls of people accompanying it on hired trucks. Like families and friends going to the airport to see off the visiting NRI. Across the road, TV channel vans had already taken positions.

The beach was being spruced up for the gods.

This is where it would end tonight. Chowpatty would be his final killing field. The stage was being set, literally and figuratively. He came for one last recce before the curtain went up. And he wanted to hide the Rampuri. Find some safe place from where he might retrieve it when he returned. The security would be unprecedented tonight. And he had no wish to be stopped with the knife on his person.

But where to hide it?

The public toilet on the beach? No, too public.

Chowpatty's famous Bhelpuri Plaza was shut.

Outside it, a murder of crows was sifting food crumbs from grains of sand. He liked the collective noun 'murder' for crows. It went with his plan.

He shuffled and limped down the beach.

A lot of activity was going on. Excavators were digging up the sand and road rollers were flattening it out again. Iron sheets were being laid out to form a ramp for trucks to take the idols to the water. There were cranes standing by. And generator vans to backup the eight light towers that would illuminate Chowpatty like floodlights at a stadium. Municipal sweepers were halfheartedly passing brooms over the sand. Conservancy staff were setting up mobile toilets. The beach would be a royal mess soon. The time to clean it up would be tomorrow morning.

Where would he be tomorrow morning?

He had no idea. Who cared about tomorrow? Tonight was the night! There was no telling how it might end. His mind was not wired to consider the consequence of his actions.

Tonight would be more Ramlila than Ganeshotsav.

When the dramatic folk enactment of the Ramayana was staged on Chowpatty every October, it ended in the death of the Demon King Ravana on these sands.

Like was going to happen tonight!

Chowpatty would provide a spectacular stage for the finish.

When you kill a king, you don't stab him in the dark. You kill him where the entire court can watch him die. DiCaprio's dialogue in *Gangs of New York*.

Chowpatty was perfect.

The venue of the city's first Sarvajanik Ganeshotsav. Lokmanya Bal Gangadhar Tilak brought Ganeshotsav to Chowpatty. The British called it Kennedy Seaface. After Lt. Col. John Pitt Kennedy of the Royal Engineers' Regiment who was a big wheel in the Bombay Baroda & Central India (BCCI) Railway. Kennedy also had the bridge leading to Chowpatty from Opera House named after him.

Chowpatty was where Tilak defied a British ban in 1893 on Indians congregating in public places to prevent their unity from sparking off a rebellion. The ban excluded religious festivals. So Tilak introduced the Sarvajanik Ganeshotsav on Chowpatty. It connected the people and fired within them the urge for *Swaraj* that later escalated into the freedom struggle.

He had great reverence for Tilak. A tall and handsome statue of the freedom fighter stood in a memorial garden alongside the beach. This is where Tilak was cremated in 1920. The garden was a horticulturist's dream. Among the greenery stood the Lokmanya, walking stick in hand, one foot forward, alert and gazing down the road for the first Ganpati to arrive.

He shuffled and limped down the beach. Where to hide the knife?

He considered the Nana Nani Udyan. Next to the Weather Bureau's old coastal warning tower with its intriguing system of flags for the day and lamps at night to alert small craft out at sea of cyclones.

No, the Udyan was too far.

That's when he noticed the huge and ugly plaster urns on the beach for devotees to dump garlands and *puja* waste in before immersing their Ganpatis. This waste was later converted into compost by the BMC. The urns looked like squat sentinels guarding the shore.

He went up to one and looked around. Nobody was watching.

The urn was as tall as he was. 'Nirmalya Kalash' was painted on its side. It rested on a small tripod metal stand. He quickly dug a hole in the damp sand beneath. After looking around again, he dropped the Rampuri into the hole and covered it.

There, it was done. He shuffled and limped off the beach.

From the road, he turned and looked at the Nirmalya Kalash. It was next to the HAM Radio Operators' Tower. The others were 25 meters to the left and right. He would find it easily tonight.

FERRAZ WAS arguing with Jackie.

They had woken up early.

She, like a good Catholic to go to church.

He was uncatholic. He woke up after she left.

By the time she returned, he had read the papers over a mug of black coffee. To it he had added a jigger of brandy. The effect was bracing. The papers were scattered on the floor and two inches of a cigar was dying in the ashtray.

"You should have come to church," Jackie said as soon as she entered.

"Why, what happened?" he asked. "The earth stopped? The angels wept?"

"Bandra Fair begins tomorrow. The basilica was packed. Traffic is a mess. There are roadblocks. And ridiculous police *bandobast!* This is a place of peace. People of all faiths come here. Which terrorist would target it?"

Ferraz marveled at her innocence.

She was wearing a simple, figure-hugging navy blue frock that ended above her knees, a wide white leather belt and matching patent leather pumps; her hair had been combed and tied in a ponytail, and she had only the faintest hint of makeup on her young, attractive face.

He thought she looked pretty as a picture.

Jackie thought he looked like he had died in his sleep.

Ferraz had on a rumpled ochre Osho robe in which he liked to laze about at home. He was unwashed. Also sleepy and tired. His indefatigable spirit had taken a beating. He felt like hell. His back was hurting like the devil. And when he yawned, he could taste stale cigar smoke. He was feeling his age and imagined he looked 20 years older.

Jackie was sniffing the air. The cigar smoke, cognac bouquet and coffee aroma were a heady cocktail for a sensitive nose.

"Have you been drinking?" she demanded, hands on her hips.

"Me? Drinking!"

"Really Angie, if you arrive at the Gates of Heaven with your breath smelling do you think the Lord will let you in?" she asked in exasperation.

"Honey, if I go to Heaven, I expect to leave my breath behind!"

Squealing with laughter she hurled herself upon him.

After she had pummeled Ferraz, she told him breathlessly, "Tomorrow I want to go to this new Yoga Café I discovered in Bandra. It has an organic power breakfast on its holistic menu."

He hadn't heard of a holistic menu before.

"Organic breakfast," he said in disbelief, going for a shower. "What shit! Oat muffins, tapioca porridge and herbal tea – that kind of *kachra*? I'd rather starve to death than be poisoned."

Twenty minutes later he stepped out with his hair still wet.

Breakfast aromas wafted out of the kitchen. Jackie had laid out the table.

"I smell *idli sambhar* and *chutney*," Ferraz said. "And what's that? Is it coffee? Praise the Lord! Whatever happened to our anti-jet lag green tea?"

Jackie ignored him.

She was bent over the Jumbo Crossword in *Afternoon*.

Ferraz helped himself to breakfast and poured out coffee.

He looked at Jackie expectantly, knowing it was coming.

He didn't have to wait even a minute.

"What kind of clue is this?" Jackie said, frowning.

Here it comes, Ferraz thought.

"It says, '*I'm the First. But I'm no Michelle. She's a Lady, I'm just a Citizen*'. The answer is three words. You know it? No! What do you know? Why do they make crosswords so complicated?"

Ferraz sighed.

She hated it when he had to work on Saturday. But the Cobra was out there stalking his tenth and last victim. Something terrible was going to happen today. Ferraz could feel it in his bones. And he wanted more than anything else in the world to stop the Cobra somehow. It was sickening to feel helpless. To know despite the entire Mumbai Police being on the job, the killer was going to strike again today.

And there was nothing they could do to stop him.

"I prayed you would –" Jackie blurted out and stopped…

… suddenly shy to admit she had appealed to God to help Ferraz today. He would laugh.

Ferraz looked at her questioningly. But Jackie turned away embarrassed. At the door she hugged him fiercely, feeling the 9mm S&W pressing into her ribs. He held her tenderly and kissed her forehead.

"May your hand not tremble, your aim not falter, and your judgment not fail," she said tremulously, surprising him with this hackneyed Bollywood dialogue.

Strangely, he found it touching.

THERE WAS a casserole of *modak* on Arun Rathod's table.

What Maharashtrians called *ukadiche modak*, the steamed variety made at home, with rice flour, grated coconut, jaggery, a touch of nutmeg, lovingly molded in hands greased with *ghee* and shaped into small dumplings. Not the *Kaju Modak* available at Ghasitaram's for 1,000 rupees a kilo.

The hands that made these *modaks*, Ferraz guessed, were those of Sheena Rathod, the Joint CP's (Crime) wife, whose concern for the welfare of her husband's cops was legendary in the Crime Branch.

Pushing the casserole forward, Rathod said, "Help yourselves."

He was looking terrible. His eyes were bloodshot and ringed by dark circles. He was slumped in his chair, legs stretched out beneath the table, his chin almost resting on his chest. He was rolling a packet of Gold Flake cigarettes between thick fingers, his mind working furiously.

The Joint CP (Crime) had given up smoking.

This was an SOS packet. Kept for when the shit hit the ceiling. The cops wondered whether Rathod would light up now. He looked at them grumpily from over glasses that had slid down his nose, far from being his debonair self.

"Okay, no speeches," Rathod said suddenly, "let's pray to Ganpati for help!"

The policemen laughed.

Rathod was relieved. Everyone looked grim. Like pallbearers at a funeral. He would be glad when this day came to an end and Ganeshotsav was over. Whatever happened, he told himself.

They had tried. They were still trying. But this psychopath had showed them that if you were insane enough to dream it, then no crime was big enough. Anybody could get away with murder. The Cobra made it seem like child's play.

They had come up empty-handed in their probe into Ajit Narkar's murder. There were no witnesses, the killer's finger print on the windshield where he had hastily scribbled a message for them in Narkar's blood was smudged, and the family could tell the police nothing extraordinary. Life was going on smoothly for Narkar. One moment the temple trustee was there – next moment he was gone. Without warning.

In Rusi Batliwala's case, the only lead they had was the phone call the Cobra had made to the astrologer to fix up yesterday's appointment. The cops got the CDRs for Batliwala's mobile from Idea and his landline from MTNL. Feverishly, they checked every call made to these two numbers over the last three weeks. Philip Varghese, the astrologer's attendant, knew all Batliwala's social and professional contacts. He helped the police identify all the people on Batliwala's call lists.

Only one number couldn't be accounted for.

The call was made from an old yellow STD-ISD-PCO in Dalal Street outside the Bombay Stock Exchange at Fort. It had been made on Monday, August 29, at 1.30 pm.

The cops visited the once ubiquitous public phone kiosk. They knew at once the lead was hopeless.

Rathod wondered what would happen after today. Would the killings stop? Would the Cobra disappear, leaving them relieved but shamefaced?

He helped himself to a *modak*.

Across him sat the cops in charge of the DCB-CID's 12 Units. Ordinarily the Crime Branch didn't do *visarjan* duty. But this Ganeshotsav had been unusual. They had nine undetected murders. And the killer was out there. Making plans to commit the tenth. Rathod wanted every DCB-CID cop on the road. He hadn't any strategy for them. But Mumbai had 72 immersions sites and some 49,879 Ganpatis were going for *visarjan*. There were already 35,000 sectional policemen, 12 companies of State Reserve Police, seven of the Rapid Action Force, two battalions of the Indo-Tibetan Border Police, and 3,500 Home Guards on this *bandobast*. Another 150-plus Detection cops wouldn't hurt.

"There's no use worrying," Rathod assured his men.

He had spent the night doing just that. Worrying who the Cobra's last victim might be. Going by the killer's terrifying track record, this condemned person was bound to be a citizen of consequence. Rathod had grown weary thinking of names. The police had provided an armed constable to every eminent Mumbaikar who was an established Ganesh *bhakt*. Several others had approached them for security. The police advised them to stay indoors till the festival was over.

Rathod was hoping that like on Anant Chaturdashi in 1968, when the Bombay Police miraculously nabbed Raman Raghav who had murdered 41, the DCB-CID might get lucky today.

"May Ganesha be with us," he said fervently.

LALBAUG WAS Lord Ganesh's catwalk.

The road sweeping through this labor class neighbourhood of old chawls and ghostly mills was Ganpati's ramp of fame. The idols passing by were hailed by people, filmed and photographed by the media, and showered by rose petals from the terraces of buildings.

"I don't know what we are doing here," Ferraz yelled in Navroze's ear.

The big Parsi cop nodded. He felt at home. The riotous celebrations had reached unprecedented decibels as the festival wound down to a thundering and spectacular finish. Devotional music blared from all Ganpati *pandals*. Bollywood songs rocked processions on the road. The sound was deafening. The blast of firecrackers added to the racket. The Maharashtra Pollution Control Board would declare Lalbaug as the noisiest area in Mumbai tomorrow. Ferraz and Navroze watched the Ganpati processions from outside a beat *chowki* near Lalbaug Market.

Lalbaug wasn't their beat.

But Lalbaug was home to the two original Rajas of Ganeshotsav.

The Lalbaugcha Raja, Mumbai's pride since 1934, the most famous Sarvajanik Ganpati of all. Its idol was believed to fulfill every visitor's wish. Devotees came from far seeking its favor. Ministers and movie stars lay prostrate before it. The idol was unveiled for the media at a press conference shortly before the festival. Like the trailer of a big budget Bollywood movie. This was the richest Sarvajanik Ganpati in Maharashtra. It collected crores of rupees and gold jewelry in donations every year.

Navroze insisted that they pray to the Lalbaugcha Raja for help. On Thursday, Shadab Khan had led them to the Mahim Dargah where the cops had invoked the blessings of Sufi saint Baba Makhdoom Ali Mahimi. But the serial murders had continued after that. The Cobra killed Batliwala. The gods were not listening. Or the Cobra had the luck of the devil.

The other Raja at Lalbaug pulling in the crowds since 1928 was the Mumbaicha Raja of Ganesh Gully. For years its 22 feet idol was the tallest in Mumbai. Then in 2000, the Khetwadi Ganraj beat it with a mammoth Ganpati 40 feet tall.

By noon, both Rajas were on their way.

The Mumbaicha Raja went first. The Lalbaugcha Raja followed. Both led by a swelling wave of singing, dancing and jostling people. The processions were agonizingly slow and would reach Chowpatty in the early morning. The idols were ceremoniously transported on large trucks decorated to resemble grand chariots. They were fitted with towering neon lights and huge music speakers. A cordon of Rapid Action Force commandos led and followed the Lalbaugcha Raja in battle gear. Weighed down by bulletproof jackets, helmets and combat boots, they marched stoically with fingers on the triggers of automatic weapons. Their presence was both intimidating and reassuring.

Whether Anant Chaturdashi was sunny or rainy, people waited in feverish excitement for a final *darshan* of the Lalbaugcha Raja. The windows, balconies and terraces of the small buildings and chawls in Lalbaug were crammed with peering faces. Shiv Sena supremo Balasaheb Thackeray, and Chhatrapati Shivaji the great Maratha warrior king, also watched from posters. People were perched on bus-stop roofs, they had climbed lamp-posts and trees, and were precariously balanced on the awnings and signage of shops. The Lalbaug Flyover was also packed to capacity with people leaning over the parapet. TV cameramen shot the Ganpatis from above. People on the road took pictures on their cells. The cacophonous but magnificent spectacle of ritual and celebration had to be seen to be believed, Ferraz was thinking. He was sweating like crazy. He could feel the 9mm S&W pressing uncomfortably into his waist.

"Let's go," he told Navroze.

27

THE CALL on the landline came at 6 pm.

Vishnu Shetty took it. He listened, then told Salvi, “Sir, Control Room has got some constable from Kolhapur who wants to talk to you.”

“Me?” said Salvi, astonished. They were in the Unit I office.

“PI Salvi,” he said, taking the receiver..

The Control Room operator said, “Sir, a head constable from Karvir Police Station in Kolhapur is on the line. He wants your mobile number. We advised him to call the Station House. He’s refusing to hang up.”

“Put him through,” said Salvi.

There was a crackle of static, then from the other end a faint and excited voice, “Salvi *saheb*, this is Head Constable Nana Phadtare from Kolhapur.”

“Yes Nana,” Salvi said. He couldn’t place the constable at all. And the last time he was in Kolhapur…

“Salvi *saheb*, the 2005 encounter… *remember*… that Mumbai gangster? I was in the Kolhapur Crime Branch team that gave you backup.”

Salvi winced.

He was unlikely to forget that encounter. Pointed questions had been raised in the Assembly. Weren’t there policemen in Kolhapur? If the Mumbai Police had gone to arrest the gangster, why did they shoot him dead?

Now Salvi said with irritation, “Yes, so… ?”

"Just wanted to remind you, *saheb.*"

"About the encounter?"

"No, *saheb*… about me, you remember me, *na*?"

"Is this why you called?"

"No, *saheb.*"

"*Then what*?" roared Salvi, making Vishnu Shetty and the other cops jump.

"Sorry *saheb*… I meant to tell you… the Mumbai Crime Branch notice sent to all police stations seeking information on Ganesh *bhakts* with police records, that request was made by you, I recognized your name."

"Yeah, what about it, Nana?" asked Salvi testily.

"My brother-in-law was a Detection constable at Khade Bazaar Police Station in Belgaum and came up against somebody like that," Nana Phadtare reported.

"In Belgaum?" asked Salvi in surprise. "How many years ago?"

"I don't know," the Kolhapur cop said, "but easily eight or nine years."

"How do you know about this Belgaum incident?"

"My brother-in-law, who is a Lingayat from Dharwad, told me *saheb.*"

"I see. But I meant, why did he tell you?" Salvi explained.

"Oh, I can't remember. It was so long ago. You want me to ask him, *saheb,* he has now been transferred to the Belgaum Rural Police."

Salvi sighed.

He was thinking, eight or nine years ago, that too in Belgaum. It was too long a shot. Why hadn't this dimwit cop got all the details before calling Mumbai?

Masking his disappointment, Salvi said with false enthusiasm, "Listen Nana, call your brother-in-law. Is he sure this Ganesh *bhakt* *was* a psychopath? Was he arrested? Where is he now? I want names, numbers, addresses, whatever the Belgaum police have."

"I don't know if he was a psychopath, *saheb*…"

"Then why did you call?" Salvi asked with real vehemence now.

Nana Phadtare laughed uneasily.

"Salvi *saheb*, according to your notice the suspect goes by the alias Cobra. Er, the Ganesh *bhakt* in Belgaum was a Chitpavan Brahmin from the Konkan region."

"So what?" shouted Salvi.

"I remember my brother-in-law, Mallikarjun Subhedar, saying this man was a staunch Konkanastha Brahmin. A KoBra, spelt K-o-B-r-a. Maybe the Mumbai Police confused KoBra for C-o-b-r-a…"

"What are you saying?"

Salvi was out of his seat in excitement. He realized in his irritation he had almost missed this amazing tip.

"Nana," he said quietly, "tell me about this Konkan Brahmin."

"Yes *saheb*. Konkanastha Brahmins are known as KoBras, they come from the coastal districts of Karnataka, Maharashtra and Goa in the Konkan region," Nana Phadtare said importantly. "They worship Lord Parshuram. But the KoBras from Ratnagiri, Chiplun and Pune are also Ganpati *bhakts*. I don't know if the Belgaum man was a psycho, but he was a Ganesh *bhakt* and a KoBra for sure."

Salvi let his breath out with a whistle.

"Nana," he said urgently, "call your brother-in-law. You got my cell number? *No!* Take it down…"

TWELVE HOURS later he was back at Chowpatty.

And amazed to see the crowd. The beach was spilling onto the road. He had taken the train to Grant Road and joined a surging mass of humanity going to say farewell to Lord Ganesh. The road was jam-packed. Like peak hour at Churchgate Station. One side meant for devotees going to Chowpatty; the opposite for those returning. Policemen kept the crowd moving. Water drums spaced several feet apart and linked by rope acted as a road divider. He followed a truck carrying 12 small idols. Behind it a Maruti van, its rear swing door open, had people huddled in the boot cradling a Ganpati, their feet dangling out. There were foreigners in the procession, bemused expressions on the faces, taking videos to show back home. It was one joyous, flowing movement.

No way the police could manually check anybody.

Reaching the beach, he went for the knife.

But the Rampuri wasn't there!

The Nirmalya Kalash near the HAM Radio Operators' Tower, beneath which he had buried the knife, was missing. There was nothing in its place. He dug up the sand there frantically. But no Rampuri.

His blood ran cold with fury.

He stood up not seeing or hearing the *tamasha* all around. Boisterous revelers waving orange flags banged into him. He felt nothing. Just his seething rage.

He saw what had happened.

As the plaster urns were filling up with garlands and other *puja* waste, the BMC's Operation Clean-Up staff was emptying them into garbage trucks. But they weren't putting down the urns where they had picked them up from. All the Nirmalya Kalashs had new positions. No amount of digging would produce the knife.

He shuffled and limped away slowly, his anger mounting.

He missed the cold, comforting feel of the Rampuri in his pocket.

That's when he remembered the gun!

He had pocketed Nikhil Sanyal's .32 Webley Scott before leaving home. Hoping there wouldn't be checks at Chowpatty. Policemen conducing body searches. But now he was thankful for the gun. He felt a surge of power suddenly. Like a hot sexual turn-on.

He had figured out how to fire the revolver.

YouTube made it seem so easy. He had done dummy runs with shaking hands. Following step-by-step instructions until he was comfortable handling the .32. The instructor in the video said even novices could learn to shoot accurately with online lessons. He wasn't surprised. Any fool could pull a trigger. Would the gunfire be loud? No matter, the evening had to end with a bang, he thought.

THE DAY that had started out bright and sunny…

… was now turning out to be a real bitch.

All evening a lazy drizzle had teased Chowpatty. At 6.30 pm, it turned into a heavy downpour. The cold, grey slanting rain lashed the beach viciously. It turned the coffee-with-milk sand into cocoa brown muck that splattered angrily as raindrops whipped it, stinging the ankles of people dashing for cover. Trucks taking Ganpatis to the dancing waves, where volunteers waited in boats, slithered in the slush and left deep groves on the beach.

Mumbai seemed to be bidding Lord Ganesh a teary goodbye.

But that was the message of the *visarjan*. It taught people to let go of something they had loved deeply and nurtured. And to surrender to faith, because what they loved, they had to eventually leave.

When the rain began, he didn't know what to do.

He slipped into the Police Control Room hoping the cops there didn't turn him out. Instead, one big, inspector offered him a plastic cup of tea. Gratefully he accepted it. He heard the cop telling someone he was on loan from D B Marg Police Station.

He had never seen so many policemen at once before.

Many wore raincoats. Yellow with 'Mumbai Police' written on the back. Traffic cops wore white with black stripes. There were trainee constables. Young and gawky. Not yet policemen, still acting like awestruck boys. They had their cells out and were taking pictures. And plainclothes men with identity cards around their necks. Also safari-suited cops of the Protection Branch who were some VIPs' bodyguards. A yellow Maruti Gypsy with Tourist Police written on its sides patrolled the beach. The Bomb Squad was there as well with their Labradors comically observing the *visarjan*. There was an equal representation of women police constables; looking like the sullen attendants at multiplexes and malls.

The rain thinned out to an inconsequential drizzle.

He switched on the transistor hoping for news from the Pallekele International Stadium in Kandy where the second Test between Australia and Sri Lanka had been stopped because of bad light and rain.

Here too, he chuckled, but there would be no stopping him.

There was a commotion outside.

He stepped out of the Control Room…

… and found himself face-to-face with Angelo Ferraz.

He caught his breath. He recognized Ferraz from his pictures in the press. But there was a quiet deadly air about the Crime Branch cop that the pictures didn't convey. Ferraz looked directly at him, holding his gaze for a moment.

No recognition in his hard, cop eyes.

He didn't expect there to be. He saw the eyes shift to the transistor in surprise. And he knew in that glance Ferraz had scanned his face and filed the impression away somewhere.

Then he was roughly pushed aside by a constable.

Police Commissioner Baburao Nawalkar entered the Control Room in a white raincoat and gumboots followed by four constables carrying carbines.

Shaken by this encounter, he moved away.

The floodlights had come on painting the beach an unnatural yellow. At the water's edge, a white Chetak helicopter of the Indian Coast Guard hovered, its downdraft churning the waves. He watched it for a while. Then made his way through the throng towards the road. Walking past the BMC's VIP Stand filled with foreigners, the BEST Stand, the HAM Radio Tower.

A loudspeaker voice told people not to shoot the immersions. The Ganpatis could only be photographed from the foot over-bridge outside. He looked at the foot over-bridge. A long banner on its side by the Mayor and Deputy Mayor welcomed all Ganesh *bhakts*. A hundred faces looked back at him from behind TV cameras. Tomorrow they would return to take videos of the Ganpatis regurgitated by the sea. They would insensitively show them wallowing in the waves with broken arms and trunks. Waiting for the BMC's garbage dumpers.

He reached the road where a folk band welcomed every big Ganpati with a triumphant blast of the *tutari*. They came in trucks, tempos, cars and cabs, with busloads of people to see them off. Volunteers directed them to dedicated lanes. The Ganpatis then waited their turn for immersion. Queuing up like planes at the airport awaiting the Air Traffic Control's clearance for take-off. NCC cadets held hands on either side, giving the Ganpatis a guard of honor. In the distance, the Saifee Hospital stood out in a blaze of lights, looking like the Atlantis Hotel in Dubai.

He shuffled and limped up the beach again.

To his left was the elevated Mayor's Pavilion, decorated with red and white streamers and lights, a wooden staircase leading up to a dais with chairs and a viewing gallery. It was guarded at the bottom by Home Guards. And on top by BMC security men. Among the VIPs expected here tonight were the Chief Minister, the Home Minister, other ministers of the state, MLAs, MPs, Municipal Corporators, and His Excellency the Governor of Maharashtra. It couldn't get bigger than that.

Mayor Yamini Olwe was the evening's hostess.

In Mumbai, the Mayor's role was ceremonial. Yamini, as the head of the BMC, enjoyed Cabinet Minister status. And as First Citizen of Mumbai, she received Presidents and visiting heads of state at the airport. But the Mayor couldn't sanction municipal works. That power was with the Municipal Commissioner. However, Yamini was a dynamic civic representative. A first-time Corporator of the ruling party in the 227 member BMC, and a Scheduled Caste who practiced

Buddhism, she had won the mayoral poll with a thumping majority. She had a degree in Political Science. Yamini had her eye on state politics. Tonight, she was the presiding deity at the *visarjan*. Every VIP to her Mayor's Pavilion was welcomed by the Police Brass Band stationed below with Bollywood tunes.

He wandered around aimlessly.

He was running over the script. Rehearsing the scene. Now that he was actually at the theater where it was happening, and the stage was set, he felt a little nonplussed by the sound and lights and the activity of hundreds of extras.

He hadn't imagined it would be like this.

A man walked past in a yellow T-shirt and black shorts, a straw hat on his head, a fishing rod on his shoulder. He wondered where he was going. Another chap with a red bandana carried a sledgehammer. Students from Wilson College across the road rushed about with black canvas bags picking up litter. And lifeguards in red bathing trunks, running in slow motion like they were on *Baywatch*, headed for the H2O Water Sports Center down the beach. An ambulance reversed into the parking lot reserved for Police, BMC and BEST vehicles, a dozen nurses in starched white stepped out.

The man on the mic was warning policemen not to let any vehicle with dark glasses enter Chowpatty. He wondered whether this had anything to do with the poster of 'Wanted' men put up by the Anti-Terrorism Squad. He didn't want any jihadis gate-crashing his party. Any shooting to be done, would be done by him. His hand went to the .32 Webley Scott again.

That's when he saw the shooting star.

He was looking up to see if it would rain again…

… and he saw the heavenly body darting across the night sky.

One moment it was there, the next it was gone. Was this portentous? He had heard stories. About seeing a shooting star and making a wish. *Wishful thinking!* A shooting star wasn't a star. It was a meteorite that moved so fast in space it burned up the atmosphere. He put it out of his mind.

NANA PHADTARE didn't call Salvi again.

Mallikarjun Subhedar, his brother-in-law with the Belgaum Rural Police, called instead. It was 7 pm and Salvi was ready to climb the wall.

"Yes Mallikarjun," said Salvi eagerly once he had established the caller was none other than the original source of this hot and promising tip.

"*Saheb*, I'm sorry," Mallikarjun began regretfully, "I understand you are searching for a psycho. But this Ganesh *bhakt* was a college professor. He abused a student for allegedly insulting Ganpati. The incident was witnessed by the entire class. Both, the professor and student came to Khade Bazar Police Station. Police Inspector Vishwanath Hande, who is now dead, didn't know what to do. They made such a commotion. Both were shouting at the top of their voices!"

"What did Hande do?" asked Salvi impatiently.

"The professor was adamant that an FIR be lodged. He advised Hande that the police had a case against the student under Sections 295 and 295A of the IPC for defiling a sacred object with the intention of maliciously insulting his religious sentiments," Mallikarjun said. "He said this was a non-bailable and cognizable offence."

"What was the professor teaching, Law? And which college did this ruckus occur in? Also what year was it?"

"He was a Psychology professor in the KLE Society's Lingaraj College, *saheb*. I think it was 2003, I can check that out."

"And what was the student's complaint?"

"She alleged that the professor had abused and threatened her."

"She! Now you're telling me the complainant was a girl?"

Salvi breathed heavily through his nose.

"Give me the whole case, Mallikarjun," he said, regretfully thinking this tip was turning out to be a real bummer.

"Yes, *saheb*," the constable said, "the student had worn a tight T-shirt to college on whose front there was a Ganpati image. She was, er, well-built, *saheb*. You understand? The professor objected. He said the T-shirt was blasphemous and insulting to Lord Ganesh."

"Did he threaten to harm her?"

"I can't recall, *saheb*. The girl was politically connected. She also advised us the professor could be charged under Section 506 of the IPC for criminal intimidation and Section 509 for insulting the modesty of a woman."

"The people of Belgaum are a law unto themselves!"

"Inspector Hande thought prima facie there didn't appear to be grounds to file an FIR against the student under Section 295. Clothes bearing images of gods were quite in fashion then. At the same time the professor had not obscenely abused or criminally intimidated her by word or gesture."

"I would have taken legal opinion," Salvi said.

"Inspector Hande did that, *saheb*. He recorded their statements and went to the Chief Public Prosecutor of the District & Sessions Court in Belgaum."

"What did the CPP advise?" Salvi asked, hurrying him up.

"To threaten the professor with Chapter Proceedings under Section 107 of the CrPC, *saheb,* and subsequently file a C-Summary Report in Court."

"Hmnn, I would have done the same," admitted Salvi.

The Khade Bazar police told the professor and student that a criminal offence could not be registered against either for lack of evidence. The Court was informed that while the allegations made by both were not untrue, there was no substance in the case. The police filed a C-Summary Report for discharge under Section 169 of the CrPC stating lack of evidence and reasonable grounds of suspicion to register an FIR. The professor, being the aggressor, was asked to execute a bond swearing not to commit a breach of peace again in Belgaum.

Mallikarjun recalled, "The professor was either dismissed in disgrace or resigned in disgust, nobody knows, but he disappeared from Belgaum and we didn't bother to find out where he went."

Salvi digested this information in silence.

Had the dishonored Belgaum professor resurfaced in Mumbai as the avenging psychopath? It seemed unlikely. But the professor and the killer were both Ganesh *bhakts,* and now it transpired also KoBras. That was too much of a coincidence.

The Belgaum policeman interrupted his thoughts.

"*Saheb*, the Lingaraj College principal… he retired and migrated to Vancouver where his married daughter is settled… but there is another professor who used to teach History, his name is Vinay Kore, he knew the Psychology professor fairly well."

"Where is Prof. Kore now?" asked Salvi.

"He also has retired and stays in Jagalbet – it's a jungle on the highway between Belgaum and Goa. I got his number… in case you're interested."

"Hmnn, yes… that would be a help," said Salvi. "Tell me, what were the names of the Psychology professor and the student?"

"*Saheb*, I don't remember. It was long ago, and it was such a *faltu* case."

"I understand," Salvi told him. "Maybe this Prof. Kore will know."

"I'LL BE damned," Ferraz said.

Salvi had just narrated his conversations with the Kolhapur and Belgaum policemen. Ferraz didn't know what to make of them. But there was no harm in checking out the information.

He looked at his watch. God, it was 7.15 pm.

"Datta, you talk to this Belgaum professor," he told Salvi, "the

History chap, what's his name, Prof. Vijay Gore, *no*, oh it's Vinay Kore. Okay, you talk to Prof. Kore. But, I'm afraid, the case is cold, even that Belgaum cop didn't remember too much detail. Tell me if I should ask the Joint CP (Crime) to call the SP of Belgaum who I'm sure won't know what we are talking about. No need to speak to the Kolhapur SP, we just got the tip from there. Smart constable, that fellow Nana Phadtare from Kolhapur. If this turns out to be the real deal…"

28

PROF. VINAY Kore had Alzheimer's.

That was the first thing his wife Suman told Salvi when he called up the Kore residence in Jagalbet. He could hear birds twittering in the professor's coconut plantations.

"He's losing his memory," the old lady said, to Salvi's dismay. "He does strange things, like right now he's sitting in the garden having a gimlet and expecting lunch. When it's close to dinner and more the hour for a hot toddy to go with this wet and cold weather we are having."

Salvi cleared his throat not knowing what to reply.

She had answered the phone after he had tried several times and was beginning to get worried. He had identified himself and explained why he was calling.

"Just a moment," she had said reluctantly.

Salvi imagined a distinguished, silver-haired woman carrying the cordless out to Prof. Kore in the garden. He strained his ears to listen. There was a mumble of low voices.

He heard a man imperiously say, "Who? *The police from Mumbai!* Don't they know it's lunch time and not to disturb me? Where's Jambudkar? He's getting lazier by the day! How long to prepare lunch, it's intolerable I tell you…"

And then Suman Kore was whispering to Salvi, "Make it short, he doesn't hold conversations for long and his memory wanders. He is impatient for lunch, he is hungry all the time, doesn't remember when he had his last meal. Also, we are in the middle of the jungle. At the slightest hint of rain, the phone goes dead and we lose electricity. Hurry it up. I think it's going to pour."

Ominously, there came the growl of thunder in the distance.

"Hello, hello, *arre* hello," a fretful voice at the other end was impatiently bellowing into the phone. Salvi was almost deafened.

"Prof. Kore, *namaskar*, this is Inspector Datta Salvi of the Mumbai Crime Branch. I'm sorry to be disturbing your–"

"Hello Inspector, how's Hiremath?"

"Hiremath! Who's Hiremath, sir?"

"Hah! Don't you know Hiremath? You said you were a policeman from Mumbai? Strange kind of policeman, I must say..."

"Is Hiremath also a Mumbai policeman, sir?"

"You're asking me! *Who the hell is this?* Is this you again, Miranda? Up to your usual mischief? I'm wise to you, aha! Won't be fooled by this police story of yours."

Salvi passed a hand across his face. Talking to the policemen from Kolhapur and Belgaum had been trying enough. He was feeling the strain a bit. He had not called up Jagalbet for this.

"Sir, I am a bona fide CID officer from Mumbai, I assure–"

"But you don't know Hiremath, what's the use!"

"The Mumbai Police has 47,000 men, sir."

"Doesn't matter," Prof. Kore said loftily. "Thousands of students passed out under me, but I'm sure I would be able to recognize and name them all still."

Salvi seized the lead.

"Do you remember the Psychology professor who got dismissed because of that unfortunate Ganpati incident, sir?" he asked breathlessly.

"Who, Gajanan?"

Gajanan! Salvi was thinking.

"Of course, I do," Prof. Kore continued. "But where is he? Haven't seen him in a while. He called once long ago to say he was coming over. Then silence for years. What happens to people? Do you know where he is?"

"No, sir. I am looking for him myself."

"Try Goa."

"Why Goa, sir?" said Salvi quickly.

"What do you mean '*Why Goa*' you silly ass?" Prof. Kore said irritably. "What a foolish thing to say. Gajanan is from Goa, where else would you find him? If you're looking in Guwahati or Gurgaon, you'll come back empty-handed, I tell you. Are you a policeman or what?"

"I've forgotten his surname," Salvi said humbly.

"Murtikar," Prof. Korc said promptly.

Salvi felt a chill run down his spine.

Gajanan Murtikar – the Ganpati idol-maker.

"Ah, yes," he said enthusiastically, "whereabouts in Goa is he from?"

"I think Cansaulim – isn't that where the Chitpavan Brahmins congregate? Or Caranzalem? Something like that. All these places sound and look the same, really, all they have is a church, a beach, a couple of taverns, one village and some fields, but to hear the hotels promote Goa..."

"Gajanan is a KoBra, isn't he?" Salvi interrupted softly.

"Yes," Prof. Kore chuckled, "like Phadke, Gokhale, Savarkar and Ranade, also Gajanan's hero, Bal Gangadhar Tilak. And Acharya Vinobha Bhave, the spiritual successor to Gandhi. The vanguard and old guard. KoBras and social reformers, educationists and thinkers, revolutionaries and Independence activists. Men of high moral character and utter determination. Men of sacrifice and courage who totally lacked greediness and would rise to the top of any situation. The Chapekar brothers – Damodar, Balkrishna and Vasudeo of Chinchwad near Pune, who were hanged for murdering the British plague commissioner Walter Charles Rand, you remember? Must be in your police records. Of course, the KoBras had their black sheep.

Not every one of them was a hero who leaped from between the pages of History textbooks. Godse, for instance, *that* Chitpavan terrorist!"

He fell silent, lost in his thoughts.

"You mentioned Tilak was Gajanan's hero," Salvi prompted him. "Why did you say that, sir? Because both KoBras worshipped Ganpati?"

"Hmnn, something like that," Prof. Kore said. "Tilak was also a teacher, you know, like Gajanan and me. He taught Math in a Pune school and later at Fergusson College. And like Gajanan in our Belgaum college, Tilak also had ideological differences with his colleagues and withdrew from teaching for a time. If you ask me, the KoBras are a community of fiery patriots but not a single saint. Rather full of themselves, I tell you!"

He laughed hysterically.

In the background, Salvi could hear the professor's wife tut-tutting in concern. And he heard another sound that made him catch his breath. The loud clap of a bolt of lightning and the long, angry drumbeat of thunder.

The thundershower sounded like it was at Prof. Kore's doorstep.

Quickly Salvi asked the professor, "Gajanan had trouble with his colleagues?"

"Trouble! Who said he had trouble?"

"I mean ideological differences, sir. Remember the scene he created with that student in Belgaum? Can't remember her name…"

"Ganpathy," Prof. Kore said at once, "Veena Ganpathy."

Salvi's heart began to race.

Ganpathy!

"What became of her?" he asked.

"Why, don't you know?" Prof Kore said. "She joined politics. I must ask Hiremath. He is sure to know. Policemen are like that, nosey, prying and inquisitive buggers, you can tell them by their eyes. Oh dear, it's beginning to rain…"

"*Sir...*" Salvi's voice was urgent.

"What now?" the professor asked querulously.

"What happened to Gajanan? Did he take up a job elsewhere?"

"I don't know. Haven't seen him in ages. A good Psychology teacher, you know, and much younger than me. Got a few years of teaching left in him, I would say."

"What kind of person is he?" Salvi persisted.

"What do you mean?" the professor demanded suspiciously.

"Personally – I meant, not academically," Salvi replied smoothly.

"Full of contradictions!" the professor cackled again. "He's a split personality with an inflated but righteous opinion of himself. Listen, it's starting to rain. Shall we shift indoors? Jambudkar must have got lunch ready. I guarantee you an excellent avocado salad with homemade vinaigrette. You'll have a glass of wine? A nice Chianti, perhaps, hmnn? Forget Gajanan, out of mind and out of sight, eh! But let me tell you about the KoBras of the Independence movement. Tilak, the strongest advocate of Swaraj. Phadke, who led the armed struggle to overthrow the British. And Gokhale, the non-violent reformist. Not to forget Savarkar, who created Hindutva. And Justice Govind Mahadeo Ranade, Sane Guruji..."

And the telephone went dead.

ANTONE DE Azavedo was a Goan...

... as zesty as Caju Feni. There was no keener aficionado in the Mumbai Police of the good life than this colorful and excitable character from that hospitable state of open doors and open hearts. *Mhojea ghar, tujhe ghar.* His Goan vim and vitality apart, de Azavedo was a resourceful cop. He had the natural inquisitiveness of his people and he was also unassuming. People trusted him instinctively.

He brought a give-'em-hell attitude to work. Like the rustic Sardarji out of whom you could not separate Punjab, de Azavedo carried the din and clamor of Goa's rousing celebrations in his blood. He had a dark, funny and roguish face, black curly hair, and sparkling eyes full of mischief. He was small and wiry. And he walked with a strut. Like he was dancing the *fandango* at some party going on in his head.

He was carefree, happy and lighthearted.

But he had boundless enthusiasm for field work and proved to be uncommonly brilliant when asked to shake a leg in an investigation that wasn't moving.

This evening, de Azavedo would be a hero.

He was enjoying the Ganpati festivities at Chowpatty with the same gladness of heart that he felt for the riotous revelry in Goa during the Carnival. He looked as if he wanted to shout *"Boa festas!"* instead of *"Ganpati Bappa, Morya!"* each time another idol went past in song and dance.

Spotting him, Ferraz got an idea.

"Antone," he shouted over the racket a troupe of *lezim* dancers was making as it led a Ganpati on a palanquin to the sea.

de Azavedo came up at a trot.

He was dressed in blue jeans and a Hawaiian shirt meant for Calangute, not Chowpatty, a .38 Colt tucked at his waist. He had a big red *tilak* on his forehead and was wearing a marigold garland around his neck. He looked utterly mad.

Ferraz and Navroze led him off the beach where the arrival of each Ganpati was taking the noise to a new climax. They entered the sanctuary of Wilson College. Police vans and an ambulance were parked on its basketball court. Commandos in fatigues roamed around with automatic weapons slung across their shoulders. They looked at the DCB-CID cops incuriously.

Urgently, Ferraz apprised de Azavedo of the situation.

"He can't be from Caranzalem," de Azavedo said, "must be Cansaulim."

"How can you be sure?" Navroze asked.

"'Coz I'm from Caranzalem, sir," de Azavedo said, grinning

proudly. He snapped his fingers, "I know everybody there. Professors, doctors, bankers, *mestre*... the church choir-master, the *tiatr* artistes, bookkeepers, the *batcar* – your landlord. My village was famous for bull fights earlier, what to tell you. You should see our football ground. And the Church of Our Lady of the Rosary. The Goa Science Museum and British Cemetery are–"

"Okay, okay," said Ferraz irritably.

de Azavedo left Goa 25 years ago, but his music was still in him.

"*Santa Marie – Devache Maie*, I've thought of something," de Azavedo said in awe. "How do you know this bugger's from Cansaulim?"

"That's what the professor from Belgaum told Salvi."

"*Eh mhojea Deva*, he could have said Candolim, it sounds the same. Perhaps Salvi sir got it wrong," de Azavedo said doubtfully, causing Ferraz and Navroze to look at each other in dismay.

"Or maybe Canaguinim, Chinchinim, perhaps Cortalim, huh? You think about that? There is also Carambolim, Canvoreim and Chicalim. What if the *chedyecho* is from one of these places? And how do you know the professor didn't say Conquirem, Corchirem or Cunchelim," de Azavedo asked with a dizzy burst of inspiration.

Navroze felt like smacking him.

"I don't think Salvi heard wrong," Ferraz said quietly. "Listen Antone, all we have is the suspect's name and possible village."

"What you want me to do, boss?" de Azavedo said uncertainly, distracted by a string of firecrackers that was exploding on the road.

"Let's stick to Cansaulim," Ferraz said. "You know anybody at the police station there? Make a call, speak the language, play the brother card, do whatever it damn well takes. If this Prof. Gajanan Murtikar is from Cansaulim, I want to know where the hell he is now."

"There's no police station in Cansaulim, boss," de Azavedo said, "the village could be under many possible police stations."

"What the fuck do you mean?" Navroze asked.

"*Arre*, it's like our Bhendi Bazar. There's no Bhendi Bazar Police Station but the police stations of Nagpada, Dongri, J J Marg and Pydhonie are all close by, get it? What's the use? The common man doesn't know where to go when he gets robbed in Bhendi Bazar," de Azavedo explained.

Navroze cursed under his breath.

Unperturbed, de Azavedo continued, "Cansaulim has the police stations of Colva, Ponda, Verna, Margao and Vasco around it. I will try and find out which one it comes under. But you know cops, we pass the buck. When a complainant comes we say, '*Amchea Bapa, sorgincha*, the crime happened in the neighboring police station – not ours, men. Go there, what you're chewing our brains here, you're fucking mad awot?'"

"Antone…" said Ferraz, cutting him short.

"But… *Goencho Saib*, I've a better idea!" he exclaimed, clapping his hands and gazing at them in wonder.

"What?"

"The Cansaulim Post Office! They would be able to tell us if this *gandi votto*, this Prof. Gajanan Murtikar, is from there. And whether he is alive or is dead and was buried at St. Thomas Church or cremated at Ponda."

"*Kutreya*, your pop is the postmaster of Goa," yelled Navroze. "Which fucking post office would be open at this hour!"

"*Christa aamchi…*" said de Azavedo looking crestfallen.

But never underestimate the perseverance of a Goan.

de Azavedo was beaming freely again.

Smacking his palm against his forehead, he exclaimed, "*Mhojea Deva*, I am forgetting. But there are hotels in Cansaulim."

"Antone, don't try me," Ferraz said wearily.

"Boss listen," de Azavedo pleaded, "there is the Park Hyatt Goa Resort & Spa in Cansaulim where my friend Joao Pascal de Santana Barbosa is the resident manager."

He grinned at them slyly.

"So what?"

"*Noman Rannie Kakutiche Maie*," exclaimed de Azavedo, "the hotels in Goa are compelled by trade unions to employ locals, don't you know, so Park Hyatt is bound to have Goans from Cansaulim."

Ferraz and Navroze looked at each other blankly.

"Somebody in Hyatt will know this *zonyachea* if he is from Cansaulim."

"*Maara baap*," shouted Navroze catching on finally. "Then call your friend, this Pascal bugger, what the fuck are you waiting for?"

de Azavedo took out his cell phone.

He dialed, muttering "*Soresvora Deva, amchi kakut kor*", then shouted in joy, "Pascal, thank God! What men, *keso asa? Hanv boro asa.* I got work for you, *re patrao, madat kar.* Now listen to me carefully… *amhi ek pishya khoonik sodhta…*"

ANTONE DE Azavedo had fervently said a prayer.

He had grown up in Caranzalem in the shadow of the Church of Our Lady of the Rosary, leading a life guided by rituals and commandments, and solemn High Mass on Sunday sung by choir and congregation. Everybody prayed everyday in Goa. And everybody had a relationship with the saints.

He had silently prayed to St. Anthony.

"*Saiba mhojea Sant Anton… mhojea magne aik…*"

St. Anthony was the patron saint of lost people. He was also the saint of travelers, pregnant women, elderly people and fishermen, a vigilant guardian of the harvest, and a guaranteed rain-fixer. Goans took their angst to him. Any prayer made to St. Anthony in faith was met by a miracle.

Perhaps there was some truth in that. They needed a miracle. de Azavedo was invoking St. Anthony's assistance to locate a missing man. His friend Joao Pascal de Santana e Barbosa of the Park Hyatt in Cansaulim was hip. *Madre de Deus!* He didn't know this Murtikar dude, hadn't heard of the *putachea*, but of course he would join the investigation.

"Kasle prashna asa?" Pascal wanted to know.

What questions do you have?

Quickly, de Azavedo told him.

Pascal was Portuguese, but he knew what a Konkanastha Chitpavan Brahmin was. His front office manager, the lovely Sonali Tamhankar, was a KoBra from Chiplun staying with her uncle in Cansaulim village.

And, *Onond Bapak, ani Putak, ani Povitr Otmeak…*

Glory be to the Father, and to the Son, and to the Holy Spirit.

… St. Anthony was in rollicking form, ask and ye shall receive.

Sonali's Uncle Vishnushastri Sahastrabuddhe, an elderly and much respected Konkanastha Chitpavan Brahmin, was the postmaster of Cansaulim!

The policemen could not believe their luck.

A phone call was made by Pascal to Sonali. Uncle Sahastrabuddhe was at home. There not being much by way of entertainment in Cansaulim on a rainy Saturday evening, the postmaster had settled down before the TV in his pajamas. Now his niece was asking him to remain on standby for a call from the Mumbai Police. He wondered why.

SAHASTRABUDDHE WAS a garrulous old man.

Almost greedily, he took de Azavedo's call.

"Mamu Sahastrabuddhe, tumche shi ulon koshi zale," de Azavedo said, genuinely delighted to be talking to the postmaster.

"Does he speak English?" Ferraz whispered.

"Tu English ulaita?"

"Vhoi," said the postmaster.

"Bore, mhojea Senior Inspectoranshi uloi," de Azavedo said, reluctantly passing his phone to Ferraz.

Sahastrabuddhe told Ferraz that his post office was not to be confused with the Velsao one, they both shared the same Pin Code – 403712. Cansaulim was a large town and it was natural for it to be serviced by two post offices, but Velsao was just a SO.ND.

"What's a SO.ND?" Ferraz asked curiously.

"Sub Post Office Non-Delivery," Sahastrabuddhe said. "My post office in Cansaulim village opposite the fish market is a SO.D, that's Sub Post Office Delivery. Velsao doesn't deliver mail, we do."

He further informed Ferraz that his post office was in Salcete *taluka* of South Goa district. Its postal division was Goa and its postal region was Goa-Panaji, but its postal circle was Maharashtra.

Ferraz was appreciative, "*But what–*"

"Our Pin Code is 403712," Sahastrabuddhe reminded him. "Most people don't know that PIN stands for Postal Index Number. Know why this is important in an address? To accurately send and receive mail. The Pin Code indicates the precise location of a post office. The first three digits are of the postal circle and region; the last three are of the exact delivery end post office."

"I see," said Ferraz. "Sir, the Mumbai Police is looking for a Konkanastha Chitpavan Brahmin by the name of Prof. Gajanan Murtikar. We believe he is from Cansaulim."

"Murtikar," the postmaster said, "yes, of course. He is a KoBra and grew up in Cansaulim. The family's original surname was Modak. They had an ancestral home here but it's been sold. I don't know when Gajanan became a Murtikar. It's not a Chitpavan surname. I haven't seen nor heard of Gajanan in years."

Ferraz sighed heavily.

"What can you tell me about him, sir?" he asked.

"What has he done?"

"Maybe nothing..."

"There's nothing to tell," Sahastrabuddhe said. "He used to teach in some college in Belgaum, I don't know the name. Then he returned to Cansaulim. One day he came to the post office – when was that, years ago, I can't remember – and said he was leaving Goa. He wanted his mail forwarded. Leaving a forwarding address with your local post office is the easiest thing in the world. All you have to do is fill a card and a diary entry is made of your old and new addresses."

"But–"

"But Gajanan had no forwarding address to give that day. So what he did was to send me a postcard later giving me his new address."

Ferraz held his breath.

"Do you remember that address, sir?" he asked eagerly.

"No," the postmaster said indignantly. "What do you think I am? A human computer!"

"I was hoping–"

"But very soon the India Post employee will be replaced by a computer," Sahastrabuddhe said bitterly. "Who cares about the post office? We are almost 240 years old and outdated. Snail mail, they call our service, because of the lag-time between dispatch of a letter and its receipt. Versus the instant dispatch and delivery of its electronic equivalent, the e-mail."

"I understand," said Ferraz sympathetically, "but this prof–"

"But who has a computer to send e-mail!" Sahastrabuddhe snorted. "Half the time there is no electricity in Goa. And some remote villages don't even get cell phone network. So there's no SMS. But the postman goes there."

"Ah, your postmen would know–"

"Goa is not like Mumbai with its skyscrapers and express elevators," said the postmaster tirelessly. "The postman has to cycle or walk for miles with his heavy bag of mail. And there are no separate postmen for registered post, telegrams and money orders; it is one man's duty. The Cansaulim postman's round takes hours. You think people are grateful? Half the time the poor postman has to watch out for dogs. They attack him on sight. One crazy old woman in Arossim Beach keeps a big billy goat. It lies in wait for the postman and charges him when he goes to make a delivery."

"About Prof. Murtikar," Ferraz said desperately.

"Yes, what about him?"

"Did your post office forward any mail to him?"

"No, I don't think so."

"Not a single article of post?" said Ferraz incredulously, "surely he must have got something?"

"I can't remember," said Sahastrabuddhe doubtfully.

"Please try, sir."

"Why is it important?"

"This is a murder investigation…"

"Khoon! Konacho khoon zaalo! Gajanan?"

"… that's why I want Prof. Murtikar's new address."

"I don't have the authority to give it to you," Sahastrabuddhe said.

"Why not?" argued Ferraz, "We are the police."

"Yes, but even then, the mail is…"

"I'm not asking to see his mail!" Ferraz shouted.

"Don't raise your voice," said Sahastrabuddhe sounding shocked.

"JUST TELL ME WHICH CITY HE MOVED TO!"

"Mumbai," replied the postmaster sulkily, "and you know that, otherwise you wouldn't be threatening an old man like me."

"I'm sorry, sir," Ferraz apologized, "I need the address. This is murder I'm investigating. Do you want to be arrested for withholding information?"

"But Gajanan's address is at the post office," Sahastrabuddhe protested.

"Then open it, please."

"*What, now!* Can't this wait till Monday?" the postmaster asked, hedging. "It's quite late here and it's raining. The post office is shut. I will have to go myself."

"I'm sorry… how far away is the post office?"

"It's not a question of how far, I'm not used to opening it, I will have to struggle with the locks and light switches and then search for the address."

"How far!"

"It's on the ground floor."

"What!"

"I stay above it."

Ferraz took a deep breath, "I will hold on."

"Bore, mhaka dah minta di."

de Azavedo nudged Ferraz.

"Tell him *'Dev borem karun'*," he said.

"What the fuck does that mean?"

"God bless you."

"That old cock… may the devil take his soul!"

Postmaster Vishnushastri Sahastrabuddhe was back in less than ten minutes.

"Yes, he is in Mumbai only – your city," he told Ferraz accusingly. "I have his forwarding address. Is there a place called Khar?"

"There is, indeed," Ferraz told him gratefully, *"Dev borem karun."*

29

IT WAS 8 pm.

They were racing against time. Afraid they were already too late. They were on their cells in a large and empty classroom at Wilson College that an obliging watchman had opened for them. Outside was madness. They would not have heard their own voices over the music and firecrackers that each Ganpati arriving at Chowpatty was being welcomed with.

Ferraz was walking between benches and telling Joint CP (Crime) Arun Rathod, "Sir, our suspect's name is Prof. Gajanan Murtikar, we don't know where he is teaching, but his address is Flat No 2, Cornell, Ground Floor..."

"... the Junction of 18th Road and Main Avenue," Navroze was perched on the lecturer's table and giving the address to Sr. PI Ramesh Jamkhande of Khar Police Station...

"... near Rajesh Khanna Garden, Khar west," de Azavedo was passing it to Sanjay Chhabria and Sangeeta Kadam who were with a Unit IX team at the old fishing village of Khar Danda where immersions were taking place.

A DRAGNET was urgently spread.

Rathod informed the Main Control Room. The police had five regional Control Rooms in North, South, East, West and Central Mumbai, too. They could locate any mobile patrol van or beat marshal of the police stations in their region on GPS and raise them on the wireless.

An alert for Prof. Gajanan Murtikar was put out.

He was to be arrested without a warrant. The police had reasonable suspicion that he had committed a cognizable offence. Under Section 41 of the CrPC, they could arrest the professor and produce him before a magistrate within 24 hours.

The cops rushing to Cornell on the Junction of 18th Road and Main Avenue reached simultaneously. A Khar police team in a Bolero and beat marshals on their motorcycle. Chhabria, Sangeeta and the Unit IX officers in a Qualis. They all stood around uncertainly. Not believing what they were seeing.

They were outside a slum called Narali Agripada. Its residents were the Agri community originally of Raigad and Thane districts. The ghetto looked large and ugly at night, its single and two-storey brick and tin shanties were covered by blue tarpaulin for the monsoon. Outside was a public toilet and autorickshaw garages. Horses used for joyrides at Juhu Beach were tethered to trees and neighed nervously. Dogs barked angrily. A big rooster strutted around them clucking irritably like it was the landlord of the slum and didn't care for their presence. The junction stank of horseshit, engine oil, human sewage, the wear and tear of slum life, and illicit liquor. Some bootlegger was distilling hooch in the slum.

The Agris were traditionally salt-makers. In time they had taken up fishing and agriculture. But right now nobody was minding the salt pans, casting their nets in the sea or out in the fields. They were outside Narali Agripada dressed in their gaudy festive finery. It was party time and they were creating a hullabaloo with unrestrained gaiety.

Disco lights perked up the gala party. Multiple colorful beams twisted up and down the junction, strobe lights flashed intensely and laser shots lit up the sky. Hanging from a lamp-post was a rotating mirror disco ball of the Seventies that sent splinters of psychedelic lights darting everywhere. Dazzled by the illumination, full of drink and their own *dum*, the Agri youth were dancing drunkenly to badly-tuned Bollywood music that blasted out of gigantic speakers. The elders sat around pretending this was fun while the women gathered in quieter conviviality around a small Ganpati idol that was being readied for immersion.

The police's arrival broke up the party. The beat marshals switched off the music. The silence that followed was replaced by a babble of angry voices. Why were the police here, the buzz went around. What did they want? Why so many of them?

Chhabria looked around nonplussed. The slum was in the airport's flight path. He watched a red-tailed SpiceJet Boeing climb the sky, the roar of its twin engines coming clearly down to him.

They were at the Junction of 18th Road and Main Avenue.

Only the building Cornell wasn't there!

CHHABRIA CALLED up Ferraz.

"Sir, there's nothing here," he said.

"Nothing there! What do you mean?"

"There's no building here. Cornell has been razed, redevelopment is taking place. A bulldozer and crane with a pile-driver are parked here. Tin screens are up all around," reported Chhabria looking at the vacant plot.

"Goddamn it… Are you sure you're at the right place?"

"Yes, sir," Chhabria said. "Locals say Cornell was pulled down in February. Its residents have accepted rental accommodation from the builder nearby or taken full payments, surrendered their flats and gone."

"This is a fucking joke!" Ferraz exclaimed.

"Sir, the redeveloper is Arenja Builders. Sangeeta has gone to look for their watchmen. I will get the estate manager's name and number and call him."

"Hurry, Sanjay … you know–"

"Sangeeta's back, sir, with a watchman."

THE ESTATE manager at Arenja Builders was bewildered.

His watchman at the Cornell plot had called in panic. Blabbering about the police having come. They wanted the names of Cornell's residents.

The estate manager asked to speak to the cops.

He told the lady cop on the phone that Cornell never had a Prof. Gajanan Murtikar among its residents. He had called up his corporate office and asked the security guard to open his cabin and check Cornell's project report for the list of society members. There was nobody by that name among the 12 flat owners.

"How can that be?" snapped Sangeeta in her no-nonsense cop voice. "Who owned Flat No. 2 on the ground floor?"

"A Dr. Uddata Kher," said the distressed estate manager, rechecking the names of the flat owners he had hastily scribbled down.

"Not a Prof. Gajanan Murtikar, you're sure?"

"No madam, the flat owner according to Cornell Cooperative Housing Society's rent receipts is Dr. Kher," the estate manager repeated. "Even the Reliance Energy electricity bills are in Dr. Kher's name."

Chhabria whispered in Sangeeta's ear, "Prof. Murtikar might have been staying on rent in Dr. Kher's flat. Ask this guy for the doctor's number."

And that's how it was.

DR. UDDATA Kher was not pleased to receive a call from the police.

He was having dinner and did not know Prof. Gajanan Murtikar.

"I cannot help you," he curtly told Ferraz, who called the original resident of Cornell's Flat No. 2 himself to inquire about its suspect tenant.

"Doctor–"

"Nor do I know which college he was attached to," Dr. Kher was saying, "or what subject he was teaching. Can't say I care either."

"But doctor, you leased your flat to him."

"So what? Who says I have to know him?" Dr. Kher asked irritably.

"Then how did–"

"My wife, Dr. Meenakshi Kher, she dealt with this Prof. Murtikar of yours. She met him through our broker. She went to the Stamp Duty Office in Goregaon with them to register our agreement."

"So Prof. Murtikar stayed in your house then?"

"Of course, he did. And we had no problems with him. Our last tenant, don't ask! She was an airhostess. She kept irregular hours and subleased the flat to four friends without our knowing. My God, they had orgies there! The society complained. Boisterous parties with loud music playing late into the night, people shouting and stamping their feet, noisy gambling sessions, sex in parked cars, sex on the terrace, it all went on. We terminated her agreement. The broker got us Prof. Murtikar. From where, I don't know, I can give you the broker's–"

"That won't be necessary," said Ferraz crisply. "May I speak to your wife Meenakshi, please? Er, she too is a doctor, you said?"

"Yes, a dentist like me," Dr. Kher said. "But a pedodontist, she's a specialist dealing with the care and treatment of children's teeth. I'm an oral surgeon. We have separate practices because our practices are different. Mine is at Khar, Meenakshi's is at Lokhandwala, where we moved to from Cornell in, let me see, hmnn it was 2007…"

"Right… may I speak to Dr. Meenakshi, please?"

"About what?"

"About Prof. Murtikar."

"Why? He's not her friend," Dr. Kher said, adding angrily, "you haven't told me what this is about. How do I know you are the police? I'm just–"

"Where did Prof. Murtikar go from Cornell?"

"I'm sure Meenakshi does not know," Dr. Kher said cussedly.

"Doctor, I would prefer to ask her myself," Ferraz said sharply.

"Oh, but you can't..."

"Why not? This is a murder investigation that we–"

"Murder! Who got – was it Prof. Murtikar?"

"I cannot go into the details," said Ferraz shortly.

"You're saying what then... *shit*, I get it, you're suspecting Prof. Murtikar of being the one who... why, it's clear as day!"

"Where is your wife, doctor?"

"Meenakshi is visiting her brother is Massachusetts."

"Oh God," Ferraz sighed deeply. "Give me her number there, please. Any idea what's the time in Massachusetts now? Must be early morning."

"But she can't be reached there," said Dr. Kher aggravatingly.

"She can't, why is that?"

"Meenakshi and her brother are hikers. They have gone on this Appalachian Trail, it passes through the states of Georgia, North Carolina, Tennessee, Virginia, West Virginia, Maryland, Pennsylvania, New Jersey, New York, Connecticut, Vermont, New Hampshire, Maine and, and... hmnn, let me see, yes, of course, Massachusetts itself."

Ferraz was astonished.

Dr. Kher knew the route his wife was hiking in the US of A, but knew nothing about a tenant they had leased their flat to in Mumbai!

"I don't know why she went on this hike," he was saying peevishly. "Most of it is through wilderness, so there is never cell network, though some portions traverse towns. It's all walking, walking, walking. I prefer cycling and photography. But Meenakshi can't pedal or hold a camera straight!"

"Look doctor, I repeat, this is murder we are investigating," Ferraz said tersely, "and where Prof. Murtikar went after Cornell is more important to me than your engaging hobbies and where your wife currently is, I hope you understand."

"I'm afraid I can't help you," Dr. Kher brusquely replied.

"Then who can? You have no idea who we are–"

"Ask Shantabai."

"Who the fu– who is this Shantabai, doctor?"

"The old woman living in the slum across Cornell. She was our housekeeper for decades. I believe Prof. Murtikar retained her."

"What! She still lives opposite?"

"I believe so," Dr. Uddata Kher said, adding sarcastically, "surely that should not be too difficult for the police to ascertain."

SHANTABAI HAD gone to the *gaon* for Ganeshotsav.

"Where is the *gaon?*" Sangeeta wearily asked the community members who were waiting for the police to go so that they could resume their party.

"Alibaug," one old man said.

"What's Shantabai's cell number?" Chhabria asked.

"Cell number!" the old man cackled. "Shantabai doesn't have a mobile."

"Okay, what's the dammed Alibaug residence number then?" Chhabria said irritably, his pink face dripping sweat under the burning halogen lights.

The old man gave a toothless grin, "*Saheb*, they don't even have electricity in the *gaon*, water is still drawn from the well, what phone number you are asking!"

"This old fucker's the Prophet of Doom," Chhabria muttered to Sangeeta. "He's hopeless, ask him anything and he comes up beaming with a pessimistic, negative reply. I want to smack him in the mouth, the loser."

"What's Shantabai's address?" Sangeeta asked. "We can get the Raigad District Police to search for her."

But the old man suggested, "Why don't you contact Shantabai's son Santosh, instead? He is a plumber at Bhatia Hospital in Tardeo."

"He is?" said Chhabria in surprise.

RATHOD HAD them making calls.

Every cop was on the phone. Calling up colleges for Prof. Gajanan Murtikar who taught Psychology. They had no numbers. And this being a holiday, the Mumbai University was shut, so they got no help from there.

"Try the Net," the Joint CP (Crime) suggested. He was directing the operation from Unit I. He had earlier had a grand time dealing with the Belgaum and Goa police.

The Belgaum Superintendent of Police knew Rathod outranked him. An SP in the districts was equal to a DCP in the city. Whereas a Joint CP in the city was on par with an Inspector General of Police in the districts.

He passed on Rathod's call to his IGP, Northern Range.

The IGP was having none of it. He had enough crime in the 123 police stations and 57 outposts of the districts of Belgaum, Bijapur, Bagalkot, Dharwar, Gadag and Haveri in the Northern Range of Karnataka.

"Karvir Police Station, huh?" he said, "when was this case?"

"Maybe eight or nine years ago, perhaps more, I don't rightly know," Rathod admitted, "that's the reason I'm calling you."

"Hmnn," the IGP said meaningfully, "eight or nine years ago… maybe more… you don't rightly know… so you're calling me. You think we don't have crime here, Rathod?"

"It's not that–"

"Then why are you sending me on this wild goose chase?"

"All I'm asking is whether–"

"You think your student in the Ganpati dress is all the crime we deal with in Belgaum? This town is an education hub. We got three reputed universities here, the KLE University, the Visvesvaraya Technological University, and the Rani Channamma University," the IGP said.

"I'm aware, and this college professor we–"

"We got students from across India and all over the world in Belgaum. You know what mischief they get up to over the weekend? Half the rapes on campuses don't get reported. And you want me to go back eight or nine or God knows how many years to locate a student who wore a Ganpati dress?"

"Actually we are trying to locate a Belgaum professor," Rathod said.

"Why? What's he done?"

"He's a suspected psychopath–"

"Suspected psychopath," the IGP gave a short, barking laugh. "Come down here, Rathod, and see the psychos we get over the weekend from Goa. Everybody goes to Goa for the weekend. Know what the Goans do?"

"They visit Belgaum?"

"Exactly! It's a short drive. They bring their tax-free alcohol, they carry Feni. Our hotels are full, our car parks are overflowing, they come for shopping and entertainment, they come to our hospitals."

"I understand," said Rathod weakly.

"So do me a favor, huh," the Northern Range IGP said, "shoot this through the official channel, okay? I've got immersion *bandobast* happening, let's hunt for your psychopath and Ganpati fashion girl later, huh?"

Courageously resolute, Rathod tried the Goa Police HQ in Panaji next.

The Director General of Police was in Sao Paolo.

"On some human rights work for the UN," his duty officer informed Rathod.

Next in line was the IGP of Goa. Who was in hospital with a

broken leg. After him was a DIG who was on leave. So the duty officer directed Rathod to the South Goa SP because Cansaulim was in South Goa.

"Is this to do with drug-trafficking?" the South Goa SP asked, "because the major crime in Goa today, let me tell you, is drug-trafficking."

"No, no… it's homicide," Rathod said.

"Yeah, who got killed, sir, a drug lord or some junkie?"

"Nobody related to drugs," Rathod assured him.

"Then what is this about?"

"We are trying to locate a professor wanted in a series of killings."

"In Goa or Mumbai?"

"Mumbai," said Rathod, thinking that was a dumb question.

"What's it got to do with us?"

"We think he's from Cansaulim."

"You think!" the South Goa SP was respectfully incredulous. "That's an inquiry you ought to be making with our CID, sir. It has a Research Unit that compiles data from our 24 police stations, analyses it, and provides crime trends and vital clues to field officers so they can take appropriate action in an investigation."

"Can't you help me?" Rathod asked with some pathos.

"How? Does your professor have a record, sir?"

"Not that I know."

"Sure he isn't into drugs?" the South Goa SP asked, "almost everybody is here. Especially in North Goa. And I'm not talking users – the big criminals are the traffickers and peddlers. The hippie culture of the 1970s left behind the menace of drugs. We have more foreign peddlers than Indian. Goa gets more tourists every year than the state's population. The Tourist Police, the Anti-Narcotics Cell and the Crime Branch are in a tizzy."

"I'm not talking organized crime," Rathod said in exasperation.

"Is your professor into the sex trade with the Russian mafia?"

"I'm sure he isn't!"

"How do you know? There's a lot of that in Cansaulim because of the hotels there," the South Goa SP said. "Millions of dollars from slush funds are being routed into Goa through *hawala* channels to fund the Russian mafia. They are buying huge tracts of land through *benami* companies to set up bases for their arms and sex trades. Soon Goa will be a haven for international criminals and terrorists, that day is not far."

"Why isn't the Goa Police doing something?" asked Rathod, so intrigued by the neighboring state's crime that he quite forgot his own circumstances.

"You think this has got to do with poor policing?" the South Goa SP asked indignantly, "No sir, it's because of our lax administration."

"Thank you, it's been a real education," Rathod said hanging up.

Now he told his DCB-CID cops to go to the Yellow Pages, JustDial, Sulekha, AskMe and Dialkaro for college numbers.

The help lines had numbers for movie halls, restaurants, car rentals, hospitals, 24-hour petrol pumps and ATMs. Those were easy to give. Colleges took longer. But in 20 minutes, to the cops' surprise, they had the names and numbers of all colleges in Mumbai.

"Divide the colleges among you area wise," Rathod suggested.

They realized there were colleges for BA, B.Com, B.Sc and BMM, for Engineering, Management, Law, Applied Arts & Architecture, Medicine, Dentistry, Ayurveda, Homoeopathy, Home Science & Social Work, Physical Education, Vocational Studies, Aviation, Hotel Management & Catering Technology, Nautical Science, Hospitality & Tourism, Heritage Management, Fashion Technology, Pharmacy, Population Sciences, and Education, Social, Clinical, Counseling, Industrial & Organizational Psychology.

Salvi whistled softly.

"In my day there was no choice," he said. "Who did Arts? Only the duffers! You went in for Science or Commerce."

"Rule out every college that does not teach Psychology," Rathod said. "So we're left with only the Bachelor of Arts, Science and Commerce colleges, right?"

He was right. But they were left with very little time.

"Datta, call our 12 DCB-CID Units," Rathod said next, "ask them to send men to all the colleges in their Zones. They are to inquire if Prof. Gajanan Murtikar teaches there and report back to me."

Salvi looked at the clock on the wall.

With sinking hearts, the cops hit the phones again. They rang in empty college offices. Or calls got diverted to the gate where the watchmen engaged them in conversation.

"Calling from the Crime Branch…" Tushar Pandit was saying.

"… do you have," Vishnu Shetty was inquiring…

"… a professor teaching Psychology," Arun Sawant was asking…

"… whose name is Gajanan Murtikar," Dinakar Salian was informing…

"… he is from Goa," Dhananjay Gadkari was adding…

"… and lives in Khar west," Puneet Singh was disclosing.

Then Rathod had another idea.

"Who's got college-going teens?" he said. "Spread the word. Tell them to ask their friends to ask their friends and friends' friends, some kid's got to know this professor and in which college he teaches. Tell them to call, text, tweet, to put this up on Facebook and BBM. Give our Station House number for anybody wanting to share information."

Salvi looked at him in wonder.

"What if the professor gets to hear of this, sir?" he asked.

"Doesn't matter, we will have him soon," Rathod replied confidently.

"And what if *this* professor is not the right man?"

It was Rathod's turn to look at Salvi in wonder.

30

SANTOSH PATIL was scared of the police.

He was fixing a geyser in the Maternity Ward when Ferraz and de Azavedo reached Bhatia Hospital. The reception paged for him. He came wiping his hands on his trousers, an honest-looking, puny, middle-aged man, perturbed to find his visitors were cops.

They had come on Ferraz's motorcycle. Bhatia Hospital was a kilometer from Chowpatty but it still took them 15 minutes. The road was almost impossible. Traffic policemen stood blowing whistles. But the processionists were also blowing whistles. Also small bugles, and banging drums. Nobody knew what was happening. All along the road political parties had set up booths like they did during elections, offering devotees free water. Their leaders were on mics, extolling the virtues of their political outfits while welcoming Ganesh *bhakts* to the *visarjan*.

Somebody flung a handful of *gulaal* at de Azavedo and his wet hair was now a dirty red and standing on end. It matched his colorful Hawaiian shirt.

"I know PI Cyrus Irani of Yellow Gate Police Station," Patil told them.

Ferraz wondered why the common man when confronted by the police quickly established his own connections in the force. It was like insurance against whatever was going to come.

"Don't worry, this is just a routine inquiry," he assured the plumber.

"Into what?" Patil asked nervously.

"Actually, we want to speak to your mother Shantabai–"

"Why? What has she done!"

In another moment the alarmed plumber would be screaming blue murder to his friend PI Irani at Yellow Gate Police Station, Ferraz was thinking.

"Relax," he said. "You know the professor who rented Dr. Kher's flat in Cornell? Your mother was his housekeeper, right?"

"Murtikar? Yes, but what has that–"

"Nothing. Where did he go from Cornell? Your mother might know."

"Oh," said Patil in surprise.

"Comes the dawn," muttered de Azavedo.

"Has he… the professor done… is he in trouble?" asked Patil.

"Never mind that," Ferraz told him. "How do we contact Shantabai?"

"The professor lives in Khar… close to Cornell, he took another flat on rent. He likes the area. Also, it's close to his college. Mother still works for him."

"What? Still in Khar! Where? Do you know his college?"

"College… ask my mother… she does *jhaadu-kadka-pochha* for him."

Ferraz grabbed him by the shoulder, making the diminutive plumber wince.

"Look Patil, where is Shantabai?" he asked.

"She is sick and in hospital."

"Which hospital? In Alibaug?"

"No – this one."

They thought they heard wrong, he said it so softly. As if the son was afraid his admission might lead to his mother's arrest.

"What did you say?" Ferraz asked in a hushed voice.

"Mother is admitted in hospital."

"This hospital, Bhatia you mean?" Ferraz shouted, shaking Patil.

"Yes," cried the plumber, wriggling in Ferraz's iron grip. "Let go of me! She got chest pain. I brought her from Alibaug by taxi this morning. The ferry doesn't run in the monsoon. The cardiologist wants to keep her under observation for 24 hours. She is in the General Ward, resting."

They ran upstairs, not waiting for the elevator, ignoring the protests of the night nurse at the General Ward who stepped forward stiff with starch, attitude and indignation, saying, "Visiting hours are..."

Shantabai was not in bed, resting. She was at the window. Watching the Ganpatis passing by on their way to Chowpatty with great interest.

"This is better than Alibaug," she told her son. "Does the Lalbaugcha Raja pass here or go from Opera House? The ward boy says last year it reached Chowpatty only at 6 am next day."

The policemen regarded her carefully.

At 80, Shantabai was a sprightly old bird.

Hawk-eyed, dark and skinny, with stringy muscles from years of doing people's vessels, dusting their homes and washing their clothes, she was perched on the window ledge like a gargoyle, chewing *paan*.

Her cardiologist would have a heart attack, Ferraz was thinking.

"*Aiyee*, these are policemen," Santosh said apologetically, "They have some questions for you about Prof. Murtikar."

"Gajanan, *what* happened to him?" the old woman asked, turning away from the outside world of song, dance and drama into the antiseptic ward of bedpans, pills and needles.

"Nothing, *aiyee*," Ferraz said gently. "We want to know where he stays now. Where's the new place where you go to work for him?"

Shantabai was a gasbag and the mainspring of local gossip.

"*Arre baba*, it's the next road only," she told the policemen. "He was at the Kher's *kholi* in Cornell. I used to look after Uddata since he was a boy, you know. And Uddata's mother Meera is my great friend. I was sad when the family moved. But what to do? Meenakshi came, they had their son Saatvik. The family was growing and needed more space. To live, to practice their *daatancha* business. It runs in the family, you know. Uddata's father is also a doctor. And his sister Sharvari… she does that medicine with the white *golis*… what's it called, Santosh? No, it's not ayurveda – yes, homoeopathy, that's it. Meera and Meenakshi used to visit Cornell after they shifted. But now the building has gone…"

Shantabai shook her head sorrowfully.

"*Aiyee*, where does the professor stay now?" Ferraz asked again.

"On 21st Road," she replied, "the last building, Seagull. I don't know the flat number but it is the middle one on the third floor, I think it belongs to some *presswallah* who gave it on rent."

"Does he have a mobile number?" Ferraz asked, hearing de Azavedo behind him giving Chhabria the professor's new address in Khar.

"I don't know," Shantabai said.

"When did you see him last?"

"Last week on Thursday. He paid me in advance for September."

"Why?"

"*Why? I don't know, I didn't ask.*"

"How does he look, this professor? Describe him for me."

"Like anybody else! He's not Amitabh Bachchan. He reminds me of that fellow, that politician… no, he's not a politician, they are all *halkats*. This man is a nice man. No, not the professor, he's also a nice man. I meant the politician… *arre deva*, what am I saying, he's not a politician this man who the professor looks like. But he fights for the poor, you know who I mean?"

"No, who?" asked Ferraz, thinking the old woman had lost it.

"*Arre,* that man you *policewallahs* arrested for going on *satyagraha.*"

"You mean–"

"Anna… Anna Hazare."

Anna Hazare! Shit, Ferraz was thinking.

While describing the killer to the police sketch artist, the rag-picker had said that he looked like the man in the poster. And the man on the poster at Bandra Reclamation had been Anna Hazare.

Shantabai was tugging at his arm.

"Oye Inspector," she was saying, "when the Lalbaugcha Raja reaches Chowpatty, can you take me for *darshan* before the *visarjan* please?"

CHHABRIA WANTED to kick the door down.

But Sangeeta called for a locksmith. The Khar Danda pavements were occupied by labourers like carpenters, painters, electricians, plumbers and masons sitting with their tools. Among them was a *chaaviwallah* smoking a *beedi.*

"What if this professor is the wrong man?" Sangeeta had argued, "We just can't break down his door."

They were outside Flat 11 in Seagull on 21st Road. Their phones were on silent. The building watchman was standing nervously behind. They had offered him no explanations. Parking at the end of the quiet road that was shielded by a canopy of trees, they entered Seagull swiftly and in deadly silence. They had brought the watchman up to point out the right flat.

On the landing, they drew their guns.

Sangeeta rang the doorbell of the middle flat.

Just in case *he* was inside… you never knew.

She rang again, twice. Silence.

Tucking her gun under her *kurti*, she nodded to the locksmith.

He looked at the cops fearfully, then examined the keyhole on the outer door. He brought out tweezers, a thin file and tiny hammer from his pouch. In three minutes, the lock made a soft click. Swinging the door open, the *chaaviwallah* bent his back to the stouter, formidable inside door that had a more challenging lock.

It took him 15 minutes.

He kept jiggling the lock with his tools. Working it. Trying to find some purchase on the tumblers inside, twisting tiny curving instruments left and right, removing them and replacing them with others. All the while he kept muttering to himself. Down on his knees, head twisted to one side, one eye shut and the other close to the keyhole. Twice he dropped his tools with a noisy clatter.

"Come on, come on," Chhabria whispered irritably, "A fucking burglar would have broken into the flat in two minutes!"

It was funny, Sangeeta was thinking, the police using a *chaaviwallah* to break into a house like burglars do. There came a solid double click in the woodwork and the door yielded. Chhabria immediately elbowed the *chaaviwallah* aside and pushed the door open.

Sangeeta and the others waited, guns drawn, what if he *was* at home and had seen them entering the building and was now standing in the dark… knife in hand? The door opened into a broad passage. On its wall, immediately before them and illuminated poorly by the staircase light were three large Ganpati frames.

Standing sideways, Sangeeta felt along the wall and found the lights.

The passage came ablaze with two overhead yellow lamps.

The Ganpati frames were actually jigsaw puzzles, bright and vivid, 1,000 tiny pieces each, Sangeeta guessed, and they had been mounted and framed.

From close, they were spectacular and mesmerizing.

To the left was the kitchen and hall.

To the right, the bathroom and bedroom.

Swiftly they spread out, guns fanning the rooms.

The house yawned emptily at the police team.

"*Sanjay,*" Sangeeta called out from the hall.

Chhabria came blundering down the passage from the bedroom.

It was a largish hall with big sliding glass windows from outside which the trees of 21st Road peeped in. Two chest of drawers, a divan, a sofa and chairs, a small glass center-table, a flat screen TV on the wall, above that a split AC unit, a couple of paintings. Chhabria took it all in with a glance.

"See this," Sangeeta jerked her head.

It was the professor's work table.

A desktop computer stood on the polished wooden surface which extended behind into a bookshelf on the wall. Behind the computer was a pin board covered in red felt.

And tacked up on it, *oh dear God…*

Chhabria holstered his gun.

Sangeeta was calling Ferraz urgently.

"YES, SANGEETA?" Ferraz answered immediately.

He was waiting for the call… not knowing what to expect.

He knew nobody would be at home. If it was him, if Prof. Gajanan Murtikar was the Cobra, then he would be out in the city, stalking his tenth and last victim.

"It's him, sir!" Sangeeta breathlessly confirmed.

"What! How do you know?"

"On his writing desk, he's got a pin board with newspaper cuttings of the nine murders. Wherever your name is mentioned, he's circled it in red."

"Really!"

"Yes, sir. He's been following us. The cuttings are up-to-date, with this morning's papers reporting Batliwala's murder," Sangeeta added. "And guess what else we found?"

"Sangeeta, is there anything to indicate who his last victim is?" Ferraz asked suddenly. "Any diary with names? Anybody's picture on the pin board? A name on the calendar? You know what I mean? Look around quickly, there may be something."

"Right, sir. And I was saying, *guess* what we found?"

"Anything lying around to tell us which college he teaches at? Like an identity card, a salary slip, appointment letter, there must be something."

"Sanjay is looking through the drawers in the hall. I will check the bedroom. And, sir, I was saying… *guess* what we found?"

"Tell me – I hate suspense."

"The cell phones!"

"Of his victims? Oh my God!"

"Isn't that a solid bit of evidence, sir?"

"You bet! I had forgotten the phones. Don't touch them, his prints are bound to be all over, leave them where they are for the forensic guys. We need every shred of evidence to build up the case against this guy."

"Right, sir."

"Another thing," Ferraz said, "if he kills his tenth victim today, he will return to the flat at night, and I want to lay a trap for him. I want Sanjay and you waiting in the dark. Get Unit IX to cover every entry and exit, even the way to the terrace. I will get the Khar cops to seal the area with additional backup in civvies. There's no way he must escape."

"Right, sir," Sangeeta said, "I'm sending the others down. What time should we put out the lights, lock the doors and sit in the dark?"

"Immediately," Ferraz said, "we don't know where he is and when he will get back. Can the apartment be seen from the road? *It can!* Fuck, switch off the lights at once, take the building watchman into confidence or throw a scare into him. Any cops in uniform should get under cover. He spots khaki, he'll smell a trap."

"Ok, sir."

"And keep your phones on silent," Ferraz warned. "I want minute-to-minute updates. Navroze and I are leaving Chowpatty and heading for Khar."

THE FIRST time Jackie called Ferraz, it was to exult.

He took her call reluctantly.

"Hey cop, guess what?" she asked chirpily.

"What? You've been invited by Amitabh Bachchan to take the *Kaun Banega Crorepati* hot seat and match your extraordinary IQ with his Computerji?"

"No," she giggled, "don't be funny, Angie."

"Then what?" Ferraz asked impatiently.

A large orange and white helicopter hovered noisily above him. It belonged to a charter air service and was taking people on joyrides over Mumbai for an aerial view of the *visarjan*. The clatter of its rotors was tremendous.

"Remember that crossword clue?"

"What fucking crossword clue?" he yelled.

"Angie! If you're going to swear, I'm not going to talk to you!"

"This noise and the crowds are driving me nuts!"

"Where are you?"

"Chowpatty. What crossword clue?"

"Remember you didn't know the answer to, 'I'm the First. But I'm no Michelle. She's a Lady, I'm just a Citizen'?"

"I didn't know? Who was solving the fucking crossword!"

"*Angie!* I told you the answer was three words."

"Yeah, so what, three words or five, you didn't know the fuc–"

"I solved it!"

"No shit!"

"The answer is Mayor Yamini Olwe. The clue said, 'I'm the First. But I'm no Michelle. She's a Lady, I'm just a Citizen'. Michelle as in Michelle Obama, US President Barrack Obama's wife. The 'First Lady' is an unofficial title traditionally held by the President's wife. She's the White House hostess during his term–"

"*Yeah, who the hell cares!*"

"Wait," Jackie warned, "the answer is Mayor Yamini Olwe because

Yamini is also a 'First' – not a 'Lady' like Michelle Obama – but a 'Citizen' as the clue hints. The Mayor of Mumbai is ceremonially known as the city's 'First Citizen'. Did you know that, you duffer?"

"All the bloody while!"

"Liar! Why didn't you say so then?"

"What? And ruin your day?" Ferraz asked and disconnected.

MINUTES LATER Jackie called Ferraz in alarm.

"Yeah honey?" he snapped, his cop voice making her flinch.

"Angie!" she cried, *"You ordered a search for my professor?"*

"Whaaat?"

"Uncle Navroze's daughter Zeenia just called..."

"I didn't–"

"... to say the police are looking out for Prof. Murti. Why?"

"Who's Prof. Murthy? That Madrasi who tipped me about the poetry?"

"Yes, Prof. Murti's been a very–"

"What's his surname? Ramamurthy? Krishnamurthy? Narayanamurthy?"

"No, it's Murtikar, the professor is from Goa not the South..."

Ferraz was suddenly silent.

"... his name is Prof. Gajanan Murtikar, he's no Madrasi."

Jackie could hear cymbals clanging, drums beating and cries of *"Ganpati Bappa Moryaa! Pudchya Varshi Lavkar Ya!"* as another idol reached the shore.

Then suddenly Ferraz exploded.

"THAT FUCKING SONOFABITCH!!!"

Jackie almost dropped her phone.

Shocked by his sudden outburst, she quavered, *"Angie, wha–"*

"Jackie," he barked, "where does this professor live?"

"Somewhere in Khar. But what di–"

"That cold-blooded, psychopathic bastard!"

The rage in his voice frightened her. He sounded dangerous. Like she'd never heard him before. She asked tearfully, "Angie, what did I say that–"

"My God, honey, your Prof. Murti is the serial killer we're hunting."

She stifled the sob and squeaked, *"Prof. Murti?"*

"Yes, and he pretended to help me with the investigation!"

She found it hard to comprehend what he was saying.

"What are you… are you sure, Angie?"

"Yes. Tell me about him, quick."

"What do you mean? He teaches us Psyc–"

"What does he look like?"

"Look like? Oh, I understand. He's… wait, I have an idea," she said in sudden excitement, "I can send you a recent picture of him."

"Prof. Murti's picture, from where?"

"It's on my phone!"

"Why do you have it?" he asked surprised.

"I took it on Monday in college, it was Teacher's Day!"

"Oh, but how will you send–"

"On BBM… but *shit*, you don't have a Blackberry!"

"One minute," Ferraz said. She heard him talking to somebody. Then he was saying, "Navroze has a Blackberry. Send him the picture. He said his BBM pin, write it down, is 2510LB33."

"I'm sending it right now. God, Angie… I can't beli–"

"Jackie," said Ferraz sharply, "does the professor know where we stay?"

"I may have mentioned it. Has Uncle Navroze received the picture?"

"Listen to me carefully, honey. Lock the door right now. And stay in. I'm sending somebody for you. Call me when he comes and…"

"Why?"

"… don't open the door unless you're convinced he's a bona fide cop."

"But why can't I–"

"Listen to me!"

Jackie meekly shut up.

"Prof. Murti is dangerous. We don't know where he is. Or who he is after. But his cover is blown. There's a manhunt for him. He can't return to his flat. Every cop is on the lookout for him. I don't want him trying to take a hostage..."

Jackie gasped.

"... once he realizes he's cornered. He'll stop at nothing then."

"You mean me... because of you!"

"Possibly, hon. I can't take that risk. He lives not far from us."

"Is Zeenia also at risk because of Uncle Navroze?"

"No, she isn't."

"Okay," she sounded subdued.

"Just do as I say and don't be scared."

"Angie... why can't I just go down and wait at the Police Control Room? There are bound to be dozens of policemen there. Surely I will be safe."

"Oh, okay, I didn't think of that!"

"What, what are you going to do to... ?"

"I've got to get him first," Ferraz said honestly.

"You received the picture?" she asked again.

Ferraz nudged Navroze.

The Parsi cop was holding his cell at arm's length and staring at it.

"The network sucks here," Navroze complained.

"Not yet," Ferraz told her.

HE got on the phone to Joint CP (Crime) Arun Rathod next.

Quickly, Ferraz narrated the conversation he had with Jackie.

"Where's the picture?" Rathod asked.

"It's downloading, sir."

"Good work, Angelo," Rathod said, suddenly excited. "Send it to

Datta. He'll forward it to all DCB-CID Units and police stations with the request that prints be made and given to every cop on *bandobast*. Somebody has had to have seen this bastard. Send it also to Chhabria and Sangeeta at his residence. Let them show it to the watchman and neighbors and confirm he's the man staying there."

"Sir… I also want to put the picture on TV."

"Do it, then!"

THE PICTURE was buffering on Navroze's phone.

"I could have done a painting of him by now," he growled.

"Let's go on the road, the network may be stronger," de Azavedo said.

"Bawa, forward it to Datta, Chhabria and Savde," Ferraz shouted.

He called Nahida Shaikh next.

"Hey, ssup?" she asked cheerily.

She was at home. He could hear the TV in the background.

"Nahida, I need your help," he shouted, coming to the point.

"Is everything all right?" she asked immediately. "Where are you?"

"I'm at Chowpatty. We've identified the killer!"

"*What?*" Nahida said stunned, thinking she had heard wrong.

Quickly, he told her about the calls from Kolhapur and Belgaum. About the Psychology professor and his Ganpati-abusing girl student.

"Who's the girl?" she interrupted.

"I don't know, her name's Veena Ganpathy," Ferraz said.

"Amazing coincidence – the name. Haven't heard of her."

"Yeah, she's believed to be in politics somewhere."

"You will need her statement later. How did you track him to Mumbai?"

He told her how Salvi had spoken to the History professor in Jagalbet. And he, Ferraz, to the Cansaulim postmaster. How they got an old address for the professor in Khar that was now non-existent.

And after a runaround involving many people, how they located his current address. He wasn't at home. They didn't know which college he was teaching at. So the Joint CP (Crime) had come up with this idea to hookup college kids in their search. Then he told Nahida how Jackie had called…

"*Jackie?" she said, amazed.*

… and told him this professor was from her college. Now they had launched a manhunt for him, he was out stalking his tenth victim, but no cop knew what the fuck he looked like. Jackie had a picture…

"*Give it to me, I'll flash it on TV," Nahida said.*

… and it would help if the city was warned, maybe there was still time.

"My God, this is fantastic," Nahida said, "almost like a movie."

"It's taking forever to download on Inspector Navroze's phone. Jackie will send it to you. Will you pass the word around, give it to the other channels also, please?"

"Yes, immediately," Nahida said, "my BBM pin is 3153KJ58."

"Thanks Nahida," he said gratefully, "I owe you."

"After this is over!"

31

HE CALLED Jackie back.

"Angie, have you–"

"What picture you sent? It's taking forever to download. I want you to send it to the TV girl Nahida Shaikh also right now..."

"Angie, there's something I–"

"... her BBM pin is 3153KJ58. What is it?"

"This Prof. Murtikar... he's cricket crazy. He carries a small pocket transistor and listens to commentary of matches from around the world all the time."

For a moment Ferraz was speechless.

"A red-and-grey transistor?"

"Yes! How did you–"

"Oh my God!"

It was coming back to him now.

The commentary in the elevator of Nicole Raja's building that fateful afternoon. He had been trudging up the stairs and the lift had been going down, unknown to him with the killer in the cage.

And... just now!

The man outside the Control Room right here on Chowpatty...

Limping away with a red-and-grey transistor held to his ear!

... a tall, fairer version of Anna Hazare, oh fuck!

Something about him had caused Ferraz to stare.

"Jackie," he said urgently, "does he look like Anna Hazare?"

"Anna Hazare?" she said doubtfully, "I don't know..."

"Think!"

"But Angie, I've never seen Anna Hazare."

"Dammit… you've seen pictures!"

"Er, vaguely… I think maybe he does, but he's taller and fairer."

"On a scale of one to ten?"

"Hmnn… I'd say five," she said, still uncertain.

"That's a 50 per cent likeness. God, I have to see his picture."

"Angie, one more thing…"

"What!"

"Prof. Murtikar limps! He walks funnily. And–"

But Ferraz was running, crashing into people unapologetically.

His heart was pounding with fear.

The killer was here! That could only mean…

Navroze and de Azavedo were on the road.

"Look," Navroze said, waving his phone.

Ferraz looked.

The man from outside the Control Room!

"Bawa, he's here!" he panted.

"What! Here on Chowpatty? Maara baap, how do you know!"

There was awe in Navroze's voice.

Ferraz told them.

"Who's in charge of the Control Room?" he asked, breathing hard. "Maybe this cop noticed him and can tell us something."

"Who's he after?" Navroze wanted to know.

"The beach is crawling with fucking VVIPs."

"In this crowd, you won't know if the man next to you has been stabbed!"

"Bawa… he's got that TV actor's gun," Ferraz remembered with horror.

"Fuck, how do we stop him if we don't know who his target is?"

Ferraz looked around Chowpatty in despair.

The man on the mic was yelling something unintelligible. Like he had seen a tsunami approaching and was warning the people to get out of the water. But Navroze was right. There were at least ten thousand noisy, celebrating people on the beach. And a grand parade of big Ganpatis on trucks was coming down Kennedy Bridge, bringing thousands more.

How to search for him in this sea of people?

"Sir, the Police Tower," shouted de Azavedo.

A watchtower had been erected for policemen to monitor the *visarjan*. It offered an uninterrupted view. But it was packed to the edge. Some senior officer was up with night vision binoculars. They could see the light reflecting on its lenses.

Navroze grabbed Ferraz's arm.

"Next to it," he yelled.

Next to it was the HAM Radio Operators' Tower.

"Wait, I'm telling Joint CP (Crime)," Ferraz shouted.

At that moment, there was an uproar at the entrance.

They quickly turned to look.

The Khetwadicha Raja, one of Ganeshotsav's big attractions, was entering Chowpatty regally. Firecrackers announced its arrival. Devotees wearing Gandhi *topis* led it in proudly with *band-baaja* and dancing. Like a wedding *baraat*. A DJ on the truck with his music console and speakers added to the din. Over 2,000 Khetwadi residents, among them Gujaratis, Marwaris and Christians, followed at an easy pace waving saffron flags.

The *tutari* squealed its note of welcome. As the man on the mic announced the new entrant, a loud roar went up from the crowd and the Mayor's Pavilion got up in excitement to take pictures.

Looking at the pavilion Ferraz suddenly remembered…

… the Chief Minister was expected here tonight.

God, the killer was after him!

He didn't want to find out. He called Rathod.

"*Yes, Angelo?*" said Rathod buoyantly.

"Sir," shouted Ferraz over the noise, "stop the CM from coming here!"

"Why? What happened?"

"He's at Chowpatty, sir, the killer! And he might be armed with a gun. "

The Joint CP (Crime) thought he would have a stroke.

"At Chowpatty? Shit! How do you know?"

In a few quick sentences, Ferraz told him.

Rathod swung into action. Ferraz could hear him ordering somebody to check with the Control Room if the CM had left for Chowpatty.

"What! He's already left?" Rathod said in alarm.

"Angelo," he said, getting back, "he's on his way. I'm calling the CP and telling him to stop the CM. Look out for him, he'll be there any moment."

"Sir," Ferraz shouted desperately, "the Home Minister and Governor are–"

"Oh hell, I know," Rathod cut him short. "I'll inform the Addl. Chief Secretary Home and request him to cancel all VVIP engagements there right away."

The Joint CP (Crime) hung up with his hands full.

Ferraz looked across the dark waters.

Several boats were taking the Ganpatis out at sea for immersion. In the light of their bobbing lanterns, he could make out the towering idols. Beyond them the Walkeshwar skyline of illuminated high-rises rose in luxurious elegance. Some with neon hoardings that would tease and dance till dawn. He saw a convoy of speeding cars with flashing lights approaching from that direction.

"Bloody hell, the CM's on his way," he shouted.

Navroze was shaking him vigorously by the arm.

"There are also consul generals in the BMC's VIP Stand!"

Ferraz looked at him blankly.

"Consul Generals?" he said.

"Remember he killed the British envoy's wife!"

"That's why those Special Protection Unit cops are here!"

"Maybe he's after the American Consul General!"

"That fucking piece of shit!"

Ferraz called Rathod again.

"Angelo," the Joint CP (Crime) said in a taut voice, "we stopped the CM from entering Chowpatty. He's turning back. The Governor and Home Minister have been advised to wait until further notice from us."

"That's good, sir," said Ferraz with relief. "It might have been–"

"Some big fish who's always protected?" asked Rathod. "Or somebody he couldn't approach without raising suspicion. But the opportunity's there at Chowpatty."

"Sir, there are several Consul Generals here as well."

"What? They too!"

Ferraz resisted the urge to laugh.

"Can you ask Protection Branch to–"

"I'll get Mugbe to send a wireless message meant for all SPU officers on bodyguard duty at Chowpatty," Rathod said wearily. "He can caution them about what's happening and advise them to get the hell out."

"That would be best, sir. If we take care of probable victims–"

"What's the crowd like?"

"It's a sellout, sir. Tens of thousands. We'll be lucky to spot him."

"I'm ordering all exits of Chowpatty to be sealed," Rathod said.

"It's an open beach, sir," Ferraz pointed out, surprised.

"Additional forces from Local Arms at Tardeo will rush there and form a chain between the beach and the road. Datta is making copies of his picture which will be circulated among all the cops. We have an advantage, Angelo. The Cobra doesn't know that we know his real identity."

"Okay, sir," said Ferraz doubtfully.

"And I'm coming," Rathod said determinedly. "I've also called all South Mumbai DCB-CID Units to Chowpatty. Angelo, we'll have a hundred of our men there. This is it. He's got no more targets left. Let's flush out this bastard."

DE AZAVEDO was asking, "What's HAM?"

Half-way up the HAM Radio Tower ladder.

Navroze pushed him impatiently from behind.

"Chal ni," he said irritably, "a HAM is an amateur radio operator. What you thought, *halkat?* Something to eat from Goa? Like your *Pork Vindaloo*?"

Worldwide, amateur radio operators were called hams. Nobody understood why. The HAMs of the Mumbai Amateur Radio Society (MARS) voluntarily assisted the police, fire brigade and lifeguards by coordinating emergency services on Ganpati *visarjan* over their radios.

The Crime Branch cops weren't interested in HAMs…

… they wanted to use the radio tower to look for the killer.

Ferraz was following Navroze and de Azavedo up when his phone buzzed.

Cursing, he stopped. *Nahida Shaikh!* Now what?

"Inspector!" her voice screamed emergency. *"I know who he's after!"*

Ferraz's heart lurched, he wasn't expecting this.

"At Chowpatty?" he asked breathlessly.

"Yes! He's going for Mayor Yamini Olwe!"

"Mayor Ya–"

"Inspector, she's that girl Veena Ganpathy from Belgaum…"

"What are you saying!"

"… the college student who got him sacked, now she's married and has changed her name!"

Mayor Yamini Olwe, whom they hadn't considered at all.

"Nahida, are you bloody sure?" he yelled…

… because explanations could wait, meanwhile the Mayor was unprotected, a sitting duck for any whacko. He knew some Indian women took on new first names also while customarily adopting their husbands' surnames after marriage. Changing their identities. Like Veena Ganpathy became Yamini Olwe. How the fuck were the police supposed to know?

"Yes, Inspector," Nahida said flatly, "no mistake!"

He stood there thunderstruck.

It made sense. The last victim was the first one the professor intended to kill. After all these years. Revenge is a dish best served cold. But he saved her. He had kept Mayor Yamini Olwe for the last. The other victims were a cover-up. Practice for the big kill tonight. Nine innocents, people unknown to him, killed for similar reasons. Now he had come full circle. That sick bastard.

Ferraz was in two minds.

Securing the Mayor was not their responsibility.

His duty was to inform Rathod of the latest development.

And let the Joint CP (Crime) take it from there.

But the police was like any government department. Rigidly devoted to details of administrative procedure. By the time the Control Room was apprised of the threat to the Mayor's life, and it informed the police station nearest Chowpatty, precious seconds would be lost.

Which could cost Yamini Olwe her life.

There must have been close to 200 policemen on Chowpatty. All on specific duties. Ferraz couldn't order any of them to drop what they were doing and cover the Mayor. By the time he made himself heard, and understood, anything might happen to her. He would have to take care of her himself. Then wait for back-up. Like in the movies.

"Bawa!" he hollered, "it's the Mayor, come down!"

He leaped off the ladder. Navroze and de Azavedo joined him. The watchtower was near the shore. The Ganpatis waiting for immersion were making a terrible racket.

"What about the Mayor?" Navroze shouted.

Ferraz pulled both closer and yelled in their faces, "She's that student of his from Belgaum – Veena Ganpathy! Her name's changed to Yamini Olwe after marriage. The professor's going to kill her here. Let's go!"

They stared at him dumbfounded, then began running.

Pounding blindly after them, Ferraz hoped he was doing the right…

Oh God! He crashed headlong into Navroze and de Azavedo.

"What the fuck!"

They stood there catching their breath.

The gigantic Khetwadicha Raja blocked their path.

It waited in queue before the Mayor's Pavilion, this breathtaking Ganpati of Khetwadi's 12th Lane, a 28-feet-tall behemoth, like Tyrannosaurus Rex from *Jurassic World.* It made everybody and everything else look small and powerless. An impassable barrier of thousands of Khetwadi residents danced around it to a mesmerizing, warlike beat of crashing drums and clashing cymbals.

Shielding their eyes against the dazzling lights, they searched the Mayor's Pavilion over the heads of the dancing crowd and waving orange flags. The pavilion was heaving with people. Many were standing on chairs to take pictures of the Khetwadicha Raja.

"There she is," de Azavedo shouted suddenly, pointing.

And there Yamini Olwe indeed was.

The Mayor of Mumbai sat on a red velvet throne in the front row. A strikingly attractive and buxom woman, stylishly dressed in a bright orange sari, wearing an elaborate hairdo adorned by jasmine flowers.

She was smiling and waving to the crowd like a film star. Surrounded by laughing, happy people and BMC security men in khaki uniforms and brown berets.

Seeing her, Ferraz felt the tension drain out of him.

Navroze put one hand on his heart and said dramatically, "Baba Angelo, I've had enough excitement to last me a lifetime. I can retire in peace and go to my farmhouse in Dahanu, eh?"

Breathing heavily, Ferraz called the Joint CP (Crime).

"Angelo?"

Rathod's voice carried the weight of his apprehension.

He was on his way, stuck in traffic on the Princess Street Flyover from where he could see Chowpatty all lit up. Salvi was following with Vishnu Shetty, Arun Sawant, Dhananjay Gadkari and Detection cops from Unit 1. Khan was coming from the *visarjan* site near Badhwar Park in Cuffe Parade with Dinakar Salian, Puneet Singh and Detection staff from Unit II.

Ferraz smiled at the sensation his words would cause.

Cupping his hand over the phone, he shouted, "Sir, we know who the professor's last victim is."

"Who!"

"It's the Mayor!"

"Who? The Mayor! Yamini Olwe? How do–"

"She's his ex-student Veena Ganpathy from the Belgaum college… because of whom he was expelled. Her name's changed to Yamini Olwe after marriage."

The Joint CP (Crime) drew in his breath sharply.

"Veena Ganpathy! How do you know this?"

Ferraz told him, as briefly and loudly as he could.

"Oh, thank God! Are you – is she safe?"

"Yes, sir. And in our sights. She's surrounded by BMC guards. We can't get across to her because our path is blocked by the Khetwadicha Raja, but–"

"The Khetwadicha Raja!"

"Sir, it's the–"

His words were lost in a thunderous crash that rattled the sky.

Startled, Ferraz took his eyes off the Mayor and looked up fearfully, almost expecting to see a monstrous 747 Boeing in flames hurtling down to earth, like that scene from *Superman Returns*.

"*What the hell was that?*" the Joint CP (Crime) demanded.

It was lightning…

… white-hot and brilliant, spitefully remonstrating with the forces that had reined it in all evening. Another jagged bolt tore the sky in half, turning night into day, chased by a louder ripple of thunder threatening to crack the world in pieces.

A strong wind roared in from the sea, pushing big dark clouds before it. Suddenly it was raining. A stormy downpour that came in great torrents taking Chowpatty by surprise, causing chaos and disrupting the *visarjan*.

The band stopped abruptly, and in the silence the rain poured heavily.

The cops looked for shelter, wondering what to do.

They were caught in the open like everybody else.

People scattered hastily, but there was nowhere to hide.

The Khetwadicha Raja watched impassively, knowing that no matter how hard it rained, this couldn't go on forever. At some point the storm would blow over. The music began to play again, this time over the public address system, somebody had switched on devotional songs.

Sheltering his eyes with his hand, Ferraz swore softly under his breath.

"It's the rain, sir," he told Rathod, "a thundershower."

"That's all we need," the Joint CP (Crime) sighed bitterly.

Navroze and de Azavedo continued to watch the Mayor's Pavilion.

As rain battered the exposed front rows, guests began crowding at the back.

Rathod was telling Ferraz, "I'm informing the CP and Mugbe. Let them move her to safety. Ideally, they should let her be and set up a trap. Then wait for him to show up."

"We'll get to her in a minute, sir."

He glanced at the pavilion through the rain, searching for Yamini Olwe.

A bobbing movement in the restless crowd caught his eye.

But the weather got worse.

The wind turned into a howling gale. It raged in from the sea. Stirring the waves violently and bringing a halt to the immersions, swaying the pavilions and towers on the beach, bending the trees. More jagged bolts of lightning shot out of the utter blackness of the night. Earth-shaking claps of thunder rolled across the sky seconds later.

Ferraz wiped his face and his eyes swept the Mayor's Pavilion again. He could make out Yamini Olwe even through the wall of water because of her bright sari, it was like a smudge of orange in the rain-laden air.

Again he noticed the bobbing movement, closer to her.

Was that…

A fireball of lightning broke free from the tar black sky. With a whip-like crack it viciously spat at Chowpatty with the forked tongue of a serpent, sending people screaming in panic.

"Angelo," yelled Navroze, "what do we do?"

Ferraz hated electrical storms.

He looked at the Mayor's Pavilion in fear.

It was in pandemonium, packed many times beyond its capacity now. More and more people were trying to go up. Seeking shelter from the rain. Afraid to stay in the open because of the zigzagging lightning. The BMC's security men stood at the top of the stairs pushing them back. The Home Guards struggled valiantly to restrain the surging crowd below.

The cops watched in horror as the pavilion swayed.

Over the storm they heard a sound that chilled them. The pavilion groaning in protest. Its wooden flooring and supporting beams creaking. Heated voices in a fierce argument came across as belligerent people challenged the security guards. Some of Yamini Olwe's guests confronted the intruders. A scuffle broke out and immediately the Mayor's Pavilion became a pitched battleground.

The man on the mic began shouting for the police.

"Fuck," said Ferraz, "let's go."

"Angelo, what's happening?"

"Sir, a fight has broken out on the Mayor's –"

"Between who – is she safe?"

Ferraz looked to see. But Yamini Olwe was swallowed up by the crowd. The fight had trickled down to the beach also now. What was a surge of dancing, celebrating revelers minutes ago, was now a melee of rebellious, scrappy people. The Police Band picked up its instruments and fled.

Thunder rattled the sky again and lightning lit up the disturbing scene.

Anxiously Ferraz checked the pavilion.

Again, it was de Azavedo who located the Mayor.

"There she is," he shouted.

Ferraz searched for the orange sari in the crush of clashing people…

… and saw through the rain that bobbing, weaving movement again.

"Angelo!" Rathod's voice cut in, "the traffic isn't–"

With a sudden sick feeling Ferraz *realized* what he was seeing.

That bobbing movement… somebody with a limp.

What was it that Jackie had said?

That Prof. Murtikar limps!

"God!" he yelled in alarm, "he's on the stage!"

"Angelo!" the Joint CP (Crime) shouted, *"stop him at any cost!"*

THEY PLUNGED into the sea of brawling people.

That was the only way to get across. And it wasn't going to part for them like the Red Sea did for Moses. The cops went in a flying wedge. Navroze in front, Ferraz and de Azavedo following. Hoping nobody would attack them. Their sodden shoes squelched in the wet sand that would do nicely to make sand castles.

From all around came frightened cries and angry shouts.

The mob was on the warpath, its blood boiling. The cops didn't know who was fighting whom. Public gatherings always had miscreants waiting to rob people and molest women. And provocateurs fomenting passions to disrupt Mumbai, the country's financial capital, at the behest of anti-national elements. Crowd control wasn't the Crime Branch's expertise. The sectional cops were there for that. But when the uniformed police arrived in riot gear, wearing helmets, carrying cane shields and *lathis*, they were violently greeted with missiles.

Antagonistic people pelted them with bottles, stones, and even chairs. The mob then ran amuck and attacked the vehicles on the beach, smashing windshields, overturning bikes. Protestors attempted to torch a police van. But the rain wouldn't let them. Irritated, they began ransacking the pavilions. A pitched battle with the police began.

This was one of the police's biggest nightmares…

… how to disperse an unarmed and peaceful crowd at a religious event that had become rowdy and was threatening life and property without it becoming a major communal row.

Standing by was the Varun, the police's 12,000 liters water cannon capable of bowling over troublemakers with a high-force water jet.

Also the Vajra, its anti-riot vehicle for firing teargas into violent, frenzied mobs. But who would deploy them? It required a senior officer to take a split second decision to meet the situation. The CP had left Chowpatty. The other cops on the spot couldn't handle it.

Meanwhile, the riot police were under attack. And when attacked by an aggressive and unrestrained mob, the police retaliate. They *lathi*-charged the agitating people on Chowpatty now furiously.

It was fight or flight in the mad, pouring rain.

Ferraz feared a stampede.

It was the worst thing that could happen. People died in stampedes. By the scores. Denser the crowd at religious functions, sporting events, music concerts and political rallies where panic broke out, higher the death toll. But there was nowhere to run. The beach was jam-packed. The road was blocked by more Ganpatis forcing their way in. Those on the beach were being herded to the shore where revelers waiting with idols were getting pushed screaming into the sea.

Tempers were running high.

Caught in the hysterical surge, the cops struggled to reach the Mayor's Pavilion which was under the onslaught of a fresh and fierce attack.

Suddenly Ferraz spotted the professor on the stage...

... shuffling and limping through the free-for-all.

Yamini Olwe hadn't noticed him.

Conscious of her duty to the city, the Mayor was playing the role of the peacemaker, frantically appealing for calm with joined hands.

While the professor advanced, slowly and menacingly.

They reached the staircase.

"Police," shouted Ferraz trying to push his way up.

The blows from the *lathis* came unexpectedly, landing on their unprotected backs and heads, dropping the cops and making them cry out in pain. His face a mask of suffering, Ferraz rolled over to confront the unfocussed constables blindly flogging everybody in front of them.

"Chooths," he yelled angrily, "we're fucking police!"

It didn't matter. The *lathis* came whistling down. He took the strike on his forearm this time, wincing in agony. As the constables raised their *lathis* again, Ferraz jackknifed himself furiously into them, kicking one in the chest and sending him crashing into the others so that they all fell in an untidy heap on the beach.

At once the crowd pounced on the constables.

This is what happened if you didn't wear uniform, Ferraz was thinking. The fucking sectional police didn't recognize you from the bad guys.

His back was on fire, his forearm stinging. But Ferraz turned to the pavilion. He couldn't see Yamini Olwe or the professor. Navroze was in difficulties on the staircase. The Parsi cop had lost his glasses. He was bleeding from the head. Two men held his arms while a BMC security man had him in a stranglehold from behind.

Navroze was roaring, "Police! Stop!"

But nobody was stopping. Or listening.

Ferraz grabbed both men holding Navroze by their collars. With a superhuman effort he hauled them off and threw them behind. While Navroze bent at the waist and sent the BMC security man sailing overhead. The grateful crowd swallowed him up immediately.

Breathing hard, they fought their way up the staircase.

As they reached the top, the staircase collapsed with a loud cracking sound, taking down 50 screaming people. The cops were on top of the heap. They tumbled down with everybody else, one mass of rolling bodies, struggling arms and legs, landing painfully on the beach.

Ferraz thought his back was broken.

He lay groaning, trying to avoid the struggling, running feet all around. Additional forces had arrived. The rioters scattered and the police gave chase. Navroze bent to help him. But somebody kicked the Parsi cop in the ass, sending him rocketing into Ferraz with a startled yell.

Cursing, Ferraz rolled aside and looked at the pavilion.

The professor was closing in on the Mayor…

… a maniacal, drooling expression on his face.

But Yamini Olwe still hadn't seen him.

Freaked out by this, Ferraz got shakily to his feet.

When he looked up again…

… the professor was confronting the Mayor.

And there was shocked recognition in her eyes.

Yamini Olwe's red, painted lips were opening in a silent 'O' of terror. Nobody heard her wail of fear in the pandemonium. The professor grinned evilly at her. He was reaching into the folds of his clothes.

Ferraz looked around urgently, his eye catching the Khetwadicha Raja's.

"Help me please, Lord Ganesh," he implored in desperation.

When he turned it was to see de Azavedo clambering onto the pavilion and wildly sending a chair flying through the air. Miraculously, it struck the professor on the side of the head and sent him reeling.

The Mayor should have fled. But she stood there paralyzed.

"Bawa, come on!" Ferraz hauled Navroze up.

But now they were blocked by angry members of the crowd.

Beyond them, Ferraz could see de Azavedo struggling with two security men on the pavilion. The professor had gained his feet. He was holding the gun by his side uncertainly. As if making up his mind to take the shot. Nobody noticed him except the uncontrollably screaming Mayor.

"Police!" Ferraz yelled at the men they were up against.

Like a Bollywood cop, he was reaching for his identity card. When somebody whacked him hard on the back with a bamboo.

Ferraz staggered, the excruciating pain squeezing his eyes shut. His hands went behind in reflex action. The welt would remain for weeks. Incensed, he whirled and kicked the attacker savagely. Left and right in the ribs, with scything feet. The man collapsed holding the broken bamboo. Another one charged but Ferraz knocked him out with a spinning back fist. Then he jump-kicked one more in the chest. Navroze kneed a fourth in the balls.

Gasping for breath, both cops turned to the pavilion again.

And then they watched in stupefaction as it swayed and pitched alarmingly, like the Titanic in distress, creaking horribly. Petrified, the far-over-capacity crowd clutched one another like they were doing the rock and roll on a far from stable dance floor. Everybody was screaming in fright.

First the supporting beams broke.

Then with a loud resounding crash, in slow motion the huge pavilion collapsed on itself like a house of cards. It swallowed the dais, pulled down the big colorful shamiana, and uprooted electric poles causing sparks.

With a mighty explosion the catering unit below preparing snacks for the guests went up in flames. Helplessly, the people fell headlong as the pavilion collapsed onto the beach.

The cops stood stunned in the eerie silence that followed.

For the moment the fighting on Chowpatty stopped. The rain hesitated, giving the fire a chance to rapidly spread, assisted by the sea breeze. As more policemen ran up with waving *lathis* and fire engines with clanging bells tried to make their way through, the restless mob rallied itself and went into attack again.

Ignoring the fighting, running figures, Ferraz and Navroze plunged into the ruins. NCC cadets and Home Guards, joined by NGO volunteers, were rummaging in the wreckage for the injured.

From under the debris came heartrending cries of trapped people begging to be rescued. The unhurt crawled to safety where ambulance attendants waited with stretchers.

de Azavedo rose from the debris suddenly, as if resurrected.

Grinning, he was giving them a thumbs-up, when his eyes suddenly shifted. They knew even before his hand went to the .38 Colt at his waist that de Azavedo had spotted the professor.

"Gun!" yelled de Azavedo, drawing out his revolver.

"No, Antone," Ferraz snapped. This was not the place to pull a gun.

The professor was crouched like a wounded animal 20 feet away, his face a snarling mask of blood, the .32 Webley Scott held limply by his side.

"Professor Murtikar!" Ferraz shouted loudly.

He jerked his head in their direction, confused at hearing his name.

"Professor Murtikar, we're the police. Please drop your–"

To their horror, Mayor Yamini Olwe got up shakily in between them.

She came out from beneath a table, her hair disheveled and without the jasmine flowers, her sari in disarray, it had fallen off her shoulder and was trailing, the blouse slashed in a deep V exposing recklessly abundant breasts. She had a livid bruise on her forehead and looked disoriented and frightened.

She spotted the professor at once and froze.

Thwack!

de Azavedo gave a howl as a constable's *lathi* crashed down on his hand. Dressed as he was, looking the way he did, de Azavedo resembled one of Chowpatty's great unwashed. Nobody would have guessed he was a cop. His finger tightened on the trigger. The .38 Colt went off with a tremendous bang making people flinch. The bullet burrowed itself in the sand.

The constable leaped on de Azavedo and they went down. The gun exploded again. People who thought they had just escaped death in the pavilion crash threw their hands up in fright.

"Police!" bellowed Navroze, rushing to de Azavedo's rescue.

But nobody heard him in that confusion.

There was another loud bang and Ferraz jumped.

The professor had fired and missed the Mayor by a mile.

Ferraz's 9mm S&W was in his hand now.

Navroze stopped and was turning, his .38 Mauser revolver out.

Without taking his eyes off the professor, Ferraz lifted a hand to caution Navroze. There were too many people around to risk random gunfire. Public shootouts with the baddie was strictly for the movies. Policemen couldn't just unholster their service weapons and fire in public. There were regulations. The reason had to be a threat of life-and-death proportion. To the cop himself or to the public. And the shooting had to be below the waist. Meant to injure and not kill. After a statutory verbal warning had been given. If a cop defied these orders, he faced automatic suspension, an endless departmental inquiry and further action.

The gunfire sent people running helter-skelter.

Survival instincts kicked in. An alarm sounded in everyone's mind. There was danger here. All they wanted was to escape with their lives. The gunfire also attracted more policemen who charged up shouting loudly. Caught in this mad swirl, Ferraz was lifted off his feet and carried right into the vortex of the riot.

Crushed from all sides, he grimly held onto the 9mm S&W and tried not to fall. The pressure from the crowd was squeezing the air out of his lungs. He struggled for breath. People got killed standing in stampedes. Death occurred from compressive asphyxiation. Not just trampling.

But Ferraz hadn't come to Chowpatty to die.

Using all his strength, he struggled to find firm footing on the beach. People tumbled all around him. When somebody went down in a stampede, more people fell over them, that's how bodies piled up killing those below. Helplessly, Ferraz toppled over too. As he fell, he saw on the fringes of the mob the Mayor crawling madly to get away. She was screaming for help. Chillingly, the professor was going after her, lurching in the crowd, holding the .32 Webley Scott out with both hands and trying to take aim. Nobody stopped him.

That was the shitty thing about Mumbai.

A hundred people would gape in awestruck horror as a jilted lover stabbed his girlfriend multiple times on a busy road and then poured acid over her. But nobody would even raise their voice in protest. Fuck that, they'd be whipping out their cells to take videos instead!

Ferraz rolled over and over in the scrimmage, protecting his face and head with both arms, drawing his knees in to shield his groin, desperately clearing space for himself, the wet sand sticking to his clothes.

Where were Navroze and de Azavedo, he wondered.

Squinting through the legs of people, he saw the professor like a hunter stalking the Mayor, making sure his target stayed in sight. People continued to run around them in confusion. Those that fell down, stayed down, crushed beneath the rest. Somebody kicked sand into his face.

Momentarily blinded, blinking in panic, Ferraz struggled onto one knee, still not taking his eyes off the professor. A hand closed around his face and somebody yanked him backwards. A boot thudded into the back of his neck. Knocking him flat on his back. Causing him to see blinding lights and exploding stars.

Groggily he turned over.

Somebody stepped on his head, lost balance, and crashed heavily on his back. Ferraz cried out in agony. He felt the muscles of his back, shoulders and neck clenching. God, he was going into a spasm.

He twisted and turned frantically to free himself.

A foot stamped on his forearm, almost making him lose the 9mm S&W. Somehow Ferraz rolled free. He rose quickly in a crouch, gun leveled, holding it steady in both hands. For just a second. The tide of people turned suddenly, ploughed right through him, knocking him off his feet and flat on his back again. But Ferraz recovered at once.

And just in time…

… for the Mayor's escape had come to an end, stopped by a hundred feet stepping on her trailing sari and pinning her on the beach, like an animal helplessly ensnared in a trap waiting for the hunter to come.

And he was coming – the professor was shuffling and limping up to her. Lining up the .32 Webley Scott for the kill with unsteady hands.

Ferraz was too far away to stop him.

"Professor Murtikar, no!" he yelled desperately.

But the professor didn't hear him. He fired at the Mayor blindly.

The bullet went low, he had been aiming at her chest. It struck her thigh. Over the hullabaloo and loud Ganpati music that was still incongruously playing, Ferraz heard Yamini Olwe scream.

His heart stopped. *Was she dead?* He had heard the gunfire. But Ferraz didn't know how badly the Mayor was hurt. She was lying flat. Even from a distance, he could see her orange sari turn a darker shade as the blood began spreading in the sheer fabric.

His own blood ran cold.

Where were the hundreds of policemen on *bandobast* here tonight?

Then he saw Yamini Olwe sitting up with a tremendous effort.

And Ferraz began running.

He skidded at once and fell heavily on one knee.

The Mayor stared at the blood disbelievingly.

Then looked up in bewilderment at the professor.

He was lifting the .32 Webley Scott again with wildly shaking hands.

Yamini Olwe shuddered, too overwhelmed to scream any more.

She closed her eyes and her head sank on her chest.

Prof. Murtikar was taking aim again…

… from point-blank range.

So was Ferraz from 15 feet away…

… praying for a clear shot between the crowd.

He couldn't remember when last he had gone to the police firing range. But now Ferraz held the 9mm S&W tight, his arms extended to full stretch, the gun level with his eyes, feet spread and bracing himself for the recoil. Like in the *Dirty Harry* poster of 1971, because that's how shooting was done, not with one hand and one eye closed in the cavalier fashion of Bollywood.

Except Ferraz wasn't Clint Eastwood.

He was a real cop. And he was aiming very carefully…

… taking his time, because Ferraz was shooting for the gold.

What was it Jackie had said this morning?

About his hand not trembling, his aim not faltering?

The professor was also taking his time.

A cold dread clutched Ferraz's heart.

The professor was saying *"Moryaa Re!"*

He couldn't hear him, Ferraz was reading the professor's lips.

And over the uproar of the rioting people, the wail of police sirens, the shouts of familiar voices from behind him, and the whisper of waves pounding the beach, he could hear the Ganpati *bhakti geet*…

"Vakratunda Mahayaya, Suryakoti Samaprabha
Nirvighnam Kuru Mey Deva, Sarva Karyeshu Sarvada…"

"O Lord Ganesh… please make my work free of obstacles always."

Ferraz didn't know if he was reciting the Ganesh *mantra* or hearing it in his mind when he pulled the trigger.

They both fired simultaneously.

The boom of the guns echoed loudly over Chowpatty.

And Mayor Yamini Olwe screamed…

SUNDAY

32

FERRAZ AND Jackie were having breakfast.

Sundays, breakfast was always special. This morning it was batter-fried Bombay Duck with tartar sauce. And bread and butter pudding, his favourite dessert. The coffee was Madras. Black and strong. He had smelled the fish frying in his sleep. And stumbled out of bed, bleary-eyed, sore and stiff in every joint, his body aching everywhere.

It hurt just to walk.

It was 7.15 am.

The middle of the night!

He had only gone to bed at 3.30 am.

Jackie thought he looked like death warmed up. She had held out a steaming mug. No fuss about brushing his teeth first this morning. Ferraz had accepted it gratefully.

Now he was sitting by the window, chewing on a smoldering cigar, listening to the squawking call of the gulls outside. The paper pinwheel Jackie had stuck into one of her potted plants on the window whirled colorfully in the breeze. Looking at it made Ferraz happy.

The monsoon showed no signs of relenting after last night's fury.

It had rolled up its sleeves and was whipping up a storm. Gusts of wind were bringing in sheets of rain from the sea, ruffling the white crests of the waves, thunder boomed in the sky.

Ferraz was tired of the rain.

He wished it would go away. The lakes were overflowing, the city didn't want any more water. Yawning loud and long, he turned away.

Jackie had laid out the newspapers for him.

Sundays they took the lot. She had pored over them while he was asleep. Ferraz had heard the doorbell ringing in his dreams. Later he would learn that his neighbors, senior cops like himself, had called to congratulate him. All early risers. Jackie had shooed them away. He looked at the headlines upside down. He could make out his picture on the front page of *Newsday*. Nahida had written the lead. Evocatively describing the nerve-wracking final moments of chaos and utter craziness on Chowpatty last night without actually being there.

It had been do-or-die for Ferraz.

And had required a supreme ice-cold effort to avoid the dire consequences of failure. With all the odds and elements stacked heavily and unfairly against him in that pandemonium.

Only Lord Ganesh on his side…

… and that had been enough.

He would never forget that moment.

The 9mm S&W bucking in his hands as he fired.

Once only, he knew there would be no second chance.

His trigger finger twitched at the memory.

Hearing again the crash of gunfire over the wild uproar on Chowpatty.

Joint CP (Crime) Arun Rathod had suddenly been at his side. With several other cops Ferraz didn't recognize. Navroze, Khan and Salvi too, and de Azavedo still ridiculously wearing that marigold garland. All with guns drawn, tension on their white, strained faces.

It hadn't been necessary.

They had hurried Yamini Olwe to hospital…

… bleeding from the gunshots to her thigh and left forearm.

But heroically alive.

She thanked the cops brokenly and in a choked voice.

Then dramatically appealed for the *visarjan* to continue, because the Mayor was the heroine of the story, and Yamini Olwe had seen the media invading Chowpatty from the foot-overbridge across the road. Like public spilling onto the field after India had won the World Cup. Jostling, elbowing one another, mics reaching out in the unrestrained disorder, cameras angled for the best shot to carry the story outside in real time.

Ferraz had made three calls in this confusion.

First to Jackie, telling her it was okay to return home.

Then to Nahida, to say "Thank you".

And finally to Sanjay Chhabria and Sangeeta Kadam.

Prof. Gajanan Murtikar's home had to be secured, police *bandobast* increased at the building and on the road, the forensic experts would descend there. Also the press. And curious people. There would be no case for trial, but the evidence of his unspeakably horrific and chilling crimes was there. The police were already calling his college authorities. They were taking care of business.

Baburao Nawalkar had addressed a press conference in his chamber.

The CP had to stop to take calls from the Chief Minister and Home Minister. He had told the room packed with reporters that it had not been an encounter. Daring them with a flinty look to say it was otherwise. There were hundreds, no thousands of witnesses. The police were forced to take evasive action. The identity of the killer had been a mystery till that last climatic moment. Thankfully, the tip from the Kolhapur police came through just in time. He told them who it was. A psychopathic professor with an old grudge against the Mayor. The Belgaum police had the details. He had killed nine innocent people first as a cover-up before attempting to murder her that night on Chowpatty. It had been impossible for the police to detect who might be next and stop him. Even though they learned of his motive by the fourth murder. Mumbai was full of Ganesh *bhakts*. It could be anyone. Turned out he was gunning for the Mayor!

The police hadn't been able to interrogate him, Nawalkar added.

Prof. Gajanan Murtikar was declared DOA at the hospital.

Yamini Olwe's life had been hanging by a thread. If Inspector Ferraz's aim had not been true, had it been a couple of inches here or there, or had he fired a millisecond later...

"You're a hero in my college," Jackie was telling him over breakfast. "All my classmates are *fida* on you, those shameless bitches! My phone has crashed with taking their messages!"

She was looking at him in awe, eyes shining.

"But we will miss the Prof. Murti we knew," she said quietly. "He was a good Psychology teacher even if he hid behind the mask of sanity, like the press is saying. We never saw that personality of his. I can't imagine him–"

"I understand," Ferraz said gently.

She hesitated and looked at him.

"Today is Bandra Fair, the Feast of Our Lady of the Mount."

"Is it? Happy feast!"

"Angie, you promised to come to church after..."

"I know," he quickly said.

"Today's the perfect day," Jackie told him.

"In this rain?"

His phone rang. It was Nahida Shaikh.

"Awake, Inspector?" she asked teasingly, "What's your story?"

Ferraz smiled, "You wrote it already."

"Why was he taken to Nair Hospital? To confuse the media?"

"For the post-mortem."

"Isn't it done at JJ Hospital?"

"Nair was closer to Chowpatty."

"But it took you two hours to get there!"

"Traffic jams, the Ganpati processions were everywhere."

"The police released no pictures of his–"

"We never do."

"Uh-huh, what's the real story, Inspector? C'mon, you owe me."

He had been in the police van with Navroze, Khan and Salvi.

That's how it was always done.

The police team that encountered the criminal took him to the morgue.

They had taken their time.

And a circuitous route.

Along the way…

Joint CP (Crime) Arun Rathod had scripted this part.

… Ferraz nodded imperceptibly at Salvi.

Navroze, Khan and he looked out of the van.

The Lalbaugcha Raja was on the opposite side of the road.

The Encounter Specialist pulled out his 9mm Browning emotionlessly.

Prof. Gajanan Murtikar lay on the floor of the van, gasping. Grievously injured, bleeding profusely. But not mortally wounded. Ferraz had shot him in the chest. The professor had been saved by the transistor in his pocket. Now he knew with the terror of doom what was coming.

Whispering Death, that's what.

He shut his eyes and died with a smile on his face.

The bang of Salvi's gun was loud in the close confines of the van.

But the roar of *"Ganpati Bappa Morya! Pudchya Varshi Lavkar Ya!"* was a hundred times louder outside and drowned the gunfire.

"I'll tell you over a Cappuccino someday," Ferraz promised Nahida.